Joss ... ̇ loves books and travelling—especially to the wild ... ̇es of southern Africa and, well, anywhere. She' ... wife, a mum to two teenagers and slave to two cats. ... ̇ter a career in local economic development, she now ... rites full-time. Joss is a member of Romance Writ ... s of America and Romance Writers of South Afri

Cha ... **Sands** is a *USA TODAY* bestselling and awa ... ̇nning author of more than forty romance nove ... ̇ ̇ writes sensual contemporary romances and stori ... ̇f th ... ld West. When not writing, Charlene enjoy ... ̇c ̇fic beaches, great coffee, reading books from ... authors, and spending time with her "hero ... and family. You can find her on Facel ... and Instagram. Sign up for her newsletter ... 'enesands.com for ongoing giveaways, disco ... ̇nd new releases!

Facebe ... acebook.com/CharleneSandsBooks

Twitter ... ̇ter.com/CharleneSands

D1353677

Also by Joss Wood

Love in Boston
Friendship on Fire
Hot Christmas Kisses
The Rival's Heir
Second Chance Temptation

Dynasties: Secrets of the A-List
Redeemed by Passion

Also by Charlene Sands

Sunset Surrender
Sunset Seduction
The Secret Heir of Sunset Ranch
Redeeming the CEO Cowboy
Texan for the Taking
Stranded and Seduced

Discover more at millsandboon.co.uk

RICH, RUGGED RANCHER

JOSS WOOD

VEGAS VOWS, TEXAS NIGHTS

CHARLENE SANDS

MIX
Paper from
responsible sources
FSC
www.fsc.org
FSC C007454

This book is produced from independently certified FSC™
paper to ensure responsible forest management.

For more information visit www.harpercollins.co.uk/green

Printed and bound in Spain
by CPI, Barcelona

MILLS & BOON

First Published in Great Britain 2020
by Mills & Boon, an imprint of HarperCollinsPublishers,
1 London Bridge Street, London, SE1 9GF

Rich, Rugged Rancher Copyright © 2020 Harlequin Books S.A.
Vegas Vows, Texas Nights © 2020 Charlene Swink

Special thanks and acknowledgement are given to Joss Wood for her contribution to the *Texas Cattleman's Club: Inheritance* series

ISBN: 978-0-263-27910-8

0120

RICH, RUGGED RANCHER

JOSS WOOD

One

"So, have you bagged your cowboy yet?"

Seraphina Martinez whipped the rented convertible onto the open road leading to Blackwood Hollow Ranch and punched the accelerator, ignoring Lulu's squeal of surprise at the sudden burst of speed.

"Slow down, Fee. I don't want to die on a lonely road in East Texas," Lulu grumbled.

"Relax, it's an empty road, Lu," Fee replied, glad she'd wrangled her thick hair into two fat braids—as opposed to Lulu who was fighting, and losing, the war with the wind.

Lulu held her hair back from her face and glared at Fee. "I'm going to look like I've been dragged through a bush when we get there."

Fee shrugged.

Perfect makeup, perfect clothes, perfect hair...being a reality TV star took work, dammit.

"Well, have you?" Fee demanded.

"Found a cowboy? No, not yet," Lulu replied.

"What about the lawyer guy who seems to be everywhere we are lately?" Fee asked. While scouting filming locations for *Secret Lives of NYC Ex-Wives*, the attorney for the Blackwood estate had been everywhere they looked, keeping his lawyerly eye on Miranda Blackwood and the rest of the cast and crew.

"Kace LeBlanc?" Lu asked, aiming for super casual and missing by a mile.

Fee darted a look at her best friend, amused. Of course she had noticed the looks Lulu sent Kace when she didn't think anyone was looking. Lu thought the attorney was hot. And, with his unruly brown hair and those gorgeous brown eyes, he was…until he opened his mouth. Then he acted like she and her costars and the crew were going to break his precious town of Royal or something.

"The guy is a pill," Lulu said before sighing. "God, he's hot but he's so annoying."

Fee agreed but she also admired Kace's determination to look after the late Buck Blackwood's interests and to ensure the terms of his will were followed to the letter. And the terms of the will were, from the little she'd gleaned, astonishing. She couldn't blame his kids for being pissed off at Buck for leaving everything he owned to Fee's costar Miranda, who was his ex and as New York as she and Lulu were. It had to be a hard slap to their born-and-bred Texas faces.

If they'd scripted this story for *Secret Lives*, their viewers would think they were making it up—aging billionaire leaves much, much younger second wife everything at the expense of his children. Buck also, so she'd heard, had an illegitimate son and this news didn't seem to surprise anyone. Buck, apparently, had liked the ladies.

This plot twist was ratings gold, pure made-for-TV drama.

Lulu looked to her right, her attention captured by a herd of Longhorn cows.

"Did you ever live in Texas?" Lulu asked her, still holding her hair back with two hands.

Fee took some time to answer, trawling through her memories. Being an army brat and having a father who jumped at any chance to move, she'd lived all over the country and attended fourteen schools in twelve years. But she couldn't recall living in Texas.

"I think we did a stint in New Mexico," Fee replied. "But I was young. I don't remember much of it."

Lulu turned in her seat and Fee felt her eyes on her. "I'm still amazed at your excitement over visiting a new place. We've been doing this for years, Fee. Aren't you sick of all the traveling? Don't you miss your own bed?"

Fee sent her a quick smile. "I rent my apartment furnished, Lu. You know that I don't get attached to things or places." She might live in Manhattan but she wasn't as attached to the city as her co-stars were.

"Because you moved so often when you were a child."

"I learned that if you get attached, it hurts like hell when you have to leave." Fee shrugged. "So, it makes sense not to get attached."

"Do you think you'll ever settle down?"

That was a hell of a question. Maybe, possibly, she might one day find a town or city she didn't want to leave. But, because she was a realist, she knew that, while she might stay in a place a couple of months or a few years, she would probably end up moving on. It was what she did.

The grass was always greener around the next corner...

And if you didn't get attached, you couldn't get hurt, especially by people. Her nomadic parents and her own brief marriage to the philandering son of one of NYC's most famous families had taught her that.

She loved people, she did, but underneath her exuberant personality still resided a little girl who knew that relationships (and places) were temporary and believing that any commitment would last was crazy.

She was currently living in Manhattan, in a gorgeous but expensive fully furnished rental in Chelsea. Her practical streak hated the idea of renting when she could easily afford to buy an apartment but Manhattan wasn't a place where she could put down roots. When *Secret Lives* ended, she'd move on, but for now she was comfortable. Not settled but, yeah, temporarily okay with where she laid her head.

She was the captain of her own ship, the author of her own book. And if she was using *Secret Lives* to feather her own nest, to make bank, that was her business. She might be loud, frequently over-the-top, but she was also pragmatic and fully understood how quickly things could change. And if her situation did change—*Secret Lives* was popular now but that could change tomorrow—she wanted her nest to be well feathered.

Because, as she knew, moving from place to place, town to town, wasn't cheap.

And that was why she took every opportunity to maximize her little taste of fame: first with the line of accessories she'd created using her husband's famous last name. Her *Not Your Mama's Cookbook*, written last year, was still on the bestseller lists. Maybe she should think about doing another cookbook…or something else entirely.

It was something to think about.

"Have you decided on your Royal project yet?" Lulu asked her, breaking her train of thought.

"I have no idea what you are talking about," Fee answered, injecting a healthy amount of prim into her tone.

Lulu rolled her eyes. "You can't BS me, Fee. I know it

was you who organized giving last season's intern a make-over. Who set Pete, our lighting director, up with Dave, the sound guy. Who read the scriptwriter's—what was his name?—screenplay? Miranda might be our Mama Bear but you are our Little Miss Fix-It."

Fee wrinkled her nose. Little Miss Fix-It? She opened her mouth to speak then realized she couldn't argue the point. She did tend to identify a need and try to meet it.

"I don't know if I'll find anyone to fix in Royal. I think I'll take a break from meddling while I'm there."

Lulu's laughter danced on the wind. "Yeah, right. That's not going to happen."

Fee frowned at her. "What? I can back off!"

"You cannot!" Lulu retorted. "Honey, we're always getting into trouble because you can't leave a situation alone! We nearly got arrested when you jumped between those two guys fighting in Nero's, and we did get arrested when you—" Lulu bent her fingers to make air quotes "—*confiscated* that abused horse in Kentucky. You are con-stantly getting trolled on social media because you stand up for LGBT rights, women's rights, immigrants' rights. That's not a criticism, I admire your outspokenness, but you don't have to fight every fight, babe."

Fee knew that. But she also knew what it was like to have no one fighting in her corner, no one to rely on. She knew how it felt to feel invisible and when she stepped out of the shadows, how it felt to be mocked and bullied.

God, she'd come a long way.

"I guarantee you will find a project and you won't be able to resist meddling," Lulu told her, blue eyes laughing.

"Want to bet?" Fee asked her as they approached the enormous gates to what was Buck Blackwood's—now Mi-randa's—ranch. The gates to Blackwood Hollow appeared and she flung the car to the right and sped down the long driveway. Lu hissed and Fee grinned.

"What's the bet?" Lulu asked, gripping the armrest with white fingers. "And you drive like a maniac."

"You give me your recipe for Miss Annie's fried chicken for my next cookbook, if I decide to do another one." She'd been trying to pry Lulu's grandma's recipe from her since the first time Lulu fed her the delicious extra-crispy chicken at a small dinner five years earlier.

"She'll come back and haunt me." Lulu gasped, placing her hand on her chest. "I can't. Just like you can't stop yourself from meddling…"

"I can. And you know I can or else you wouldn't be hesitating…"

Lu narrowed her eyes at Fee as they approached a cluster of buildings that looked like a Hollywood vision of a working ranch. A sprawling mansion, guest cottages, massive barns. Despite visiting the spread days before, it was still breathtaking.

"There's the crew's van." Lulu pointed toward the far barn and Fee tapped the accelerator as she drove past the main house that went on and on and on.

"What could be so interesting down by the barns?" Fee wondered.

"That."

Fee looked where Lulu pointed and…holy crispy fried chicken. A man riding a horse at a gallop around a ring shouldn't be a surprise, but what a man and what a horse. Fee didn't know horses—she thought the speckled black-and-white horse might be a stallion—but she did know men.

And the cowboy was one hell of a man. Broad shoulders, muscled thighs, big biceps straining the sleeves of his faded T-shirt. She couldn't see the color of his hair or the lines on his face, the Stetson prevented her from making out the details, but his body was, like the horse, all sleek muscles and contained strength.

Hot, hot, hot...

He also looked familiar. Where did she know him from?

Fee took her foot off the accelerator and allowed the car to roll toward to where the other vehicles—the crew's van, a battered work truck and a spiffy SUV—were parked. All her attention was focused on the horse and rider, perfectly in sync. He seemed oblivious to his audience: a couple of cowboys sitting on the top railing of the fence and Miranda, Rafaela and Zooey standing with their arms on the white pole fence, their attention completely captured by the rider hurtling around the ring in a blur of hooves and dust.

God, he was heading straight for the fence. They'd either crash through it or he'd have to jump it because there was no way he'd be able to stop the horse in time.

Fee released the wheel and slapped her hands over her mouth, her attention completely caught by the drama in the paddock. She wanted to scream out a warning and was on the point of doing so when the rider yanked on the reins and the stallion braked instantly, stopping when his nose was just an inch from the fence.

That collision didn't happen, but another did when Fee's very expensive rented Audi convertible slammed into the bumper of the battered farm truck.

Lulu released a small shriek and Fee flung her arm out in a futile effort to keep Lulu from lurching forward. Their seat belts kept them in place but metal scraped against metal and steam erupted from her car as the hood got up close and personal with the back of the rust-covered truck.

"Are you okay?" Fee demanded, looking at Lulu.

"Fine," Lulu replied, then winced at the carnage in front of her. "Your car is toast, though—the hood is crumpled."

"I can see that." Fee nodded, releasing her seat belt. "How come it's always the crap cars that sustain the least damage?"

"That crap car is a seventy-two Chevy pickup I am in the process of restoring."

Fee yanked her eyes off Lulu and turned her head to the right, looking straight into faded denim covering strong thighs and a very nice package.

Strong, broad hands rested on his hips, the veins rising on his tanned forearms lightly covered with blond hair. The red T-shirt had faded to orange in places but the chest underneath it was broad and those biceps were big and bitable. His horse—had they jumped the fence to get to her so quickly?—laid its chin on the cowboy's shoulder but neither she, nor the cowboy, were distracted by the animal's interference in their conversation.

Fee kept her focus on him, utterly entranced by his strong face, the blond stubble covering his chiseled jaw, the thin lips, the long, straight nose. The feeling of familiarity coalesced into certainty, she'd seen him before, this cowboy—here at Blackwood Hollow a few days before—but she couldn't recall his name. Probably because he'd just fried most of her brain cells.

She wanted to see his eyes; no, she needed to see his eyes. On impulse, Fee clambered up to stand on her car seat.

God he was tall. Fee pushed the rim of his Stetson up with her finger, her eyes clashing with the deepest, saddest, green-gold-gray eyes.

Hard eyes, angry eyes, sad, sad eyes.

Fee couldn't decide what she wanted to do more, hug him or jump him.

Save the horse and ride the cowboy, indeed.

* * *

Clint Rockwell was a guy of few words but if Buck Blackwood were magically resurrected, he'd have had more than a few to hurl at his friend and mentor's head. What the hell had he been thinking to ask Clint to mind the property during his long illness and after his death?

Since Buck's funeral, Clint had been coming over to Blackwood Hollow a few times a week, to check on the hands and to exercise Buck's demon horse, Jack.

He and Jack were finally starting to bond and their skills were improving. Clint lifted his hand to hold Jack's cheek, enjoying the puffs of horse breath against his neck.

Animals were cool; people were not.

People hurt people—and sometimes things, his pickup being a case in point. Ignoring Jack, Clint walked over to the hood of the Audi convertible and dropped to his haunches to inspect the damage to his pickup. He didn't much care about the damage to the convertible, they were dime a dozen, but his truck was vintage and worth a pretty penny.

Hey, Rock, if I don't make it, finish my truck for me. Only original parts, man, gold and cream.

You are going to make it because if you don't, I'm going to paint it pink and white, Clint had told him, his hand in the hole in Tim's chest, trying to stem the river of blood soaking his hand, Tim's clothing and the dirt road beneath them.

They'd both known Clint's optimism was a lie, that Tim needed blood and a surgeon and that he was out of time.

I'll haunt you if you do anything stupid to my baby, Tim had muttered.

This accident probably qualified as a haunting.

Hell, Clint didn't sleep anyway, so Tim was welcome to pop in for a chat. His army ranger buddies were the only people Clint liked being around for any length of time, the only people on the planet who understood. They'd seen what he had, had watched men they loved be blown apart, women and children die, buildings being ravaged and lives destroyed.

They got him.

Civilians didn't.

Oh, the people in this town tried, sure. No man with his money and property ever had to be lonely if he didn't want to be. He wanted to be. His army days were behind him and he was now a rancher and oilman—more rancher than oilman, truth be told. His land and animals were what mattered.

Shaking off his thoughts, Clint stood up, automatically using his good leg to take his weight. He had to stop doing that; he had to start treating his prosthetic as another leg but, shit, it was hard. Leaving the force had been hard, losing a limb had nearly killed him and being forced to deal with people, civilians, was the cherry on his crap sundae.

Clint turned and cursed when he saw he was the focus of much attention and quickly, and automatically, took in all the salient details. Since he was still ignoring the driver of the convertible—he wasn't ready to deal with her yet—he turned his attention to the passenger. Sporting glossy black hair with dark eyes, she'd left the car and was standing with Miranda Blackwood, Buck's ex-wife. With them was also a fresh-faced beauty and an Italian bombshell who reminded him of one of Grandpa's favorite actresses, Sophia Loren.

The four women, Buck's ex-wife and her reality TV co-stars, watched him with avid interest. They looked as out of place as he would on a catwalk, their spiked heels digging into the grass, designer sunglasses covering their eyes.

The Blackwood ranch hands couldn't keep their eyes off them…

He uttered a low, sharp order for them to get back to work and they hopped off the fence with alacrity, tossing admiring looks at the New Yorkers as they ambled off.

The next problem was to get the cars untangled so he could accurately assess the damage to Tim's truck. But first he had to take care of Jack: animals first, things later.

Clint called out to a hand and when he jogged back to where Clint was standing, Clint passed him Jack's reins. "Can you cool him down, then brush him for me?"

"Sure, boss."

Clint didn't correct him since he was, by Buck's decree, the temporary boss. And ordering people around wasn't something new to him; he'd been the owner–operator of Rockwell Ranch since he was eighteen and a lieutenant in Delta Force. Despite their enormous wealth, thanks to ranching and business acumen and large deposits of oil, serving was family tradition: his great grandfather saw action in France in 1917, his grandfather fought the Japanese in the Philippines. His father did two years in the military but never saw any action. His dad didn't see much of anything, having died shortly before Clint's fifth birthday.

Anyway, it felt natural to join the army, and then it felt natural to become one of the best of the best.

Excellence was what he did.

Jack stepped on his foot as he walked away—bastard horse—and Clint didn't react. If he'd been alone, he'd have told Jack he'd lost his leg above the knee and having his foot stood on barely registered on his pain-o-meter but there were people about. He never discussed his prosthetic leg, ever.

Mostly because he was allergic to pity and he was terrified of people thinking he was weak. He might be half the man he'd once been but he'd rather die than allow people to coddle him.

He didn't need anybody or anything…not anymore.

But he did need this damn car moved.

"Look, I'm sorry, I lost focus."

She sounded more defensive than sorry, Clint decided as he walked back to the driver's door of the Audi. The driver was now sitting on the top of the front seat, brand-new cowboy boots on the white leather. Clint started there, at those feet, and slowly made his way upward. Now that the red haze had lifted from his vision—he was still mad as hell but he was in control—he could take in the details.

Holy crap…

Slim legs in skin-tight blue jeans, curvy hips and a teeny waist he was sure he could span with his hands. She wore a lacy, button-down shirt and a heap of funky necklaces. Two thick braids, deep brown at the top and lighter at the ends, rested on a fantastic pair of breasts.

He lifted his eyes to her face, his mouth dry. Yep, she had a rocking body but her face was 100 percent gorgeous. A stubborn chin, a mouth made for kissing, high cheekbones and merry, mischievous, naughty eyes—deep brown—framed by long, long lashes and a cocky pair of eyebrows.

A straw Stetson covered her head.

She might be pint-sized but Clint just knew every inch of her was trouble

He jerked his head sharply. "Move."

She cocked her head and sent him a slow smile. "No."

Okay, admittedly he hadn't had a lot of interaction with people lately but when he used his don't-mess-with-me voice, people generally hustled. "What?"

"Say please."

Clint stared at her, not sure he'd heard her correctly. Shaking his head, he tried again. "Lady, move."

The smile grew sweeter. And deadlier. "No."

What the everlasting...

"Have you heard of the phrases *please* and *thank you*?" she asked, cocking her head.

She was lecturing him on manners? She'd dinged his truck, probably putting back his restoration by months and months, had barely apologized herself and then had the balls to throw his manners in his face?

Red haze descending again, he didn't trust himself to speak so Clint took the next easiest option. Stepping up to the car, he swiftly slid one arm under her knees, the other around her slim back and swung her off her perch.

But instead of placing her feet on the ground, he held her to his chest, fighting the wave of lust running through him. There was something about the soft, fragrant give of a woman, the curve of her hip beneath his fingers, the softness of her breast pushing into his chest. Her minty breath, the surprise in those deep dark eyes.

Soft, sexy lips he desperately wanted to taste...

God, he needed sex. It had been a while...another thing that changed when he lost his leg. He hated pity, from others and loathed a woe-is-me attitude but experience had taught him that normal women, women who weren't loons and gold diggers, weren't crazy about one one-legged guys with too many scars to count. His girlfriend sure as hell hadn't.

"So, this is comfortable," she purred, looking as relaxed as if she was stretched out on a lounger by a sparkling pool, margarita in her hand.

Did anything faze her?

Wanting to find out, Clint loosened his grip on her and she fell a few inches before he caught her again. Instead of squealing she just tightened her arms around his neck and those eyes, the color of his favorite dark chocolate, met his. "You wouldn't drop me."

"Watch me." Knowing there was a half decimated, now loosely packed hay bale behind him, he whipped her around and released her. Her face reflected her horror and anger as she braced to hit the hard ground. When her pretty butt landed on the hay, her eyes widened and her comical what-just-happened expression almost made him smile.

But he didn't. Because smiling wasn't something he did anymore.

Pulling his eyes off his faux cowgirl, he hopped into the convertible, cranked the engine and released the brake. Slapping the car into Reverse, he pulled away from his truck and stared down at the dashboard, noticing the flashing warning lights. Water, oil, temperature were all going nuts. Yep, she wasn't going anywhere, anytime soon.

Not his problem...

Clint cut the engine and exited the car. Ignoring the tiny woman who was trying to extract herself from the inside of the hay bale, he walked over to his truck and slapped his hand on his hip. It wasn't as bad as he'd feared. The tailgate was damaged but he was pretty sure he could find another. The lights were broken but he knew a guy who had spares. It would cost him but he could afford to pay for the damage.

Actually, he should just get the peanut to pay. Judging by the rocking diamond ring on her right hand and the fat diamond studs she wore in her ears, she could afford to pay the bill out of pocket rather than forcing him to haggle with an insurance agency.

He tossed a look over his shoulder at her. "I expect you to pay for the repairs. Twenty grand should cover it." Twenty thousand was ten times more than he needed but he figured she should pay for inconveniencing him. "I don't want to wait for the insurance company, so you can pay me and fight with them."

Her head jerked up and she pushed up the brim of her cowboy hat to glare at him. "What?"

"I want twenty K. Preferably in cash."

Those eyes hardened. "Are you off your meds? I'm not paying you twenty grand! You could buy a new truck for less than that."

Sure, but could he buy a 1972 Chevy pickup with an original, hardly used engine, original seats and fixtures? Not damn likely.

"You can find me at Rockwell Ranch. Don't make me come looking for you," Clint warned her as he walked around the hood of his truck to the driver's door. He climbed in, grabbing the steering wheel and pulling himself up, his upper body strength compensating for his missing limb. Slamming the door closed, he rested his arm on the window, surprised to see she was still glaring at him, utterly unintimidated.

Now that was a surprise because Clint knew his hard face, gruff voice and taciturn attitude scared most people off.

Instead of being frightened, she stomped over to him, pieces of hay stuck in her braid. Intrigued to see what she would do, or say, he held her hot gaze.

"You need a lesson in manners."

"Probably. I also need sex. Are you offering that too?"

Instead of blushing or throwing her hands up in the air, insulted, she narrowed her eyes. "In your dreams, cowboy. Who do you think—"

"Who are you?" he interrupted her, purely to be ornery.

"Fee… Seraphina Martinez."

Fee suited her. Seraphina didn't.

And that mouth. It was sassy and sensuous and made for sex. Talking? Not so much.

"Bring the money to my ranch—don't make me come looking for you," Clint told her, thinking he'd better leave before he did something stupid, like using his own mouth to cut off the tirade that was, obviously, coming.

Shit, he was losing it.

"I'm ten miles down the road. You'll see the gates." Clint cranked the engine and placed his hand on the gear stick. He tapped his Stetson with two fingers.

"Ma'am," he said, purely to irritate her.

Annoyance and frustration jumped into her eyes. "Don't you 'ma'am' me! I *will* get you to learn some manners."

Hell, if she was under him, naked, he'd learn anything she wanted him to. *Enough now, Rock, drive off.*

"Honey, I don't do people so I don't do manners. I just need my twenty K."

"When pigs fly," Fee muttered, her hands on those curvy hips. Clint looked at her mouth again and fought the urge to leave the car, haul her into his arms and taste it. To inhale her sweet scent and pull her into his—he looked down—rock-hard erection.

Over the roar of his engine, he heard one of the women shout across to the fake cowgirl. "Is he going to be your next project, Fee?"

Fee looked at him and her smile chilled him to his core. "You know what? I rather think he is."

What the hell did she mean by that?

Time to go.

Clint slammed his pickup into Reverse, conscious that all the New Yorkers were still staring at him. But he only wanted to see the brunette with the smart mouth and tempting curves in his rearview mirror. She was sexy as hell and, because he wasn't a total idiot, he'd noticed her attraction to him.

Clint barreled down the driveway and tossed his Stetson onto the empty seat next to him. He'd seen her checking him out and suspected she liked what she'd seen, up to a point. He'd worked hella hard to build his core, chest and back muscles. Women liked his top half but, these days, his bottom half caused him problems.

Hell, both the women—his mom and his girlfriend—he'd ever loved had been unable to come to terms with his disability…

The memories rolled back and Clint forced himself to face them. On returning from Afghanistan, he'd spent a couple of months in hospital recovering after his amputation and when he got back to the ranch, he'd spent a few more months in bed, sleeping and smoking and drinking.

Carla, his long-time girlfriend, had immediately moved in to take care of him and she'd run around, waiting on him hand and foot. It didn't matter to her that he could afford to hire teams of nurses, doctors and physiotherapists. Family money, lots and lots of money, gave him access to the best health care on the planet but Carla only allowed the bare minimum of people to have access to him.

She'd insisted on fussing over him herself, coddling and mothering him. But, as his depression lifted, he realized that he didn't like the flabby, bloated, unhealthy man he saw in the mirror. He'd always been a fitness fanatic and because he was sick of feeling sick and miserable, he turned two rooms of his ranch house into a state-of-the-art gym.

As he got fitter, and more adept with his prosthetic, he became more independent and Carla had mentally, and physically, retreated. And when his sex drive finally returned, she'd retreated some more. When he'd finally convinced her that he was well enough, strong enough, for sex and taken his prosthetic off, she bolted.

Never to be seen again.

Thanks to his frequent absences due to his career in the military, they'd drifted apart and his accident pulled them back together again. She adored his dependence on her, loved being so very needed and had he stayed that way, she might've stuck around. But being weak wasn't something Clint did. Weakness wasn't part of his DNA.

His sex life didn't improve after she left. He'd tried a couple of one-night stands and neither were successful. One woman left when she saw his leg, another, the next morning, acted like she'd done him the biggest favor by sleeping with him and Clint decided that climaxes with strangers weren't worth the humiliation.

It had been two years since he got laid and, yeah, he missed sex. And when he met someone he was instantly, ridiculously attracted to, as he'd been to that brunette back there, he missed it more than ever.

But sex was just sex; he wouldn't die from not getting any.

He didn't think.

Clint felt his phone vibrating in the back pocket of his jeans and lifted his butt cheek to pull it out. Glancing down at the screen, he saw the Dallas area code and recognized the number as one of his mother's.

The mother he no longer spoke to.

Clint briefly wondered why she, or more likely her PA or another lackey, was calling. It had been years since they'd last spoken but he didn't answer the call. He had nothing to say to his mom. Not anymore...

Mila had blown into the hospital to visit with him before his operation and he'd been cynically surprised by her show of support as she'd never been an attentive, involved mother.

Back in his room after the operation that took his leg, he'd hadn't felt strong enough to deal with his intense news-anchor mother and he'd pretended to still be under the anesthetic, hoping she'd go away. He'd just wanted the world to leave him alone but his hearing hadn't disappeared along with his leg and Mila's softly spoken words drifted over to him.

So, I'm here, he's still out so what now?

I've arranged for the press to photograph you leaving the hospital after visiting your war-hero son. Clint had recognized the voice as Greg's, Mila's business manager, whom he'd met a few times over the years. He was, so Mila said, the power behind Mila's rise to being one of the most famous, powerful and respected women in Dallas.

So, try to look worried, distressed. And proud.

I'm going to have to act my ass off, Mila had moaned. *He's, like...repulsive.*

Jesus, Mila, he's your son, Greg had said, sounding, to his credit, horrified.

I like pretty and I like perfect. He's never been perfect but before he went off to play at war, he was at least pretty, Mila had retorted. *Thank God he has that girlfriend because I'm certainly not prepared to be his nurse.*

Wow. Her words laid down just another hot layer of pain.

With her words bouncing off his brain, Clint had slipped into sleep and a six-month depression. Carla and his mother were the reasons he'd worked his butt off to become, as much as possible, the person he was before the surgery. He never wanted to be dependent on anyone ever again, not for help, sex or even company. Carla had wanted to help him too much, his mother not at all, but Clint was happy to be shot of them both.

All he wanted was for the few people he chose to interact with to see past his injury to the man he was. And he couldn't do that if he flaunted his prosthetic so he never, ever allowed anyone to see his bionic leg.

And if giving up sex was the price he paid for his independence then he'd happily live with the lack of below-the-belt action. Nothing was more important to him than his independence. And his pride.

But some days, like today, a woman came along who made him wonder, who made him burn. But he was nothing if not single-minded, and like the others he'd felt a fleeting attraction to, he wouldn't act on it.

No woman was ever worth the hassle.

Two

Fee slid into a booth in Royal's diner and nodded her appreciation. Every time she walked through the doors, she had the same thought: that this was what a diner should look like: 1950s-style decor, red fake-leather booths, black-and-white checkerboard linoleum floor and the suggestion that gossip flowed through here like a river.

She rather liked Royal, Texas. It was, obviously, everything New York City wasn't—a slow-paced small town with space to breathe.

From being yanked from town to town with her parents, Fee had honed the ability to immediately discern whether a town would, temporarily, suit her or not. She'd hated Honolulu—weird, right?—and loved Pensacola, tolerated Tacoma and loved Charleston. But something about Royal called to her; she felt at ease here.

She would never belong anywhere—Manhattan was where she'd chosen to work and socialize but it still wasn't home, she didn't think any place would be—but Royal was intriguing.

Strange that this small town with its wide, clean streets and eclectic mix of people and shops was where she felt more relaxed than she had in a long, long time.

Fee grinned. If she kept on this mental train, soon she would be thinking she could live on a ranch and raise cows. She snorted and looked down at her manicured fingers and soft hands. This from a girl who believed meat came from the supermarket and eggs from cardboard cartons?

Now, crotchety Clint Rockwell looked like he was born to ride the range. The man was one sexy cowboy. Pity he had the personality of a rabid raccoon. Fee put her hand on the box lying on the table and grinned.

Twenty thousand to fix a heap of rust? Ok, that wasn't fair, it was vintage truck and probably rare but the repair, from her research, wouldn't cost that much! She knew she was being hustled; she wasn't the village idiot.

Well, she might be a reality TV star but she was a pragmatic reality TV star and she didn't hand out money like it was M&M's.

If he hadn't been such a snot she might've tossed in a few extra grand to compensate him for the inconvenience but the guy had taken jerk to a whole new level...

He needed to be brought down a peg or six.

Fee heard the door to the diner swing open and watched as Lulu threaded her way through the tables to fall into the seat opposite her. Like her, Lulu had also dressed down in jeans. In her case, they were topped with a simple white, thigh-length jersey, a brightly colored scarf in a complicated knot around her neck. Lu slapped a paper folder on the table between them and frowned at the board game Fee had purchased from the toy shop down the road. It was a game to teach kids about money and, importantly, the notes inside looked remarkably real.

"I'm sure we can find something to do in Royal that doesn't include board games," Lulu stated.

Fee grinned. "I'm not playing with you. I'm going to play with someone else."

"You're going to pay him in toy money?" Lulu caught on instantly. That was one of the many reasons they were best friends. "Oh, clever."

Fee put her hands together as if to pray and bowed her head. "Thank you. Did the *Secret Lives* researcher dig up any information on Clint Rockwell?" she demanded, pulling the folder to her. "I mean, I don't think he's one of Royal's leading lights—not with a personality like his— but maybe he made the papers because he did something stupid. I can see him busting up a bar or racking up speeding tickets, maybe breaking and entering…"

"You have a hell of an imagination," Lulu commented, thanking the waitress when she offered coffee.

Fee was certain that Clint Rockwell was not the boy next door, not someone who was part of the Chamber of Commerce or a member of the illustrious Texas Cattleman's Club.

He was an outsider, a loner, someone who didn't do group events. Someone mysterious, possibly dangerous…

Fee flipped open the folder and looked down to see a photograph of Rockwell looking very un-farmy. In this photograph, his short dark-blond hair was covered by a tan beret immediately identifying him as an army ranger. He wore a dark blue dress uniform with about a million medals on his chest, including a Purple Heart.

Well, she'd gotten one thing right—as part of that elite regiment, he was definitely dangerous.

Fee was about to move the photograph to the side when

she heard the waitress sigh. Fee looked up to find the young girl's eyes firmly on the photograph. Fee couldn't blame her for taking a moment. Rockwell, looking like Captain America in his dress blues, was definitely sigh worthy.

"It's so sad."

Fee exchanged a look with Lulu and frowned. "What's so sad?" Lulu asked the waitress, whose name tag stated she was Julie.

Julie gestured to the photograph with her coffee carafe. "Clint Rockwell. Poor guy."

Ooh, gossip. Fee leaned back, her full attention on the waitress. "Why? What happened to him?"

"He's a Rockwell, so obviously there's no shortage of cash. Like his daddy, his granddaddy and his granddaddy before him, Clint is an oilman and a rancher. But he leases his oil fields and occupies himself with his ranch. And with coordinating Royal's volunteer fire department."

Fee's head spun with all the information. She held up a hand. "He's a fireman too?"

"Apparently, he did some firefighting course in California before he enlisted." Julie pulled her eyebrows together, looking a little confused. "Where was I? Right, his daddy died when he was young, really young, and he and his mama don't talk."

Yeah, that was sad. Her parents might have hauled her from pillar to post and back to pillar but they were now settled in Florida and she saw them occasionally. In fact, she was heading there shortly to spend Christmas with them. They weren't super close but she knew she was loved, in an abstract kind of way.

"The Rockwells are a Royal institution, a founding family and really rich."

"How rich?" Fee asked, as direct as always.

"Mega," Julie replied.

And he was stiffing her for twenty grand? The bastard!

"What else can you tell me about him?" Fee asked, her temper bubbling.

"He lost his leg in a helicopter crash. That's how he earned his Purple Heart. His leg was mangled. His whole unit was seriously injured. Apparently, the helicopter crashed in an enemy-controlled area and he, and another guy, held off the bad guys until reinforcements arrived. Half of his unit survived, but Clint lost his leg."

Fee frowned at Julie, not understanding. "He lost his leg?" She'd noticed he walked with a slight limp but never suspected he wore a prosthetic.

Julie nodded. "Yeah. That's why he left the army." Julie shrugged. "Ever since he got back, he's become a bit of a recluse and doesn't have much to do with Royal residents, except for the volunteer firefighters. And he never, ever talks about his tours, his regiment or his injury. Like, *ever*."

Someone called Julie and she sent them an apologetic smile. "Sorry, got to go."

Fee transferred her gaze to Lulu, who looked equally disbelieving. "He's disabled?"

"He looked plenty abled," Fee replied. "I would never have thought…"

"Holy crap." Lulu rested her hand on her heart. "Hot, brave and sexy—I think I might be a little in love with him."

Fee felt a surge of jealousy and did an internal eye roll. What was wrong with her? Flipping the folder closed—why had they sent the researcher to the local library when the source of good information could be pumped for details over coffee?—Fee stared out of the window and watched the activity on the street outside.

Did this information change anything? She was as much a sucker for a wounded war hero as the next person and she had a million questions. Why was he a loner? How had he managed to master his prosthetic leg to be able to ride as he did? Why was he holding her up for twenty grand if he was loaded? But mostly, she just needed to figure out whether this changed her plans.

If he hadn't lost his leg, she wouldn't have hesitated to confront him and toss the fake money in his face. But should this revelation really hold her back? Her thinking she should go easy on him because he'd lost a leg was insulting in the extreme. He'd already proven he could more than handle her, and lost leg or not, the guy needed to learn some manners.

"You're still going to confront him," Lulu stated, sounding resigned.

"Damn straight I am."

"He's pretty intimidating, Fee," Lulu said, concern in her voice. "I'm not sure whether you should go out to his ranch alone."

Fee instinctively shook her head. "He's not going to hurt me, Lu. Oh, his tongue might raise some blisters, but he'd never raise a hand to me."

"How do you know?"

Fee lifted both shoulders and ran her hand through her hair. "I have a strong gut feeling about him. He's not dangerous…sad, confused, bitter, sure. But he won't hurt me."

Lulu sighed. "And you see his lack of manners and his rudeness as a challenge."

"Sure. Someone needs to set him straight. I'm sorry he lost a leg but it doesn't give him the right to act like an ass."

Lulu pinned her to her seat with hard eyes. "Oh, I know you, Seraphina Martinez—and I know what this is really about. Yes, bad manners and rudeness annoy you, but you also see him as a challenge. You want to know if you can be the one who can break through to him, make him more sociable."

Fee avoided eye contact, waiting for Lulu to drop the topic. But her friend wasn't done.

"I don't think he's going to like being one of your projects, Fee," Lulu told her, worry coating every word. "He's not going to bend under the force of your personality and if he wanted friends, he would make his own. You don't need to rescue every stray who comes across your path, Seraphina."

Lulu's use of her full name was a solid clue to her seriousness. Fee wrinkled her nose. "Do I really do that?"

"You know you do! You have the strongest rescue gene of anyone I know! He's a veteran, you have a soft spot for soldiers because you grew up on an army base. Add hero and wounded to the mix and you want to wrap him up in a blanket and coddle him."

"I'd rather unwrap him and do him," Fee admitted. She pulled a face and forced the words out. "I'm crazy attracted to him, Lu."

"Any woman, and more than a few guys, would be," Lulu replied. "And that's okay. Although you're not big on one-night stands or brief flings, if you want to sleep with him, do. But when he puts his clothes back on, don't try to fix him, Fee. Respect his right to be alone, to choose how he interacts with the world. From the sound of it, he's gone through hell and back. If he wants to be left alone, he's earned the right." Lulu gripped her hand and continued. "Fixing him might make you feel better but it's not about you, it's about him."

Lu's words smacked her in the chest. She stared down at the folder, her breath a little ragged. She did like the feeling of accomplishment she got when she managed to solve someone else's problems. Sometimes it felt like she was filling in pieces of herself. But Lu was right, this wasn't a makeover, or a blind date, or a rescued horse. This was a man of pride, honor and discipline who'd served his country with distinction. He'd trained hard, sacrificed much, seen and experienced situations no one should have to see and she had no right to make judgments about his life. Or to presume she knew what was best for him.

Fee pulled in a deep breath and met Lulu's eyes. "Okay."

"Okay...what?"

"Okay, I won't try to fix him, to rescue him from his lonely life," Fee clarified. "But I *am* going to confront him about his rudeness and his lack of manners. You can be a hermit without being an ass."

Lulu slapped her hand against her forehead and groaned. "And are you still going to pay him off with toy money?"

Fee nodded. "Damn right I am."

"And are you going to sleep with him?"

She couldn't lie, she was very tempted. Fee lifted one shoulder and both her hands. "He's tempting, so tempting, and I shouldn't..."

"But?"

Fee didn't want to be attracted to him, and as God and Lulu knew, she wasn't in the habit of falling into bed with guys on a whim—or at all—but she didn't think she could resist the sexy, sad, rude cowboy. "But if he asks me, I just might."

Clint hated surprise visitors—he never wanted to be caught without his prosthetic or using crutches—so he'd installed cameras all over the ranch and had them wirelessly connected so they sent an alert to his phone whenever he had company. He grabbed his cell from the back pocket of his jeans, pulled up the screen connecting him to his camera feed and saw another convertible—red, this time—flying up his driveway.

Yep, she was back.

Clint, walking a mare that had colic, whistled and when Darren's head popped out from a stall, he jerked his head. "Can you carry on walking Belle for me?"

Darren's eyes widened with concern. "LT, I have no experience with horses and this one is, so I hear, one of your best."

Clint smiled at the familiar nickname for *lieutenant*. "It's just walking, Darren, and we're civilians now—you can call me Clint. If you run into trouble with her or you think something is wrong, just yell for Brad. He'll hear you and take over."

Brad, his foreman, didn't always agree with his policy of hiring out-of-work veterans instead of experienced hands but Clint insisted that learning to muck out stalls and fix fences didn't require experience. The ranch needed people who wanted to work and there were so many vets needing to find a way to support themselves and their families.

And, as he knew, open skies, fresh air and animals were a great way to deal with the memories of war.

"I'll be back as soon as I can."

Darren nodded, took the reins and led the horse to the entrance of the stable. Clint broke into a jog, heading for his dirt bike parked just outside. Gunning the accelerator, he headed back to his house, cutting around the back of the stables to arrive at the main house at the same time she did.

They both cut their engines at the same time and Clint rested his forearms on the handlebars of his bike, watching her from behind his dark glasses and the brim of his

Stetson. The sun was starting to dip and he could probably ditch both but they provided a shield he badly needed...

He couldn't let her know how attracted he was to her, how he wanted nothing more than to take her inside and get her naked and horizontal.

Actually, he just needed her naked because vertical worked too.

Clint watched as she shoved an expensive pair of designer shades into her hair, the arms raking her loose curls off her face. She wore less makeup today than she had yesterday. Her lips were a pale pink instead of bright red and her outfit consisted of a cranberry-colored jersey that worked well with her creamy skin and those brilliant dark eyes.

God, she was hot. He couldn't invite her into the house: first, because his crutches were leaning against the wall in the hallway—he'd put on his leg while sitting on the bench in the hallway early this morning—and second because he wasn't sure he could resist her.

Fee opened the door of the rental and climbed out, shapely legs in tight blue jeans tucked into low-heeled, knee-high boots. The jersey clung to her breasts and curves of her hips and Clint felt all the moisture leave his mouth.

He'd stormed houses filled with terrorists in Afghanistan, had faced down a Somalian warlord and protected his guys while they waited for an evac after the crash but he'd never experienced such a dry mouth.

But this woman, with her black-brown hair and expressive eyes, managed to achieve what a dozen treacherous situations hadn't...

And that scared the crap out of him, which added another layer to his grouch.

"Have you got my money?" he demanded, staying where he was.

"Hello, Fee, how are you? Did you find the place okay?" Fee singsonged, calling attention yet again to his lack of manners.

Tough. He didn't have the time and energy to play nice; he just wanted her to be gone before he made a stupid suggestion like, "Let's go to bed."

Because that was a disaster waiting to happen. He'd have to explain he was missing a limb and then, if she didn't rabbit, he'd have to wait and see if she could deal with his stump and scars.

Such fun…

Nope, it was a game he was better off not playing.

"You're wasting my time, Martinez," Clint warned, dismounting the bike and pocketing the keys. He waited for her at the bottom of the stairs leading up to his wraparound porch and the front door. He wouldn't invite her inside but they could, at least, get out of the sun.

Instead of following him, Fee placed her hands on her hips and tipped her head back to look at the house he still thought of as his Grandpa's—the place where he'd visited the family patriarch every summer from the time of his dad's death when Clint was five until he turned eighteen and enlisted.

At the time he hadn't cared where the army sent him, as long as it kept him away from his mother's hounding to study law or something equally boring. He couldn't have known that shortly after he enlisted, his beloved grandpa would die, and Clint would become the fifth Rockwell to own the land.

Grandpa Rockwell always said that he didn't want the land to be a burden, to be a noose around his neck. He'd been the biggest supporter of his military career so Clint hadn't felt the need to rush home when he died, comfortable to place the ranch in Brad's capable hands until his return.

He'd always preferred the ranching side of his inheritance so he'd leased his oil fields. Years later, he was still happy for someone else to deal with that side of the business.

"I like your house," Fee said, and he frowned at the note of surprise in her voice. "It's big, obviously, like everything else in Texas, but it's not ostentatious. I don't do ostentatious."

"Says the girl driving another fast, expensive convertible," he drawled.

Fee looked back at the car and her husky laughter surprised him. "Touché. But I'm a real gearhead and I don't get to drive as often as I'd like to."

"I'm sure all the residents of New York City are eternally grateful for that fact, because you have a lead foot," Clint said. "And how did you charm the rental company into trusting you with another fast car after your crash yesterday?"

"I apologized sincerely and asked them nicely," Fee retorted, her eyes flashing with irritation.

"You didn't apologize to me," Clint pointed out.

"I tried to! But then you started barking orders and tossing me into hay bales!"

Clint lifted his index finger. "One. One hay bale."

Fee rolled her eyes. "Whatever... Anyway, you should try this thing called charm or, this is a radical idea so beware, a smile. Oh, your face might crack but I think you'll survive the experience."

Clint felt the corner of his mouth twitch with amusement. He loved her sassy mouth and now rather liked the fact that he didn't intimidate her. He walked up onto the porch and gestured to a cluster of outdoor furniture to the left of the door.

"Take a seat."

Fee's winged eyebrows shot up. "Ooh, manners. There's hope for you yet."

"Don't bet on it," Clint replied, putting his hands into the back pockets of his jeans. He watched as she sat on the arm of one wicker chair, casually draping one gorgeous leg over the other and tucking her foot behind her calf. Such a female, sexy movement, full of grace and charm.

Clint waited her out, knowing silence was usually a good way to hurry the conversation along by forcing the other person to talk. But Fee confounded him again by ignoring his scowl and silence, seemingly content to watch the mares frolicking in the paddock closest to the house.

Why couldn't this woman do what he expected her to?

Clint rocked on his heels, his eyes constantly dropping to her lips, wondering whether she tasted as spicy as she sounded. He eventually broke their silence. "Why are you here, Seraphina?"

Fee flashed a smile and leaned down to tuck her hand into her very large leather bag—big enough to carry a change of clothes, a bag of groceries and a saddle or two—and pulled out a couple of rolls of cash. He saw a fifty-dollar bill under the rubber band of one and a hundred-dollar bill around the other. He sucked in his breath.

He'd been annoyed yesterday and tossed out twenty thousand as a figure, hoping to annoy her. But, judging by the cash she'd brought along, she'd taken him seriously.

He couldn't take her money, not now and not ever.

Clint was about to tell her to put it away when he noticed the rolls seemed irregular, that not all the edges of the bills lined up. If he hadn't been so distracted by her, he would've immediately noticed that something was wrong with the roll, that her sweet, innocent expression was as fake as hell.

Oh, hell no, she wouldn't dare...

He held out his hand and instead of handing the first one over, she threw it at his chest. He caught the first one, then the second and tucked it under his arm, snapping the rubber band off the first.

Yep, as he thought. A real note covering fake money. Toy money...

Clint felt a bubble of laughter rise within him, tried to swallow it and failed. When his husky-from-lack-of-use chuckle filled the space between them, he was as surprised as Fee.

He couldn't remember the last time he'd laughed...

He heard Fee's smothered laugh, a cross between a hiccup and a giggle. And because he wanted to taste his laughter on her lips, because he wanted to taste her, Clint moved quickly and, after placing his hands on either side of the arm of the chair, bent down and kissed her.

And immediately wished he hadn't.

Because, as their lips touched, as her mouth opened and her fingers came up to touch the scruff on his jaw, he knew he'd never be satisfied with just one kiss...

He wanted more. Much, much more.

He was a grouch and a grump, curmudgeonly and contrary, but hellfire, the man could kiss. Fee found herself surging to her feet, her arms looping around his neck, her breasts pushing into his chest. She felt his big hand on the top of her butt, pulling her into a very thick, concrete-hard erection, and she whimpered in delight.

He was so big, everywhere. Fee found herself on her tiptoes, straining to align their mouths, knowing they'd both have cricks in their necks at the end of this make-out session. Clint solved the problem by placing his hands on her hips and boosting her up against his body, holding her weight with ease. What else was a girl to do but wind her legs around his trim waist, hook them behind his back and slide her most sensitive spot over his impressive bulge?

Fee heard Clint's moan of appreciation and then his hand encircled the top of her leg, his fingers on the inside of her thigh, and Fee wished he had his hands on her naked flesh, that she could feel his clever mouth sucking her nipples, maybe even going lower.

His mouth, as she was coming to learn, was a weapon of mass temptation. Fee knew that if he asked, she'd eagerly follow him into his house and down the hallway to his bedroom, or whether he decided to stop. She would take whatever he'd give her, grateful to be the recipient of the profound pleasure he managed to pull to the surface.

They didn't need to talk, their bodies were better at communicating than they were. Fee felt Clint take a step and she felt the hard coolness of wood through her jeans, dimly realizing he'd planted her on the wide sill of a window.

He lifted his hands to hold her face, his thumbs caressing her cheekbones as he feathered kisses across her eyelids, down her temple. Fee closed her eyes, enjoying the moment of tenderness. Then Clint covered her right breast with his hand, and her nipple tightened, rising against the fabric of her sweater to press into his palm. Clint jerked his head back, looked at her with stormy eyes and muttered a quiet obscenity.

"Why aren't you pushing me away?" he hoarsely demanded.

"Why would I, since you kiss like a dream?" Fee responded, her voice just this side of breathy. Hearing his sharp intake of air, Fee decided to rock his boat a little more. "You are abrupt and annoying but, God, you know how to touch me."

Clint ran his knuckles up her ribcage and across her nipple. "Like this?" His fingers burrowed under her sweater and landed on her bare skin.

"Exactly like that," Fee murmured. Then Clint pulled down the lacy cup of her bra and pulled her nipple with his fingers. Fee couldn't help crying out.

Fee put her hand behind his head and shook her head. "No, don't stop! Do it again."

Clint's repeated the action and Fee arched her back, dropped her leg and banged her heel against the back of his lower thigh, just above his knee. Instead of bone and sinew, the heel of her boot bounced off metal hidden behind the fabric of his jeans.

Clint reacted like he'd been scorched. Leaping backward, he put a healthy amount of distance between them. He stared down at the floor as Fee tried to make sense of why he stopped.

The answer came to her on a quiet whisper: she'd kicked his prosthetic leg.

Well, okay then. No big deal…

"Come back here and kiss me, Rockwell," Fee suggested, wanting, no, needing his mouth on hers. She wasn't done with him, not yet.

Clint had frozen, his big arms folded across his chest, his face a blank mask. She didn't like the lack of emotion in his eyes, in his expression. She could handle pissed off and irritated, turned on and taciturn, but she didn't like this cyborg standing in front of her, acting like she was a fly he was getting ready to swat.

"I think it's time you went home," Clint said, in the blandest of bland tones. "You can take your gag money with you and start arrangements to pay me the twenty thousand we agreed upon."

They were back to this, really? "That number is just something you pulled out of your ass to piss me off, we both know it's stupidly excessive. As for leaving…"

Fee jumped down from the windowsill and walked up to Clint until her breasts brushed against his arms. She saw the flare of heat in his eyes and knew he was nowhere near as unaffected as he was pretending to be.

Good to know.

"I don't like mixed signals, Rockwell. You can't devour me one minute and ask me to leave the next."

"On my spread, I can do anything I damn well like," Clint muttered.

Fee cocked her head at his statement. "Now you're just sounding petulant. It's not a good look on you, Rockwell."

Clint rubbed his hand over his face. "Will you just go? Please?"

"No, not until we talk about why you jumped away from me like you were hit by a bolt of lightning."

Annoyance and frustration jumped into Clint's eyes and Fee didn't mind. She could deal with those emotions. She far preferred anger to his impassivity. "Let's break it down, shall we?" she continued.

"Let's not."

Fee ignored him. "You touched my boob and I banged the back of my heel against your prosthetic leg. Now, because I know that couldn't hurt you, there has to be another reason why you're overreacting."

Clint handed her a hard stare, his eyes reflecting confusion and more than a little fear. At what? What was the real problem here?

"You know I have a prosthetic leg."

Yes, she did. It was the least important thing she'd discovered about him. "I also know you are a billionaire, you were some sort of super soldier and now you are a semi-recluse, much to the dismay of the Royal residents, who've placed you somewhere between God and Friday-night football."

Finally, a hint of amusement touched his lips. "That's a huge exaggeration since I have little to do with them."

"Trust me, ten minutes dealing with your sarcasm and general orneriness would have them reevaluating your wonderfulness," Fee said, her tone tart. She slapped her hands on her hips. "But we're getting distracted from the point of this conversation."

Clint looked past her at something beyond her shoulder. "You're not going to let this go, are you?"

Damn straight. "No."

"I lost my left leg above my knee. When you kicked it, I realized I should stop this, now."

"Why?"

"To save both of us the embarrassment of you running out of here squealing when you see me, and it, fully exposed. It's not a pretty sight." Clint's smile was hard and his eyes glittered with pain-laced fury. "I don't need your sympathy or your pity. I just need sex."

Fee felt anger boil inside of her. She was angry at the people who had so obviously hurt him by making him feel less than, and angry at him for projecting those people's feelings onto her. Yes, she was a reality TV star but she wasn't shallow, dammit.

To make her point, Fee gathered a handful of Clint's T-shirt in her fist. She knew with a quick twist he could be free of her grasp, he did have a hundred pounds of muscle on her, but she was trying to make a point here.

"You just keep pissing me off, Rockwell. It's quite a talent," Fee murmured.

"Just get to the point, Seraphina. I've got work to do."

Fee pulled him over to the steps and pushed him down two of them so they were eye to eye, face to face. "That's better. Now, listen up because I'm only going to say this once…"

"Man, you're bossy."

"If I were a man, you'd call my behavior assertiveness," Fee quipped back.

"If you were a man, I would've had you in a headlock by now."

Fair point, Fee thought.

"And I certainly wouldn't have kissed you and we wouldn't be having this conversation," Clint continued.

Fee waved his words away. "I'm not going to get into an argument about semantics with you, Rockwell. Not right now anyway." Fee was surprised that Clint—a taciturn, will-only-use-one-word-when-three-are-needed man— was even arguing with her.

Fee placed her hands on either side of his face and rested her thumbs against his mouth. "Be. Quiet."

"Nothing makes me angrier than when someone who doesn't know me compares me to someone else," Fee told him, keeping her voice low but intense. "I'm lots of things—I have a hundred faults—but I am, one hundred percent, my own person. That means I make up my own mind and I get very pissed when people assume they know what's inside my head."

Clint narrowed his eyes at her and pulled his head out of her gentle grip. Fee held up her hand to silence him when he opened his mouth to speak. "Not done. I kissed you because, although you are annoying and frustrating, you're probably the best-looking guy I've stumbled across in a long, long time. You're tall, built, ripped and you kiss like you're in contention for an Olympic medal. You've got skills, Rockwell. I'm not going to deny that. And, yes, had you not behaved like a jerk—which seems to be something you specialize in—we might be naked right now. But you did, so we're not.

"I already knew you lost a leg, Rockwell, and I got the Royal diner version of how it happened. If I was turned off by your missing leg, I wouldn't have started something we couldn't finish. Again, I am lots of things, but I'm not a tease."

Fee handed him a hot look. "Fact, I want you. I wanted you the first time I saw you days ago when I first visited Blackwood Hollow. I wanted you yesterday when I saw you barreling around the ring on your demon horse, looking sweaty and hot and, God, so alive."

His eyes heated and Fee forced herself to continue, to not go with her impulse and cover his mouth with hers. She needed to say this; she had to get her point across.

"I wanted you when you castigated me about my driving. I wanted you when I was showering, and in my dreams last night. When I heard about your having lost a leg, I felt, momentarily, sorry for you." She saw him jerk at the *S* word and shrugged it off. "I felt sorry for you because that's how nice people feel when they hear about something tragic happening to a good man. But that was quickly replaced with the 'how the hell does he ride so well with one leg?' thought."

"Seraphina—"

Since he was calling her by her full name, Fee knew she hadn't broken through yet. "I'm not done, Rockwell." Fee took a deep breath. "Judge me on my own words, Clint. My own actions. Don't judge me on someone else's stupidity. It's not right and it most certainly isn't fair."

Clint rubbed the back of his neck and stared down at

the ground. It was a hell of a conversation to have after such a short acquaintance and a bruising kiss.

"And know this…" Fee concluded. "If I start something, I always finish it."

Clint raised his head, looking mystified and a little amused. "Where the hell did you come from, Seraphina Martins?"

"Martinez," she corrected. Fee stood up straight and just managed to drop a kiss on his jaw. "And I'm from everywhere. And nowhere."

She tapped her fingers lightly against the side of his jaw. "If we do this again, make sure you're prepared to let me in, to see you, to see all of you. Otherwise, don't bother."

A little bit of misery seeped into Clint's eyes. "I don't know if I can do that."

Fee rubbed her cheek against him, loving the feel of his scruff gently scratching her cheek. "That's your prerogative, Rockwell. If you can't, that's cool. But, for me, it's an all or nothing deal. You see me naked, I see you naked."

"You're whole, Fee, and I imagine you look glorious naked."

"Damn right I do." Fee dropped a small kiss onto his lips. "But beauty, as they say, is in the eye of the beholder, Clint."

She pulled back, spun around and picked up her tote bag from the floor. She looked down at the fake bundles of cash on the floor and picked up the real money and tucked the bills into the back pocket of her jeans. She tossed Clint a look over her shoulder.

"Also, while you are deciding whether you want to sleep with me or not, how about you stop messing with me about how much the repairs are going to cost and give me a figure that's in the ballpark of reasonable?"

"Of course I *want* to sleep with you, Fee," Clint said.

Fee sent him a small smile. "But not enough, Clint, not just yet."

And that was okay, she'd allow him a little time to get there. Men always needed a little extra time to get with the program.

Her program was simple—rope a cowboy, ride him hard and get him out of her system.

Really, this shouldn't be so hard.

Three

Whoever had the bright idea that the New York social-ites should learn something about ranching should be shot, Clint decided. And the person who decided Clint should oversee the process should be tortured, then shot.

Back at Blackwood Hollow, Clint fought to hide his impatience as he stood outside a stall in the bigger of the two stable blocks and listened to Miranda DuPree-Blackwood and her Italian bombshell colleague bitch about the smell, the dirty hay and the smell of horse.

Well, it was a stable, and to be fair, only the brunette was bitching. Miranda just had a determined look on her face as she pitched hay into a barrow while the brunette—Rachel, Rafel… *Rafaela*—examined her nails. Clint turned around to glare at the director who was making notes on her clipboard, her iPad tucked under her arm.

Damn you, Buck, for complicating the hell out of your death.

"You do realize we have work to do and we can't hang around here all day waiting for these—" he bit back the word he really wanted to say "—*ladies* to get out of our way?" Clint demanded. He had his own ranch to look after once everything was running smoothly at Blackwood Hollow. Yet again, he cursed the day he'd agreed to keep an eye on the place after Buck got sick. He should have stuck to his role as the town hermit and said no, but while his grandfather's old friend was irascible and hard-assed, he'd had, under his prickly exterior, a heart of gold few people got to see. Buck had also kept an eye on Rockwell Ranch after Gramps died, so Clint owed him.

And he always, always, paid off his debts.

"Miranda owns this place, there's an inheritance saga, a family feud and, on top of that, the *Secret Lives* stars know nothing about ranching. I know this is frustrating but it will make fantastic TV."

Great, because that was what he cared about, making fantastic TV. He had cows to feed, fence stays to cut for repair work and he wanted to put a new wood stove in the calving barn so the calves born in late winter had a better chance of survival.

Thank God the oil side of his business was leased and the day-to-day issues associated with that business weren't his problem.

Miranda, with hay in her hair, poked her head out from the stall. "You don't need to be here, Clint. I'm sure Gabe can show us the ropes."

Gabe, Buck's longest employee, gave him a *don't leave me alone with them* look. While Miranda had inherited Blackwood Hollow and everything else from Buck, she knew diddly-squat about ranching and she couldn't afford to annoy the staff, especially Gabe.

Gabe knew the ranch inside out and Miranda, whether

she knew it or not, needed him. And the man looked frustrated and irritated and was, obviously, itching to leave.

Clint sighed. "Gabe, you carry on with the rest of your work. I'll look after this lot."

Gratitude flashed in the older man's eyes and he didn't bother to argue, he just hightailed it out of the barn as fast as he could. Clint fought the urge to run after him.

He turned back to the director, who held a clipboard to her chest. "How much more do you need?"

"Well, I thought we could film Rafaela learning to saddle a horse and taking her first riding lesson, Miranda collecting eggs from the chicken run and Lulu filling the horse nets with food."

Yeah, because that's what ranching was really about. Collecting eggs and feeding horses. What about counting the livestock, branding, checking for pregnancies, land management? Worrying about too little rain, too much rain, stock theft, beef prices, whether they had enough feed to see them through the winter after a very dry summer?

"I need to film Seraphina doing something farmy, too."

Clint held back his snort. *Farmy?* God help him.

"I can assign hands to show the ladies the ropes for the tasks you had in mind, and I can show Fee how we transport bales of hay to the pastures so the cattle have enough to eat during these winter months," Clint suggested.

"Someone mention my name?"

Clint turned and his heart kicked up when he heard her chirpy voice. He slowly turned around and he had to smile at the sight of Fee in cowgirl mode again. Her long hair was in two thick braids hanging down over her flannel shirt, which was worn over an old pair of jeans. She wore rain boots printed with—Clint leaned forward and squinted at her feet—ducks wearing rain boots.

She had a streak of dirt across her cheek and she looked

like she'd actually been doing some work instead of just playing at it.

"Lu and I are done in this stall. What's next?" Fee asked, rubbing her hands on the seat of her pants.

Clint used his height to peek over the stable door and was impressed by the full water trough and clean floor covered by fresh straw.

And they hadn't taken forever to do it.

The director consulted her clipboard. "Why don't you go with Clint and Jimmy? He can film you taking something somewhere."

Clint summoned the little patience he had left. "Hay bales to the feed stations in the pastures," Clint told her.

"Cool. How do we get the hay out there? Do we put it in wheelbarrows?"

Clint had to smile. "Since the bales are over a ton each, that would be difficult. We use a lifter…" He closed his eyes at the thought of Fee operating the lifter with its two massive forks. With her lead foot, who knew what damage she'd do?

"Yay, I get to drive." Fee bounced on her toes, looking excited.

Worst idea ever, Clint decided, as Fee bounded for the door. Clint turned to the director. "I hope your insurance and liabilities policies are up to date since Fee is a maniac behind the wheel."

"Don't break anything, Fee!" Miranda shouted from the inside the stable, obviously listening to their conversation.

"Yeah, Fee, don't break anything," Lulu said, coming to stand in the doorway of the stall. She smiled at Fee and then her expression changed and her eyes cooled. Clint looked over his shoulder to see Kace LeBlanc, standing by the sliding door at the entrance of the stable block, a dark brown Stetson throwing shadows across his face.

LeBlanc seemed to be everywhere the socialites were. Clint couldn't decide if he was taking his job as Buck's lawyer to heart by hovering around Miranda, or if his true motive was because the NYC tourists were all stunningly attractive.

But Kace only seemed to have eyes for Lulu.

Clint pulled his eyes back to Fee, who stood with her hand on her heart, her eyes full of mischief. A cameraman stood behind him, the camera pointed in Fee's direction. Clint stood aside so he wasn't in the shot. "I am truly saddened by your lack of faith in me, Miranda."

"I came by it naturally," Miranda said as she walked out of the stable, trailed by another cameraman and Rafaela who, judging by her still spotless clothes, hadn't lifted a finger to help muck out the stall.

"You did put your hand into Abby's wedding cake, and you did nearly set the kitchen on fire when we were filming in the Hamptons because you left oil on the stove. You did fall off a bar in Cancun," Miranda pointed out. "You really should stop dancing on bars."

Fee pulled a face. "That was Lulu."

"We both fell off the bar in Dublin," Lulu corrected her. "You fell off the bar in Cancun because you were flirting with the bartender and weren't looking where you were going."

Fee shook her head and her braids bounced off her shoulders. "I dispute that." She looked around and frowned. "Where's Zooey?"

"Present."

Clint turned at the faint voice drifting over to them and he saw another woman standing at the entrance to the stable, a cowboy hat tipped over her eyes, her booted foot resting against the barn wall behind her.

Clint heard Fee's huge sigh and watched as she walked

over to her friend and pushed up her hat. The cameras would pick up what he saw: a pale blonde with blue-ringed eyes, looking like she was dealing with the hangover from hell.

"Aw, honey," Fee crooned, stroking her arm from shoulder to elbow. "You look like crap, Zo."

"Feel like crap. Too many shooters with too many cowboys," Zooey replied.

That would do it.

The director turned to Clint. "I need something for Zooey to do. I have to film her doing something, preferably sitting down."

What was he, a friggin' consultant? "Get her to clean some tack." He walked up to where Fee was standing and put his hand on her back. When she looked at him with those delicious brown eyes, his heart spluttered.

Stupid thing.

"I really need to get going. You coming or not?"

"Always so gracious," Fee murmured. She looked back at the director and flashed a smile. "I'm going to feed the cows."

"Excellent. Take Jimmy with you."

Clint looked at the tall, lanky man holding a camera to his shoulder and rolled his eyes. Fabulous.

No, super fabulous.

Because, how exactly was he supposed to kiss the hell out of her when he had an audience?

Fee parked the lifter where she'd found it and slapped her hands on the steering wheel, immensely pleased with herself. She'd thought she'd be driving a tractor but could see why this machine was so effective. She shoved the prongs of the lifter into a massive bale of hay, lifted it up and transported it to a feeding trough in a nearby pasture.

She'd cut the twine off the bale—using Clint's multi-tool—and returned the lifter to its parking spot, all without injuring herself, Clint, Jimmy or the machine itself.

Nothing to this ranching stuff!

Jimmy dropped his camera and held it to his side. "I'm going to take off, Fee. Do you want to walk with me back to the barn?"

Fee glanced at Clint, who'd hopped off the lifter. "No, I'll catch up with you." She glanced at her watch. "Where are we filming this afternoon?"

"We've got the afternoon off," Jimmy reminded her.

"Excellent." She glanced at Clint who was staring down at his phone, his expression intense. "Tell Lu and the rest that I'll see them when I see them."

"Cool."

When he was out of earshot, Fee hopped down from her seat and walked around the back of the machine to where Clint stood, still looking troubled. "Problem?"

"I was just checking the weather app—it's an occupational hazard." Clint looked a little distracted. "There's a forecast for high winds."

"Winds are a problem?"

"They can be," Clint replied. "We experienced a drought this past summer, and the grass and lands are dry. We typically start to worry about fires later in the season but even now, because it's so dry, one spark can set off a hell of a blaze."

Fee looked around, saw the brown grass and the cattle in the pastures and shuddered. "That wouldn't be good."

Clint handed her one of his almost smiles. "It wouldn't." He gestured to the lifter. "You did well. Now, you have to do that another fifteen times today to feed all the livestock in the paddocks closest to the house. And we haven't even started getting feed to the livestock in the far pastures."

Fee looked aghast. "How many more times?"

Clint's slow smile caused her stomach to flip over. "Relax, I'm not going to ask you to do it. Gabe and the hands will finish up."

"Thank God," Fee said, putting her hands on her lower back and stretching. "That seat is not good for my back."

She noticed his eyes went to her breasts, and she didn't mind. In fact, she loved the flash of desire in his eyes. "Back problems?" he asked, his voice lower and huskier than before.

"Yeah. A gate fell on me when I was a kid and I've struggled with back issues ever since. Especially when I do something different and, trust me, mucking out stalls and hopping on and off machinery is very different from my normal exercise routine."

Clint walked behind her and placed his hands on her waist, his thumbs digging into two spots in her lower back. Fee groaned as sweet pain flooded her system. God, his fingers felt so good.

He moved his hands up, holding her rib cage, thumbs pushing into another set of knots and she moaned again.

"You're as tight as a drum," Clint murmured, his breath warm against her ear. She shivered, wanting to turn around and slap her mouth against his.

Hellfire, she wanted him.

Without turning around, she lifted his big hands over her breasts, arching her back to push her nipples into his broad palms. "I still want you."

Clint's thumbs swiped over her, eliciting a groan of pleasure. "Are you sure?"

Fee whipped around, instantly annoyed. "What do you need me to do, take out an ad in your local newspaper?"

Clint's mouth twitched. "Point taken." She saw him hesitate and she waited for his next excuse. Yeah, she understood his reluctance to get naked, but unless he was resigned to a celibate lifestyle, he was going to have to get over it.

Clint pulled her back into his chest, the ridge of his erection pushing into her lower back. "Come home with me."

Finally. Fee allowed her lips to curve upward. "An excellent plan. We'll take my car—it's parked out front."

"I've got a better idea."

Fee stiffened. "Not by horse, please. Firstly, it will take too long since I don't ride and also my back is already killing me.'

"Not by horseback, not today anyway," Clint told her, taking her hand and leading her to the back of the barn and then behind the stables to where a muddy dirt bike was parked.

Clint slung his leg over the seat and tipped his head. "Climb on, peanut."

Fee placed her hand on his shoulder, swung her leg over and felt herself sliding down the seat into Clint's back, her breasts pushed against his flannel shirt. When she wrapped her arms around his waist, he rested his big hand on her thigh and squeezed. "You okay?"

Fee wiggled and she smiled when Clint tensed. Yep, she was pretty sure that if she dropped her hand and allowed it to fall lower, she'd find something long and hard and ready to play. "I'm good. You?"

"My jeans are suddenly about two sizes too small," Clint admitted.

Before she could reply, he gunned the accelerator and Fee squealed as they took off. She tightened her hold on him, instinctively realizing she had to move as he did, trusting him to keep them upright.

After a few minutes, she knew Clint was as good on a bike as he was on a horse and she relaxed, spreading her fingers across his stomach, allowing one hand to drift up his chest. Instead of taking the main road, Clint cut across the ranch, using trails, skirting trees and rocks.

When they hit an open piece of land, Clint lifted one hand to cover hers with his, holding it against his heart.

It was such a small gesture but, in that instant, she felt utterly connected to this man, and to the land he knew so well.

And seemed to love as much.

They passed through a gate and Clint informed her she was now on Rockwell land, pointing out the oil derricks in the distance.

"The Rockwell wealth was built on oil and ranching," Clint told her, above the noise of the engine and the whistling wind.

"Is your father not involved in the ranch at all?"

Clint's grip on her fingers tightened. "He died when I was five. My folks separated when I was a baby and my dad, initially, had custody. When he died, I moved to Dallas with my mom but I spent every holiday here at the ranch with my grandfather. My grandfather left the ranch to me when he died."

They were getting personal and that wasn't supposed to happen. She didn't do permanent and he didn't seem to do people, so this was a one-off thing.

"So, all this land is yours?"

"Yep." Clint slowed down to allow a cow to cross the trail they were riding and sent her a mischievous look over his shoulder. "I also own a ranch close to Austin."

She loved his bad-boy look, his charming half smile, his closeness. Fee was surprised her ovaries hadn't exploded yet. "Good thing I'm only interested in your body, not your acreage," Fee lightly replied.

"Good thing," Clint quipped as he swung the bike

off one trail and onto another. Within a few minutes Fee caught glimpses of his sprawling house and she swallowed a burst of panic. What was she doing, literally riding off with a cowboy? Despite her party-hearty reputation, she didn't do one-night, or afternoon, stands; she never hopped into bed with strangers.

But there was something about Clint, something that called to her. Maybe it was the hint of vulnerability she'd heard in his voice or the sadness and loneliness she'd seen in his eyes.

She wanted him, sure, but she also wanted to make him feel a little treasured, a little cherished, even if they were only destined to spend a few hours together. Because she suspected it had been a long time, if ever, since Clint was cherished, treasured.

He probably wouldn't recognize either one if it bit him on the butt.

Clint skirted his barns and the paddock, beautiful horses with patterned coats raising their heads at the sound of the bike. He sped toward the imposing front of the house with its wrap-around veranda and stately front door.

Fee heard his low curse and saw a white SUV parked next to a quad bike and a brand-new pickup with a Rockwell Ranch logo on the door.

He parked his bike next to the SUV, hopped off and scowled. "Is today the twentieth?"

"All day," Fee answered, climbing off the bike.

Clint ran his hand through his dark blond, windblown hair. "My physiotherapist is here. I forgot she was coming today."

Ah. So, no afternoon sex then. Damn.

"You're still having physio?" Fee asked as she followed him up the stairs and through the big wooden door into a spacious hallway.

"Only once a month now. Sam comes to check up on my progress and to make sure I am not overdoing it."

"In what way?" Fee asked, looking into the luxurious great room with floor-to-ceiling windows, massive, comfortable-looking couches and a huge fireplace. Bright art adorned the walls and Fee was grateful she couldn't see any dead animal heads mounted on the walls.

She wasn't a fan of taxidermy in any shape or form.

"She's both a physio and a trainer, so she was able to get me back in shape after too long lying around, recuperating. Sam also helped me with my various prosthetics, learning how to use them, to program them."

He frowned slightly, looking a little embarrassed. "I don't know what I would've done without her these past two years so, as much as I want to whip you off to bed, I'm going to have to take a rain check, just for an hour or two."

Fee wondered what she was expected to do while she waited for him. Or if she should wait for him at all. Maybe this wasn't such a good idea.

She glanced at the front door. "Maybe I should go. But I'd have to borrow a vehicle from you."

Clint grinned and her heart sighed. "You're a maniac behind the wheel, Martinez, so that's not going to happen." Clint took her hand in his and squeezed. "Don't run off, Fee. Please?"

Before she could answer him, Clint tugged her down the long, cool hallway. Where were they going? Surely he wasn't intending to stuff her into his bedroom and expecting her to wait for him like a good little girl?

"Maybe we should table this for another day."

"Nope." Clint stopped in front of a half-open door, and he closed his eyes. "You might as well come in, meet Sam, see me. After Sam's tortured me, you can then decide if you want to stay or go."

Fee immediately knew what he was saying. If she watched his physio, she'd see him wearing his prosthetic, a prelude to seeing him naked, which was his most vulnerable state. He was giving her, and him, a gentler way to back out if she changed her mind.

Which he clearly kept expecting her to do. But he didn't know she was stubborn, and once she set her mind on something, she generally never backed down.

And, she knew with every fiber of her being, no matter how bad his leg looked, she would still want him.

Because she wasn't only attracted to his fallen angel face and his wide chest and big arms, flat stomach and thick legs, she was attracted to his soul, to his determination, to his unwillingness to stop doing what he wanted to do because he was missing a limb.

He rode horses like a crazy person, worked his ranch, rode his dirt bike. He wasn't sitting in a darkened room refusing to face life—people, maybe, but not life—and she admired his drive and persistence.

So many people would just throw their hands in the air and embrace being a victim of life's unfairly dealt cards.

Fee wouldn't change her mind about sleeping with him and the only way to prove her intention was to *not* change her mind.

She gestured to the door and bumped his shoulder with hers. "Rockwell, we're only going to get to the fun stuff if you hop to it."

The words flew out of her mouth and she only realized what she'd said when they hovered in the suddenly awkward silence between them. Fee glanced at Clint, hoping he didn't think she was mocking his disability, and she sighed in relief when she saw a flash of amusement in his eyes.

He might've lost half his leg but he hadn't, entirely, lost his ability to smile.

Thank God because she seldom thought before she spoke and she was known to be occasionally inappropriate. And irreverent.

But, hopefully, never cruel.

Four

Clint saw Sam out, and when he returned, he found Fee curled up in the easy chair in the corner of his expensive home gym, one leg dangling over an arm. Earlier he'd changed from jeans into exercise shorts and a tank for his training session with Sam, and he was conscious of his matted hair and damp chest but mostly of his matte black prosthetic.

Do or die time.

Clint pushed down the panic threatening to close his chest. Fee was one of the few women he'd allowed to see the stump tucked into his prosthetic for a long, long time. Would she bolt? She kept saying she wouldn't, but he'd learned to trust what people did, not what they said. Time for the truth, he thought as he stood in front of her, his arms folded over his chest. She'd either handle it or she wouldn't; he wouldn't allow himself to care either way.

He'd stopped caring about his mom's opinion—*I like*

pretty and I like perfect—and he shouldn't care about Fee's since she was leaving in a few weeks to go back east, so why was his heart in his mouth? Why was his stomach twisted like a pretzel?

He was so pathetic, because, dammit, when he saw female appreciation in her eyes, when she looked at him like she wanted to devour him whole, he felt like the man he used to be.

He felt strong and capable and powerful and whole... He wasn't, but she made him feel that way.

Fee swung her legs off the chair and leaned forward, examining his prosthetic. It was one of the most advanced devices on the planet and he had a full range of movement; it was just a marvel of modern technology.

But, funny thing, he'd still prefer his old leg back.

Fee rested her fingers on what should've been his knee, allowing her fingers to drift up to the suction cup. "Is it sore?"

"No. Not anymore," he answered. "It's an ugly wound but not sore."

"Phantom pains?"

Someone had done their research. He was both pleased and terrified. "Yeah, I get those but less often than I did. They are pretty annoying."

"Why do I suspect that's your way of saying they hurt like a bitch but that you would rather die than admit it?"

She was spot on. They *did* hurt like a bitch but he wasn't one for whining. Fee kept her hand on him and looked up through long, thick lashes. "I went online and read up on what you did to save your teammates, Clint. You were amazing, so focused and so brave."

There was nothing amazing about it. He'd done what he had to do to save his friends; he would not let them die in a tangle of metal in a foreign country. "Any of them would've done the same."

"Maybe, maybe not. But you were the one who did and, I know this sounds weird, considering we barely know each other but—" Fee hesitated and he saw the glint of tears in her eyes. Or a crapload of emotion. Suddenly he really wanted to know what she was about to say...no, he *needed* to know.

"But?"

Fee dropped her hand and looked at the floor, shaking her head. He cupped her jaw and tipped her face up. "What, Fee?"

She looked embarrassed. "I was just going to say I'm proud of you but that sounds weird because, you know, we don't know each other." She waved her hand in front of her eyes as if to dry the moisture. "Anyway, I'm sure your family is very proud of you."

He almost laughed at her statement. Proud? Definitely not.

He was good PR—Mila frequently mentioned her wounded war hero, Purple Heart–recipient son on her prime time news slot—but his mom hadn't want to deal with the reality of having a son who'd needed numerous operations, spent months in the hospital and who had to undergo rigorous rehabilitation to get back on one foot. Even before he was injured, he'd always been too much trouble for her, distracting her from what was important, which was making sure she was the most visible, most powerful, journalist in Dallas.

Fee was the first person he'd allowed to broach the subject, to talk about the past. And being Fee, she just looked him straight in the eye and spoke with pity and sentimentality.

"Thank you," he said, his voice husky. He felt her hand

drift onto his thigh, above his suction cup, her fingers resting lightly on his scarred skin.

"Let me see you, Clint. All of you."

It was such a big step…she was asking him to strip down, to show his most vulnerable self. With his prosthetic removed, he either needed to sit down or use his crutches, neither of which screamed rampant sex god. He would be vulnerable…

He reminded himself that she was half his size and he was trained; she couldn't hurt him if she tried. He was still a highly trained army ranger and she wasn't dangerous, not to his safety anyway. His heart maybe, but he wasn't going there…

What was the worst she could do? Laugh? Run away? Well, that had happened before and he'd survived. He'd survived his mom's lack of interest and, after losing his friends and his limb, knew he could survive anything.

But, still…

I like pretty and I like perfect…

Clint cursed, not sure if he could do this. He wasn't ready.

He didn't know if he'd ever be.

"It's okay, Clint, really," Fee said, standing up and wrapping her arms around his waist she placed her forehead on his sternum and he looked down at her mass of black curls. "I'm really pushy—it's one of my worst traits."

Clint laid his hand on her head. "I'm not pushable."

"I know," Fee said, looking up at him. "You're the most stubborn man I've ever met."

"Pot calling the kettle black, Fee?"

Fee smiled at him and his heart cracked, just a little. He'd patch it up later, before the chasm widened and he started to think of this woman in terms of tomorrow and more.

He just wanted a night, maybe a few nights, and then he would say goodbye, wave her on her way. They had today, maybe tomorrow, and he didn't intend to waste any time. But right now, he wanted to lay hands on this woman, and not in the way she thought he would.

Giving her a massage would give him some time to think, to gather his courage to let her see him, to take a chance.

"Why don't you lie on the massage table, face down?" Clint suggested.

Fee looked at the massage table in the corner of the gym, the one where Sam had worked on him earlier. "Why?"

"Trust me," Clint said, taking her hand and leading her across the room. Fee sat on the edge of the bed and he yanked off her rain boots—taking a moment to inspect the ducks. Shaking his head, he tossed them to one side and reached for the button on the band of her jeans.

Fee stopped him by frowning, placing her hand on his. He looked down and grimaced. "Sorry, I have heard about foreplay, I promise—but that's not what this is. I just wanted to loosen your pants a bit so I can massage your lower back."

"You're going to give me a massage?" Fee asked, her eyes round with surprise.

"Well, yeah." Why else did she think she was on this table? He was out of practice but he hadn't forgotten everything he knew about women. Their first time deserved a bed, not a hard table in a gym. "I've seen you grimace a few times and you keep stretching as if you are cramping."

"You really have to observe less and explain more, Rockwell," Fee said, flipping onto her stomach and pushing her jeans down to her hips. Clint's mouth dropped open when she lifted her torso and whipped off her shirt, baring the crisscross straps of her purple bra to his very appreciative gaze.

Acres of creamy skin, three freckles just below her left shoulder blade, the bumps of her spine. Clint wanted to kiss the hollow of her back, the two small dimples he could see at the top of her butt, and he would, sometime this afternoon.

But, for now, he wanted her loose and liquid. Not wanting to ruin her beautiful bra, he asked her if he could unhook it and when she nodded, he separated the hooks and eyes, allowing the purple fabric to bunch on the bed at her sides. He picked up her hair, draped it over her shoulder and lifted a few loose tendrils off her elegant neck.

He had no idea how he was going to massage her without getting distracted. Clint poured some massage oil into his hands, rubbed them together and took a deep breath as he stroked the oil onto her skin. He sucked in a hot, aroused, confused breath as he dug his fingers into her muscles. He'd had women before, lots of them and he'd never felt this turned on, this on edge.

This was life changing, important, breath stealing…

And she shouldn't be. He wouldn't let her be.

He had to stop giving her more importance in his life than she had. This was about sex, about a moment in time, about physical release.

Stop thinking, Rockwell, your head is going to explode. And that wasn't the explosion he was most looking forward to. That one would happen three feet lower…

Fifteen minutes later and he was nearly done. Clint dug his fingers into a knot beneath Fee's shoulders and heard her low groan, felt her shudder. He couldn't wait any longer, he needed her, here, now…

He couldn't deny himself any longer…

"Roll over, Seraphina," he commanded and she did,

holding her sexy bra to her breasts as she sat up. He cocked an eyebrow, amused by her reticence. She was loud and bold—he hadn't expected shyness. He hooked a finger under a cup of her bra and gently tugged. Fee sucked her bottom lip into her mouth and allowed the fabric to fall into her lap. Clint felt the punch to his heart, another to his stomach as she leaned back on her hands, allowing him to look…

And look.

She was cream and Cointreau and he knew she'd taste as good as she looked. "You are the most beautiful woman I have ever seen."

The flash of surprise in her eyes told him too few lovers had mentioned her beauty. He dragged his finger across her collarbone, down the slope of her breast and over her puckered nipple. *So responsive*, he thought. He placed his hands on her breasts, tested their weight, enjoying their fullness. Man, she was hot and yeah, he wanted her.

But not here…

Clint banded his arm around her waist and pulled her so that she sat on the edge of the massage bed and he stepped into the space between her legs. "Let's take this to the bedroom. Hook your legs around my waist."

"Okay but…first…" Fee scooted closer, draped her arms around his neck and Clint sucked in his breath when she slid her mouth across his. Her tongue traced his bottom lip and all his good intentions to take this slowly evaporated.

He needed her…now.

Clint took control of the kiss, plundering her mouth as if this were the last time he'd kiss a woman, the last time he'd have this experience. Instead of pulling back, Fee met him stroke for stroke, twisting her tongue around his and pushing her bare breasts into his chest. Frustrated at the lack of skin-on-skin contact, Clint pulled his tank over his head and then her hands were on his ribcage, sliding up and over his chest, moving around to his back. She pushed her hand under the band of his exercise shorts, growling her frustration.

"I need you, now," Fee muttered and Clint's last shred of control was obliterated.

This was going to happen in his gym, on a Tuesday afternoon a week before Christmas. Best present ever.

Clint dropped his hands to her jeans and this time she didn't stop him when he slid the zipper all the way down, pushing the opening apart so he could slide his hands inside. He sucked a nipple into his mouth and laved it while working her jeans down her hips. Fee lifted one butt cheek to help him, then the other and soon her jeans and panties were on the floor, and Fee wasted no time in making sure his exercise shorts and boxer briefs joined the pile of clothing.

He stood naked before her and, not wanting to give her time to think or pull back, reached for her, needing passion to take over, to take them away.

But Fee placed a hand on his heart, those exquisite eyes connecting with his. "Let me see you, Clint. I need to see you."

Clint knew he could distract her with a quick, hard kiss but Fee's request was powerful, sweet and not easy to deny. Tensing, he watched her face as he stepped back, feeling her eyes on his chest, his groin area and finally his leg. A part of him was relieved that he was standing, that he couldn't take off his prosthetic.

He wasn't quite ready…

"You are so beautiful, so powerful," Fee murmured, her finger running over the biceps in his left arm. "You're so ripped, so muscular but not too much. Your body is… God, spectacular."

He couldn't remember when he'd last blushed but knew he was damn close to it now. "You need your eyes tested, Martinez."

Her eyes collided with his and she shook her head. "Don't do that, okay? Don't minimize how far you've come, how hard you've worked. You took a hit, one direct to your leg, and you not only survived, you goddamn conquered. I'm in awe of you, Clint. What's happening with us might only be a ships-passing-in-the-night thing but I can still appreciate your determination, your persistence."

He felt ten feet tall, like he could take on the world. To have such a woman—gorgeous, smart and mouthy—talk this way about him, lust and admiration and appreciation in her eyes, filled his soul with something that might be happiness.

Happiness…not an emotion he was terribly familiar with. And it scared him. He didn't want to get a taste of it and have to live without it. It was better to strive for contentment, for comfort and satisfaction.

And talking about satisfaction…

"You're pretty spectacular yourself," Clint said. "Can we please stop talking now?"

Fee's eye roll was accompanied by a smile. "I like to talk, Rockwell, get used to it."

"I noticed." Clint held her face in her hands. "Now, shut up and kiss me."

"I can do that."

Still standing in front of her, Clint covered her mouth with his, pulling her legs around his waist so skin met skin, breast to chest, the V of her legs pressed into his cock. This…man.

Touching Fee was what he never knew he needed.

Clint wrenched his mouth off hers, his attention on the warmth and moisture heating his cock. "I need you, Fee. I need to be inside you but I need to protect you. And the condoms are in my bedroom."

Fee just hooked one ankle behind the other and pressed her heels into his back. "I'm on the pill and I'm clean. If you can say the same, let's not move."

Could he risk it? Should he? He knew he was clean but he never, ever placed so much control in someone else's hands. But it would also take a momentous effort to disengage, to walk away. Just this once, this one time, he would take a chance.

Clint kissed her again, his hand sliding between their bodies to test her readiness and when she bucked into his fingers, moaned in his ear, he pushed into her, keeping his thumb on her clit.

Fee's moans were incomprehensible, a mixture of English and Spanish and girl-on-the-edge groans. She scooted even closer to him and dug her fingernails into his butt.

Clint kissed her with a ferocity he took to a firefight and buried himself to the hilt, his eyes crossing at the wonder of being in her, holding her, kissing her...

She was falling apart in his arms and he loved it.

Fee's nails dug deeper, her hips lifted and he felt her inner channel clench, demanding his response. She was close, and he couldn't wait. Needing her to come, he surged into her, placing his hands under her butt to tilt her up and she gasped and...

Yeah, gushed. On him, through him, around him.

Clint felt the pressure build in his balls, at the base of his spine, and he plunged deeper into her, needing more, needing everything.

Fee released an *oh-oh-oh* in his ear, and he came with

all the force of a missile strike. Earth was destroyed, he was the conqueror...

Clint buried his face in Fee's sweet-smelling neck, the thought occurring that, by not being able to resist her, he might be the one who was vanquished, the one who was obliterated.

And right now, at this moment, he was okay with defeat.

Five

Unlike her costars who worked with personal trainers in air-conditioned gyms, Fee preferred running to keep herself in shape. So, after a meeting with the producer, director and the rest of the cast, she strapped her phone to her arm, pushed wireless buds into her ears and hit the road.

Running through Royal was a pleasure. It was a pretty town and the traffic was light at eight thirty on a Monday morning. Christmas, thank God, was over and she'd spent the holiday with her parents in Florida. Her visit had been short, less than thirty-six hours, and because her parents left for a cruise the day after Christmas, she didn't have to make excuses to return to Royal.

Her costars were also back in town and it was business as usual. The feud between the Blackwood siblings and Miranda raged on unabated, Buck's illegitimate son had yet to be found—Miranda had told her about Buck's request for him to be found and asked she not repeat that news to anyone, not even Lulu (and she hadn't)—and the director of *Secret Lives* was milking the tension for all it was worth.

And, bonus, they didn't have to write the storyline…

Trying to relax, Fee looked at the Christmas decorations still gracing the homes and lawns of Royal residents. Their yards were well tended, the Christmas decorations were picture-postcard. It was obvious the Royal residents were proud of their homes and their town. She could see why. It really did seem like the perfect place for someone looking to settle down and build not just a life but a legacy for generations to come. The sheer permanence of everything—the post office that had stood for more than a century, the diner that had been on Main Street for decades—continued to surprise her.

Fee knew nothing was permanent—her parents had taught her that lesson—and for her, putting faith in a relationship, in a town, in a friend, was asking for trouble.

She didn't belong anywhere, not even in New York City. Manhattan was just a place to temporarily lay her head and when *Secret Lives* ended—and she was a realist, it would end—she would find another city, another place to live while she wrote the next chapter of her life.

That could be in Barcelona or Bogota, Riyadh or… Royal.

Fee stopped abruptly, her expensive running shoes scraping the pavement. Where on earth had that thought come from? Yes, Royal was a pretty town but it was too small, too farmy for her. She wasn't a small-town girl, she needed the energy of the city, to be able to browse specialist bookstores, visit art galleries and museums, go to cocktail parties and to the ballet.

But when last did you go clubbing, or to an art gallery? she asked herself. *When last did you go to a party*

*that wasn't work related? You claim to love the city but
you don't avail yourself of what it offers...*

Fee started jogging again, wondering why she was so at
odds with herself. She'd been feeling this way since before
Christmas, since leaving Clint Rockwell's bed.

They had, after making very good use of his massage
table, moved to his room where they had spent the rest of
the afternoon, and a good part of the evening, in a haze
of orgasmic pleasure. She, obviously, noticed that he kept
his prosthetic on throughout and she hadn't asked him to
remove it.

His leg, his choice.

At ten, she'd dressed and Clint had, without argument,
driven her back to her hotel. They'd parted with no prom-
ises to get in touch, skipping the obligatory *I'll call you*s.
Through silent but mutual agreement, they both knew one
night was all they could have, was all either of them could
cope with.

She because Clint was too compelling for comfort, he
because...who knew?

It didn't matter. They'd slept together, it was fun and it
was over. It was all good...

And a little confusing because, since that night, rogue,
stupid thoughts kept jumping into her brain, causing her
to falter, to question her freewheeling life. What was up
with that?

Fee stopped at an intersection, looked both ways and
noticed a large construction site down the road, next to a
smaller building with an old fire engine parked outside.
The new building looked mostly finished but what caught
and held her attention was the tall figure dressed in dark
blue chinos and a pale blue button-down shirt under a
gray pullover. Her heart kicked up and started to thump
erratically.

Clint was dressed up, looking good and spending the morning in Royal. The town's most reclusive citizen had graced the town with his presence. Why?

You're just curious, Fee told herself. *You are not excited to see him. You are not desperate to hear his deep voice, to see whether his hazel eyes are green, gold or gray today. He's just a guy you had carnal relations with...*

And Shakespeare was just a writer, and Mandela was just another activist.

Annoyed with herself, Fee debated whether to run past the fire station. If she went left instead of right, it would add another three miles to her run and she'd already run three. Running past the fire station was the shorter route and she couldn't afford to take the extra time.

She had a full schedule today. They were filming at Blackwood Hollow and she and Lulu were scheduled to do a scene where they'd discuss what they intended to wear to the Texas Cattleman's Club New Year's Eve ball. Miranda had persuaded Nigel Townsend, owner of the production company responsible for *Secret Lives of NYC Ex-Wives*, to sponsor the event, to say thank you to the good residents of Royal for allowing them to film their town and have cameras and microphones shoved in their faces.

Fee had a schedule and she was, despite what the world thought, a professional. She hated being late so she'd have to run past Clint and the men he was talking to.

It had nothing to do with the fact she really, really, desperately wanted to speak to the sexy cowboy again.

Annoyed with herself, Fee ran down the road, pretending not to have noticed Rockwell. But she knew the exact moment when he noticed her. She felt her skin prickle, then flush with heat.

What if he ignores me? What if he pretends he hasn't seen me?

"Hey, peanut."

Although she wasn't crazy about the nickname, she was grateful to hear his voice seeping past the buds in her ears. Stopping, she turned around slowly and pulled them from ears. Crossing the road, she walked up to the construction fence and brushed a curl off her cheek. "Hey."

Oh, scintillating opening line, Seraphina. Use your words, girl.

Clint's eyes traveled up her body, taking in her skin-tight exercise pants and sleeveless crop top. Her eyes connected with his and she saw passion flicker gold in all that green. Gesturing at the suits with him, Clint quickly introduced his companions, who were architects from Dallas.

"I think we're done here, Clint," the oldest of the trio said, holding out his hand for Clint to shake.

"Thanks. And I can expect the building to be fit for occupation by the middle of January?" Clint asked.

"Absolutely. If not sooner."

As they said their goodbyes, Fee walked down the fence until she found a gate and went inside the construction site, staying close to the perimeter so she wouldn't be in the way of any of the busy crew.

She placed her hands on her hips and when Clint joined her, she pulled her eyes off the building to his face. "So, this project has to be fairly important to drag you off your ranch—" she gestured to his elegant clothes "—and into a nice outfit."

Clint jammed his hands into the pockets of his blue chinos. "I'm also meeting the suits leasing my oil rich land later so I thought I'd leave the battered boots and old jeans at home."

"And your Stetson?"

Clint's eyes crinkled at the corners. "In my car." He

gestured to a fancy SUV across the road, solidly black and engineered in Germany.

Nice wheels. "Where's the beloved rust bucket?"

"In for repairs."

Fee wrinkled her nose. "Tell me what it costs and I'll pay."

"Don't worry about it."

"Clint, I damaged it, I need to pay for those damages."

Clint surprised her with his quiet okay. "It won't be twenty grand," he added.

"What a shock," Fee replied, her tone dry. She saw his mouth kick up in a half smile and her ovaries quivered.

I want him. Again. Some more. A lot more.

Calm down, Martinez, you fool. That ship has sailed. Wanting to get her mind off the fact that Clint had seen her naked, and that she wanted him to see her naked again, and vice versa, she glanced at the half-constructed building.

"What are you building here?" Fee asked, rubbing her hands on her arms, conscious that the wind had picked up and that it was on the wrong side of chilly.

Clint, being the observant soldier he was, noticed her shivers, pulled off his sweater and placed the opening over her head. Fee didn't argue, she was grateful to be warm, and threaded her arms through the sleeves, rolling back the excess material. "Thank you."

"Pleasure. This wind is picking up," Clint commented, looking at the swaying trees to the side of the building.

"Isn't that what wind does?" Fee asked, confused.

Clint looked down at her. "Farmers don't like wind, especially not when it's dry. It just takes a stray spark and the right wind and we're in trouble, fire wise."

Oh. That made sense. Fee nodded to the building. "So, this?"

Clint placed his hand on her back and Fee forced herself not to react, not to move closer so she could soak up his heat or inhale more of his aftershave.

"It's a new fire station. The old one is too small, too cramped and too outdated."

"And why are you here, having on-site meetings?"

"I spent some time in California, ages ago, doing a smoke jumping and firefighting course. Because nobody in Royal forgets anything, I ended up coordinating Roya's firefighting efforts. It's my contribution to the community," Clint told her. His small, sexy smile flickered. "I do, occasionally, interact with the folks of Royal."

But only on his terms. And he was fudging, she could tell. "I still don't understand why you were having an intense discussion with the architects."

She saw him flush, felt his hand drop away. Rockwell didn't like talking about himself, didn't like anyone seeing below the surface. But he wasn't difficult to figure out.

"Just admit it, Rockwell, you're building this fire station," Fee stated, her tone brooking no argument. "From your own pockets, I presume?"

"Yep," Clint eventually replied, lifting his shoulders in a casual shrug.

"Those are pretty deep pockets, Clint," Fee murmured, impressed. Knowing there was more to this story, she pushed. "What else are you funding?"

Clint narrowed his eyes at her. "That's none of your business."

"Fire trucks? Water tankers? New equipment?"

Clint rolled his eyes. "If I say yes, will you shut up?"

She grinned, enjoying his discomfort. "What else? New uniforms, a secretary, hmm, maybe some permanent staff since I've heard the town uses volunteers?"

"All of the above and two helicopters outfitted with the latest firefighting and crime-fighting tech—so the police can use them too," Clint admitted, sounding resigned. He stared up at the bright blue sky and shook his head. "It's something I've been working on since I returned home. How the hell do you get me to tell you stuff I don't tell anyone else?"

"It's a skill," Fee said, sounding, and feeling, smug.

"War hero, rich, sexy as hell and generous," Fee added. "You are too much, Rockwell."

"I'm not a hero. I have the money and I'm sure as hell not sexy."

He uttered those words with complete conviction. Fee shook her head in disbelief. She met his eyes and arched her eyebrows. "Did we not have this conversation? Did I not see you naked?"

Clint rubbed the back of his neck. "Holy crap, Martinez, stop."

"Why?" Fee demanded, wanting to see what he'd do, whether he was going to slam his mouth on hers, like they both were desperate for him to do. Dammit, the attraction hadn't faded; they still wanted each other as much as before.

"I want some more naked time, with you," Fee stated, holding his eye.

And her breath.

"Another one-night stand?"

Fee just nodded, unable to talk for once, since her heart sat on her tongue.

Clint looked at his watch and took forever to answer. "I have an appointment now but I can reschedule."

It was tempting—it really was. Fee was considering whether she could duck out of her commitments when Clint's phone jangled. He cursed before pulling it from the back pocket of his pants. Frowning, he quickly answered the call and his terse one-word replies gave her no hint of the subject of the conversation. Clint finished his call, told her he needed a rain check and started to walk toward his SUV across the road.

"What's the matter?" Fee demanded, walking quickly to match his long stride.

"There was a lightning strike yesterday and it set some land alight on the outskirts of town. We thought we had it under control but it sparked up again and if we don't get it under control quickly, it can become a big problem," Clint replied, sounding terse.

"Because of these winds, right?"

Clint nodded and pulled his keys from the pocket of his chinos. "I'm going to head over there, assess the situation, decide whether we need more people to fight it. So, about that rain check?"

It wasn't the right time to discuss this, he was in a hurry, but she didn't want him to think there was a possibility of anything growing between them. This was just about a passionate attraction, she was leaving soon.

She always left…

"We're still ships passing in the night, right?"

Clint cupped her jaw, ran his thumb across her lower lip. "I kind of think we're still in the harbor, on furlough, needing to have some fun before we both move on. Can I call you?"

They exchanged numbers and Fee sighed when Clint's lips met hers in a hard, passion-filled kiss. He pulled back and cursed. "I shouldn't, I don't have time but…hell."

He gathered her close, kissed her thoroughly, his tongue sliding into her mouth as if he owned it. Fee didn't mind, she was happy to stand on any pavement, anywhere being kissed by this man.

The sound of a honking car broke their kiss and Fee heard catcalls and whistles and the rich laughter of four elderly women slowly driving past. Fee, mortified, closed her eyes and wondered how long it would take for this news to hit the gossip airwaves. Ten seconds? Twenty?

"Well, that's going to cause some talk," Clint said.

Fee winced and stepped back. "Sorry."

Clint sent her a rare smile. "Worth it," he said, before climbing into his SUV and driving off.

The fire on the edge of town was under control…not extinguished but under control. Clint stamped on a burning tuft of grass as he retreated toward the road, watching the other firefighters with a critical eye. They had all worked like fiends and he was grateful for their effort since this was a volunteer gig.

As he had back in the unit, Clint felt himself taking command, keeping an eye out, feeling responsible for all the men and women who'd pulled on the safety gear he'd donated and gone out to beat back the fire threatening the houses and land on the west side of town. Somehow, because of his military training, he'd become their temporary Fire Chief. He was proud of Royal, proud of the residents and proud they were prepared to get their hands dirty.

It was nearly over and they could soon go home.

Clint turned at the beep of a horn and sighed when he saw the van pull to a stop behind the cordon. The exhale turned into a muttered curse when he saw those spectacular legs, those black curls. Fee was now dressed in black designer jeans and knee-high heeled boots and wore a thigh-length leather jacket over a white silk top. He'd give her ten minutes, tops, before the flying soot stained it beyond repair.

Clint narrowed his eyes as two men also jumped out of the van, cameras on their shoulders. Fee spoke to one cameraman, her eyes moving from the camera to the swathe of burned land beyond the cordon. She pointed to where the fire stopped on the edge of Mrs. McPherson's garden and her hands moved as fast as her mouth. He wondered what she was saying.

They started to move in his direction and Clint swallowed a curse. He glanced back at his crew, then turned to face Fee and the dreaded cameras.

"Don't have time for this, Martinez."

"Two minutes, Rockwell," Fee said, holding up her finger. "Is everything okay?"

Clint nodded "Yeah, mostly."

"Mostly?"

"There are still a couple of spots burning. We're working on them," Clint said, his tone terse. He felt a fresh gust on his cheek and frowned. The wind had died down ten minutes ago but it was picking up again. He looked around, saw wind whipping the trees and released a series of violent, army-based curses.

Fee reached across the cordon to lay her hand on the yellow sleeve of his fire jacket. "Clint? What is it?"

"The wind has changed direction and is strengthening. If we don't kill the fire now, we're going to have a helluva problem on our hands. We need more hands, and we need them quickly."

Fee handed her microphone to the cameraman—Jimmy?—and spread her hands. "Let me help."

Clint frowned at her. "What?"

Fee pointed to a firefighter who was smacking the grass with the back of a shovel. "I can do that. I want to help. And you just said you need hands."

He did. Not to mention, Fee was wearing her stubborn face and he didn't have time to argue. He wasn't about to put her to work fighting flames—hell to the no!—but there were other ways she could help. He thought for a moment. If the fire turned and started heading back in the direction of the houses, they could find themselves in a world of trouble.

"I need you to go down this street, go house to house and ask the residents to prepare to vacate their houses. I don't want to create a panic—it's a precautionary measure. Make a list of who will go, who won't and get it back to me as soon as possible. Note down any injuries, any sick people, anyone who needs special care. Basically, anybody who can't move fast."

Fee nodded. "Sure, I can do that for you. Where will you be?"

Clint gestured to a strip of flames to the east of the original fire and sighed. "There. Hang around once you've gotten your list. If I need your information, I'll find you."

"Okay." Fee grabbed his hand and squeezed. "Be safe."

Another hard kiss and she didn't seem to mind that his face was covered in grime, that he smelled of fire and smoke and burned grass. "You too. And thanks. I appreciate you pitching in."

Fee smiled. "Hey, the sooner we get this done, the sooner we can play our ships game again. Hurry the hell up."

Clint smiled and then laughed.

Fee was, at the very least, entertaining.

The small fire turned into something bigger than he'd expected, but six hours later they'd managed to contain the blaze. While it wasn't the hardest challenge he'd ever faced, it had been a long day. He was desperate to get home, take off his prosthetic, slide into his tub and stay there until his muscles were lax and his washing-machine brain stopped churning.

Clint walked toward his vehicle and pulled off his jacket. He ran his forearm over his filthy face, grimacing at the streaks of dirt covering his arm. He'd have to take a shower before he sank into his tub. Man, he couldn't wait to get home. Clint looked around, saw many of his crew were also stripping down, guzzling water, all looking tired and played out. The *Secret Lives* van was gone and Clint sighed at his surge of disappointment.

Fee had, obviously, left as well.

Good thing he hadn't needed the list of evacuees from her. *Dammit, Fee, I trusted you with a task and when you got bored, you bailed. What if I had needed that information, what then?*

Annoyed with her, and with himself for believing in her, he flipped open the back door of his SUV and pulled out a cooler. Slamming the lid up, he yanked out a bottle of cold water and furiously cracked the top. This was why he shouldn't trust people, why he should keep to himself, be alone. Because people always, always let you down.

"Can I have one of those?"

Clint lowered the bottle from his mouth and turned around slowly, his eyes widening at the sight of the tiny figure in the fire suit. Her hair hung in strings down her face and her face was as dirty as his, possibly dirtier. The blue rings under her eyes told him she was beyond exhausted.

It looked like she'd been fighting the fire but that was impossible because he was in charge and he hadn't authorized her to fight the goddamn fire! He was going to find the person who put her out there and string him up by his balls! How dare he put her in danger?

"What the hell, Fee?" he roared, causing heads to turn and eyebrows to raise.

"You needed help, I helped," Fee said, placing her hands on her lower back and stretching. Her fire jacket hung past her knees and her boots were at least two sizes too big for her. "And, before you erupt like a volcano, I wasn't in any danger. I just went over ground the guys had already cleared, making doubly sure there were no sparks."

Okay, relief. Maybe he wouldn't have to kill any of his volunteers today.

"Still not happy," he told her, rubbing her cheekbone with his thumb. But he was relieved to know she hadn't bailed and that she'd taken his request to stick around seriously.

"I appreciate your willingness to help, Seraphina, I do. But I didn't know you were in the field and that's a problem. Firstly, because I need to know exactly who I'm responsible for so I can ensure that the head count I had at the beginning is accurate, that the people who walked into the path of the fire are the people who walked out. If you got into trouble, I wouldn't have known to even look for you."

"Dav—" Fee winced as she let slip the name of the volunteer who'd allowed her to work. Clint would deal with him later. "He knew I was there."

"And if he got into trouble and couldn't tell me?" Clint asked, trying to keep his tone conversational. He was trying to be reasonable, reminding himself she was a civilian and he couldn't rip her a new one like he would one of his unit.

She'd also, he admitted, had the best intentions at heart and didn't know any better. Still, she'd never learn if no one told her, so he continued his lecture.

"I have to take every variable into account, think ten steps ahead. And I needed to know where you were in case the fire got out of control and headed for the houses. You had information I might've needed."

"I knew where you were every minute," Fee said, lifting her chin. "I watched you, and I would've known if you were looking for me."

Well, that was something. And, really, they were arguing—discussing—a possibility that hadn't, thankfully, materialized. And she had pitched in, gotten dirty, shed her socialite skin to help when help was needed. He admired and respected her for it.

Clint handed her his all but full bottle of water. "Drink. And when you're done, drink some more."

"Aye, aye, Lieutenant."

"Smart-ass," Clint muttered as he reached for another bottle.

Fee's eyes twinkled at him. "I thought you rather liked my ass."

He did. And every other inch of her body. Fee chugged back her water, wiping her mouth when she was done and creating a new streak of dirt across her chin.

He grinned and shook his head. "You are something else, Seraphina Martinez."

"I know," Fee replied, her tone jaunty. She arched a thin, dirty eyebrow. "Think you can handle me, Rockwell?"

"I never start something I can't finish, Martinez," Clint said, not caring the local media were milling about. He'd spotted a cameraman from a nearby TV station hovering around earlier but that didn't stop him from reaching for the zipper on her fire suit and pulling it down.

Fee just laughed. "I wouldn't do that, cowboy."

"And why not?"

Fee laughed at him. "Look down."

Clint looked at her chest and saw she was only wearing another sexy bra. This one was lacy and transparent and the color of a tangerine. His mouth, dry from the fire, felt like it hadn't tasted water in years. He looked again, he couldn't not, and zipped her up.

"Why aren't you wearing anything under your jacket?" he asked, sounding like someone had a very strong pair of hands around his throat.

Fee looked at him as if he'd lost his mind. "Because I was a wearing a very expensive designer silk shirt and it would not survive the soot and dirt." She grinned at him. "You see, I was taking all the variables into account, thinking ten steps ahead."

"As I said, smart-ass."

"Yeah, but you like it."

God help him, he did. And, this time, he wasn't only talking about her very fine butt.

Six

They stripped off in the mudroom off Clint's kitchen and walked through his lovely house in their underwear. Fee was quite glad Clint held her hand and led the way; she wasn't sure whether she'd be able to find his bedroom again in the ridiculously large-for-one-person house.

Fee glanced through open doors as he tugged her along past a library, a study, a sunroom, a kick-ass media-slash-theater room. Another sitting room.

They all but sprinted past the gym containing the massage table where he'd made love to her. At the end of one wing, separate from the rest of the house, Clint pulled her into his bedroom and, once again, she looked around, enjoying the masculine space. The walls and floors were finished to look like concrete and two massive frames, splitting the canvas with a view of a snow-covered mountain, formed the headboard. The room itself was a study in gray and neutral colors but the focal point was the floor-to-ceiling views out over the paddocks to where Clint's award-winning Appaloosas grazed.

It suddenly occurred to Fee that they'd made love in this bed where anyone approaching the paddock could see them.

"While I'm not a prude, I don't feel comfortable standing in front of the window, dressed like this. Or naked."

Clint's teeth flashed white in his soot-covered face. "We can see out, they can't see in."

Thank God. There was reality TV and then there was providing sex shows to Clint's ranch hands. In her book, that was a step, or five hundred, too far.

"Let's get you cleaned up, Seraphina," Clint said, leading her into his gray-and-black bathroom. Stepping into the massive shower cubicle, he flipped the taps to one of the two shower heads and gestured her inside. "Take your time, there's plenty of water."

Fee immediately sensed he was uncomfortable. She saw a pair of crutches within easy reach of the shower stall and noticed the wooden bench running the length of the massive shower. She glanced at his prosthetic and realized Clint would have to remove it to shower. With all its electronics, it couldn't be waterproof.

She'd finally see him without his bionic leg. The last time they made love, he hadn't removed it but it was time. Fee tipped her head to one side and handed him a gentle smile. "Come and shower with me, Rockwell."

Clint looked indecisive and she could see the excuse on his lips. "Clint, c'mon. I'm dead on my feet and we can kill two birds with one stone. We can get clean together and have some fun."

"I—"

Fee placed her hand on his bare chest and sighed.

"We've been over this, Rockwell. I'm not going to faint and run screaming into the night. Trust me, just a little."

Clint scowled and stared at the stream of water falling inside the cubicle. When he cursed and sat down on the bench outside the shower, she knew she had won. The trick was, Fee decided, not to let him see a hint of surprise, a smidgen of doubt. If he did, he'd rabbit and they'd be back to square one.

She needed to distract him so she bent her head for a kiss. Clint pulled back from her and grimaced. "I'm filthy, Fee."

"So am I." She smiled against his lips. "I don't think I've ever been this dirty in my life but it's good dirt, you know? Dirt gathered while I did something important... or am I being silly?"

"I understand exactly what you mean," Clint replied, his eyes serious. "Good dirt is the sweat and dust after rounding up cattle, after spending the day checking fences, training horses."

"It's strange but nice," Fee said. Hearing the release of air, she looked down. Clint's bionic leg was in his hand and she could finally see what was left of his leg. Dropping to her haunches, she examined his injury. The top of his thigh was pure muscle, right down to where his leg ended, an inch or two above his knee. There were scars, sure, lots of them but...

It wasn't a big deal. It wasn't ugly or pretty or strange or unusual, it was...it just was. It was Clint. Fee risked placing her hand over the end of his leg, gently squeezed it and stood up. Handing him a crutch, she quickly stripped out of her underwear and ducked under the spray, groaning as she tipped her face up to receive the hot water.

Bliss.

After a minute, she opened her eyes and looked at Clint,

who looked shocked. She was not going to make this a big deal, because it wasn't. "Are you coming in? Because, you know, over here, I've got soap and skin and shower sex just waiting for you."

Clint gestured to the crutch tucked under his arm. "That's going to have to wait until I get you in my bed."

Fee ignored the tremble in his voice. God, someone had really done a number on his head. "Oh, we'll get to the bed but there's a bench in here. I rather fancy sitting on your lap…"

Clint groaned and pushed his boxer briefs down with one hand. "At the risk of repeating myself, you are something else, Seraphina Martinez."

Fee shot him a naughty grin. "So I've been told."

Turning as he stepped into the cubicle, she flipped on the other shower head and water pounded them from every direction. Fee felt like a dozen hands were massaging her muscles. "Oh, this is fabulous. I want a shower like this."

Clint pulled her to him, aligning their bodies so she was plastered against him, skin to skin. Fee ignored his crutch and lifted her hands to cup his face.

"You did good work today, Rockwell," she said, loving the gold in his hazel eyes. Gold meant he was turned on, feeling relaxed. Green was his hiding-from-the-world color. When his eyes turned gray, as they did earlier when he heard she'd been fighting the fire, she knew he was angry.

He was such a protector, such an alpha male. God, she adored him.

Shaking off the unsettling thought that she was allowing Clint to sneak too far under her skin, Fee lifted her mouth for a kiss and sighed when he covered her lips with his. Passion sparked, flared and exploded. His tongue wound around hers, demanding that she keep up as he feasted on her mouth. Fee fell, whirling and swirling, into this magical world he created, allowing their mutual fascination to take her on a magic carpet ride.

This was as close to love as she'd ever felt since those first heady days with her ex. A little scared but a lot turned on, Fee ran her hands down his sides, across his hard stomach and down to capture his hard cock between her hands. He used his free hand to hold one breast, his thumb swiping her nipple before running the backs of his fingers down her ribcage, and down her hip to a small patch of hair at the top of her sex. Then his long fingers parted her, tested her, and she whimpered as her magic carpet lifted her higher. Clint found her bundle of nerves and gently, so gently, stroked her. Fee dropped her forehead onto his sternum, panting softly. There were so many sensations hitting her—the hot, hard streams of water, the sooty scent of his fabulous skin, the harshness of his ragged breath as she stroked him from base to tip, his warm mouth on the ball of her shoulder.

It was all too much, too intense. She was so close and, judging by his soft curses and the urgency with which he thrust into her fist, so was he.

Fee let out a whimper as he slid a finger into her, then another and she released a low scream when he curled his fingers to hit a spot deep inside her. His thumb brushed her clit and she moaned against his chest, instinctively increasing the pressure on his cock, rubbing her thumb across the head every time he thrust his hips into her hard grip.

"So close, Fee," Clint muttered.

"Me too."

"Fly, sweetheart." Clint tapped her inner walls and Fee, flying on her magic carpet, hit the sun and shattered into a million sunbeams. From somewhere far away she realized Clint had also found his release and it felt like they were dancing on the rainbow, riding streams of sunlight.

The rainbow slowly disappeared and gray tiles and black walls replaced the shimmery sunbeams. Eventually, Fee blinked, realizing she had collapsed against Clint who, in turn, was using the wall to hold up their combined weight. He still held his crutch under one arm but the other was wrapped around her back, holding her tight. The side of his face rested on the top of her head.

"What the hell was that?" Clint muttered.

"Mutual madness," Fee sleepily replied. Now, if he could wash her, dress her and let her sleep, that would be great.

"Well said." Clint lifted his head up. Fee managed to raise her own head to smile at him.

"Was that amazingly good or was that just me?"

"It was good," Clint responded, dropping a quick kiss on her lips. He touched her lips with his fingers before pushing some wet curls off her forehead. "Let's get you clean and dressed, Martinez, and I'll see what I can heat up for supper."

Fee yawned and reached for the loofah and soap. "Don't worry about food. I'm too exhausted to eat."

"Food, then sleep."

"Sleep, then more sex—we can skip the food."

Clint smiled at her and her stomach rolled over. Really, the man should smile more since his smiles had the power to light up the sun. "I know my housekeeper cooked up some mole poblano earlier today."

Fee narrowed her eyes at him in mock outrage. "You're trying to tempt me to eat using Mexican food?"

"Well…yeah."

Fee was suddenly ravenous. "Well, it worked. I adore

mole. Let's get clean and eat. Okay, new plan, food, sex and sleep."

Clint sent her a look of mock horror. "Woman, you're insatiable."

She needed to remind them why they were here, what they were doing. "Well, if this is just our furlough together then I've got to get in as much as I can before I leave. Don't you agree?"

Clint's eyes took on a hint of green. "Absolutely." He reached for the shampoo and, using the wall for balance, dolloped some into his hand. "Because we're both not looking for a relationship."

Fee stared down at her pink toes. Exactly.

Because she wasn't…

Was she?

It was past midnight and Fee had yet to fall asleep. The moon was high in the sky and provided them with enough light to pick up the movement of the wind blowing in the trees, the individual slats of the white paddock fences.

It was a stunning night and if she only had a little time with Clint, she didn't want to waste it sleeping.

"Are you asleep?" Fee whispered, her words bouncing off Clint's chest. Her head was on his shoulder, her thigh rested across his leg, her knee tucked into it. She'd never felt so comfortable, so at peace, in her life.

"Nah. But if you want more sex, I doubt I can oblige. I'm done."

Fee doubted that. She was sure she could persuade him but she was too relaxed to make the effort. She just wanted to lie here, in his big arms, feeling happy and relaxed and, yes, protected.

Despite having parents, she'd been—mentally and emotionally—on her own for most of her life and she could count, on one hand, the number of people with whom she could fully relax. But Clint made her feel more than relaxed; he made her feel safe, like trouble would have to go through him before reaching her.

It was both a heady and a dangerous feeling. She couldn't allow herself to get used to it. She was leaving, sometime soon after the New Year's Eve bash at the famous, original TCC clubhouse. Within days she'd be gone and Clint would be nothing more than a delicious memory.

"I can hear you thinking," Clint said, his fingers running up and down her spine.

She couldn't tell him the truth so she hunted for another subject. "Did you ever think about following your mom into journalism?"

Clint tensed. "Hell, no."

Fee frowned, remembering she'd seen footage of him on one of his mom's shows. The research she'd done on him since their first time together had been extensive. And, no, she wasn't creepy. Or weird.

Just curious.

She might as well be upfront about it. "I like to know with whom I'm sleeping so I did a little research on you. For someone with no social media presence, there's a lot about you on the 'net."

Clint answered with a sleepy "yeah" but didn't sound like he cared much.

"I watched some old reruns of your mom's show. She often talks about you. She's even shown videos of your graduation ceremony and some from your childhood. She spoke about you often during her series about wounded soldiers and their heroism. They were heart-wrenching and rather wonderful."

"Yeah, my mom is a great BS artist."

Fee pulled her head off his chest to look up into his hard eyes. "What do you mean by *that*?"

Clint's sigh whispered over her hair. "My mom talks a good line but she doesn't like getting her hands dirty. Her sympathy and her patriotic spirit are all BS. She doesn't care about me, or about any of the veterans she interviewed for that series. She's all about her ratings and understands that wounded soldiers are a great way to get viewers."

He made the harsh statement in an ordering-coffee voice and Fee knew that she had to choose her next words carefully. "How do you know that, Clint?"

"Because she was in my room after I had my leg amputated and I overheard her telling her manager that I repulsed her. That she liked pretty and she liked perfect and I didn't hit either mark anymore. And she was happy I had a massive trust fund to fund me and a girlfriend to nurse me because she had no intention of helping my suddenly incapable ass." His voice was rough with disappointment and anger. "And I realized that if she couldn't care about me, how much can she care about the other vets?"

God, that explained so much. Fee suddenly understood why he was so independent, why he pushed himself so hard. It made her heart ache for him even as she reeled at his mother's callous attitude. While her parents had been a tad neglectful and a lot self-absorbed, they were never cruel.

His mother was a witch of epic proportions. "Man, that's cold."

Clint's fingers dug into her spine. "She really is. She's all about the packaging, not the gift."

"Is she the reason you keep to yourself, why you don't interact much with people? Why you don't…date?"

Fee knew there was more to his story, a lot more, and she wanted to know every detail.

"As I said, I had a girlfriend when I returned home," he admitted. "We'd been together for a while, but after the surgery, she moved in. She really looked after me. Saw to my every need…except one."

Fee winced. "Sex?"

"Yep."

Ah, no.

"She couldn't, with me, and after she left, I tried to date but that didn't turn out so well. So, I figured it was easier not to."

No wonder he'd had doubts about her reaction to seeing him naked. Who wouldn't?

"Between my mother and my ex and my inability to get lucky, I kind of lost my faith in people after that. I suppose that's also why I avoided Royal and people in general. I hate feeling less than, weak, incapable, disabled."

Fee tightened her arm across his chest and kissed his shoulder.

"I vowed I would do everything and anything I was able to do before. And I vowed I would never let anyone see me as anything other than fully capable."

And that was why he never allowed anyone to see his fake leg, to see him using crutches, to view him as being disabled. Because he wasn't disabled. He was one of the most able people she knew. "You've just lost half of your leg, that's all. To me it's no more important than a scar or a birthmark. It's a part of you but it doesn't define you."

Clint didn't reply—she hadn't expected him to—but she felt his appreciation in the way he tightened his grip on her, in the way he rested his lips in her hair. It was all she needed.

Clint's voice, when he spoke again minutes later, was rough with emotion. "How was your Christmas, by the way? Where did you go?"

Back on stable conversational ground. "I went to see my folks, in Florida. I gave them a cruise for Christmas, they gave me a voucher from Target. My mom bitched about my antics on *Secret Lives*, I tried to explain, again, that the show is scripted, that I'm playing a part. She doesn't get it."

"Not much reality in reality TV, huh?"

"Not so much, no," Fee replied. "But it's provided me with a healthy nest egg and a platform. I'm thinking about writing another cookbook, maybe trying to get a gig as a celebrity chef when the show ends."

"You cook?"

"I cook damn well," Fee told him. "I spent a lot of my childhood comfort eating and I wanted to learn how to make the foods I loved. We moved around too much for me to be able to revisit favorite restaurants or bakeries so I had to figure out how to cook everything myself. I make a mean red velvet cupcake and my fish tacos are to die for."

Clint moaned. "I love fish tacos." He pulled away from her to lie on his side, his head resting in his hand, facing her. "Why did you comfort eat?"

Time for her to get personal. Fee thought it wasn't clever to be exchanging confidences when she was leaving—but then, maybe that was what made it okay. In a few weeks, he'd just be a lovely memory, so what was the harm in telling him things she'd never told anyone before?

"We moved a lot and there was a new school—sometimes more than one—every year. Coming into a new school as a fat Latina was like putting a bull's-eye on your head and handing the kids a bow and arrow. I learned to fade into the walls, to make myself as invisible as possible. Even if I'd wanted to make friends, it wouldn't have been easy. And I didn't want to. Getting attached meant getting hurt... I don't allow myself to become attached, Clint."

"Because it hurts too much when you leave. And you always leave."

She nodded. "I tried to tell my parents I was unhappy, but they brushed me off. I told school counselors, and they did the bare minimum, which basically amounted to nothing."

Fee rested her head on the pillow, her hand on his chest. "I desperately wanted a stable base as a child but thanks to the way I grew up, I was equally terrified of being trapped. While I was going through hell at one school or another, the only way to survive was to believe I was only there for a set time, that the next school, town, situation would be better. I built up this idea that the grass is always greener just around the corner."

Clint stroked her from shoulder to hand and back up again. "Parents and the many ways they manage to mess with their kids' heads."

"Do you want kids, Clint?" Fee sleepily asked.

"Yeah, sort of. Bit difficult to do when I'm not so keen on the wife and the relationship that goes along with them. You?"

Fee yawned. "Sort of, for the same reasons." Her eyes drifted close. "I'm so tired, Clint."

Clint's fingers drifted across her jaw. "Then sleep, sweetheart. I've got you."

He did, but just for tonight. Because that was all she had, all she was allowed.

Situated in Royal, The Bellamy was the establishment all Fee's future visits to hotels would be measured against. Sitting on fifty or more acres of ruthless landscaping and lavish gardens, it had more than two hundred lusciously appointed suites, containing every gadget known to man. As well as staying at the resort while in Royal, she and her friends had been filmed dancing, and drinking, in The Silver Saddle bar and eating tapas from their award-winning menu. They'd eaten at the hotel's amazing farm-to-table restaurant The Glass House and today they were going to be filmed enjoying a spa day at Pure.

The Bellamy had it all.

After a night long on sex and short on sleep, Fee hoped she wouldn't snooze her way through the filming.

Deciding she needed coffee—preferably intravenously injected—she popped into the small, intimate coffee shop to the left of the dining room and smiled when she saw Lulu sitting at a small table by the French doors, scrolling through her phone. Kace LeBlanc sat at the table next to hers, reading a newspaper, and they were both studiously, deliberately ignoring each other.

What was their problem?

Pulling out a chair opposite Lu, Fee sat down, reached for Lu's coffee mug and took a large sip. Black and sweet, just the way she liked it.

"Hey!" Lu complained, her head jerking up.

"I need it," Fee told her, taking another drink. When the waitress approached them, she quickly ordered a stack of pancakes and a cup of coffee of her own.

"Nigel will freak if you put on weight," Lulu pointed out.

Fee smirked. "I worked it off last night and I'll go for a run later."

"God, I hate you," Lulu told her, raising her voice so the next part could be heard clear across the room. "I think I'm a born-again virgin, it's been so long."

Because Lulu was rarely so brash, and never at that volume, Fee quickly realized she was trying to make Kace feel uncomfortable. Fee darted a look at him but the man gave no indication he was listening to their conversation.

"I'm so jealous," Lulu told her. "I still haven't bagged a cowboy of my own."

Kace abruptly stood up and threw his linen napkin onto the table. They both watched as he quietly and deliberately folded his newspaper before finally tucking it under his arm. When he lifted his head, he only had eyes for Lulu.

"Can you, possibly, drop the reality star persona for five seconds?"

Lulu draped an elegant arm over the back of her chair. It was no accident that the movement made her chest lift. Kace's eyes dropped and he looked his fill. He shook his head when their gazes clashed again. "Like what you see, LeBlanc?"

"Any man with a pulse would," Kace replied. "But that's all surface, Ms. Sheppard. Is there anything beneath your pretty exterior? Like a brain? Or a heart?"

Lulu's eyes narrowed and Fee leaned back. She'd experienced Lulu's temper before and Kace was in her firing line. But instead of unloading, Lulu just stared at him with wide, round, hurt, eyes.

Worried that Lulu was genuinely upset, Fee opened her mouth to defend her friend against the stuffy lawyer, prepared to rip his heart out. But Lu shook her head and Fee shut her mouth.

Lulu had this.

One tear, perfect and devastating, rolled down Lulu's cheek. Fee hid her smile knowing Lulu could cry on demand and did it oh, so well. Lulu blinked, allowing another two tears to roll down her face.

"That's such a hurtful thing to say," Lulu whispered, her hand on her heart.

Instead of falling to his knees and begging her forgiveness, LeBlanc just arched one eyebrow, his brown eyes cool. "Cut the crap, Ms. Sheppard, your tears don't fool me."

Fee gasped, then winced. Nobody, and especially no man, had ever looked past Lu's tears. When she turned on the waterworks, every single one of them had begged for her forgiveness.

Huh.

So maybe the stuffy lawyer could see past Lu's particular brand of BS.

Lu's tears instantly cleared. "Well, well, well...you aren't just a pretty face."

Lulu resumed her languid, arm-over-the-back-of-her-chair pose. She crossed one long, gorgeous leg over the other and tipped her head to one side. "What is your problem, LeBlanc? With me, specifically?"

Kace shook his head. "Dammit, you're gorgeous. But you're also vain and superficial and shallow."

"So decisive in your opinions and we haven't even had a proper conversation," Lulu drawled. "Well, if we're making snap judgments, you're buttoned up, stuffy and have a stick up your ass."

Kace sent her a tight smile. "Glad to have that cleared up." Picking up his briefcase, he abruptly turned and marched out of the coffee shop.

Because she admired the back view of a built guy as much as the next girl, Fee sighed. "He's seriously hot."

Lulu reached across the table and pinched the skin on the back of her hand. Fee yelped and jerked her hand away. "What is wrong with you?"

"He's annoying, and stuffy, and condescending and annoying—"

"You said that."

"—and patronizing and buttoned up and very, very annoying."

"You're repeating yourself," Fee said, enjoying herself hugely. Lulu usually had men eating out of her hand and it was fun watching her deal with the one man who refused to grovel at her admittedly beautiful feet.

"You're attracted to him," she added.

"I. Am. Not," Lulu told her through gritted teeth.

"And you both love and hate the fact he's not super impressed by you."

Lulu glared at her. "Stop. Talking."

"You want what you can't have," Fee said, risking her friend's legendary temper.

"I hate you so much right now."

Fee leaned back as the waitress placed her plate in front of her. When the girl was gone, she dug into her pancakes.

"And you're jealous I spent the night having spectacular sex and you…didn't." Come to think of it, that really was strange. Even if she was trading barbs with the stuck-up lawyer, Lulu normally, at the very least, had a handful of men wrapped around her baby finger.

Fee chewed, swallowed and waved her fork around. "This town is full of sexy men and you're telling me you haven't managed to date one of them? Why is that, Miss Lulu?"

Lulu picked up a fork and Fee hoped she wouldn't use it as a weapon. "Nobody has caught my eye."

"Oh, someone has caught your eye and you're just pissed you can't bring him to heel, and worse, can't BS him," Fee told her, leaning back as Lu raised her fork. "Don't stab me."

"It's tempting but not today," Lulu retorted. "I am not attracted to LeBlanc. He's so not my type."

Fee hooted, amused. "He's smart, rich and stunningly good-looking. He's *so* your type."

Lulu's fork missed Fee's hand by half an inch and landed in her stack of pancakes. She cut through the fluffy stack with the back of her fork then lifted a huge mouthful and shoved it into her mouth.

Lulu glared at her as she chewed. When she was done, she narrowed her eyes at Fee. "You have me eating pancakes."

"Not me. You always comfort eat when you're upset."

Lulu went back for another bite and Fee whipped her plate away. "Prove LeBlanc didn't upset you by not having another bite."

Lulu held her stare but, after ten seconds, dropped her eyes and waved the waitress over. "Bring me my own pancakes please, heavy on the bacon and the syrup."

"Thought so," Fee said, smirking.

"Fee?" Lulu asked, super sweetly.

"Mmm?"

"Shut. The. Hell. Up."

Seven

What in the name of all things holy was he doing?

Clint stood in front of the door to Fee's home away from home, her suite at The Bellamy, and glared at his highly polished wingtips. He was dressed in a tuxedo, bow tie perfectly knotted, hair brushed and his face clean of its habitual scruff. He'd spent more time dressing for this one night than he had the entire week.

All because Fee had asked him to accompany her to the New Year's Eve ball at the Texas Cattleman's Club. He didn't do balls, the TCC or people, so why on God's great green wonderful earth was he standing outside her hotel door prepared to do all three?

All because a gorgeous brunette with a huge heart and wild curls asked him. And he couldn't blame a post-sex haze for his saying yes. They hadn't even been in the same room. She'd called him up, issued the invitation and he hadn't hesitated.

He was definitely losing his mind.

Clint jammed his hands into the pockets of his tuxedo pants and rocked on his heels. He and Fee had spent all their free time together lately—including very slow horse rides (Fee had never ridden before and was taking forever to learn), quiet dinners and sitting on the porch, drinking wine and talking—and it had been the best time of his life.

The Fee he was coming to know was nothing like the fast-talking, over-the-top character she played on the two episodes of *Secret Lives* he'd managed to watch. Oh, she was a firecracker in either incarnation, and wasn't scared to share her opinions, but one-on-one she was softer and gentler than her on-screen persona.

Clint raked his hand through his hair. She was… amazing.

Uncomfortable with that thought, Clint tried to distract himself by thinking how much had changed, in Royal and in himself.

The Blackwood siblings versus Miranda war was still raging, Kace LeBlanc was still, he presumed, doing what lawyers did to resolve the situation. The *Secret Lives* crew was still milking the drama for reality gold.

All the players in that saga would be present tonight and arguments and snide comments were, as he'd heard from Fee, expected. The situation was tense and everyone was on edge.

Not his problem.

But, at some point the buzz would die down—probably sooner rather than later—and Fee would return to Manhattan. That was a given.

He'd miss her, that much he knew. He also accepted they couldn't have a long-distance relationship. What they had wouldn't survive her leaving Royal. It was a long way from Manhattan to Texas, and if he could barely cope with the small town of Royal, he'd go mad visiting New York.

And, for Fee, Royal was a quirky place to visit but she was too much of a city girl to settle down in a smallish agricultural town.

Not that she had any plans to settle down anywhere. Fee, as she'd told him, liked having options, being able to move on when she needed to. Despite his career in the military, he'd always know he'd return to Royal and his land. He was emotionally tied to his ranch, to his grandfather's and great-grandfather's legacy. He belonged in Texas, on his ranch, raising cattle and horses and avoiding people as much as possible.

They were all the opposites—sun and moon, light and dark, city and country. They didn't have a hailstone's chance in hell of making a relationship work. He didn't want a relationship...

People, he reminded himself, hurt people.

So why was he standing here? Why wasn't he back on the ranch, listening to the wind whistling through the trees, sitting on his porch as one year rolled into another?

Because she'd asked him...

It was a short-term fling, a flash in the pan, a brief, fun affair. There was no need for self-analysis or deep intro-spection. He wasn't expecting more, neither was she. He was overthinking this...

Just stop, Rockwell. Right damn now.

Annoyed with himself, Clint rapped on the door and heard the click of heels on the tiled floor on the other side of the door. He heard the snick of a lock opening and, when he saw what she was wearing, reached for the doorframe to steady himself.

It was a dress, floor-length, embroidered, with long sleeves, the color of a fiery Rockwell ranch sunset.

The dress plunged to her navel in an enormous V, showing a considerable amount of her fantastic breasts. Clint couldn't decide whether he should rush her downstairs to show her off or take her back inside to see what that dress looked like on the floor. Instead, he just stared at her and reminded himself to breathe. *Holy crap.*

"Hi," Fee said, sounding a little shy. Clint pulled himself together and noticed the hesitancy in her eyes, her need for reassurance. Strange, because he'd never seen her question herself. She'd always seemed to be thoroughly confident in her body.

Could she, possibly, be waiting for his approval, wanting to hear whether he thought she looked good?

She didn't look good—she looked magnificent.

"Uh…um." He could think the words, apparently, but verbalizing them was giving him difficulty.

Fee stroked the lapel of his tuxedo. "You look wonderful, Rockwell. Very debonair."

Say something, dammit. "Thanks. You… Jesus, Fee, that's a helluva dress."

Fee held the edges of the skirt and winced. "Too much?"

He shook his head and ran his finger down the curve of one breast. "Yes, no… My head is spinning."

"In a good or bad way?" Fee asked and he caught her hesitancy again. *Get over yourself, Rockwell.*

Clint held her face in his hands and looked her in the eye. "You look amazing, perfect, gorgeous…too sexy for words. As you might have gathered."

Delight jumped into her brilliant eyes. "Really?"

"Oh, yeah," Clint answered her, looking at her mouth. "Can I kiss you or am I going to find myself wearing your particular shade of lipstick?"

Those plump lips curved up. "It's stay-fast so you should be good."

Clint touched his lips to hers, sighing when she grabbed the lapels of his jacket, holding on while he ravaged her mouth. Yeah, skipping the ball sounded like a fine idea. He'd take his time removing her dress. He'd leave her heels and her dangly earrings on while he kissed her from top to toe...

"Ah, get a room. But later, because we're going to be late."

Clint reluctantly pulled his mouth off Fee's to look over his shoulder at Lulu, who was closing the door to her own suite. She wore an aqua-colored dress with a coral band across one shoulder. Even to someone as fashion-challenged as him, the hues were a perfect complement to her warm Caribbean island-girl skin.

Fee stepped away from him and walked over to her friend, taking both her hands as they each gave the other a critical once-over.

"Love that color on you," Lulu said.

"Ditto. Your makeup is fantastic."

Clint had to smile at their mutual admiration society, appreciating how easily they communicated, how in tune they seemed to be. This was friendship, he realized. The give and take, the easy, genuine compliments. He didn't have a friend like hers, not anymore.

And whose fault was that? The vets who worked for him were his employees and he'd isolated himself after leaving the military, he'd brushed off offers of help, of company, the invitation to join the TCC. Fee had become his closest friend since leaving his unit and she'd be leaving soon and he'd go back to his solitary life.

Or maybe he didn't have to. Maybe, when she left, instead of brooding at home, he could invite some of the volunteer firefighters to Rockwell Ranch for a barbecue. He could join the TCC. He could start, slowly, to reintegrate himself into the community.

He'd need a distraction to keep him from missing Fee… But, still…*people*.

He'd see. Fee needed to leave and then he'd re-evaluate his life. Hell, for all he knew he might just slide back into being the crotchety bastard he'd been before Hurricane Fee blew into his life. That was definitely the easier option—interacting with people took work…

But sometimes, like with Fee, the result—laughter, a connection, frickin' great sex—was worth it.

Fee's hand on his arm jerked him back to the present. He looked at her gorgeous, puzzled face. Did he have shaving cream on his cheek, something in his teeth? "What?"

"You just zoned out there for a minute," Fee replied, linking her fingers with his. "Ready to face the good citizens of Royal?"

Her hand felt right in his. Escorting her to the TCC clubhouse felt like it was something he was meant to do. But he did know his presence would set the gossip chain on fire.

Anything for Fee…

He smiled at her before returning his attention to Lulu. "Would you like to join us, Lulu?"

Lulu was opening her mouth to reply when they heard footsteps approaching them and Kace LeBlanc turned the corner, stopping abruptly when he caught sight of Lulu. Yep, that was what stunned looked like.

LeBlanc recovered a lot quicker than Clint had.

"Ladies, you look lovely," Kace said, approaching them with his hand outstretched for Clint to shake. He greeted Kace and returned his hand to Fee's back.

"Are you going to ride with us, Lulu?" Fee asked.

"I can give her a ride," Kace offered. "I came to collect

Miranda but she's left already. I have space for you two as well, if you'd prefer not to take your car," Kace told Clint.

Clint considered it for a minute, thinking it would be nice to have a couple of beers and not have to worry about going over the limit. Then he shook his head. "I appreciate the offer but I'd prefer to have my own vehicle in case another fire sparks and I have to leave quickly."

Kace nodded. "Understood." He looked at Lulu. "Ms. Sheppard?"

Even Clint, socially inept as he was, heard the challenge in Kace's voice. He looked at Fee and raised his eyebrows, silently asking whether he was imagining the electricity arcing between the tall lawyer and Fee's gorgeous friend.

Fee winked at him and they waited for Lulu's answer. Lulu eventually lifted her chin and nodded, with all the condescension of a Nubian queen.

"Thank you. Are you driving or do you have a driver?" Lulu demanded.

Ooh, snooty.

"I have a driver. Sorry, but you'll have to tolerate my presence for a very short time," Kace smoothly replied. "Just as I will have to tolerate yours."

Clint pulled a face at Fee, who was trying not to laugh.

Lulu looked at Fee. "Have bail money ready in case I kill him on the short drive from the resort to the club."

Fee struggle to keep her face impassive. "Always. Remember, jail orange is not your color."

Lulu picked up the skirts of her floor-length dress and arched an imperious eyebrow at LeBlanc "Shall we go?"

"Yes, your highness."

That wasn't a compliment, Clint thought as Kace and Lulu walked down the passage ahead of them. When they were out of earshot, he turned to Fee, laughter bubbling in his chest. "What the hell was that?" he asked.

Fee giggled. "Aren't they too precious for words? All growly and snarly and irritated because they are both too stubborn to admit they desperately want to see the other naked."

"Kind of like us when we first met," Clint said.

"Exactly like us," Fee cheerfully stated as she tucked her hand into the crook of his elbow. "I hope they eventually have the same fabulous time we've had. But they are running out of time—we're leaving Royal soon."

Yeah, did she have to remind him?

Miranda entered the ballroom at the TCC clubhouse by herself, choosing to make the silent statement that she was fine on her own, that she didn't need the acceptance of Royal residents, the members of the Texas Cattleman's Club or her stepchildren.

Stepchildren who were closer to her age than she'd been to their father's. Stepchildren who'd resented her role in their father's life even before he'd left her the inheritance they thought should be theirs.

Dammit, Buck, my life was perfect before you dropped this mess in my lap.

Miranda took a glass of champagne from a tray and caught a glimpse of her reflection in one of the many mirrors in this ballroom. She was pleased with her tight silver dress; it showed off her fantastic cleavage and the embroidered pattern between her breasts and hips highlighted her curves. The slit that came halfway up her thigh revealed her toned leg.

She looked good.

Looking good was great armor.

"Miranda."

Miranda turned and sighed at Kellan Blackwood's tight face. He'd found love with Buck's housekeeper and she looked around to see if she could spot the woman who'd been a faithful friend to her and Buck, in spite of Kellan's anger and resentment toward them both.

Not seeing Irina, Miranda forced a smile, knowing many eyes were watching their exchange. The cameras were also pointed in her direction, and she knew when the viewers watched this episode of *Secret Lives*, they'd wait in eager anticipation for the fireworks.

But, unlike some of her costars, she didn't seek notoriety. "Let's not make a scene, Kellan. It's New Year's Eve and this is supposed to be a happy event."

"I'm not the one who came back to Royal, determined to cheat a family out of their home and their father's wealth. I'm not the one who brought a camera crew with her to document the process," Kellan said, keeping his voice low.

He made it sound like she had complete control over the directors and producers, just as he apparently thought she'd controlled Buck. Miranda felt a headache building between her eyes. "Yeah, that's exactly what I did, Kellan. Where's Irina?"

"She's talking to Sophie." Miranda looked across the room to where her stepdaughter stood, tall and curvy, her dark hair and olive complexion the exact opposite of the Irina's pale skin, blond hair and blue eyes. Night and day, sun and moon, Miranda thought. Not unlike the way one of them liked and trusted her while the other passionately detested her.

Kellan also loathed her. So why was he talking to her? Why he was confronting her in front of everyone? He had to know their interaction would cause tongues to wag. Not that she cared about what the good residents of Royal thought, but he should.

"Say what you want to say, Kellan, and let's move on," Miranda said, giving him a tight smile.

Kellan's hand tightened around the tumbler of whiskey in his hand. "Irina and I were married in Nashville."

Whoa. Okay, then. "Congratulations?" Miranda posed the word as a question.

"We're very happy," Kellan stated, sounded defensive.

"Okay?" Another one-word answer, framed as a question. She saw the irritation flash in his eyes and smiled. These Blackwood children deserved to feel a little of the irritation, and annoyance, she constantly lived with.

"I want to make it perfectly clear I'm still going to fight you, tooth and nail, to win back my father's estate. We will claw back everything he gave you, Miranda."

This. Again. God, she was so tired. Instead of replying, Miranda just waited him out, knowing he would fill the silence she created.

"My wife wants to make Royal our base."

"What about your businesses in Nashville?"

"I'll travel back and forth to Nashville, as needed," Kellan said. "I just wanted you to know marriage hasn't made me soft. I still intend to fight you for everything you took from my siblings and me."

Same old same old. Miranda opened her mouth to blast him then remembered where she was and that the guests and the cameras were waiting for her to blow. She wouldn't give either audience the pleasure. "Noted."

Kellan waited for her to say more and when she just sipped her champagne, his frown deepened. "Is that all you have to say?"

Miranda nodded. "For now."

"What the hell does that mean?" Kellan demanded.

Just because it would make good TV, and because it would confuse the hell out of him, his siblings and everyone watching, Miranda reached up and placed a kiss on his cheek. Making sure her voice carried to both the guests, the cameras and the roving microphone held by the *Secret Lives* sound guy, she smiled at him as she wiped her lipstick off his cheek with her thumb.

"Congratulations, darling. I hope you and Irina are very happy together, like I was with your father."

Miranda heard the collective intake of breath, the murmurs following her controversial statement. Then she walked away, thinking the world couldn't prove or disprove her statement. Despite their divorce, nobody had known the true state of her marriage to Buck and she intended to keep it that way.

The cast of *Secret Lives* weren't the focus tonight and the cast wasn't miked so Fee didn't have to watch what she said. They'd been told the coverage of the ball would be minimal and they only needed to make a few direct-to-camera comments apiece and they'd be done.

And that meant Fee could have a quiet conversation with her best friend, who was, she reluctantly admitted, looking a little shell-shocked.

Leaving Clint talking to James Harrison, the TCC president—Clint being present at this party was causing a stir and everybody wanted a word with him—Fee walked over to where Lulu was standing on her own by a potted plant, looking a little dazed and a lot confused.

Fee walked up to her, put her arm around her friend's waist and gently turned her so they were both angled toward the wall and the room couldn't watch their interaction.

"Sweetie, are you okay?"

Lulu's lovely eyes met Fee's as she lifted a hand to her mouth and shook her head. "Not really."

Fee heard the panic in Lu's voice and instinctively went into mama-bear mode. Something was wrong and she was going to kick some lawyer's ass. She didn't think that Kace LeBlanc had hurt Lulu, she couldn't imagine him doing that. But something had happened…and she might have to get her ex-army ranger boyfriend—lover, fling, whatever—to knock him all the way across Texas.

"If said something that really hurt you, I will rip him apart," Fee muttered. "What did he say to you?"

Lulu shook her head and held up her hands. "Nothing."

Fee narrowed her eyes. "Then why are you looking all dazed and freaked out and crazy?"

Lulu placed her hand on her heart and gnawed on her inside of her cheek. "Because it was so damn fantastic, Fee. How can someone I loathe make me feel so…spacey?"

Okay, time to play catch-up. "What, exactly, happened on your five-minute drive, Miss Lulu?"

"Fastest, sexiest, craziest five minutes of my life," Lulu told her, pink in her cheeks.

"I swear, Lu, if you don't spill, I'm going to beat it out of you."

Lulu sighed and sighed again. "We didn't speak, at all, from the time we left you until we reached the limo waiting under the portico of The Bellamy. He opened the back door for me, I got in and he sat opposite me. The driver pulled off, Kace looked at me and…bam!"

Bam? What did that mean?

"I'm not sure whether he moved first or I did, but our eyes just connected and the next minute my dress was up around my waist and I was straddling his thighs and his hands were on my butt and his tongue was in my mouth and… *God.*"

Whoa. Hot damn.

"Not one word, we just kissed and kissed and…" Lulu saw a waiter carrying a tray of champagne and snapped her fingers to grab his attention. Lulu picked a glass up from the tray and downed the contents. She snagged the waiter's arm before he could walk away, handing Fee a glass before gulping a second one herself.

Fee stopped her from reaching for a third. "Nope, no throwing more liquor down your throat. Tell me what happened next."

The waiter finally escaped and Lu held her empty glass to her chest. "The limo stopped. Kace—" he was Kace now, Fee noticed, not Mr. Stick-Up-His-Ass as Lu normally called him "—put me back on the seat. He climbed out of the car, looking super cool, and helped me out. He walked me into the ballroom in complete silence, handed me a glass of champagne and a sarcastic smile and then walked away without looking back. I've been in a daze ever since."

Interesting. Lulu wasn't the type to lose her head over a man. "Wow. Just…wow."

Lulu frowned. "How can someone who irritates me so intensely set my panties alight? Fee…" She held her index finger and thumb an inch apart. "I was this close to letting him nail me in the back of the limo. It's stupid, and silly, and annoying and incomprehensible."

"It's chemistry."

"Or I have multiple personalities and the crazy woman inside me is making her presence known," Lulu muttered. "Maybe I'm simply psychotic."

"Chemistry," Fee insisted.

"I'd prefer to be psychotic," Lulu retorted. She tossed back her hair, straightened her spine and lifted her chin. Yep, Queen Lulu was back. "I will not let him affect me. I will not make a big deal about a hot kiss from a man who doesn't like me enough to try and make conversation. I deserve to be treated better."

"You do," Fee said. Then she looked past her friend to

see Kace watching Lulu with all the intensity of a Category 10 storm. He looked as flustered as Lu had earlier.

Yeah, she didn't think Kace was as unaffected as Lulu assumed.

Oh, this was going to be fun to watch.

"He's looking at you," Fee told her and Lu jerked her head around to scan the room. Kace had turned his attention back to the group of men surrounding him but his smirk told Fee he was very aware Lu's eyes were on him.

"This is so high school," Lu muttered, closing her eyes.

Nope, unlike Fee's experiences of high school, this was *fun*.

Eight

Sophie Blackwood stood between her two brothers, dwarfed as she always was by their height and good looks. It had always been the three of them and she was the baby, protected and, she guessed, cosseted. But now Kellan had his arm around the very beautiful Irina. While Sophie liked her brand-new sister-in-law, she felt like everything was changing too quickly and their lives were spinning out of control.

She wanted her dad to be alive, to be able to call Blackwood Hollow home again, to not have to fight Miranda Blackwood for what should be legally theirs. What the hell had their father been thinking leaving everything to Miranda and nothing to them? Had he really hated them that much?

Sophie looked across the room and watched the redheaded woman flirting with someone whose name she couldn't recall but whom she recognized as being a past president of the TCC. The man looked like his tongue was about to fall on the floor at her feet.

Miranda was a beautiful woman and beautiful women had always been her father's weakness. She'd been aware of his affairs from a young age, had met many potential stepmothers but Miranda, thirty years younger than Buck, was the one he'd married minutes after the ink on his divorce papers to Sophie's mom were signed.

Buck had moved on from his wife quickly and it seemed, by leaving everything to Miranda, he'd moved on from his kids as well. His relationship with all of them had been distant at best—problematic at worst—but she'd always thought they'd have a chance to resolve things. That chance was gone now. God, it hurt.

Sophie felt Vaughn's hand on her back and she looked at her brother, gorgeous with blue eyes and his sharp-enough-to-cut-glass jaw. She saw the worry on his face and tried to give him a reassuring smile.

When Vaughn asked her if she was okay, she knew he wasn't fooled.

Sophie shrugged. "As well as can be expected." She tapped her fingernail against the glass of her flute and frowned. "I'm so angry at him, Vaughn. And at her."

Vaughn knew exactly to whom she was referring. "I know, kiddo. We all are. And now we have to deal with meeting, at some point, a half-brother. Jesus."

He looked at Kellan and Irina, who were exchanging a long, loving look. Sophie rolled her eyes at Vaughn. "At least something good has come out of this mess."

"Yeah, they look happy."

Kellan turned his attention to them. "We are happy."

"Very happy," Irina said, laying her head on his shoulder.

Sophie, never having experienced love like that, tried to

control her jealousy. How amazing would it be to feel so at ease with someone, to find the one person you clicked with? She was happy for Kell, she really was, even if she wasn't happy about not being at their wedding.

"I cannot believe you got married on the sly," Sophie stated.

Kellan sighed. "Here we go again."

Sophie ignored him and looked at Irina. "Didn't you want the pretty dress and the vows said in front of a pastor?" Sophie demanded. "The presents and the first dance?"

"I just wanted Kellan," Irina said simply. "The rest is just icing on the cake."

"Icing on the wedding cake you never got to eat," Sophie muttered.

Vaughn laughed. "Give it up, Soph."

Sophie saw Kellan look across to Miranda and his eyes hardened. "I told her we were married and our fight is far from over."

"Good for you," Sophie replied. "Did you also tell her we think she's a classless, over-exercised fortune hunter and that we will wrest her grubby hands off Dad's assets if it's the last thing we do?"

Vaughn smiled at her bloodthirstiness but gestured to draw Sophie's attention toward Irina, who looked uncomfortable. "Easy there, tiger."

Irina excused herself to go to the ladies' room, and Sophie released a huff of exasperation. "I didn't mean to upset Irina—I just get so frustrated with this whole mess! The inheritance, the fact that we have a half-brother out there somewhere. I need answers to how this all happened. But we've only run into dead ends in Royal."

Kellan placed his hands on her shoulders and squeezed. "I understand your frustration, Soph, I'm equally pissed off. But, to be honest, I'm not sure how to unravel this mess."

"I could go to New York City and see if I could dig up some dirt on Miranda."

"And how would you do that, Soph? You're not exactly a PI," Vaughn scoffed.

"I have another idea," Sophie said, choosing her words carefully. "I've been researching reality show TV and I know they film everything and they have hours and hours of outtakes stored…somewhere. I'm pretty sure there will be some compromising footage somewhere. I just need a plan to get it," Sophie mused. "But I'll have to go to New York, I can't do anything from here."

"I don't think that's such a good idea," Kellan responded.

"Why not?" Sophie demanded.

"It's New York, Soph." Vaughn immediately sided with Kellan, both going into protective mode.

"And I'm twenty-seven years old, not a child," Sophie replied, her tone heated. "I need to do something, guys. I can't just sit on my hands, hoping something will change."

Vaughn rubbed the back of his neck. "I don't like it, Sophie."

"Me neither."

"You don't have to like it," Sophie informed them, her determination only growing in the face of their resistance. "I'm an adult and if I want to go to New York, or any other city, I can. If I want to try and track down some footage, that's my prerogative. All you can do is support me. And say thank you when I find something."

When, not if. She refused to accept any other option.

Clearly realizing that she wouldn't back down, Kellan sighed and gave in, shoulders slumping with resignation.

"Don't do anything stupid or illegal, Soph. And if you find yourself out of your depth, you come home."

Sophie rolled her eyes at his comment but she knew when to retreat, when to quit when she was ahead. "I'm a Blackwood," she reminded her brothers. "I'll do whatever is necessary—nothing more…and nothing less."

Fee loved her Bellamy hotel suite, from the bright purple door to the spacious hallway, the cool tones of the lavender-and-white color scheme and the natural light. She loved the French doors and high ceilings but she still would prefer to be on Rockwell Ranch, in Clint's gray-and-black bedroom, rolling around on his sheets.

Having sex in a hotel room brought home the impermanence of their relationship, made what they had feel more like a hookup and a fling…

But it *was* a hookup and a fling, wasn't it?

Fee kicked off her heels in the luxurious sitting area and switched on a lamp. She was leaving soon, leaving Royal and leaving him, and if she was thinking this could be more, that they could have more, she was setting herself up for a hard fall.

She would move on; it was what she did. Always.

She couldn't forget that.

Fee watched Clint shed his jacket and silently admitted a part of her loved the fantasy of being Clint's, of being one half of a whole. They'd had a magical evening and Clint, despite his loner personality, had seemed to enjoy himself, even slow dancing with her to one of her favorite songs. Despite the avid interest of the other guests, he'd kissed her—a kiss that was far too heated and went on for far too long for propriety—when the old year flipped over into the new.

The society columns and entertainment sites would be buzzing with speculation.

She hadn't cared then and she didn't care now. She was with Clint and that was all that mattered.

"Fun evening," Clint said, loosening his bow tie and flipping open the button holding his collar together. He looked around, saw the crystal decanters on a bar set up in the corner and his long strides covered the distance in a few steps. "Would you like a nightcap?"

"Cointreau, thanks," Fee answered him, sinking into the corner of the sofa and tucking her feet under her.

Clint handed her a drink and sat down next to her, pulling her legs over his thighs. He held her ankle as he sipped his drink.

"Happy New Year, Fee."

Fee smiled. "You too, Clint. I hope this year brings you so much happiness."

She wouldn't be around to witness what direction his life would take but she hoped he wouldn't retreat back into his lonely world—she hoped he'd make an effort to be more sociable. She could tell he'd had fun tonight; he'd enjoyed the company of his fellow ranchers, of the businesspeople in Royal, his town.

It wasn't hers. She'd like it to be but she wasn't the type to settle down, and she didn't think she could live in a small town where everyone knew each other's business, where you couldn't sneeze without someone across town sending a *bless you* your way. She'd hate it, she'd feel confined and hemmed in and claustrophobic…

But Clint was here and he made her feel free, accepted, protected.

What was the point in even considering it, though? Even if she could wrap her head around staying in one place—a massive "if"—Clint had never, not once, hinted he'd like her to stay. She was just a fling, someone to share a little of the holiday season with, some fun in the middle of a harsh winter.

Even if she wanted to, it wouldn't be fair to change the rules of the game on him now.

Fee rested her head on the back of the sofa and sighed, enjoying the way Clint's thumbs pressed into pressure points in her foot. She moaned, feeling heat slide into her veins and sparkles dance across her skin. They'd made love often but she still felt a hit of anticipation. He made her feel new, precious, undiscovered.

Even, she thought, *a little loved.*

But love was out of the question, and not something either of them was looking for. So why was she feeling this way? "You're looking a little pensive," Clint commented, placing his glass on the coffee table in front of them.

"It's a fresh start, a new year. A perfect time to feel pensive," Fee replied. She took a sip of her liqueur, sighing when the warmth hit her stomach.

Clint lifted her legs off his and stood up. Bending down, he pushed one hand under her thighs, another around her back and lifted her, with no effort at all, into his arms.

She still had her drink in her hand.

"Where's your bedroom?" Clint demanded.

Fee waved her glass in the direction of the hallway. "Last room on the right."

Clint carried her past the dining table and stepped into the dark hall while Fee continued to sip her drink, very confident in his ability to carry her. He kicked open her door and walked her across the luxurious room to lay her in the middle of her enormous, too-big-for-one-person bed. Clint took her drink from her hand, threw the last sip of Cointreau down his throat and placed the glass on the bureau behind him.

"I can't think of a better way to start a new year, Martinez," Clint stated, his voice extra growly. "You, a splash of orange on that white bed, eyes dark and mysterious in the shadows. Take down your hair."

Fee blinked at the unexpected command but she lifted her hands, pulling the pins out of the complicated knot her stylist had created at the back of her head. She placed the hairpins on the bedside table and allowed her heavy mass of curls to fall over her shoulders, down her back.

"You are so beautiful, Seraphina. I'm always going to remember this night."

She would too. She would remember him standing in front of her bay windows, moonlight highlighting the blond in his hair, turning his eyes from green to gold.

She'd remember the way his white shirt caressed those broad shoulders, how well he wore his tuxedo.

"I don't want this to end, Clint," Fee admitted, bending her legs and wrapping her arms around her knees.

"I know. I don't either," Clint said, coming to sit beside her on the bed, his fingers sliding into her hair. "But it has to end, sweetheart, because neither of us can change."

She could, maybe, if she tried hard enough. Clint shook his head when she suggested it.

"You're a beautiful butterfly who needs to experience the taste of different places and I need to be here, in Royal. Neither of us can—should—change."

His words hurt but the truth always did. "I know." Fee pushed her cheek into his palm, turning her head to kiss his calloused skin. "I just can't imagine not doing this again."

Clint held her cheek, his eyes a soft green-gold. "We've just got to enjoy the time we have and make some great memories."

He was right, they couldn't waste a second. Life was too short and their remaining time was minimal. Fee placed her hand on his knee, feeling the outline of his prosthetic under her fingers. Clint looked down and smiled. "You make me feel whole, Fee, normal."

Fee placed a gentle kiss on his lips. "You are whole, and you're better than normal—you're extraordinary."

Clint held her face and gently kissed her lips, in a caress that was as magical as it was erotic. "I want to make this last," he murmured against her lips, "I want to savor, to commit every caress to memory."

While that sounded wonderful, Fee knew herself all too well. "I'm not very patient, Clint."

"Suck it up, cupcake." Clint smiled against her mouth. Tipping her face, he changed the angle of his kiss and slid his tongue into her mouth, tangling with hers in a languid exchange that seemed to last for days, years.

Fee leaned back against the pillows and Clint covered her body with his as they kissed, fully dressed. This wasn't just sex; he was making love to her and Fee's heart expanded to explosion point.

She would take this night, and the memory, and thank God that, at least once, she'd known true passion.

Clint undressed her slowly, sliding her dress off her body and dropping the magnificent garment to the floor. She lay on the bed in her tiny flame-colored thong and gold spiked heels, her body flushed with pleasure. Clint stroked her from neck to foot, committing every curve, bump and freckle to memory. Fee tried to touch him in return but he moved her hands back to her sides, telling her this was his time to feast.

He loved her breasts, pulling her nipple between his teeth, easing the sting with his tongue. He buried his nose into her belly button, gently nipped her hip. He kissed the back of her knees, nibbled her ankle just below the strap of her heels.

Somewhere along the way he shed his clothes and allowed her to use her hands, her mouth, to torture him as he had her.

By the time she'd finished paying his body the same attention he'd paid hers, they were both vibrating with need, desperate to fly. Clint settled himself between her legs and rested his weight on his elbows next to her head. "Fee, look at me."

Fee lifted her heavy lids, sighing when he slid into her, hard and masculine, filling her, completing her.

"Remember this night…when you feel lonely or less than or sad, remember this night, remember me. Remember that I was profoundly, deeply grateful to share this with you. Remember that I think you are amazing and how your beauty makes my heart stutter. Remember this, remember me," Clint said, placing a hand under her butt to lift her up and into him.

Fee held his face as he rocked her up, and up. "I will. I always will. Will you remember too?"

Clint nodded, his eyes foggy with desire, his back tense from holding back. "I'll never forget you, Fee."

Fee smiled, nodded and closed her eyes as she followed him over the edge.

Nine

On the first day of the New Year, Fee, curled up against Clint's broad back, heard the beep of an incoming message on her phone and released a long groan. She gently banged her head against Clint's spine before rolling away from him to scoop her phone up off the bedside table. Pushing her hair out of her face, she squinted at the screen and cursed.

"Such ladylike language on the first day of the New Year," Clint teased, slinging a leg over her thigh and covering her breast with his big hand.

Fee dropped the phone onto the mattress and rolled her head to look into his pretty eyes. "We need to do some filming today, and I really don't want to. I'd rather spend the day in bed with you."

Clint lifted his wrist to look at his watch. "It's barely six. What time do you need to report for duty?"

"Ten."

"I need to get back to the ranch." He dropped his mouth

to her shoulder, nuzzling his cheek against her skin. "Do you want to come with me? I can check on my guys, the animals and I'll feed you breakfast. I'll have you back in town by ten."

She couldn't think of anything she'd like to do more. "Yes, please." She sighed as she rolled onto her side. "I'd much rather spend the day with you than filming."

"I don't know how you cope with having those cameras in your face all the time."

"You get used to it."

"It would be my worst nightmare." Clint stroked her arm from shoulder to elbow, his touch light and soothing. "Do you enjoy it?"

"Enjoy what?"

"Being a reality TV star? Having to look good all the time, being careful what you say and how you say it?"

Fee thought for a moment. Before she came to Royal, she would've quickly responded she loved it, that going to work every day was fun. And in many ways, it was—she'd had a lot of experiences she never could have had without the show opening doors for her, as she explained to Clint.

"I've traveled, a lot, seen places that would've been out of my budget on a normal salary. I've earned a lot of money over the years. Money that will allow me to keep traveling, to keep being able to see new places, do new things. To keep moving."

"And that's important to you, being on the move?"

Was it? She was no longer so sure. "It's what I know, Clint. As a kid, we moved every six to eight to ten months. The longest we stayed in one town was just over a year." Fee sat up and pulled the sheet over her breasts. "I like being with people, probably because I spent so much of my childhood and teenage years on my own. The show, the people working on it, are my family."

"But you will lose them if you leave the show and move on."

And that was something that still worried her... They'd been such a part of her life for so long. Could she could cope without being part of a group, not having people around her 24/7? Yeah, she thought she'd be okay. She'd miss her friends, miss the crew and the constant company, but she wouldn't be completely lost without them.

"Being here in Royal, learning the basics of ranching—"

Clint snorted. "Please. You didn't even scratch the surface of what it means to ranch..."

"Okay, point taken, we didn't take it very seriously."

"Or at all," Clint muttered.

Fee ignored his interruption. "But I would've like to have learned more. It's an interesting process. And I think I could be good at it."

"Mucking out a horse stall and counting cattle doesn't make you a rancher, Fee."

"I know that. I just said it's interesting. I like being in the fresh air, doing something with my hands, seeing immediate results. It's...life-affirming, I suppose." Fee looked through the open drapes at the day starting to unfurl outside. "I like the animals, the big sky, feeling grounded."

"Careful, you're starting to sound a little in love with Royal, with the ranching lifestyle," Clint teased.

That might be because Fee *had* fallen a little in love with Royal, with the town and the land and the relaxed lifestyle. And she was, terrifyingly, more than a little in love with Clint. Fee nibbled on the inside of her lip as she watched the sun's weak rays touch the huge lake she could see from her bed.

When had that happened? She couldn't tell; it had slowly crept up on her. Maybe it was his refusal to be pigeonholed by his disability. Maybe it was because he was strong and decisive and a natural leader. His superfine body played one part and his skill as a lover another. Under his taciturn exterior was a guy who just wanted the world to see him for what he was and not how he looked.

The residents of Royal did see him for what he was— it was only Clint who thought they were judging him by his disability.

They admired him and Clint still couldn't see it. He was still convinced they only saw the guy with the prosthetic. That was why he pushed himself so hard, why he was determined to fund the fire station, to act as their temporary Fire Chief. He wanted the world to see he was more than a guy who'd lost half his leg.

Fee could relate. She wanted the world to know she was more than a pretty face, a party animal, the high-spirited, loud-mouthed, fast-talking delight she was shown as on TV. Up until her visit to Royal she'd been content with the way the world saw her but after a few short weeks in this town, she understood, on a fundamental level, Clint's need to be recognized for who he was and not what he looked like.

She got it, she really did. Because the world didn't see her clearly either.

So was she confusing love with understanding, blowing their mutual connection out of proportion? She'd never been in love before so she wasn't sure, but it was something to think about. She also needed to give some thought to her future, to what she did next. But she'd need to leave Royal to do that. She needed to see if she still felt this way when she was back in New York, back in her apartment.

Back in Manhattan, she'd be able to think clearly again.

Turning back to Clint, she saw his eyes were closed and his breathing had evened out. His eyelashes were long on his cheeks and she could see hints of gold in his stubble. In sleep his lips were relaxed, his hair messy. Fee pulled back the sheet and looked down at the hard muscles of his stomach, his early morning erection, her eyes wandering down his thighs, over his knee and to his long, elegant foot.

His prosthetic was propped up against the bedside table and she was so thankful he had the money to pay for one of the most advanced systems in the world. She had no doubt Clint would've gotten by on a cheaper version, or on crutches, but his variety of robotic legs gave him amazing freedom of movement.

"You're thinking too loud," Clint muttered, kissing her shoulder again.

"I thought you were asleep," Fee replied.

"Dozing," Clint said, sitting up. He kneeled and, gripping her under her thighs, pulled her down the bed. Then he rolled on top of her, his cock settling within the V of her legs.

Fee lifted her eyebrows, instantly aroused. "I thought we didn't have time."

"We don't but I need you. I need to have you again."

Fee turned into his embrace and sighed when Clint kissed her.

Best way to start a New Year, bar none.

Clint heard the twang of a country song coming from the speakers of his SUV and hit the button on his steering wheel to mute the music. He smiled when Fee hit the radio to bring the song up again so he flipped the station to a heavy rock channel. "It's too early in the morning for slit-my-throat music, sweetheart."

"It's country—you're a rancher and a Texan, you're supposed to like country music."

"I don't," Clint replied, lifting his take-out cup of coffee to his mouth.

"It tells a story, and it's moving."

"It's depressing," Clint said, amused. His city slicker was really throwing herself into country living. He looked at her outfit and shook his head. Okay, it wasn't quite so over-the-top country as her first cowgirl outfit, but her jeans were tucked into a brand-new pair of tooled brown cowboy boots and she wore a sleeveless navy padded vest over a long-sleeved, pale pink T-shirt. The voluminous scarf in greens and blues made her eyes seemed darker and edgier.

She was the sexiest cowgirl he'd ever met...

Clint sipped his coffee and thought about their evening spent in Royal. Despite his bitching about the camera crews and dressing up in the tux, he'd had fun the previous night. He'd met several new members of the Texas Cattleman's Club and he'd enjoyed talking ranching and oil and beef prices. Despite the wealth, the glitz and the over-decorated ballroom, he'd felt more at home than he'd thought he would.

But the after-party in Fee's suite had been the highlight of the evening. He'd sipped champagne from her belly button, from the hollow of her back, trickled drops over her hard nipples. They'd loved and laughed and talked and loved and laughed and talked some more. He really wished they could spend the whole day on his ranch—saddle up two horses, go for a ride and, later, fall asleep, preferably naked, in the afternoon sun, hitting his bed in the middle of the afternoon.

He'd had little to no sleep and, God, he wasn't seventeen anymore. He needed to recharge...

"Clint?"

Something about Fee's voice jerked his attention back and he looked at her, frowning. "What is it?"

"Smoke."

The single word hit him with all the force of a bullet and Clint pulled his foot off the accelerator and looked toward where she was pointing. A massive black cloud hovered over the ridge and he cursed. That wasn't good, not at all.

Clint pulled over and reached for his cell phone. As he picked up the device to make a call, it rang. He swiped the screen to answer. "Jeff, yeah, I see the smoke. Blackwood Hollow?"

Jeff, one of his more experienced volunteers and the guy he wanted to be appointed as Royal's first permanent fire chief, didn't waste time with explanations. "The fire was started by kids smoking at the reservoir."

The reservoir was in a secluded area to the north of town where teenagers frequently met to party and let off steam. Clint cursed.

Jeff ignored him and continued. "These dry and windy conditions aren't helping. The fire is moving rapidly towards Blackwood Hollow. There are also fires north of Royal, and there's another one heading towards the TCC clubhouse."

Clint ignored Fee's big eyes and her inquisitive expression. He rapidly accelerated. "I'm heading toward Blackwood Hollow. When can I expect help?"

"Twenty minutes, maybe thirty?" Jeff replied.

"Tell them to hurry the hell up," Clint told him. He barked out another list of instructions, including a request for surrounding counties to send their people in to help. It was a crap start to the New Year but they'd have to deal.

And get the damn fire under control.

Clint cut his call to Jeff, made a few more calls and handed his phone to Fee. Keeping an eye on the column of smoke, which was to his left and growing bigger, he whipped into the driveway of Blackwood Hollow. He looked at the wind causing the trees to sway and felt dread curl in his stomach. The direction of the wind would push the fire directly toward Blackwood Hollow, and the house, stables and barn would be in its fiery path in no time at all.

"Is Rockwell Ranch safe?"

"Right now it is," Clint tersely replied. "The wind is sending the fire this direction, not toward my spread. But if the wind changes, everything could change."

"Don't you need to be there?" Fee asked, her hand on the dashboard in front of her.

"I spoke to my foreman. Brad has it under control. We go where the biggest threat is."

"Understood. What's the plan?"

"The plan is that you go into the underground bunker and stay put."

Fee's hard "No" shot out of her mouth. "That's not going to happen."

"Jesus, Fee, I can't be effective while worrying about you."

"Understood," Fee replied. "And I will get in the bunker when there's nothing more I can do, when I'm getting in the way. But there must be something I can help with now. I'll go mad sitting on my ass in a bunker."

Fair point. She could help, and it wasn't unsafe for her yet. Clint thought for a moment as he drove past the house toward the stables. He jerked to a stop and released his seat belt. "Okay, it's early so the horses should still be in the barn. We're going to get them out."

"And take them where?" Fee asked, following him out of the car. She unwrapped her scarf and threw it, and her vest, onto the passenger seat.

"We'll take them into the north pasture for starters.

Then I'll take the dirt bike and open a few gates and get them out of the paddocks and onto the range. Their instinct will take them away from the fire, to safety. We've just got to get them onto the open land and they'll head, hopefully, in the direction of Rockwell Ranch."

Clint saw the Blackwood hands pouring out of the bunkhouse and gestured them toward the other barn where all the working horses were stabled.

Clint headed to the second, smaller barn and Fee had to jog to keep up with his long legs. But he couldn't slow down, time was of the essence.

Clint headed into the first stall and ran his hand down the already sweaty neck of Buck's favorite stallion, Jack. "You can smell the smoke, can't you boy?" Clint kept his voice steady. "I need you to take your mares to safety. You can do that, can't you, Jack?"

Clint looked behind him to see Fee with her hands full of bridles. "Good thinking, sweetheart."

He quickly placed one over Jack's massive head and when he was done, handed the reins to Fee. "Lead him outside—do not let him bolt."

Fee took the reins and nodded, her eyes filled with fear. The horse was enormous next to her but Clint didn't have a choice, he needed to put bridles on the other ten horses.

His phone jangled and he pulled it out of his back pocket and didn't bother to greet Jeff again. "Yeah?"

"The intensity of the fire is building and it's quickly spreading. We need helicopters in the air, we need water dumps urgently. Blackwood Hollow is in immediate danger, Clint."

Clint ran over to the open door of the stable and saw the fire was so much closer than he'd believed. Smoke stung his eyes and he tasted the heat in the back of his throat.

They were out of time. Cursing, he retraced his steps and flipped open the latches to all the stalls.

"Unhook Jack's reins and slap his rump, tell him to go," Clint yelled at Fee. "And stay out of the damn way!"

He poked his head out of the stall, saw Fee following his directions. The horse bolted. Fee waited until the huge horse passed her and ducked into the stall opposite. A heartbeat later, another horse, this time a black filly, galloped out. Within minutes they managed to clear the stable. Clint grabbed Fee's hand and they ran out of the building. Clint watched as Jack led his mares away from the fire, all of them easily clearing the low white fences.

Yeah, they'd be fine.

They moved to the other stable block and helped the hands release the rest of the stock. In minutes the barn was finally cleared of animals but the air was getting thicker, smokier by the minute. They needed to burn a firebreak to keep the fire from hitting the house but he also needed to be up in the air. He was one of the few helicopter pilots in the area and before donating a few birds to the town of Royal, he'd made sure his certification was current.

Clint grabbed Fee's hand, heard her cough and knew she needed to get underground as soon as possible. The hands would start burning a firebreak but there was still a damn good chance that Blackwood Hollow would be burned to the ground.

"Are there any people or animals in the main house?" Fee asked, after coughing.

Clint thought for a minute. "Miranda? She's living here now, isn't she?"

Fee nodded.

"Can you call her, get her out here? Then both of you can go into the bunker."

Fee shook her head. "I left my phone in the car. I'll just run over to the house and get her out."

Clint saw a convoy of cars speeding up the long driveway and nodded. Thank God, help had arrived.

"You have ten minutes. I'm serious, Fee, ten minutes to get her out. Meet me by the front door."

Fee nodded and turned to sprint toward the main house. Clint fought the urge to run after her, to keep her at his side, and told himself she was running away from the fire, that he needed her to get Miranda out. She'd be fine, there was no need to worry.

Kellan Blackwood was the first person to exit a vehicle, closely followed by his brother, Vaughn, and Clint nodded, grateful. Despite having been estranged from Buck, they were, at heart, ranch boys who loved this land. They had an added incentive to save Blackwood Hollow. Gage, Buck's foreman, who'd spent the night in town with his honey, hopped out of the second vehicle and Clint sent up another prayer.

Gage was old school, had fought the massive fire of eighty-two and knew exactly what to do.

Running over to them, Clint spoke directly to Gage. "You're in charge. Burn a break, slow the fire down. If you can't fight it, get everybody to the bunker, make sure your people are safe. Human life is what's important, buildings are not."

"Got it." Gage nodded. "We need a bird up in the air."

"I'm on that. Jeff let me know he's got a pilot out of Deer Springs to fly the other chopper."

Gage nodded. "That'll work. Right, let's beat this bastard."

Okay, they had a plan. Clint raised his hands at the other volunteer firefighters as he jogged to his vehicle but didn't stop to talk. There was no time. He needed to get Fee and

Miranda into the bunker; she would be safe in the shelter Buck built to protect his people from tornadoes, storms and the end of the world, and Clint could do his job not worrying about his woman.

His woman…

Well, for now, today, she was.

Clint whipped his car around, punched the accelerator and drove up to the main house. He exited his SUV as the front door opened and he jogged up the steps to see Fee's white face. "She's not here. She must've stayed at The Bellamy last night."

"You sure?" Clint demanded, wondering whether he could spare the time to search the house himself.

Fee's look was sour. "I can search a house, Rockwell, even one as ridiculously big as this."

Point taken. "I trust you. Let's go."

Fee followed him into the kitchen and then down the stairs that led to a basement converted into a games room. Ignoring the massive TV and the billiards table, Clint headed for the far corner and twisted the painting to a forty-degree angle. Like magic, the wall slid away to reveal a steel door, complete with a brightly lit keypad. Clint punched in some numbers and light filled the room beyond the door.

"The code boots up the generator and filters the air coming into this safe room," Clint told her, gesturing her to step inside. It was a hell of a room, Clint thought. Couches, chairs and bookshelves filled the space. Bunk beds lined the far end of the room and, in the room adjoining this area were more bunks and a double bed.

If he didn't have a raging wildfire to fight, he could make good use of that bed.

"There's a shower and toilet through the door and drinks and nonperishables in the cupboards. Help yourself."

Fee folded her arms across her chest and looked apprehensive. Clint fought the urge to pull her into his arms, knowing he might not let her go. And he had to go.

"You'll be safe here, Fee. The fire, even if it takes the house, won't affect you. This room was built to hold twenty people, to keep them safe for three months or more. I promise you, you will be okay."

Fee rolled her eyes at him. "I'm not worried about me, you idiot, I'm worried about you. You're the one who's rushing into danger while I sit on my ass and do nothing."

Her obvious concern for his welfare touched his cold, shriveled heart. Clint clasped her face in his hands. "I'll be fine, sweetheart."

"Are you okay to fly the helicopter? You know, after having been in one that crashed?"

The crash was the reason he'd forced himself to learn to fly, getting back on the horse and all that...

"I've worked really hard to put that behind me, Fee."

"And you won't take any stupid risks just to prove you can?" Fee demanded. "I don't need a hero, Rockwell, I need you alive. To come back and get me."

"I won't be a hero." He'd do what he needed to do but he wouldn't take any unnecessary risks. Or he'd try not to. "And I've told Gage and the Blackwood boys, Kellan and Vaughn, you are in here. There's also a camera system for you to see whether the coast is clear. You can leave when you feel it's safe. I'd prefer for you to wait for me, though, so I'm asking you to wait for me to come and get you, Seraphina."

Fee nodded and Clint sighed at the tears in her eyes. "I'll be fine, Fee."

Fee smiled and knuckled the moisture away. "Of course, you will be. I, on the other hand, will be going crazy down here."

Clint kissed her nose.

Fee lifted herself up onto her tiptoes and brushed her lips across his. "Go now. Come back to me as soon as you can."

"That's a promise," Clint said, before dropping an open-mouthed kiss on her mouth. Allowing himself one last, quick taste, he pulled away and, without looking back, walked out of the safe room.

While he still could.

Ten

Fee stared at the TV screen, the image split into quarters, and wondered why she bothered. Twelve hours had passed since Clint pushed her into this underground bunker and night had long since fallen over Blackwood Hollow. Earlier, via the screen, she'd watched the fire reach the far barn, enveloping the structure in silky, almost pretty flames. The volunteers had allowed the structure to burn, choosing to put their efforts toward saving the newer stable block. She thought they might have succeeded, since the camera within that stable was still working while the other wasn't.

Fee folded her arms and looked at the solidly black screen. At least she couldn't see any more flames, and were those raindrops she saw on the lens of another camera?

God, she hoped so. It was time Mother Nature started working with them instead of against them.

Fee sat on the edge of one of the super-comfortable

couches and held her shaking hands between her knees, trying not to cry. Was Clint safe? Where was he? Was he still flying, fighting fires? She knew some helicopter pilots were night rated and wondered if he was too. She was in awe of his bravery and determination. If she'd been in a crash, and if said crash had killed a few of her teammates, she doubted she'd go anywhere near a helicopter, or a plane, again. Hell, she'd have trouble with anything more than two feet off the ground.

But not Clint. Clint had looked at himself, realized he was scared and instead of retreating—like a normal person would—rushed headfirst into resolving his problem. He was scared so he needed to conquer his fear by learning to fly the damned machine, exerting his control over the situation.

He was pretty damn amazing and a real inspiration and, yep, she was very definitely in love with her superhero cowboy.

Dammit.

But any woman would be. He was sexy, sure, good looking, sure, and possessed awesome bed skills. But he was also intelligent, hardworking, determined and reliable. He gave and gave and gave and all he wanted was for people to see him as capable. He didn't want medals, recognition or kudos, he just wanted people to see him, not his disability.

And they did. Clint just had to recognize that truth.

Fee stared down at the concrete floor, trying not to look at her watch again. Not ten minutes had passed since she last checked the time, and God knew, a watched clock didn't move any faster. She'd tried to read, she'd tried to sleep, but nothing kept her occupied for long.

She'd mostly just spent the past twelve hours pacing the floor, worrying.

Should she open the bunker? Was she safe? She didn't

know, but man, she needed to get out of here in the worst way. She needed to find Clint, to see if he was okay, to assess the damage done to this ranch, to Rockwell Ranch, to Royal itself. This might, after all, be her forever town.

But she didn't know what awaited her outside. The fire could still be raging off camera; she might be walking into hell itself. It was dark, and she didn't have transport.

She was, dammit, safe here. Safe and, since she couldn't find a phone or a radio, disconnected.

Fee tasted panic and forced it down. She'd fought occasional bouts of claustrophobia all afternoon and it had taken all she had not to wrench the door open and run out of the room.

But she wasn't a fool. She was safe here and she'd promised Clint to stay put.

He trusted her to keep her word, so she'd spend the night here, if necessary, and in the morning, she'd reassess the situation.

That meant spending more time in this box but she would deal...

Mostly because she didn't have a damn choice.

"Suck it up, cupcake." She repeated Clint's words and immediately felt steadier. Standing up, she walked into the bathroom and stared at her white face in the small mirror above the sink. There was nothing of Seraphina Martinez, reality TV star, in the mirror. She looked haggard, older, stressed.

Her man had been in danger all day; she had a right to look like crap. Fee splashed some water on her face and bent down to sip some out of her cupped hand. It slid down her tight throat and she felt a burning sensation in her eyes.

"You are not going to cry, dammit."

Fee headed into the main room, thinking of a way to

distract herself. Maybe if she pushed the couch to the side, she could do some yoga, find her Zen.

Well, she could try.

Fee bent down, put her shoulder to the heavy couch and pushed, relieved when the couch scraped, reluctantly, across the smooth concrete. There still wasn't enough space so she pushed it again, totally surprised when the couch easily glided across the floor this time.

Lifting her head, she saw his yellow trousers, his bare arm, and she squealed when she saw his sooty face, his white teeth flashing. Launching herself up, she gave him just enough time to straighten from his bent position before throwing herself into his arms, gripping his waist with her legs and raining kisses on his filthy face.

"Oh, God, you're here. You're safe."

"I'm safe." Clint pushed his hand into her hair and held the back of her head. "How are you? Doing okay?"

"Pfft." Fee waved his concern away. "I'm fine. Bored but fine. What's the damage? Is your ranch okay?"

"The fire touched some land bordering my ranch but we got lucky. It started to rain and stopped it from spreading."

"It's really raining?"

"Bucketing down. Thank God," Clint replied. "It'll kill the last few sparks, the small fires."

"What about Blackwood Hollow? How much damage is there?" Fee demanded, sliding down his body and ignoring the streaks of dirt on her clothing.

"The far barn is gone, as is one of the stables. The guest house lost a couple of rooms." Clint pushed the braces off his shoulders and allowing his pants to slide down his legs. He kicked them away and stood in his jeans and T-shirt, looking exhausted but satisfied.

"Is Royal ok?" Fee asked as she headed toward the big fridge on the far side of the room. She pulled out a cola and popped the tab, handing it to Clint, who sat down on the edge of the bed, clearly exhausted.

"We lost a few houses on the edge of town, the TCC clubhouse has been damaged and there's smoke damage to a few businesses on the outskirts. There's a lot of work to do, clearing up and rebuilding."

"I learned how to wield a drill and a hammer when I worked on a Habitat for Humanity project last spring," Fee told him, sitting cross-legged on the bed beside him. "I can help."

"I'm sure we can use your skills." Clint drank deeply from the can and looked down at his black hands. "I'm filthy."

"I thought you were flying—not fighting the flames up close and personal."

"I was," Clint said, standing up. "Then I landed and another small blaze kicked up not far from where I was. It was quicker to beat the fire back toward the firebreak than fly the chopper to pick up another load of water."

Clint strolled into the bathroom and Fee heard the shower. "Let me clean up and then we'll head out to my place."

Fee thought for a minute and followed him into the bathroom. He cursed when he looked down at his leg. "Shit. I don't have any crutches here."

"Hang tight," Fee said. Without giving him chance to argue, she stripped off and bent down in front of Clint to remove his leg. She heard the pop of the suction cup and gently removed his prosthetic, resting it against the bathroom cabinet. Clint leaned against the wall and Fee placed her shoulder under his armpit, letting him lean on her while he hopped into the shower, adjusting the stream of water to hit him as he rested against the wall.

He reached for the soap and loofah but jerked his hand

back to hold onto the edge of the shower door to keep his balance. "Crap, it's slippery in here."

Fee waited until she was sure he was balanced before leaving his side. She quickly stripped off her underwear and stepped into the shower. Grabbing the loofah, she dumped some liquid soap on it and started to wash Clint's body.

"Fee, I—"

Fee looked up at him, a frown on her face. "You've spent the past twelve hours helping your fellow ranchers, your fellow residents. You've fought fires, dumped water, flown a damned helicopter. You've helped and helped and served and served. Let me help you."

"I—"

"Just shut up, Rockwell," Fee told him, standing on her toes to drop a kiss on his mouth.

Not giving him more time to argue, she washed his shoulders, under his arms, across his chest and his stomach. She swiped the loofah over his private areas and down his leg, and then, equally clinically, over his short leg.

She took a washcloth, put soap on it and wiped his face. Seeing the dirty water streaming off his hair, she told him to duck his head. Picking up a bottle of shampoo, she washed his hair, once, then again.

"God, it feels so good to be clean," Clint told her, hot water pounding her head and his shoulders.

Fee wrinkled her nose. "Sorry, but you're going to have to get back into your dirty clothes."

Clint shook his head. "There's a cupboard full of clothes, different sizes and styles. I'll find something to wear."

"Buck really was prepared," Fee said, impressed.

"You have no idea." Clint wiped moisture off his face

with his hand and switched off the water. "Let's get dressed and we can go home."

Fee saw the exhaustion in his red-rimmed eyes. She touched his cheek. "Do you have to go back? Is there something you need to do on the ranch tonight?"

"No, my foreman has it covered," Clint replied. "Why?"

"Because there's a very nice bed in the adjoining bedroom and I think we could both do with a some sleep."

"I thought you would be sick of this place by now, that you'd want to get out."

Fee handed him the truth. He was a big boy and she was sure he could handle it. "You're here now and I'm fine. Let's go to bed, Rockwell. I need to hold you and be held."

Clint nuzzled his cheek into her palm. "Me too, Fee. I need to hold you too. But I can only sleep for an hour, maybe two. There's so much I still need to get to tonight."

Because, if there was work to be done, Clint was first in line to do it. Fee loved that, and everything, about him.

Sophie Blackwood, dressed in her most ragged pair of jeans and oldest, most battered sweatshirt, picked her way through the debris of what was once the original stables housing the Blackwood family horses. These days, her father's prize horseflesh was stabled in the new climate controlled, technologically advanced stable block but she'd loved the history of the original stables.

It was gone now. Annihilated. Burned to the ground.

She shouldn't be this upset about it, Sophie admitted to herself, blinking away hot tears.

Everything was changing and she didn't like it.

Sophie felt a big hand on her back and turned to see Vaughn standing next to her, concern in his expression and in his eyes. "You okay, Soph?"

She wanted to be able to tell him she was fine but couldn't speak the lie. "The hits keep coming."

He rubbed a big circle on her back. "It could've been worse. The house could've burned down."

Sophie managed a weak smile. "This stable block meant more to me than the house. I never felt at home there." Sophie pushed back her deep-brown Stetson with her wrist. She bit her bottom lip. "We owe Clint Rockwell our gratitude, Vaughn. His quick response saved Blackwood Hollow, even if it's not ours anymore."

"I tried to thank him but he brushed me off," Vaughn said, looking over to where Rockwell stood. Kace and Lulu were standing just behind him, for once not arguing. Clint looked dead on his feet, pale with exhaustion. He'd gone above and beyond and Sophie, when the time was right, would express her gratitude, in her own way.

"Blackwood Hollow will be ours again," Vaughn assured her. "We just have to find a way."

"From your lips to God's ears," Sophie murmured. "Here comes Kell."

Sophie took one of the bottles of water Kellan held out, giving him a grateful smile. Cracking the lid, she heard the arrival of an expensive vehicle. Her oldest brother rolled his eyes and Sophie turned to see the Step Witch pulling off her designer sunglasses and exiting the expensive two-door coupe. Her hair was pulled back into a ponytail, her makeup was understated and she wore jeans and a long-sleeved, emerald silk T-shirt. Despite her attempts to dress down, she still looked like the expensive trophy wife she was.

Sophie followed her two brothers as they approached their father's ex-wife.

Miranda tucked her keys into the back pocket of her jeans and sighed. "Oh, great, another inquisition."

Kellan ignored her sarcastic comment. "What are you doing here, Miranda?"

Miranda waited for a beat before replying. "I came to check on Blackwood Hollow."

"Aren't you supposed to be living here, as per the terms of the will?" Kellan demanded.

"I'm allowed to leave the property Kellan." Miranda didn't drop his eyes from his. "I had a late night and, probably, too many glasses of champagne at the New Year's Eve party. I wasn't drunk but I was over my limit and, because I am a responsible citizen, I chose to spend the night at The Bellamy." She gestured to the charred ruins. "I was told the stable block and an outbuilding burned down. Any other damage I should know about?"

"Like you actually care." Sophie snorted.

Miranda tapped her foot, obviously exasperated when none of them answered her. "Okay, I'll wake Gage up and get him to give me a status report."

Sophie knew Gage was exhausted and he'd just left, at Kellan's and Clint's insistence, to go home. He needed the rest. She'd stomach answering Miranda's questions if it meant Gage was able to sleep undisturbed.

"The stable block and outbuilding were, as you can see, destroyed. The guest house lost a few rooms but is mostly intact. We lost a lot of grazing land but you have Clint Rockwell to thank that you didn't lose more."

"I'll definitely extend my gratitude to him," Miranda answered, her expression and tone cool. She looked around. "What can I do?"

Three sets of Blackwood eyebrows rose. Vaughn spoke for all of them. "You're going to work?"

"I was planning on it."

"Hauling soggy bricks, trudging through the mud?" Kellan mocked her. "You'll last two seconds."

Miranda bared her teeth at him. "Try me."

Sophie caught the movement of a cameraman heading toward them, intent on capturing their exchange. None of them needed their harsh words to be caught on camera. "Tell your guy to back off, Miranda," she told her, steel in her voice.

Miranda turned and waved the guy away. "Sorry, they are overly inquisitive sometimes and have few boundaries."

"Oh, cut it out, Miranda," Vaughn snapped, sounding irritated. "We all know you are only here, pretending to care about Buck's ranch, as a publicity stunt, to garner more attention for your ridiculously inane show."

"Tell me how you really feel, Vaughn," Miranda murmured, a slight smile tipping up the corners of her mouth.

"They'll film here and they'll edit it to make your ten minutes of work look like you spent the day doing some serious labor. We're not fooled."

"Because nothing gets past you three."

Sophie couldn't decide whether that was sarcasm she heard in Miranda's voice or not. But the calm, smirky smile remained on her face. Miranda's smile widened as she made eye contact with all three of them. "So nice chatting with you all again. It's always a highlight of my day."

Yep, that was definitely sarcasm. Sophie watched her walk away and narrowed her eyes at Miranda's slim back and the cocky sway to her hips.

Oh, Sophie couldn't wait to get to New York City and find the footage she needed to take the bitch down.

Clint appreciated the *Secret Lives* stars' willingness to help with the cleanup of Blackwood Hollow, but honestly, they tended to create more problems than they solved. Lulu, Miranda and Fee, obviously, genuinely helped the process, but the blonde and the sultry brunette spent most of their time gossiping about the fire and chatting up any man with a pulse.

He was over it.

The rain had stopped and the wet ground had killed any embers that could spark into a problematic fire again. He was grateful for the rain, obviously, but now they were clearing waterlogged areas where mud and soot and water mixed together to create a horrible sludge.

He'd been shuttling between Royal and Blackwood Hollow since dawn and on arriving back at Buck's ranch, he found himself in the middle of a Blackwood family argument around the best way to clear the debris of the destroyed buildings.

Vaughn thought the best solution was to bring in backhoes and level the half-collapsed outbuilding and the listing stable. Kellan thought both structures could be shored up.

Both agreed they needed the insurance agent to visit the property before any decision was made.

Neither was thrilled when Miranda Blackwood reminded them that, as the owner, she would make the final decision about how to go forward.

Ugly words were exchanged and Clint walked away, not wanting to get involved in their family dynamics. They needed to work it out themselves, in their own way.

Clint tugged his heavy work gloves into place and walked back over to the burned-out barn where Fee and Lulu were hauling pieces of wood away to pile them neatly to the side. A cameraman followed their every move and their cast-mate Rafaela watched, her phone in hand.

The day was warmer than expected and his jeans were wet but he refused, like the other guys, to wear shorts. He was hot, uncomfortable and exhausted after he and Fee had spent most of the night burning up the sheets in a lovemaking session as hot as it was intense—a few hours of soul-touching, concentrated, breath-stealing emotion.

It had been magnificent, but today he was at the end of his rope: tired, mentally wiped and physically drained. He was also, he realized, peopled out. He needed to be alone, to soak in some silence, to recharge his batteries. He hadn't spent this much time with this many people since he was in the unit. He was done.

But he had work to do—his neighbor needed help, so did the town, and he would not let them down. He just didn't want to talk to anybody while he worked.

"Clint, how are you feeling this morning?"

Clint turned around at the strange voice and glared when he found a camera in his face. Putting his hand up, he shoved the camera away. "Get that out of my face."

The cameraman took a few steps back but didn't lower the device. "How do you feel about the fires, about the rain, about the mess Royal is in?"

Crap on a cracker. Clint rubbed the back of his wrist against his forehead to wipe away the perspiration.

"Any comment, Clint?"

Yeah, he had a comment. He looked directly into the camera and spoke with deadly intent. "Yeah, here it is…if you point that thing in my direction one more time, I am going to ram it down your throat. Clear enough?"

The camera lowered and he saw both fear and resentment in Jimmy's eyes. "Just trying to do my job, man."

"Do it somewhere far, far away from me," Clint told him before turning around to lift a piece of corrugated iron off a wooden beam. He walked it over to a pile he'd started and carefully placed it on top of another square piece of iron, trying to ignore the phantom pains shooting from his stump up his leg. It had been months since he'd experienced them and he'd thought they were behind him.

He'd pushed himself too hard and for too long. Clint needed to take a non-opiate painkiller—he had some in the car. Maybe the analgesic would disrupt the false signals his brain was receiving from his nonexistent limb.

He pulled off his gloves and walked toward his car, but before he'd taken a few steps, another camera appeared on the periphery of his vision. "Clint, can you comment on the cleanup?"

He was going to kill someone, he genuinely was. Clint stopped, clenched his fists and counted to ten. Then to twenty. When he thought he had his temper under control, he opened his eyes and nailed the cameraman with a hard look.

Before he had time to issue another threat, he saw Fee hurrying over to him, looking determined. Striding up to the camera, she pulled a jack from its connection and held it in her hand as the camera lowered.

"Vincent, back off. Leave Clint alone."

Vincent looked like he wanted to argue but the fierce look on Fee's face stopped him in his tracks. Fee wiggled her fingers. "Give me your radio."

Vincent dug a small two-way radio out of his back pocket and handed it over, resigned. Fee took the device, hit the button and spoke into the receiver. "This is Seraphina Martinez and I'm ordering you all to stay away from Clint Rockwell."

While he appreciated her intervention, Clint didn't need her to talk for him. He opened his mouth to blast her but a disembodied voice from the radio beat him to it. Clint recognized it as being the director's voice.

"You aren't the boss here, Seraphina. Rockwell is the hero of the hour—we need to get him on screen."

"I distinctly recall Nigel telling us all we shouldn't force cooperation from the Royal residents. Clint wants privacy, and he's entitled to it," Fee shot back.

God, he could fight his own battles. And by making her announcement, they'd attracted the interest of the *Secret Lives* cast, the Blackwood siblings and Kace LeBlanc, who was there, Clint presumed, to help with the cleanup.

"Seraphina, enough! I lost the use of my leg, not my brain or my mouth," Clint roared and he caught the hurt in Fee's eyes as she turned to face him.

Then a bright red flush climbed up her neck and into her face. Her humiliation was easy to see in her eyes as she said, "I was just trying to help, Clint."

"I don't need your goddamn help. I don't need anybody's help. All I want to do is go to my truck without tripping over a reality TV star or cameraman. I just want fifteen minutes of goddamn peace."

Fee lifted her hand and backed away as she sent him a princess-looking-at-a-peasant look. "Fine. Do what you need to do."

Shit, he'd screwed up. He started to call her back, to say—what? Apologize? Yeah, he could apologize, not for threatening the cameramen but for snapping at her in front of her friends and coworkers.

That had been badly done and he was ashamed of himself.

But Fee was out of hearing distance and his leg was killing him. Before he could make amends, he needed to take some pills and a mental break, calm the hell down. He needed to find a quiet place, maybe do some meditation exercises, to rest his body, his mind and his eyes.

He'd make amends later; right now he needed to be alone.

Clint dug his painkillers from the first aid box he kept in the car and chased them down with half a bottle of water. Walking away from the car, he skirted the damaged building and walked into the surviving stable block, welcoming the quiet shadows within the building. Yay, privacy. He saw a straw bale tucked into a dark corner and, feeling hot and miserable, decided to step out of his wet jeans for a little bit.

Sitting down on the bale, he stretched out his legs in front of him and debated whether to remove his prosthetic. Deciding to leave it on, he rested his head against the cool wall and closed his eyes, breathing deeply to calm his tumultuous brain.

It had been a tough few days but he'd endured many days a great deal worse.

Eighteen hours of fighting fires shouldn't wipe him out.

But it wasn't the fire—not really. No, what did make him feel tired, emotionally displaced and, yeah, terrified, was that he was so close to dropping to his knees—one knee—and begging Seraphina to stay in Royal.

To stay with him.

There, he'd admitted it. He wanted her to stay, on the ranch, with him. Which was, admittedly, crazy. Fee was a city girl, a TV star. She needed to be seen at restaurant openings, in clubs, dancing on bars in bohemian pubs. What could he offer her? He had wealth, sure, but comfort or even luxury couldn't turn Royal into a big, bustling city. She was not a rancher's wife, girlfriend or significant other. Jesus, the woman couldn't even ride a horse.

It didn't matter how unsuited she was to live on a ranch, on his ranch; he still wanted to beg her to stay. But that was a special type of madness.

Because, if she did, what would happen? They would have great sex for a few weeks, maybe a few months, before the isolation would get to her and she'd start to think she had someplace better to be.

Good sex would fade into dissatisfaction and her fascination with ranch life, with him, would fade too.

He refused to put himself in that position.

But, damn, it was a great dream. And because he was exhausted, and a little sad and a lot overwhelmed, he allowed himself to daydream about her cooking in his kitchen, teaching her to ride, making love to her in the flowers blooming in the high meadow in spring. He dreamed of her in his bed, in his shower…

In his life.

Later Clint realized how exhausted he must have been because he, a highly trained ex-army ranger, never once suspected someone stood in the shadows, watching him.

Eleven

The next day Fee was riding shotgun in one of Rockwell Ranch's pickups and she turned to face Clint as he drove up Blackwood Hollow's long drive. After a brief apology from Clint for his rudeness—which she readily accepted—and a solid night's sleep, he looked better than he had yesterday. He was back to being strong, fit and in control.

She needed to tell him shooting was scheduled to end in two days and she had a plane ticket back to the city that same evening. She wanted to tell him that, if he asked her to stay, she would. How did she tell him he was the only man who could persuade her not to move on, to plant her feet?

The only person she felt safe enough to risk her future on?

Clint had proved himself, over and over. He was steadfast, courageous and honorable.

She should tell him, she had to get the words out. But what if she was reading too much into the situation, seeing possibilities not there? What if he didn't want her…

like that? What if he was perfectly happy to see the back of her, to let her go?

What then?

She was driving herself crazy. Either way, one of them had to raise the subject, but seeing the entire cast and crew of *Secret Lives* waiting for them on the steps leading up to Blackwood Hollow's imposing front door, she knew their discussion would be delayed.

Fee wasn't sure whether to laugh or cry, to feel relieved or irritated. God, this falling in love business was hell on the nerves.

Clint parked his car and, seeing the excited faces of her colleagues, turned to her and raised his eyebrows. "What's going on?"

"No idea," Fee said, opening her door and jumping out. It was barely nine and nobody on set usually managed to crack a smile this early. They all needed at least four cups of coffee and a couple more hours before that happened.

Fee looked at Lulu and saw her smile was strained and she wasn't as excited as Rafaela or the producers. Gemma, their PR person, looked like she wanted to jump out of her skin with excitement.

"What's going on?" Fee asked Lulu.

Lulu didn't answer her, she just turned to Gemma and gestured for her to explain.

"Clint's photo has gone viral," Gemma gushed.

Okay, what photo? She didn't know what they were talking about. "Explain."

"Rafaela went around town yesterday, doing a photo essay of Royal, looking for the poignant, pertinent photos, the human-interest angle," Gemma responded.

Human interest? Fee almost snorted. Rafaela wasn't exactly the most empathetic or sensitive of the ex-wives.

The situation would be funny…if there hadn't been

mention of a photo of Clint. Fee felt ice invade her veins and, worse, she felt Clint stiffening behind her.

"What photo?" Fee demanded, between clenched teeth. Clint was so publicity averse, any photo of him hitting the tabloids or papers would piss him off. God, she hoped it was from a distance, and flattering.

Gemma waved her tablet around and it took all Fee had not to snatch it from her hands.

"Rafaela posted it to her social media accounts, then we shared it and it's had about half a million retweets and a million views. It's hot." Gemma sent a flirty smile Clint's way that had Fee grinding her teeth.

"Show it to me," Fee demanded.

Gemma held out her iPad and Fee took it, holding her breath. Fee looked down and read the headline first: News Anchor's Son a Local Hero, This Is What True Courage Looks Like.

In the photo, Clint sat on a hay bale, head against the wall, eyes closed. He wore plain black boxer shorts and a sleeveless tank, looking hot and sexy and dirty. He appeared utterly exhausted but a small smile played around his mouth and there was a hint of pride and satisfaction on his face.

It was a powerful photograph, soul gripping and intensely emotional, and she could see why it had gone viral. Clint looked like the hero he was.

Fee heard his sharp intake of air and immediately the atmosphere changed. She closed her eyes and waited for his explosion, for his temper to ignite. She instantly knew why he was upset—he never allowed anyone to see his prosthetic leg. He was intensely private and his disability was an off-limits subject.

But Rafaela had exposed him, showing what he tried to keep hidden from the world.

Fee turned around slowly and when she met his eyes, she saw the betrayal in his eyes, the sharp kick of shock. Then his expression turned bleak and she felt him slipping away from her.

Fee felt Lulu remove the tablet from her shaking fingers and felt her friend's hand on her back, steadying her.

Oh, God, this was bad.

This was so, so bad. Clint ignored her beseeching look and regarded her as if she were a brown recluse spider he'd found on his shoe. "Excellent work, Martinez. Fantastic publicity. Glad it all worked out for you."

Oh, no, now that was unfair. She didn't know anything about the photograph and she wouldn't be blamed for it. "I would've killed it if I'd known it would be used—or if I'd known she'd taken it in the first place."

"It's a great photo," Rafaela protested, "and it's very inspirational."

"Take it down," Clint told Gemma, whose excitement had turned to confusion. *"Now."*

Gemma exchanged a panicked look with Miranda. "I can take it down from our site but it's already out there on social media. Hundreds of thousands of people have reposted the picture, the news outlets have picked it up and interviewed the residents of Royal, who have nothing but amazing things to say about you."

She got increasingly flustered when Clint's face took on that robotic expression Fee so hated.

"I don't understand why you are mad," Gemma wailed.

"And I have no intention of explaining," Clint said, his voice a few degrees lower than freezing point. He turned his attention to Miranda. "I'm done. This stops, now… today. Either they leave or I do."

"Clint, don't do this," Miranda said, her voice soothing. "I understand you are angry, and it is a shocking invasion of your privacy, but maybe you should take a few days to cool down before you do or say something you'll regret."

Clint folded his arms and nailed her with a frigid look. "Either you get rid of them or I walk. That means no one will be around to oversee the lands, the cleanup, your hands, the stock."

Miranda held his eyes for ten seconds before nodding. She turned to the director and lifted her hand, dragging it across her throat. "We're done. Let's go."

"But I have a schedule! There are shots, interviews—"

Miranda narrowed her eyes. "I said...we're done."

Miranda told the crew and Fee's costars to head for their cars. Lulu gripped her hand and squeezed before walking away.

Clint jerked his head to Miranda. "You're going to miss your lift back to town," he told Fee.

Fee felt her anger bubble, way down deep in her stomach. "You know I'm not going to walk away without discussing this."

"I have nothing to say to you, Seraphina."

God, he'd never said her name in such a dismissive way, like he had acid on his tongue. "I did not know anything about the photograph, Clint."

"You're an integral part of the show. Are you seriously telling me nobody told you they were going to plaster a photograph of your disabled lover on social media? Please, tell me another lie! I dare you."

"Nobody told me." Fee lifted her hand when he started to interrupt her. "Maybe they didn't think they needed to because they saw what I did."

"Yeah, a goddamn cripple."

Fee grabbed his arm, trying not to feel hurt when he shook off her touch. "They saw a guy who went above and beyond the call of duty, who worked like a Trojan to make sure his community was safe, who still went to work the day after that grueling day. I saw a guy who can do everything a guy with two legs can do, and more. I saw a hot, sexy, tired guy who looked amazing."

"Bullshit, Seraphina. Stop trying to spin this!"

She was so over him putting himself down. "*You* stop! Stop assuming everyone is judging you. The only person who sees you as being disabled is you, Clint. You! No one else!"

Sparks of pure silver anger flashed in Clint's eyes. "Quit blowing smoke up my ass, Martinez. I know most women see me as only half a man. There's nothing I can do to make myself whole." He was just making her angrier and angrier.

Instead of yelling at him, Fee folded her arms and waited for him to look at her. "Are you done with the pity party?"

"What?"

She ignored the roar that had horses in the nearby paddock lifting their heads. "When you are done feeling sorry yourself, I have something to say."

"I'm not interested," Clint snapped back.

"You have yelled at me, embarrassed me in front of my friends and made a ton of assumptions that simply aren't true. You owe me the right to speak."

Clint hauled in a deep breath and she watched his big chest rise and fall. When she knew she had his attention, she pushed her words past her teeth.

"Fact, you have one leg. Fact, you are technically disabled. Fact, you lost your leg in an act of supreme bravery. Fact, your mother is a stone-cold bitch and those women you hooked up with who rejected you? Shallow and superficial. And how dare you compare what they said or did to me?"

Fee drilled a hole into his chest with her finger. "I am rude and loud-mouthed and outspoken but I am not fake, Rockwell, and that's what you're accusing me of being. I made love to you because I think you are the most amazing, inspiring, capable guy I've ever met. So, once again, the only person in the whole goddamn world who has an issue with you missing a limb is you."

"And my mother, and those women—"

"Again, superficial and shallow. Why are you even giving them headspace? I'm standing here telling you your town loves you, that I do too, and the people you are listening to are people who have proved themselves to be douches. What is wrong with *you*?"

"I hate that photo—it makes me look weak!"

"You look strong and brave."

Clint shook his head and Fee realized she was fighting a lost cause. She couldn't change his mind for him. He had to realize his worth, for himself, by himself. She held up her hand and blew air into her cheeks.

"I'm crazy about you Clint, head over heels in love with you, but I can't be with you. I can't spend the rest of my life reassuring you of your worth. I'm a strong woman. I need a man who's equally aware of his strength. Until you can accept yourself, love yourself, exactly as you are, as I do, I'm wasting my time."

Clint stared at her, obviously shocked by her honesty.

"I'm going back to New York, as soon as I can. This was fun but now it's not."

Clint nodded once. His short, sharp gesture was an exclamation point at the end of their conversation. "I think that's a very good idea. Even if I believed you about not being half a man—and I don't—we could never work. You're town, I'm country. We're exact opposites."

Fee felt like her heart was breaking but she forced a

smile onto her face. She placed her hand on his chest and felt him stiffen as she leaned into him, felt him pull back as she lifted herself onto her heels to speak in his ear.

"Coward. You can face down a band of terrorists intent on killing you and your team but you can't let people see your leg, you can't love me? Shame on you, Rockwell."

Fee was close to crying, but she refused to allow him to see her tears so she quickly turned and headed for the driveway, hoping against hope Lulu was waiting for her, that she wouldn't have to phone for a ride, leaving her waiting here with the gorgeous, broken man she loved with every fiber of her being.

Through her tears Fee saw her best friend sitting in the driver's seat of her rented Jeep, far enough away not to hear her conversation but close enough to intervene if their fight went south.

God bless her best friend, Fee thought as she slid into the passenger and burst into tears.

Lulu, because she was a goddess, just held her hand and let her weep before driving her back to a life she no longer wanted.

Twelve

Two weeks passed before Clint made a trip into Royal, and only because it was the grand opening of the new fire station. He'd dressed in a sharp white button-down shirt, a tie and black chinos, and desperately wished he was in his jeans and boots, and on one of his many horses. Or working on Tim's truck, having recently received the Chevy back from the body shop. He did not want to smile and shake hands with the Royal residents, to face their sympathetic and prying eyes, answer his questions about how he was doing.

He was alone. He was fine...

Which was all a steaming pile of bull crap.

He was alone but he wasn't fine, he was just holding on.

Ignoring the cars parked in the front of the building, Clint skirted around to the parking area at the back and slid his SUV between the two new, state-of-the-art fire engines he'd donated. The firefighting/rescue helicopters were parked at the regional airport, ready to be dispatched at a moment's notice. He had provided funds for two teams of permanent firefighters, a trained medic and a pilot, saying he would serve as backup to fly as and when he was needed.

He was giving back to his community—it was all he could do.

Clint exited his car, feeling like ants were crawling under his skin. He couldn't go anywhere in Royal without thinking about Fee and that, frankly, pissed him off. And he couldn't decide what he was most angry about— the invasion of his privacy or Fee lying to him by telling him she loved him…

Oh, wait, maybe it was the fact she'd called him a goddamn *coward*.

He'd snuck behind enemy lines in the dead of night, risked his skin a thousand times, suffered deprivations and starvation rations, endured mortar strikes and enemy fire, he'd earned medals—a goddamn Purple Heart!—and yet she'd still thrown the insult straight in his face.

How dare she judge him?

Walking into the large empty bay where the catering staff was setting up tables for drinks and food, he ran up the flight of stairs into the commander's office, hoping to hide out until he was needed. He'd say a few words and then fade away; nobody would even miss him.

Clint threw himself into the leather office chair behind the desk and rested his forearms on his thighs, staring down at the hard-wearing floor beneath his feet. His thoughts, as they always did, turned back to Fee. What she'd said was unforgivable, hurtful, cruel. This—this was why he should avoid relationships.

Because they sucked, dammit.

Well, like rehab and surgery and PTSD and everything

else he'd endured, it was over and he could put it behind him. He had work to do, a ranch to run, the fire station to oversee. All of that would keep him sane. He'd launch the fire station, and after it was up and running, he'd retreat and lick his wounds.

He'd tried, and failed, at a relationship. He should learn from it and move on.

Clint heard the sharp rap on his door and lifted his head to see Jeff, the about-to-be-appointed fire chief, standing in the doorway. Clint stood up and gestured to the chair. "Sorry, I should've asked you if I could be in here."

"Clint, you paid for everything here. You can be anywhere you like. And I don't have secrets to hide."

Clint sent him a tight smile and took a surreptitious look at his watch. The function wasn't supposed to start for another half hour so he walked over to the window and stared down at the cars streaming into the parking lot.

Damn, too many people…

Jeff sat down on the edge of his desk and picked up a signed baseball. "So, you must be pleased with the response you received from the photograph."

Yeah, *thrilled*. Not.

"I read a lot of the comments and the responses. Not sure how much of it you've seen, but hell, if it was me, I'd be floating near the ceiling," Jeff commented.

Clint frowned, confused. "What are you talking about?"

"Thousands of vets and paraplegics and disabled people—women, children and men—left comments saying you are a role model, an inspiration, and that you've given them hope. The story was picked up by a national news outlet and you're trending. God, your social media accounts must be blowing up."

He didn't have any social media accounts so he'd had

no idea of the extent of the reach of the photograph. "And the responses were mostly positive?" he asked, confused.

"They were *all* positive. You're the new poster boy for true American grit. And your mom has been hitting the radio stations and interview circuits, boasting about you and the fact she taught you everything you know."

She wished. And how typical it was for his mom to jump on the publicity he generated. But none of it mattered, not really, because he'd lost the person he loved.

It meant little without her.

"Talking about being an inspiration," Jeff said, "would you do me a favor and meet someone? He's in the gym."

Clint started to shake his head but Jeff held up his hand. "Ten minutes, Clint. Please?"

He didn't want to. He wanted to stay here and enjoy his solitude. *Coward*, a little voice inside him stated. It sounded like Fee.

Wanting to be alone wasn't an act of cowardice.

Sure it is...

Annoyed by the direction of his thoughts, Clint nodded abruptly and followed Jeff out of his office and down a floor to the gym the architects had tucked into the corner of the fire station. Clint had requested the workout room for the firefighters but had also suggested that it could be used by any veterans in the area who couldn't afford the fees at a normal fitness center.

Jeff was fully on board with his idea.

When Clint stepped into the gym, he saw a kid standing in the middle of the floor, his hand on a thick rope dangling from the ceiling. He sported a mop of bright blond hair but Clint's attention was immediately captured by his prosthetic leg.

Clint started to back away and hit Jeff's broad, solid chest.

"He's eleven years old, he's a cancer survivor and all he wants is to meet you. He won't say why or how you landed on his radar, but he's obsessed with you. His mom, a waitress, took a day off work to bring him here when they found out you'd be at the ceremony today. Apparently, it's the most excited she's seen him in months."

Clint felt Jeff's hand on his shoulder and his fingers dig into his skin. "You will not mess this day up for him, Clint."

Well, okay then.

Clint looked around and saw the boy's mom standing against the far wall, looking anxious. She also looked too thin and way too tired. A single mom, he realized, trying to cope as best she could with a kid who'd suffered through a horrible disease and was now physically challenged.

Sucked...

Clint jammed his hands into the pockets of his chinos and walked into the center of the gym, sighing when anxious bright-blue eyes met his. He held out his hand and waited for the kid to put his much smaller hand in his before giving it a gentle shake. "Hey, bud, I'm Clint."

"I'm Beck."

"I heard you wanted to speak to me."

Beck folded his arms across his chest and tipped his head to one side. "I've read every article about you and there were a lot."

Clint heard the challenging note in his voice and considered apologizing. If there were as many articles and comments about him as Jeff said, then the kid had spent a hell of a lot of his time reading.

Clint just held his gaze and lifted an eyebrow, waiting for Beck to continue.

"Did you really fight off terrorists by yourself, with half your leg missing?" Beck demanded.

Since he wasn't about to glamorize war, Clint just nod-ded. "If I hadn't, they would've killed me and my team."

"And they cut off your leg afterward?"

"They did."

"Were you mad?"

Out of the corner of his eye, he saw Beck's mother step forward and he held up his hand, telling her he had this. "At losing my leg? Sure I was. It was a shitty thing to happen."

Maybe he should apologize for his language but after enduring cancer and losing his leg, he was sure the kid could cope with some swearing.

"But you learned how to walk, to run, to ride a horse, to become a helicopter pilot with one leg."

"I did."

"How?" Beck looked at the rope in his hand and gave it a tug. "How did you know you could do it?"

"I didn't," Clint replied, keeping it honest. "But I knew I had to try. That trying and failing was better than not trying at all."

Beck shook his head. "I don't want to fail."

"Sometimes you do fail, that's life. But you have to give it your best shot. Not trying is being a coward and being a coward isn't something a soldier can be."

You had to give it your best shot. And he hadn't tried with Fee and, ergo, he *was* a coward.

Shit.

Of all the times to realize she was right and he was wrong. Clint ran a hand over his face and mentally released a stream of F-bombs. Saying them aloud would be more satisfying, but right now, he had a kid who was looking at him like he hung the moon, like he had all the answers to every question Beck had ever had.

A kid who was hurt, badly bruised and insecure.

He needed to restore some of Beck's confidence and he

needed to do it right now. Clint held up his finger and told Beck to stay put. Motioning Jeff over, he asked whether he could loan him some gear. He changed into a Royal Fire Department T-shirt, a pair of exercise shorts and running shoes, grateful he and Jeff were roughly the same size. He looked down at his bare prosthetic and shrugged off the wave of panic. If a kid could show the world his leg, Clint could too.

He jogged back into the gym and easily pulled himself up the dangling rope until he was close to the ceiling. He hung there for a sec, before sliding down and landing lightly on his feet.

He held the rope out to Beck. "Your turn."

"I can't. I don't know how. I only have one leg."

"You have just as many legs as me, and you won't know if you can do it until you try. One hand over the other, pull. Then wind the rope around your leg and pull up again."

Beck managed to pull himself up a few feet and grinned down at Clint, joy on his face. Clint high-fived him, then helped him down. "Twenty push-ups, soldier."

Beck sent him an uncertain look but copied Clint's stance, his toothpick arms managing five push-ups to Clint's quick twenty before he collapsed, his forehead on the floor. "I'm so bad at this."

"But are you trying?"

Beck turned his face. "Yeah, I am."

"I'm not asking you to be great at it. I'm asking you to try."

Clint worked with him for the next half hour, making Beck lift ropes, flip tires, practice squats and planks, vaguely aware he'd gathered an audience but keeping his sole attention on Beck. The kid's face was red and his hair was damp with sweat by the time he finished but his face radiated a sense of achievement and, yeah, pride.

Clint handed him a towel and a bottle of water and sat down next to him on a bench. "The kids at school, they call me a crip and a gimp," Beck told him, his voice soft.

Clint silently cursed at kids' cruelty. "Screw 'em. Work to be better than them and kick their asses when you're done. But don't tell your mom I said that."

Beck looked over to where his mom stood, talking to an olive-skinned brunette dressed in a flame-orange mini-dress and black knee-high boots.

She had her back to him, but he knew that body from any angle. Besides, only one person would have the audacity, the balls, to wear such a sexy pair of boots in Royal and look amazing doing it.

Clint raised his bottle to his lips, his heart stuttering. Fee was back.

Fee. Was. Back…

"Would you teach me to kick their asses? To defend myself?"

It took all he had to pull his attention back to Beck. "I'll talk to your mom, see if we can get you up here once or twice a month for some training, some lessons."

Clint darted another look at Fee and turned back to his new friend. "Look, Beck, I want you to remember you are allowed to fail, you're allowed to not be good at something—"

"What aren't you good at?" Beck interjected, his eyes bright with curiosity.

Clint didn't hesitate. "Dealing with people, checking my pride, allowing people in, being thoughtful toward the ones who matter to me. So, hug your mom, bud, I think she needs it now and again."

Beck nodded solemnly.

"I was saying you are allowed not to be good at something but you have to try. Promise me you will always try."

Beck tipped his head to the side. "Are you going to try with people?"

Clint grinned. "Touché, kid."

Yeah, he was going to try. And he was going to start with Fee.

Beck wrinkled his nose. "I don't know what that means."

Clint ruffled his hair and stood up. "It means you turned the tables on me."

He nodded toward the locker room. "Good job, bud. Go wash your face and hands."

Clint waited for Beck outside the locker room, thinking he hadn't even broken a sweat. He could go back in, change back into his clothes and carry on with his day. But he didn't want to waste a minute so when Beck walked out of the locker room, Clint placed his hand on the kid's shoulder and walked him back over to his teary-eyed mom. Fee gave Clint a brief nod of greeting and, being Fee and outgoing, immediately engaged Beck in conversation.

Beck's mom—she introduced herself as Jan—placed her hand on his arm. "Thank you for giving him your time. He's been struggling lately—he's been very sullen and uncommunicative. I haven't been able to talk to him for months and the only time he's really spoken to me was to ask to come see you."

Uncomfortable with her praise and thanks, Clint asked for her cell phone. Taking it, he programmed in his number and told Jan to call him when Beck was acting up. Or whenever she or Beck needed to talk.

Tears streamed down Jan's face. Fee handed her a tissue and she wiped her eyes as she turned her attention to her son.

"Did you see me, Mom? Did you see what I did? Clint said I have to try."

Clint watched them walk out of the now-empty gym and turned back to his biggest problem and his greatest joy. He didn't know what to say so he went for the obvious.

"I didn't expect to see you back in Royal, Fee." He looked past her, looking for the cameras. "I presume your crew is outside, filming this opening of the fire station. It's supposed to be more of an appreciation party for the volunteer firefighters, but we decided to hold both functions at once—"

"My crew isn't here," Fee interrupted him.

Clint frowned, puzzled. "I would've thought they would want to be here. It's a nice ending to the story."

"Since I'm leaving the show, I'm not part of the decision-making." She wrinkled her nose and Clint realized he wanted to watch her do that for the rest of his life. Could he ask her to give him another chance? What if he failed?

But he had to take his own advice.

But before he threw himself off a cliff, he wanted some more facts. "What, exactly, do you mean by that?"

"It means I am quitting the show," Fee told him, her tone still cool. "I still have to negotiate my exit, but I've made up my mind. I only came by today to tell you I've decided Royal is my town and I need to be here. I'm sorry if that doesn't suit you but Royal suits me."

Wait...what? What the hell?

"I'm sorry, what did you say?"

"I'm renting a cottage in Royal, working on a cookbook and I have feelers out to do a cooking show." She shrugged her slim shoulders. "Eventually I'll either buy or build a place but I felt I owed it to you to tell you I'm back. I'm not asking, or expecting, a damn thing from you."

Clint cocked his head. "Well, damn, now that's a pity."

Fee's eyes turned a shade of bitter chocolate. "You should also know I have no intention of climbing into your bed and being tossed out when you tire of me. Or when you get scared."

Fair point. "What if I just keep you in my bed, in my house, in my life for the rest of my life?"

Fee closed her eyes, color receding from her face. "That's such a cruel thing to say, Clint. You've been an ass and a jerk, but you were never once cruel. Congratulations, lieutenant, you've reached a new low."

Fee turned to walk away and Clint stared at her back, completely confused. He'd just tossed his heart at her feet and she thought he was taunting her by offering something he didn't intend to deliver? Yeah, he really, really, really needed to work on his communication skills. He might never be good at it but there was a lot of room for improvement.

"I missed you."

Fee stopped in her tracks and he heard her loud sigh. She started to walk again and he threw another truth her way. "You were right. I *am* a coward."

Oh, God, that hurt, but then the truth always did. Fee stopped again, slowly turned around and raised one dark eyebrow. "Sure, when it comes to me."

Typical Fee, never one to give an inch. But at least she wasn't walking away. She kept her eyes on him as she said, "But please, feel free to tell me how you came to that conclusion."

Sarcastic as well. He loved it. Loved her. "I worked my ass off to be capable, to show the world I could do anything I did before and more. But I didn't work at relationships and I didn't bother to work out how to deal with people. Because people are complicated, contrary, and they don't always react the way you want them to."

"We don't all jump when you bark an order, lieutenant."

He ignored her sarcasm. "So, I withdrew. I've always been solitary, Fee, always a loner. My ex, those women, their…insensitivity and my mother's comments about my disability, gave me the excuse I needed to not try, to not interact. It took a fast-talking, sexy, mouthy reality TV star to show me I'd stopped trying with people. That, when it came to relationships, I'm a coward." Clint shook his head. "It was a truth I didn't want to acknowledge."

Fee nodded. When Clint didn't say anything more, she lifted her hands before pointing to the door. "I'm going to go and I think people want to get this show on the road. James Harrison probably wants to get the formalities over with so he can have a beer."

"The president of the TCC can wait," Clint told her. "I'm not done."

"I don't know what there's left to say," Fee admitted.

Clint walked over to her and gently lifted a tendril off her cheek and tucked it behind her ear. "Oh, I have quite a bit still to say."

He saw the trepidation and the faint flicker of hope in her eyes. "Since when did you get to be Mr. Chatty?"

"Since I looked up and saw you across the room and I knew there was no way I was going to let you leave my life again." His fingers brushed her ear, ran down her neck, and he felt her shudder. "I wasn't joking earlier…stay in my house, stay in my life."

"Clint…" Fee begged him but he wasn't sure what she was asking.

So he kept talking. "I'm completely utterly, crazily in love with you, Seraphina. You brought color and warmth and a fair amount of craziness into my life and I don't want to go back to that colorless world again."

Fee's eyes glistened with tears and she finally, finally

touched him by placing her hand on his heart. "Do you mean that?"

"Those few, inadequate words don't even begin to cover the depth of my love for you." Clint cupped her beautiful face. "You just told me you are staying here, that this is your town. But did you mean it? Is this really where you want to be?"

"Why are you asking?" Fee asked, tipping her head.

"I don't want you to settle, just because I am here. I want you to be happy and if you're not going to be happy in Royal, then we'll find another place, any place." He shrugged. "I might have to buy a plane so I can come back regularly to keep an eye on the ranch but we can live anywhere."

"And you'd go with me?" Fee asked, a smile pulling her mouth up.

She was where he needed to be. Yeah, he'd miss his ranch but they'd make it work. "As long as you are happy," Clint murmured. "Making you happy is all I care about, Fee."

And it was. His life was now hers. Her happiness was everything.

"That's the sweetest thing anyone has ever said to me," Fee stated, looping her arms around his neck. "But might I remind you of one salient point you seem to have forgotten, Rockwell?"

"What's that?"

"I came back to Royal with no expectation of a relationship with you. I came back because I like this town, I like the people and I want to be part of this community. I want to live here, even though I thought I had no chance of being a part of your life."

"Oh." He was struggling to catch up, to make sense of

all of this, mostly because Fee was back and in his arms. "So, you're happy to move into my place?"

"More than," Fee said, her thumbs rubbing his jaw. "Tell me you love me before you kiss me senseless, Rockwell."

"Love you, sweetheart."

"Love you back, cowboy," Fee murmured against his lips, but before he could follow through on her command to kiss her senseless, he heard Jeff clearing his throat.

Jeff just grinned when Clint raised his head and gave him a piss-off-I'm-busy glare.

"James is chomping to get started since all the VIPs are present and accounted for."

Fee stepped back from him and Clint groaned his frustration. She slid her hand into his. "We can pick this up later, Clint." She rubbed his T-shirt between her fingers. "You need to change, darling."

Clint looked down at his exercise shorts and his faded T-shirt. Shrugging, he sent Jeff a wry grin. "Tell James I'm changing. I'll be there in five minutes."

Jeff nodded and left, but instead of heading toward the locker room, Clint pulled Fee back into his arms. "Now, where were we?"

"You're not going to change?" Fee asked him.

"I'd rather kiss you." Clint's mouth curved against hers. "Besides, it seems like the whole world has seen my leg and the planet didn't tilt off its axis."

Fee laughed and slapped her mouth against his.

And it was a good fifteen minutes before they made an appearance at the ceremony.

Epilogue

Fee looked at Clint posing for photographs with the mayor of Royal, Jeff, the new fire chief, and James Harrison, the president of the Texas Cattleman's Club, thinking Clint looked perfect in his exercise shorts and the tight fitting Royal FD T-shirt. Yeah, he should be more smartly dressed for such an important occasion, but most of the attendees had heard about his impromptu gym session with young Beck and applauded him for it.

Her man could walk down the main street of Royal buck naked and nobody would blink an eye. He was their own homegrown hero, one of their favorite sons and he could do no wrong.

When it came to her, though…well, she'd seen first-hand the challenges that faced anyone who loved this man.

Fee didn't have many stars in her eyes, and while she loved him with every strand of DNA she possessed, she wasn't naive enough to believe Life had just sprinkled a can of fairy dust over their lives. She fully accepted that, going forward, there would be problems and arguments and flared tempers and hurt feelings. That was just life. But there'd be love too. Happiness. Passion. Acceptance.

She'd found her happy place and it was here, in Royal, with Clint. And she'd told him the truth earlier. Even if Clint hadn't been part of the deal, she'd want to spend most of her time in Royal, make this town her home base. She felt at ease here, settled.

Royal was where the rest of her life began.

Having finished with the photographer, Clint made a beeline toward her, his hazel eyes more gold than green.

"You okay? Any second thoughts?" he teased, but Fee wasn't fooled by his light tone. He was worried and she couldn't blame him; this happiness was so new, it felt like it might disappear in a puff of smoke.

"Just catching my breath." Fee linked her fingers with his and rested her head on his shoulder, smiling when he dropped a kiss on her hair.

"I know. I keep feeling it's the most amazing dream and I'm going to wake up alone."

Clint took her glass from her hand and placed his mouth over the lipstick mark she'd left on the glass. He swallowed the rest of the chardonnay and handed the glass back to the waitress. He looked around and sent her a conspiratorial grin. "When can we leave? While I'm loving your dress, I sure as hell can't wait to get you out of it."

Fee grinned back. "Rockwell, really? We have to stay for a little while—it'll be rude to leave now."

"Ten minutes? Fifteen?" Clint asked, mischief in his eyes.

Fee rolled her eyes then allowed them to drift around the room, searching for a neutral subject to distract them from what they were both desperate to do. Soon…

"How are the cleanup operations going?"

"Slowly," Clint replied. "There's so much damage, Fee. More buildings were affected than we originally suspected, including the TCC clubhouse. By the way, James Harrison has asked me to join the Texas Cattleman's Club."

That didn't surprise her. "Of course he has. You're the town's hero."

"I wish everyone would stop calling me that. I just did what I needed to do," Clint replied, frustration in his voice. "I was able to help so I did."

He didn't realize many people wouldn't have, that lots of people threw money at a problem and then washed their hands of any responsibility, looking to others to find a solution. Clint used his money, and his time and his skills, and that was a rare and beautiful thing. But she liked the fact he was unaware of just how amazing he was.

"I'm surprised the Blackwood siblings aren't here," Fee commented, changing the subject.

"I heard Sophie Blackwood has left Royal for New York City." Clint shrugged. "Kellan is in Nashville, I think. I'm not sure where Vaughn is at present."

"Kace is here." Fee gestured to the lanky lawyer talking to James Harrison.

"And your friend isn't," Clint said. "Something happening between them?"

Fee was curious on that point too—but Lu had been uncharacteristically quiet lately. Then again, she'd been heartbroken and not really interested in anything but her own misery.

"I don't know. But I haven't been a great friend lately. I've been rather wrapped up in my own heartbreak," she admitted.

Clint turned her to face him and placed his hands on

her shoulder. "Hell, Fee, I have to apologize. Again. I acted like a jerk, and I'm really sorry."

"And I was a lot meaner than I needed to be but I was hurt. I'm sorry too. You're not a coward, Clint. I'm so sorry I insulted you like that," Fee said, her heart in her throat. She was still ashamed of herself, that of everything she could've said, she'd gone straight for his emotional jugular.

"But I was. When it came to you, and love, I was a total coward." Clint jerked his head at Beck, who stood by the table laden with desserts, stuffing his mouth. "I told him he had to try, that he could fail but he *had* to try. Then I realized I was crap at taking my own advice. And I looked up and there you were."

He smiled and Fee's heart jumped into her throat. Clint had an amazing smile and she was going to look at it for the rest of her life. How lucky was she?

"Your arrival damn near gave me a heart attack," Clint admitted. He looked at Beck and lifted one huge shoulder. "The fire station project is, obviously, over and we need to clean up Royal but—"

"But?" Fee asked, intrigued by the light she saw in his eyes.

"But I was thinking that, for my next project, I'd like to build a rehab center, a gym, something specifically designed for veterans and people struggling to come to terms with their disabilities. Maybe hire some physios, some counselors, have some skills training. A place of... acceptance."

Fee blinked away her tears. Oh God, that sounded perfect. "It sounds awesome, darling. You'll have my full support, Clint."

"Maybe we can call it Fee's Place, because you led me to a place of acceptance."

She was touched but...no.

"We'll find a name, a good name, but not that one." Fee rested her forehead on his chest before looking up at him, tears rolling down her face. "I'm so in love with you, Rockwell."

"As I am with you," Clint told her, spearing his fingers into her hair and tipping her jaw up to receive his kiss. "I only have one more thing to ask you…"

Oh God, it was too soon. What would she say? Yes, of course, but were they rushing things? Was she ready for a proposal?

"What?" Fee asked him, sounding a little breathless.

"Can we go home now?"

Fee released a long breath, a little disappointed. "Yeah, sure."

Clint took her hand and led her through the throngs of people, adroitly avoiding everyone who wanted to talk to them by telling them he'd catch up with them soon. Outside, in the cool evening air, he turned back to Fee and smiled at her. "So, would you have said yes?"

She didn't pretend to misunderstand him. "It's very soon but…yes. I would have said yes."

Clint brushed his lips across hers. "Good to know. Let's go home, my darling Fee."

She was already there. No matter where she was, if her hand was in his, she was home.

* * * * *

VEGAS VOWS, TEXAS NIGHTS

CHARLENE SANDS

Dedicated to my lifelong friends: Mary, Allyson
and Robin. Decades of Forever Friends,
keepers of memories, hearts of gold,
in good times and in bad, they are always there.
We are fortunate to have each other.

was living in Boone Springs again, the town founded a century ago by his ancestors. He was his brother Mason's best man, while Katie was maid of honor for Mason's fiancée, Drea. Unwittingly she and Luke had been thrown together in a joint bachelor/bachelorette party in Sin City. Vegas, baby. What happened here stayed here.

She thought about her sister again. How her scars remained. Poor Shelly faced the humiliation bravely but she'd never forgotten what Luke had done to her, how he'd betrayed her love and trust. She'd become bitter and sad and never let her mother, Diana, or Katie hear the end of how Luke had ruined her life. So the thought of Katie sleeping with Luke, her one-time friend, drunk or not, would be the worst of the worst.

Luke rolled over onto his side and braced his head in his hand, as if they were discussing what to have for breakfast. "What do you remember about last night?"

"What do I remember?"

"Yeah, do you remember leaving the party with me?"

She moved away from him as far as the bed would allow and thought about it. She remembered drinking and laughing and dancing with Luke most of the night. She'd felt guilty having so much fun with him, but they'd always gotten along, had always been friends until he'd backed out of the wedding.

The Boones had been good customers at her bakery. She and Luke also shared a love of horses and both volunteered at the Red Barrel Horse Rescue. Still, ever since his return from military service nearly a year ago, they'd been overly cautious with each other, their conversations often stilted and awkward. Katie, too, had been hurt when Luke had dumped her sister. Katie had also trusted him.

"I remember you offering to walk me back to my hotel." Which was only a few blocks away from the nightclub.

"We'd both had too much to drink."

The pain in her head was a reminder of that. "Yes."

Luke stared into her eyes; his were clear and deep blue. Kinda mesmerizing. "You pleaded with me not to take you back to your hotel. You didn't want the night to end. You…uh…"

Katie rubbed her aching head. This was getting worse by the second. "What?"

Luke remained silent.

"What did I say?" she demanded. She had to know, to make some sense out of this.

"You said you wanted what your friends had. You wanted someone to love."

"Oh God." She covered her face with her hands, her long hair spilling down. She was embarrassed that in her drunken state, she'd revealed her innermost secret desire. And to Luke no less. "And so we ended up in your hotel room?"

Luke flinched and his eyes squeezed shut. The concerned expression on his face really worried her. "Not exactly. We went somewhere else first."

"Another club?"

He shook his head. "Not according to this." He grabbed a piece of paper from his nightstand and gave it a once-over. "Another thing you said you wanted…" He handed her the paper.

She looked down at the bold lettering on the piece of parchment she held and her hand began shaking. A marriage certificate. Both of their names were listed and it had today's date. "You can't be serious."

"Hey, I don't remember much from last night either. My head's spinning like a damn top right now."

This was ridiculous. It had to be a bad joke. Where was the hidden camera? Someone was pranking her.

Yes, it was true she'd thought of her secret wishes, often. She'd wanted to find love and be married, though she'd never voiced those wishes to anyone. She didn't want her friends to worry about her or think she envied their happiness, but she wouldn't have told Luke that, would she? Certainly she wouldn't have acted upon it.

Yet, the proof was staring her in the face. Dated today, as in they'd gotten married after midnight, about the time they'd walked out of the club together. The facts added up, but she still had trouble digesting all of it.

"I can't believe this. No, this isn't happening." She lowered her voice. "We didn't…do anything else, did we?"

Was she being naive to think that she'd end up naked in bed with handsome, appealing Luke without having sex with him?

"I remember some things. From last night." The blue in his eyes grew darker, more intense. "Don't you?"

She didn't want to. She didn't want to think it possible to spend the night with the one man in the whole world who was off-limits to her. But darn it, vague memories started to breach the surface of her mind. Being held, being kissed, her body caressed, loved. She grimaced. Dear Lord, the memories were fuzzy, vague, but they were there.

"Oh no," she whispered. Tears touched her eyes. "Why didn't you stop it?" she asked.

It was unfair of her to throw this all on him. The way he flinched at her question said he thought so, too. "I… couldn't."

He couldn't? What did that mean?

"Katie, it's going to be okay. We're married. I didn't take advantage of you. I mean, from what I remember, you weren't complaining about any of it."

She gripped the sheets closer to her chest. "That's what you think I'm worried about? It's okay that we had sex because we're married? My God, Luke. Do you have any idea how bad this is? You were engaged to my sister! You practically left her at the altar. My mom and sister were devastated. I'm not worried about my virtue here. It's way bigger than that."

"Okay, okay. Calm down." Luke ran a hand down his face. "I'm going to take a shower and get dressed and we'll discuss it. Unless you want to go first?"

"No, no." Married or not, she wasn't about to let him see her naked. "You go first."

"Fine. And Katie…it really is going to be all right."

She frowned. The frown only deepened when Luke rose from the bed as if they'd been married for years and walked into the bathroom, giving her a stunning view of his broad shoulders, muscular arms and perfect butt.

Her heart pounded hard. She'd married a Boone, one of the richest men in all of Texas, the man who'd betrayed her sister, the man she'd tried hard to avoid since he'd come back and resumed his life in Boone Springs months ago.

As soon as she heard the bathroom door close, she rose and scrambled to gather up her clothes from the floor. That's when she spotted an open condom packet, the top torn off, the contents empty. Now there was actual proof they'd consummated the marriage, as if her own sated body wasn't already screaming that to her.

She dressed and waited for him. They had to resolve this immediately. She wasn't going home as Katie Boone. No, sir. When she heard the shower faucet turn off, she braced herself, finger combing her hair, straightening out her cocktail dress, her resolve as sharp as her annoyance.

The door opened and out walked Luke, his hair wet, his skin glowing in the morning light. He wore a soft white towel around his waist, but the rest of him was hard, ripped muscle and brawn.

Good Lord. Was he the man in her dreams?

No, he couldn't be. Just because they'd once been friends and they shared a love of horses didn't mean she'd ever think of him that way, even subconsciously.

"Luke, we need to talk."

He looked her up and down, his eyes raking over her black dress, and suddenly she felt amazingly warm. She shifted her attention to a drop of water making its way down his bare chest, tunneling through tiny hairs to drip past his navel and absorb into the towel.

Luke caught her eyeing him and smiled. "I need a cup of coffee. We both do. I'll order breakfast while you take your shower."

He seemed too accommodating, too casual, as if he also hadn't made the biggest blunder of his life. Where was his panic?

"And we'll resolve this then?"

He nodded. "We'll talk, I promise."

Thirty minutes later, Katie stepped out of the bathroom refreshed and feeling a little better about her predicament. Her stomach still churned, but her outlook wasn't nearly as bleak. They were in Las Vegas, after all. How hard would it be to dissolve their quickie marriage, to seek a divorce from a wedding that should never have happened? Surely there were hundreds of people who found themselves in the same situation after a wild night and too much drinking.

Luke waited for her at the rolling table that had been de-livered by room service. Thankfully he was fully dressed now, in jeans and a navy shirt that made his eyes pop an even darker shade of blue. She had only the clothes she'd come with last night and her purse. Luckily her cell phone had enough charge for her to text Drea this morning telling her not to worry, she'd explain everything later.

Or not.

But she'd have to tell the bride-to-be something. They shared a hotel room and Drea had seen her leave with Luke last night and knew she hadn't returned to her room.

"Ready for breakfast?" Luke was already sipping coffee, the pot of steaming brew sitting on the table beside dishes of bacon, eggs, French toast, roasted potatoes and a basket of fresh pastries.

Ugh. None of it looked appetizing. She couldn't eat. "No, thanks. Coffee's good."

She grabbed the coffeepot and poured herself a cup, taking a seat facing him. She dumped in three sugar cubes and stirred, Luke giving her an arch of his brow. What could she say? She loved sweet comfort food and right now, sugar was her healing balm. His silent disapproval had her reaching for a fourth sugar cube, and she stared right at him as she dumped it into her coffee.

"You're not eating anything?" he asked.

"I'm not hungry, Luke. My head's still fuzzy."

"I thought the shower would help."

"The shower made me realize that if being in Vegas got us into this mess, then why can't being in Vegas get us out of it?"

Luke gave her a long stare and slowly shook his head. "What?"

"I want a divorce. Immediately. Surely there's someone in this city that can accommodate us."

Luke scratched his head, looking at her as if she were a child asking for the moon. "That's not possible, Katie."

"How can you say that? We haven't even tried. Look, I wasn't myself last night and you know it. How long have we known each other? Ten years?"

"Twelve and a half." She stared at him and he shrugged. "I have a good memory for dates. We met at the first anniversary of the Red Barrel Rescue."

Katie remembered that day. She'd chosen the rescue to be the subject of her high school term paper and had gone there not knowing what to expect. She'd taken one look at the beleaguered and maimed horses being cared for and had fallen in love. Luke had been a mentor of sorts, and through her, he'd met her sister, Shelly.

"And in all those twelve and a half years, have you ever known me to be impetuous or wild or, as you put it today, the kind of girl who could drink you under the table?"

"No." He scratched his head. "But then, I've never been with you in Vegas."

She rolled her eyes. "This is serious, Luke. I don't recall all that happened last night, but I do know we have to undo the problem as soon as possible."

"I…agree."

"You do? Good, because for a second there, I was starting to believe you didn't think this was a big problem."

"I can't get a divorce until I speak with my attorney. I'm sorry, Katie, but this isn't going to happen today."

"Why not?"

"Because it's more complicated than that. I'm a Boone, and that means divorce proceedings can get pretty nasty. My attorney isn't going to let me sign my name to anything until he sees it."

"Goodness, Luke, I don't want anything from you or your family. If that's what you're getting at, you can go straight to—"

"It's not me, Katie. It's just the way things are when you're…"

"Rich?"

"A Boone."

"How horrible it must be for you not knowing who you can trust. I suppose you had those very same issues with Shelly?"

"Let's leave your sister out of this."

"Easy for you to say." Katie's stomach burned now, the acid churning violently. This was not going well. He was being obtuse and the implication that she was somehow out for Boone money only ticked her off. "There's nothing we can do? Maybe if you give your attorney a call—"

Luke frowned. "I can't. He's out of the country on a personal matter."

"Personal matter? You could say this is your personal matter."

He sighed. "His mother is extremely ill and he's there to help get her affairs in order. That is, if the worst happens."

"Oh. I'm sorry to hear that. Can't you use someone else?"

Luke shook his head. "I'm afraid it doesn't work that way. At least not for me."

She jammed her hands on her hips and his attention immediately was drawn there. Gosh, how much of last night did he remember? He was looking at her differently than he ever had before. As if he was taking their marriage seriously, as if she was…his wife. "I can't go back to Boone Springs married to you, Luke."

"Looks like you're going to have to. Our flight leaves in a few hours."

Katie sighed and tears welled in her eyes. "I can't believe this."

He kept silent.

She had no choice but to relent. She saw no other way out. If she prolonged her stay here in Las Vegas, the entire wedding party would get suspicious. She didn't need that. She had to keep what happened between her and Luke quiet. She'd think of something before the Boone company plane took off.

"Fine. I'm not happy about this. If the truth comes out, I'm doomed. It'll ruin my relationship with my family. And who knows how this would affect my mama's health. Promise me that no one will know about this, promise me you'll keep our secret."

Luke touched her hand, his slight caress sweet, comforting and confusing as hell. "I promise, Katie. No one will know."

Luke waited until everyone boarded the Boone company plane, keeping his eyes trained on Katie. She took a seat by the bridesmaids in the back, all the girls huddling around the bride-to-be.

He couldn't keep from admiring Katie's beautiful blond hair tied up in a ponytail, the strands framing her face making her look wholesome and sweet. She was all those things, but last night at the club, he'd seen her flirty, passionate side. Mischief had glowed in her soft green eyes, especially while she'd been dancing in her sexy black dress. Now, in a denim jacket and jeans, she contrasted beautifully with the creamy leather seats and ambience of the custom designed plane.

She was his wife now. He could hardly believe it. He was actually married to Katie Rodgers. While Mason was engaged to Drea and his other brother, Risk, was engaged to April, Luke had inadvertently beaten his brothers down the aisle.

Katie glanced his way and their eyes met. He could look at her forever and never tire of it. But as soon as she caught him eyeing her, she turned away.

He smiled inside but didn't dare appear content around a quiet, sullen Katie. She was just cordial enough to her friends to ward off questions. She'd told everyone she'd gotten sick last night, barfing up her brains and Luke had taken her to urgent care in the wee hours of the morning to make sure she wasn't dehydrated. It was a feasible fib, one everyone seemed to believe, with the exception of his brothers. While Drea had thanked him for taking care of her best friend, both Risk and Mason had given him the stink eye.

Hell, he certainly hadn't planned any of this, but hearing Katie's softly spoken desire about wanting love in her life, wanting to be married, had reached down deep inside him and wrung out his lonely heart. He'd been drunk, too, and his willpower around her had been at an all-time low. She'd flirted with him, practically asked him to make love to her, and well…he didn't have much defense against that. Not with her.

The pilot, a navy veteran, came by to say hello to the passengers and make sure everyone was ready for takeoff.

Luke shook his hand. "Hey, Bill. Hope you didn't lose too much at the tables while you were here."

"Nah, my big gambling days are behind me. The penny slots are just my speed."

"I hear you," Luke said. He'd never been a gambler. He didn't like to play games he couldn't control. And he didn't like the odds in Las Vegas, with the exception of his recent marriage.

The odds of him marrying Katie had been slim to none. Yet he'd beat them and no one was more surprised than he was. Except Katie. He'd won the jackpot and now he had to convince his new bride being married to him wasn't a big fat mistake.

"Any time you want to come up and copilot, you know where the cockpit is," Bill said.

"Maybe later. Right now I'm still feeling the effects of last night's party." Luke grinned. "I'm afraid you're the designated driver today." He was in no shape to navigate anything, much less fly the friendly skies. He'd become a helicopter pilot while living on Rising Springs Ranch and had gotten his pilot's license in flight school during his stint in the service. Yet Mason had insisted he not pilot the plane so Luke could let loose and not have to worry about his alcohol consumption. His brother wanted everyone to have a good time.

"Sure thing. I'll see that you all have a good flight."

"Thanks, Bill."

Luke buckled up and glanced back at Katie. She was all set, looking like she'd just lost her best friend, even though Drea was sitting right next to her.

He sighed and as he turned his head around, he came eye to eye with Risk in the seat beside him. "Something going on between you two?" he asked.

He'd promised Katie he wouldn't give away their secret and he wouldn't betray that vow. "Who?"

"Don't be obtuse. You and Katie."

"No, nothing."

"I'm not judging," Risk said. "And if you do have something going with her, it'd be a good thing. I can read you like a book. You're hot for her."

Luke shot him a warning look.

Risk's hands went up. "I'm just saying, if you get together with her, you have my approval."

"Like I'd need it."

"Hey, just want to see you happy for once."

"You do know who she is, right?"

Risk smirked. "The best pastry chef in all of Texas. She'd keep us silly in gourmet cupcakes."

"She's Shelly's younger sister. And she barely tolerates me."

Years ago, Katie had dragged Shelly to a Red Barrel charity function and had introduced them. There'd been instant attraction between them and Luke had begun dating Katie's big sister. The engagement had seemed to fall right into place. Until the day Luke had woken up and realized he was making a big mistake.

"You two took off together last night," Risk said, "and today, you can't take your eyes off her."

"Leave it alone. Okay?"

Risk seemed to read the emotion on his face. "Okay,

I'll back off." He slapped Luke on the shoulder. "But if you run into a problem, I'm here for you."

"Appreciate that. Why aren't you hanging with your fiancée?"

"Seems the girls won't call it quits on their bachelorette party until the plane touches down in Boone Springs."

Risk eyed April, giving Luke a chance to seek out Katie again. And there she was, trying her best not to spoil everyone's fun, trying to smile and conceal the pain she must be going through. The thought that he was the cause of her pain ate away at him. It was the last thing he wanted. But he couldn't let her go. Not now.

She was the girl who shared a love of horses with him, the girl he'd danced with most of the night, the impossible girl who'd been in his dreams for the past five years.

He needed a chance with her, and this was the best he was going to get.

One chance.

Was that too much to ask?

Two

A Boone limo picked up the entire wedding party at the airport, taking everyone directly to their homes on the outskirts of town. Katie was among the last to be dropped off since she lived in the heart of Boone Springs, her apartment just above the bakery. It was a modest place, with one bedroom, one bath, but the rooms were spacious enough and her large home kitchen served as a backup when orders in the bakery exceeded their limit. That didn't happen often. Katie ran an efficient place and there was nothing like rolling out of bed at 4:00 a.m. and working in her jammies downstairs until the bakery opened at seven o'clock.

As the limo pulled up in front of the bakery, she was struck with a pang of relief. "This is my stop," she said to her friends remaining in the limo. "I hope you all had a great time."

Drea gave her a big hug. "It was wonderful. Amazing girl-bonding, my friend. Thanks for all you've done. Love you for it."

"Love you, too."

Katie glanced at everyone and waved a farewell. "All of you made the party for our dear friends something to remember."

"After last night, I've forgotten more than I remember," Mason said, smiling.

"You had the best time with your friends and family, especially with your fiancée." Drea gave him a quick kiss on the cheek. "Just ask me, I'll fill in the blanks."

Katie had some blanks she'd like to have filled in, too.

"One thing I do know, Luke and Katie worked hard on organizing this. Thank you," Mason said. "You two make a good team."

A rush of heat crawled up her neck. "Thank you. It wasn't that hard, really, and it was fun." The only difficult part had been working with Luke. *Her husband.* Oh God.

The limo driver grabbed Katie's bags and opened the door for her.

"I'll get off here, too," Luke told the driver.

Katie glared at him.

"It's a short walk to the office," he explained. "And I need to check up on something. Benny, if you could drop off my bags at the ranch I'd appreciate it."

The limo driver nodded. "Yes, sir."

Katie climbed out, Luke right behind her.

"I'll take those." He grabbed her bags from the driver's hand.

Katie noticed some raised eyebrows in the limo and wanted to melt right into the cement. What on earth was Luke doing? She didn't want to arouse suspicion. It was bad enough she'd had to lie to her best friend about where she'd been last night. But Luke was oblivious as to how his behavior appeared to everyone.

"Bye," Drea said. "Thanks again, hon. We'll talk soon."

"Okay," Katie said, giving her friend a smile.

When the limo drove off, she turned to Luke. "Give me my bags, Luke."

"I'll carry them up for you."

"That's not necessary."

"I know, but I'd like to."

"Why?"

"Your hangover is hanging on. You're pale and looking a little weak."

"The only reason I look ill is because of what happened between us. Makes me sick to my stomach."

His mouth twitched, but she wasn't at all sorry she'd been so crude. Well, maybe she was a little bit sorry. This was just as much her fault as it was his.

"All the more reason for me to help you. I feel responsible."

"Don't."

"I can't help it, Katie. C'mon, you need to rest."

She didn't like him telling her what she needed, but his jaw was set stubbornly and they couldn't stand here all day arguing. "Okay, fine."

He had the good sense not to gloat at winning the point. He nodded and walked over to the front door with her bags.

She opened up her shop and walked in first. The bakery had been closed for three days, yet the scent of vanilla, cinnamon and sugar flavored the air. The smell of home. She sighed and her body relaxed.

"Smells like you in here," Luke remarked, as if reading her thoughts.

"How's that?" she asked.

"Sweet."

She let his comment hang in the air for a moment. She didn't feel sweet right now. She felt horrible and guilty. She kept wishing she could escape from this horrible dream. Waking up wed to her sister's ex was truly a nightmare. And the sooner they rectified it, the better.

"The stairs are in the back, through the kitchen." She led the way and he followed.

He stopped to take a look at her baking area. "So this is where the cupcake magic happens. I've always wondered what this place looked like."

"Yep, this is it. This is where I spend a good deal of my life." She couldn't keep the pleasure out of her voice. She was proud of her shop, proud of what she'd accomplished. And she loved her work.

Luke took in the huge mixer, bowls and cupcake tins, the bins of flour and sugar and the industrial-size refrigerator. Yes, this was home to her.

"I see you here," Luke said, as if he was picturing her at work.

"It's not glamourous."

"I would imagine it's darn hard work. But work that you enjoy."

"True."

"Your bakery is the best in the county, everyone knows that. But I've only known you as a horse lover. You spend a lot of time at Red Barrel. How do you find time for both?"

"You run a multimillion-dollar company, how do you find the time?"

He grinned. "You're quick, I'll give you that."

"Apparently, not quick enough," she mumbled. Or else she wouldn't have gone to bed with him.

Luke ran a hand down his face. "I wasn't lying when I said it was mutual, Katie. I know that for a fact. Don't blame yourself too much."

She squeezed her eyes shut briefly and nodded. The man she knew at the horse rescue was gentle and caring and kind. He'd been her friend at one time and that was where it all got confusing. Because he had hurt her sister and maybe what Katie thought she'd known about him was all wrong. "Okay, can we just not talk about it?"

"Talk about what?" He played along. "You were going to tell me how you find time to work at the rescue."

"My workday ends early. And I think the work we do at the rescue is important. Those animals need help." She lifted a shoulder. "I don't date. Or at least I haven't for a while and so I have all kinds of—"

"You won't be dating, Katie."

She didn't like his tone, or the implied command. "Luke, for heaven's sake. You think I want to complicate my life even more?" She fisted her hands. "And you don't get to tell me what I can or cannot do."

"It may have been a hasty wedding, but you're my wife."

She wrinkled her nose. "Don't say that."

"I'm your husband."

"For a nanosecond. Remember, you promised that you'll look into a divorce as soon as possible."

"I said it and I will. But until that time…" Luke came closer, his incredible eyes soft on her. He took her hand and squeezed. "If you ever need anything, call me."

"You know what I want."

He smiled and his blue eyes darkened. "I know what you think you want."

"What does that mean?"

His hand gently wrapped around her neck, his fingertips urging her forward. Then he lowered his mouth to hers and kissed her. It was tender and sweet, not at all demanding, and the pleasure made it hard to pull away.

"I think you should leave," she murmured, pushing at his chest.

"I was just going."

When he backed away, she stared at him. There was a moment, one tiny second, when she saw something in him that made her happy, made her wish he didn't have to go.

"When you hear from your attorney, give me a call."

He nodded and walked out of the bakery.

Maybe it was a good thing she hadn't taken him up to her apartment.

"Here's your herbal tea, Mama." Katie handed her mother a mug and took a seat beside her on the living room sofa in the home Katie and her sister had grown up in on Blue Jay Avenue. The neighborhood was close-knit, just on the outskirts of Boone Springs, about a ten-minute drive from the bakery. She'd come here as soon as she'd unpacked her bags.

"Thanks, honey. I love the pomegranate and blackberry mix." Her mother blew on the steam and then sipped delicately. "Mmm. Tastes so good going down."

"It is good," she said, concerned over her mother's health.

Diana Rodgers had tired eyes that told of sacrifice and lack of energy. Her body was a bit broken from ill health. At the age of fifty-eight, she'd suffered a minor heart attack that had taken her away from the teaching job she'd loved. Taking an early retirement had never been in her plans. She'd been a single mother most of her life, working hard at the grammar school with special needs kids. But the job was stressful, and Diana often took her work home with her, a habit her cardiologist couldn't condone.

"So why aren't you joining me in a cup?"

"I will a little later. Right now, I just want to hear how you're feeling."

"You've only been gone three days, hon. I appreciate you coming over as soon as you got home, but I'm the same as I was before you left." Her mom waved her hand. "Enough about me, how was your trip?"

"It was…nice." Katie had trouble mustering up any enthusiasm. *Oh, and one little detail I forgot to mention… I married Lucas Boone.* "Drea and Mason enjoyed it very much. I think everyone did."

Her mother moved around in her seat a bit and her mouth twisted as it did every time the Boone name was mentioned. "Too bad Drea had to fall in love with *him*."

"Mom, Mason's a nice guy."

"He's rich and feels entitled, just like all the Boones." She meant Luke.

That sick feeling in Katie's stomach acted up again. "Drea's happy and that's all that matters."

Her mother sipped her tea. "So, what did all you gals do at the bachelorette party?"

Katie shrugged. "The usual things. We saw the sights, ate like there was no tomorrow, had a spa day, went to a concert, and then on the last night the entire group got together for a party at a nightclub."

There. She'd given a short, encapsulated version of her long weekend. Enough said.

"You had to deal with Luke?"

Before she could answer, Shelly walked into the house, dropping her shoulder bag on the edge of the sofa. "What about loser Luke?"

Katie's heart started pounding. Shelly was still bitter. "Hi, sis. What are you doing here?"

"Checking in with Mom, just like you." Her sister, dressed in nurse's white, walked over to give her mother a kiss on the cheek. "Hi, Mom. How are you today?"

"Feeling pretty good. Your sister made me some tea. Would you like a cup, sweetheart?"

"Thanks, but I'm fine. Just thought I'd stop by here first, before heading home and changing clothes. Dr. Moore asked me and a few colleagues to attend his seminar tonight. I have to leave soon. So, what about Luke?"

"Nothing," Katie said.

"Your sister had to plan Drea's bachelorette party with him."

"We didn't plan the bachelorette party together. He was

in charge of entertaining the groomsmen. All we did was coordinate the party at the end of the weekend together."

"Ugh," Shelly said. "Poor you."

"It wasn't that bad."

"I feel sorry for any woman who gets involved with him," Shelly said flatly. "I should've known better."

"He wasn't ready for marriage," Katie said. God, they'd had this conversation for years. It was truly beginning to grate on her nerves. Shelly never was one for letting go. She'd never forgiven their dad for divorcing their mother. She'd never accepted their father's new wife. Clearly, a broken engagement, even if it was three days before the ceremony, was much better than a divorce later on.

"Why are you defending him?" Shelly asked.

"Maybe I just want you to move on with your life, Shel. Maybe I'm not defending him so much as I'm looking out for you."

Shelly sighed. "Okay, got it. Easier said than done."

"It's so nice to have both of my girls here with me today," her mother said softly.

"I wish I could stay longer," Shelly said. "But I'm meeting everyone at the hospital in an hour."

"That's fine, honey. You go on to the seminar. I'm proud of the way you girls are so conscientious about your work. That means you, too, Katie."

"I know, Mama." Her mother had always told her how proud she was of what she'd accomplished at the bakery. Her business was on solid ground now but it hadn't always been that way. Her mom had faith in her, had always given her support. "I'll stay and visit with you a bit longer."

"Wonderful." Shelly gave her a rare smile.

Her sister had had a rough time facing her friends after the marriage debacle and then to have her "almost" groom leave town for years, leaving her with no hope, no way to reconcile her sadness, no way to rant and rave at him. That was probably the greatest injustice. Shelly had never gotten the closure she'd needed.

After Shelly left, Diana got up to take her teacup to the kitchen. "I made soup, your favorite, chicken and dumplings. Will you stay and have some with me?"

"Sure, that sounds yummy."

Katie was beat, tired and nervous, but having comfort food and her mother's company would distract her from the giant mistake she'd made in Las Vegas last night.

Katie raced down the stairs, stubbing her toe on the last step. "Ow, damn it." As she entered the bakery, not even the soothing scents of all things sweet helped lighten her mood this morning. She'd overslept by an hour and now she was totally behind schedule. Gosh, she'd had so much on her mind, sleep had eluded her, and when she'd finally fallen asleep, it had been deep and heavy. She'd dreamed that a faceless beast was chasing her and she'd kept running and running until she'd woken up in a sweat.

Was that dream trying to tell her something?

She flipped on the light, tied on her lavender Katie's Kupcakes and Bakery apron and got to work, gathering up her ingredients, prepping her cupcake tins.

The Monday morning special was always a carrot zucchini cupcake infused with a light apricot filling. She called it her Start Smart Special, a healthier alternative to a sugary treat. It was a fan favorite for those guilty of indulging over the weekend.

Her assistant, Lori, knocked on the back door. Katie opened it to her smiling face.

"Hey, good to see you. How was your trip?" Lori asked, as she walked past her and took off her sweater.

"Uh, it was okay."

"That so? Just okay?" Lori sounded as if she had her doubts. They'd worked closely together for six years and knew each other pretty well. Now Lori was putting herself through college at night aiming for a degree in business, so the bakery hours were perfect for her. The shop closed at two in the afternoon. "Sounds like it wasn't fun. Did something happen?"

"No. Nothing. I'm just tired. I overslept."

"You never oversleep. Maybe you had *too* much fun in Vegas." Lori winked. If she only knew. "You're gonna have to give me deets. I've been cramming all weekend, stuck at my place, fantasizing about your fun weekend."

"There are no details." Katie shrugged. "We had a good time. Saw a show. Got massages, did some dancing. Usual stuff."

"You were excited about it when you left here. I thought for sure you'd have some good Vegas stories to entertain me with this morning."

Lori put on her apron and they began measuring out ingredients. She started on chocolate ganache cupcakes with marshmallow filling while Katie worked on the special. They had their routine down to a science and being behind schedule meant one or two cupcakes would have to get the boot.

"Sorry, Lori. Nothing much to report," she fibbed. "How about we eliminate anything pumpkin, since the fall season has been over for a while," she said, changing the subject.

"Good choice."

"And if there are any complaints, you know what to do."

"Always."

It was her motto to keep the customer happy by giving away a free cupcake or two to ward off hostility. Although that rarely happened with her regular Boone Springs customers. They were like family. She knew most of them by name, as well as where they lived and how many kids they had. She often catered birthday parties and other occasions.

While the cupcakes were baking, she worked on pastries, filling croissants, making cookies and cinnamon rolls. Between the two of them, working nonstop, they'd filled the bakery case shelves by 7:00 a.m. Coffee brewed and her regulars began popping into the shop.

By nine thirty, there was a lull and Katie flopped into a chair in the small lounge by the back door. Exhaustion set in and it wasn't just from lack of sleep, but acute mental fatigue over what happened in Vegas this past weekend.

Lori gave her a sympathetic look. "Why don't you go upstairs for an hour?" she suggested. "Get in a nap. I can handle things until it picks up again."

"Don't we have deliveries today?" Sometimes they'd get orders from companies or restaurants or clients celebrating big birthdays.

Lori scanned the list on the bakery wall. "It's Monday and pretty calm right now."

"Thanks, but I'll be fine in a few minutes. Just need to get a second wind."

The second wind didn't come and by closing time, Katie was truly beat. She had one delivery to make, a last-minute order for a private dinner party happening later tonight. They needed a dozen tiramisu and a dozen lemon raspberry cupcakes, and while Lori closed up shop, Katie arranged the cupcakes in a box and taped it shut.

"Let me take those for you," Lori said. "I can drop them off on my way home. This way you can go upstairs now and relax, put your feet up."

"I can't let you do that. You've got studying to do."

"It'll take me ten minutes, tops. It's my way of making up for all the days you let me off early when I had to cram for an exam. Say yes."

"You really are such a good friend. Yes. Thanks."

Lori smiled. "Welcome."

After Lori took off with the delivery, Katie climbed the stairs slowly and once inside her apartment, plopped down on her sofa. She turned on the television, struggling to keep her eyes open until she finally lost the battle.

Normally, Luke spent most of his time in the office in the main house at Rising Springs Ranch. He took a hands-on approach to running things on the property and had a good relationship with Joe Buckley, their ranch foreman. They worked well together and Luke knew Joe wouldn't let him down.

Today he was at the Boone Springs corporate office, sitting in a room with his name plaque on the desk, staring out the window.

He had Katie on the brain and he'd come into town today, just because he wanted to be close to her. Her bakery was only two blocks away, nestled in between a clothing boutique and a fabric store. Because of the location, the bakery got pretty good foot traffic. Even if it didn't, Katie would be successful, because her pastries were the best in the county and because Luke had made sure no Boone holdings would ever compete with her.

A little fact he'd kept secret.

While he was serving the country, he'd made his wishes known and his brothers had all been onboard. He'd put the Rodgers family through enough and they'd done what they could to make sure Shelly and her family wouldn't unintentionally suffer any hardships of their doing.

But for him, it had mostly been about Katie. Wanting to see her succeed, wanting her to have a good life. God, when he'd come back home, he'd wished she had married, or at the very least, been in a serious relationship. Knowing she was still single had made his return torturous, yet he'd managed to keep his distance when he saw her around town or when they volunteered at the horse rescue.

And then Vegas happened.

Frustrated, he forced himself to go over ranching reports he'd pulled up on his computer. He had to get some work done, had to feel productive today, instead of daydreaming about seeing Katie again.

A little after two in the afternoon, his cell phone rang. "Hey, Wes. How's it going?" Luke usually didn't hear from the manager of the horse rescue, so he knew this had to be important.

"Hey, Luke. Sorry for the call, but it's Snow. I'm sorry to say it might be her time. The ole girl isn't breathing real well. I've had Dr. Hernandez out. He gave her some painkillers, but that's about all he can do for her. Thought you'd like to know."

Luke's stomach churned. Snowball was a mustang who'd been severely abused and she'd come to the rescue at the same time he'd returned home. He and Katie both had sort of taken the mare under their wing. They had a soft spot for the old girl. She'd been recovering, but the abuse had taken its toll on her and unfortunately with some of the horses, there wasn't much else to do but ease their pain.

"Thanks, Wes. Sorry to hear that. I'll, uh, I'll come by. I want to see her."

"Thought you would."

"I'll let Katie know, too."

"I just called Katie. She didn't answer her phone. I left her a message."

"Okay, well, I'll try to get word to her somehow. I'll see you soon, Wes."

Luke hung up and rubbed at the corners of his eyes. Giving himself a moment to gather his thoughts, he shook his head. As much as he wanted to see Katie again, he didn't want to give her bad news.

Five minutes later, he was in his car, driving by the bakery. There was a Katie's Kupcakes Is Klosed sign on the window. Still, he parked the car in a diagonal spot right in front of the bakery and got out. He tried the shop's door handle. No luck. Then he cupped his hands to ward off the sun's glare and peered inside the window. Not a soul was around.

A car slowed on the street and a young girl called out, "Can I help you?"

He recognized her as one of Katie's employees, though he couldn't recall her name. She'd made a few deliveries to the Boone corporate office. "I'm looking for Katie."

"Hold on a sec." The young woman parked her car and walked over to where he stood by the door.

"I'm Lucas Boone."

She smiled as if to say she knew who he was; the Boones were usually recognized in town. "Hi, Lucas. I'm Lori. Do you need cupcakes or something? The bakery is closed."

"No, nothing like that. I need to see Katie. It's important. Has to do with the Red Barrel Horse Rescue."

"Oh… I see." The young woman nibbled on her lips.

"She's not answering her phone."

"No, she's probably resting up in her apartment. She was pretty exhausted today."

"It's really important. Can you help me?"

She thought it over for a few seconds. "I know your brother is marrying her best friend, Drea. So, I guess it's all right if I let you in."

"Thank you."

Lori put the key into the lock and opened the door. "I only came back because I left my textbook and notes here and I've got this big exam tomorrow night."

Luke nodded and she let him inside the empty bakery.

"I'll go upstairs and knock on her door," she said. "I'll let Katie know you're here."

And a few minutes later, Luke was face-to-face with a sleep-hazy Katie.

"W-what are you doing here?" Katie stood at her doorway, a plaid blanket wrapped around her shoulders, staring at Luke. She didn't think she'd see him again so soon. His head was down, a concerned look on his face. Her heart began to pound hard. "Lori said something about the rescue?"

"I got a call from Wes a little while ago. It's Snow. She's in bad shape."

The air left her lungs and her shoulders slumped. "Oh no. Not our girl."

"Yep. I'm afraid so." He rubbed the back of his neck. "Thought you'd want to know. Wes tried to call you."

"I—I was fast asleep. I didn't hear my phone."

"I'm on my way out to see her. Maybe for the last time."

Oh man. All she could think about was the raw deal Snowball had gotten, a life of abuse and pain. Her owner had neglected her and she'd come to the rescue undernourished, scarred and broken. It wasn't fair. They'd tried their best to save her, and now Katie wasn't about to let her take her last breaths alone. "I've got to see her, too."

"I'll take you."

"No, you go on." She ran a hand through her hair. She must look a mess. "I need to run a comb through my hair and freshen up."

"I'll wait."

"You don't have to."

"Katie, I'm here, my car's out front and we're driving to the same place. Let's not waste any more time when we can spend it with Snow. Just do what you have to do, I'll be waiting downstairs."

He was right. Snow was too important to her to quibble with him about driving arrangements. "Okay, fine. Give me a minute."

Five minutes later, she was dressed in jeans and a red shirt, her hair in a knot at the top of her head. She splashed water on her face and put on lip gloss to keep from biting her lips and then dashed down the stairs and out the door of the bakery.

Luke waited for her out front, leaning against his black SUV, his hands in his pockets, a pensive look on his face. Her stomach was still in a twist about her ultra-secret marriage to her sister's ex. And now, the sweet mare she'd tended for the past year might be dying.

"Ready?" Luke asked, opening the door for her.

"Yes… I think."

"Yeah, I know what you mean. Snow's a special one."

Katie climbed in and grabbed her seat belt while Luke closed the door and took a seat behind the wheel. They drove off in silence and as they approached the canyon, she shivered.

"Cold?" he asked.

"A little." She hugged her arms to her chest. "I forgot my jacket." She'd forgotten how chilly the canyon could get in the later hours of the day.

"I can warm you up real fast," he said, giving her a smile.

His dimpled grin brought heat to her body instantly. She flashed back to Vegas and those hours they'd spent in bed together.

He reached for the dials on his dashboard and soon a flow of warm air surrounded her. "Better?"

She nodded.

"I've got an extra jacket in the back. I won't let you freeze to death out here."

That he was talking about "letting" her do anything or

not gave her nerves a rattle. He wasn't really her husband— just thinking it seemed completely foreign to her—but he was taking care of her needs and that wasn't something she was used to, with any guy. "Thanks."

A few minutes later they approached Red Barrel Horse Rescue and Luke parked in the gravel lot in front of the small building that served as the office. "I'll go in and let Wes know we're here," he said. "You want to stay in the car and keep warm?"

"No, I'll go with you."

"Sure," he said. He stretched way back and grabbed two jackets from the back seat of his car. "Here you go."

He handed her a suede jacket lined with lamb's wool, while he took a lighter weight cotton one. They tossed them on, hers almost reaching her knees, and Wes came out of the office to greet them.

The men shook hands, then Wes gave her a gentle hug. "I knew you two would come out as soon as you heard. Snow's in the barn. I've made her as comfortable as possible."

Luke met her eyes, then looked back at Wes. "We'd like to see her now."

"You two know the way. Stay as long as you want."

"Thanks," Luke said, his hand closing over hers gently. They began walking toward the barn and Katie took note of all the other horses in the corrals on the property. They were the lucky ones who'd been given a second chance at Red Barrel. There were so many others who were sick and hungry running wild in the canyons.

Once they reached the wide wooden doors, Luke turned to her. "No matter what happens in there, just know we did the very best we could for her."

"I know that," she whispered. "It's just that she's a special one. And she's been through so much."

"Well then," he said, his eyes softening. "Let's make her final hours the best they can be."

She held on to a breath. And then exhaled. "Okay."

They walked out of the daylight and into the darkened barn. A cold shiver ran through her. It was definitely jacket weather in the canyon.

"There she is," he said, pointing to the largest paddock in the barn.

Katie moved closer to the stall and as she laid eyes on Snow, she clutched her chest. "Oh, sweet girl." It hurt so much seeing Snow weak, giving up the fight.

"She's down," Luke said. "But she's still with us."

"Yes, she still is. You've waited for us, haven't you, my pretty Snowball?"

Snow lifted her head and eyed them both before laying her head back down on a pillow of straw.

Katie took off her jacket and entered the stall, laying the jacket on the straw beside the mare. "Do you mind?" she asked Luke.

"Not at all," he said, doing the same with his jacket.

They lowered down and sat on the jackets next to Snow.

"Hey, girl. I'm here," she whispered in her ear. "You don't have to do this alone." Katie laid her hand on Snow's mane and used the gentlest touch to comfort her. "I know you're struggling to breathe. Just stay calm. I'm here."

Luke stroked Snow's flank and whistled a soft, mellow tune. He was actually pretty good and not only did the whistling relax the mare, it soothed Katie's nerves as well.

"That's nice," she said, closing her eyes. "How did you learn to do that?"

"A buddy of mine taught me when I was overseas."

Katie opened her eyes. "When you were in Afghanistan?"

He nodded. "We had time to kill when we weren't on

active duty. You know, something to fill the void from being away from home."

"Must've been hard."

"It wasn't a walk in the park," he said.

"Yet you signed up for it. When you had family here and a multimillion-dollar company to run. You didn't have to enlist."

"I felt like I did. I think the time away helped."

"Are you talking about my sister now?"

He nodded. "I never meant to hurt her. I know she hates me, but a lot of time has passed since we broke up."

"You mean, since you walked out on her? Humiliated her?"

"Yeah," he said, frowning. "If that's the way you want to put it."

"It's just that my family trusted you," she said, stroking Snow's mane. Luke hadn't stopped his caresses either. "And your decision sort of came out of left field."

"What can I say that I haven't already?"

Katie was at odds with her feelings. She wanted to support Shelly and their mom, but Luke had a point. He couldn't marry a woman he didn't love. It was just too bad he'd come to that conclusion right before the wedding was to take place.

"I know they hate me, Katie. But do you?"

The question took her completely off guard. "*Hate*'s a strong word."

"So you don't?"

"Let's just say I hate how things played out."

Luke nodded. "Fair enough."

"Speaking about the way things played out, any news from your attorney about our dilemma?"

Luke frowned. "No."

She drew a deep breath. "Too much to hope, I guess."

Snow became agitated, moving around on her bed of straw.

"I think you need to keep whistling," Katie said. "It really does help her."

Luke put his lips together again and the melodic sounds filled the barn. Soon, Snow calmed and her breaths came more evenly.

Afternoon gave way to evening, and the ole girl hung on. Snow's eyes were closed now, her breathing more labored. "That's my girl, Snow. Ease over the bridge now. You'll be in a better place soon." Katie bent to kiss her and stroked up and down her nose.

Luke took a break from whistling. "I remember when I first spotted her. She was covered with sores and bruises, yet she had soulful eyes. They were filled with such life, such hope."

"I was appalled at the way she'd been treated. For heaven's sake, the poor thing didn't have a name," Katie said.

"Yeah, I remember. Her coat was black underneath the dirt, and that circle of white on her forehead right smack between her ears couldn't be missed. It looked like she'd been struck by a fat snowball."

"And I named her Snowball."

"I named her Snowball," Luke said, raising his voice an octave.

She smiled, seeing the feigned indignation on his face. In truth, she didn't know who'd said it first, but they'd agreed on the name. "Okay, maybe we both named her Snowball."

Luke smiled, too. "I think that's the way it happened. Finally, we agree on something."

Katie liked this Luke, the one who showed compassion. A man who could laugh at himself and not put on airs. He was a zillionaire, yet he never seemed to flaunt it. "It's the magic of Snow. She's…"

They both gazed down at the mare. She was still. No longer breathing. "Oh no."

Katie looked at Luke as both their smiles faded. The mare had taken her last breath as they were conversing. Snow had heard them, recognized their voices and felt at peace enough to slip away without struggle.

Tears stung Katie's eyes.

Luke, too, was pinching the inner corners of his eyes. "She's g-gone."

"She is," he said. He wrapped his arms around her shoulders, pulling her in close. "But she went knowing she was loved."

Katie couldn't hold back any longer. She nodded, bobbing her head as the truth of his words sank in. She wept quietly and turned to Luke, her tears running down her cheeks and soaking his shirt.

"It's okay, Katie. Don't cry, sweetheart."

"I knew this day would come, but I didn't think it would be so soon. I thought we'd have more time with her."

She had never owned a pet. She'd never had an animal to care for, to nurture and love, until she'd started working at the rescue. She loved all the horses here; they all had a story. But for some reason Snow was special. She'd touched Katie's heart and they'd shared a deep connection, a bond that she didn't have with any of the others. Katie had taken it as a personal challenge to make Snow's days comfortable.

Luke clearly felt the same way. His eyes moist, his expression sad, he couldn't mask his sorrow either. He brushed his lips across her forehead. She needed his warmth right now, his strength.

"There's nothing more we can do." His voice was shaky and he seemed reluctant to release her, to let go of the bond they'd shared. "We should go."

She nodded, wiping her face with the back of her hand

and then attempting to pat his shirt dry from her tears.
"Sorry."

"Don't worry about it," he said softly.

"I hate to leave her."

"I'll let Wes know she's gone. He'll take good care of
her from now on."

It was hard to let go. To say goodbye.

Luke rose and helped her up, entwining their hands.
"Ready?"

"I think so." She glanced at poor Snow one last time,
her heart breaking.

Luke picked up the jackets and brushed the straw off
them. "Put this on. It'll be cold outside."

He gave the fallen horse one last glance, too, a look
filled with sadness and regret as he grabbed a woolen blanket from the stall post and covered her body.

Katie slipped into his jacket and he clasped her hand
again, his warmth and strength seeping into her. He led
her out of the barn. "C'mon, sweetheart. Let me take you
home."

She didn't mind the endearment this time; she couldn't
fight it. Couldn't argue. She'd had a rough twenty-four
hours and she was just too numb to think anymore. His
shoulders were there for her to lean on, he seemed to know
the right things to say and this one time she would accept
what Luke had to offer.

Without guilt.

Three

Luke stood facing Katie at the threshold of her apartment. He'd insisted on escorting her upstairs after entering the bakery, probably because she couldn't quite get her emotions in check. She'd wept most of the drive home, little sobs that broke from her lips every time she pictured Snow lying still on the ground, lifeless. In the car, Luke had glanced at her often. She'd felt his concerned gaze but she couldn't look him in the eye. She didn't like showing her vulnerable side to anyone, but tonight she couldn't help it. Her emotions were running out of control.

"Are you going to be okay?" he asked her.

"I think so." She bit her lip. "You don't have to worry about me."

He stared into her eyes, then ran a hand down his jawline. "But I do."

"You have no obligation to me, Luke. Really, I'll be fine."

"Is that what you think this is?"

He said it softly, without condemnation, and suddenly she felt small and petty. "No, no. I'm sorry. I know you're just as upset as I am about Snow. Really, I'm glad we shared her last night together. You cared for her as much as I did. Gosh, I can't believe I'm speaking of her in the past tense."

"It's strange, huh?"

"Yeah."

She stared at him, so many thoughts racing through her mind. But mostly, she was glad he was there tonight, lending her comfort, helping her come to grips with losing Snow.

"It's been a long day. I should let you go, get some rest," he said.

"That sounds…good."

"Okay, well. Good night then."

He turned to leave and Katie blurted, "Luke, wait."

He turned, his dark brows lifting.

She took both of his hands in hers and gave a squeeze. "I just wanted to thank you for coming to get me today. It meant a lot to me to be there. Honestly, I don't know how I would've gotten through it all, if you weren't with me."

Then she reached up on tiptoes and pressed her lips to his cheek to give him a chaste peck, but suddenly she turned her head, he turned his, and their lips were locked in a real kiss. Luke made a sound from deep in his chest and a warm delicious sensation sparked inside her.

She might've kissed Luke dozens of times in Vegas, but she didn't remember any one of them. *This* kiss she'd remember. This kiss she didn't want to end.

A moan rose from her throat, one of need and want, and for a moment she flushed, totally embarrassed. But Luke didn't stop, he didn't hesitate to devour her mouth. He was all in, too, stirring her deepest yearnings to be held, to be comforted. She was hurting inside and this kiss was a balm to her soul.

He moved forward, backing her into the apartment, kissing her endlessly. She went willingly, relishing the taste of him, the raw pleasure he was giving to her. He tossed his jacket off and then removed hers without breaking the kiss. Then he cradled her in his arms, holding her so close to him that his need pressed against her belly.

A surge of heat raced through her. It was astonishing how quickly he made her come alive. She was glad of it, glad of the sensations rocking her body. In Luke's strong arms, she suddenly wanted what was forbidden to her.

"Luke," she said when the kiss came to an end.

He looked deep into her eyes. "Don't tell me to stop," he whispered, grazing his lips over hers again.

"I'm not, but maybe we should come up for air?"

The quick smile on his face devastated her. He was so darn handsome. Why did it have to be him? She took a deep breath, pausing for just a few seconds. "Okay, that's enough."

"You're good with this?" he asked, brushing a wayward strand of hair off her face. "Don't answer that," he murmured. "I already know you are."

He cupped her face in his hands and gazed into her eyes, before claiming her lips again. The absolute pleasure overwhelmed her, helping to ease the pain in her heart. It amazed her how easily she welcomed him, how much she wanted more of his kisses, more of him. Her insides heated, and a spiral of warmth traveled through her body, making her hot, needy.

"You feel it, too, don't you?" he whispered in her ear.

She shouldn't. But yes, yes. She did. "Yes," she said softly, hating to admit it, but she couldn't lie to him. Couldn't try to deny how his touch shockingly turned her on. How his kisses made her melt. How she wanted more.

This was all about Snow and the loss she felt. It had to be. Because no other reason would do.

Luke unbuttoned his shirt and tossed it off. He clasped her hand and set it flat on his chest. The taut muscles under her palm intrigued her and she moved her hand over him, gently mapping out the broad expanse of his chest. He was stunning, hard, firm, tough.

Electricity sizzled between them, an invisible connection pulling her closer, making her head swim. She pressed a kiss to his shoulder and felt him shudder.

"Katie."

Her name came from deep in his throat, not a plea, not a warning, but a mixture of awe and reverence that set off a barrage of tingles.

She hadn't had a man in her life for two years, and even that hadn't been anything serious, just casual dating. And now here she was with Lucas Boone, for heaven's sake, wanting him, needing his strength and compassion. Her body reacted to his, and she was sure it was mutual grief heightening the sensations, making a hard day a bit easier.

He began kissing her again, drawing her tight into his arms, his big hands caressing her shoulders, her back and then lower yet. Everything below her waist throbbed in the very best way.

She moaned, a guttural sound erupting from her throat that she didn't recognize as her own. Yet she relished the way Luke touched her, and soon his hands were caressing her chest, undoing the buttons on her blouse, pushing it off her. His eyes gleamed as he took in her small round breasts overflowing the cups of her bra.

"So beautiful," he murmured between kisses.

His praise brought more tingles, more heat. She was lost in the moment, totally and fully engaged. He removed her bra and cupped her breasts, taking one into his mouth, stroking it with his tongue gently, reverently, making her feel more alive than she'd ever felt before.

Soon she was wrapped in his arms and being carried into her bedroom. He didn't let up, didn't stop kissing her until he set her down, her boots touching the ground.

"Invite me in," he rasped.

That made her smile. "You're already here," she whispered.

His lips quirked up in a sexy way and she wouldn't have been able to deny him, even if she'd wanted to. "I guess I am." He kissed her again and before she knew it, the rest of her clothes were off and she lay waiting for Luke on the bed.

She had a moment of panic, the realization of what was happening finally dawning. This was Luke, her sister's ex, the man she'd accidentally married in Las Vegas. Yet she'd bonded with him tonight while they were saying goodbye to Snow and shared a deep loss together. It was complicated, and she'd deal with it later, but now... now she needed the comfort he provided. The thrills were an added bonus.

He came over her on the bed, gazing down, a hungry look in his eyes. "I don't take this lightly, Katie. I... This isn't—"

"I know," she said simply. "I know why this is happening."

"You do?"

"It's about Snow."

Luke stared at her for a long second. "Yeah."

Then he covered her body with his, stroking her below the waist until she whimpered in pleasure and then shattered into a hundred pieces. Now she knew what total bliss felt like and she basked in contentment. "Oh wow," was all she could say.

"Yeah, wow," Luke said, pressing tiny kisses along her

shoulder blades, allowing her time to enjoy the aftermath of her climax.

Then he brought his lips to hers again, and she welcomed it and invited him in with her body. He wasted no time shedding the rest of his clothes and sheathing himself in a condom. "I want you, Katie."

She knew. And so when he joined their bodies and gasped, she did, too. "Oh, Luke."

He filled her full and the need inside her grew as his thrusts deepened. Each movement heightened the intensity until she cried out. Luke seemed as lost as she was, moving inside her in a deliberate rhythm that lifted her hips and took her completely home.

He wasn't far behind. His thrusts grew harder, his face masked in pained pleasure and she kept pace with him, taking the ride with him, until he finally shuddered in release.

Moments later, he fell upon the bed next to her and cradled her in his arms. He kissed her forehead and kept her close, both of them too out of breath to utter a word.

Luke woke first, and Katie's sweet scent wafted to his nose. He felt her presence beside him on the bed, and when he opened his eyes and actually saw her snuggled in tight, her honey blond strands spilling onto her pillow, he smiled. She was his wife, and they'd made love last night like they belonged together. This was his honeymoon, all he'd ever wanted. All he'd ever needed.

How many lonely nights had he spent thinking about her? During his stint in the Marines, forbidden thoughts of her would creep into his mind. He'd felt terrible for hurting Shelly, for hurting the Rodgers family. But it would've been a whole lot worse, being married to one sister while secretly craving the other. Often, when he was alone with his thoughts in Afghanistan, he'd wondered if he'd been a damn fool for falling for a woman he'd never touched, never kissed. How would he know if they were compatible? What if the real thing didn't live up to the fantasy?

Now, he knew.

Oh boy, were they compatible. Katie *was* his real thing, his fantasy come true.

He stared at her, watching her take slow peaceful breaths. He should probably leave and let her come to grips with what happened alone. But he couldn't walk out on her. He couldn't leave without seeing her reaction. Was he a fool to hope that she'd be okay with what happened between them?

It was nearing 4:00 a.m. She'd soon be rising for work, but he needed a few more minutes to savor being in bed with her, to savor the sweet serenity of her body next to his, their warmth mingling.

Luke sighed and bent over to place a light kiss on her cheek.

"Mmm," she murmured in her sleep.

He smiled and gently moved a fallen strand of hair from her face. "My pretty Katie," he whispered, needing to touch her again.

She tossed around a bit and he backed off, turning to his side and bracing his head in his hand, content to just watch her sleep.

Too soon, the alarm clock on the nightstand blasted through the peace and Katie opened her eyes and found him beside her. "Hi," she said.

Her greeting surprised him.

"Morning, sweetheart."

Clearly, she wasn't thinking straight.

Luke reached over her to shut off the alarm and then pressed his luck, brushing his lips over hers. Her lips were warm and welcoming. For a second, he held on to hope. "Did you sleep well?"

She blinked and blinked again. "What the…" And then she darted up on the bed, a pained expression on her face. "Oh no."

She glanced down, obviously noting she'd slept in the nude. She grimaced as if her world was coming to an end and then covered up her perfect body.

"Katie—"

"Luke, this was only about Snow. We were both hurting last night, but I… I should've known better. I shouldn't have let my emotions overwhelm my judgment. We can't keep doing this."

"Seems to me, we *do* keep doing this. Must mean something."

"It does. It means I'm a numbskull."

"No, you're not. You're human, and you have real feelings that you can't chuck away or hide. It was good between us last night."

Katie stared at him as if remembering. She couldn't deny the sparks and fire they'd shared last night. For him, there was nothing better.

"Yes, but it can't happen again. We were both…lost."

He wasn't lost. He'd known exactly what he'd needed. And she did, too, but she wouldn't admit it.

She shrugged and a little pout curled her mouth up. "Poor Snow."

"Yeah. It was hard losing her, but you gave her the comfort she needed."

"You really think so?"

He nodded. "I think you're amazing."

"Don't say things like that. It's already complicated enough."

"What, I can't praise my wife?"

She gritted her teeth. "I…am…not…your…wife."

Luke's good nature faded. Why was the thought of being married to him so distasteful? Of course, he knew it was because of Shelly, but was that all it was? Her harsh tone spurred his temper. "Funny, but I have a document that says you are. And, sweetheart, we've consummated our marriage more than once already."

"Don't remind me," she said, rising from the bed, taking the sheets with her. But one corner of the sheet caught on the nightstand knob and jerked away from her body. She stood before him naked in all her glory.

She hoisted her chin. "I'm taking a shower. I'm already late getting to the bakery. You need to leave before Lori gets here, which is in less than an hour."

As she turned away, he focused on the curvy shape of her bare body, her rounded cheeks and the length of her long legs.

It was a freaking turn-on. His throat went dry and his body grew immediately hard. Hell, he wasn't getting out of this bed until he calmed down. He needed to think about cattle prices or something equally benign.

And ticked off as he was, he still couldn't help wondering what she would do if he followed her into the shower.

Katie set two pots of coffee brewing on the back counter of the bakery, behind the near empty bakery case. Normally, decaf was her speed, but this morning she needed a large jolt of caffeine, something that would make her think more clearly. Obviously, last night she'd had no clarity. Not one bit. All she'd had was grief and Luke's welcoming arms.

Spending the night with him had been a big mistake, but at the time she'd needed someone. No, not just someone... She'd needed Luke.

God, she didn't want to feel things for him that would cause a world of trouble. What she'd confessed to him in Las Vegas was true. She wanted someone in her life. She wanted a partner, someone to share moments with, someone who'd have her back. But it couldn't be him. Never him. Her mother's weak heart couldn't take it and Shelly would probably disown her as a sister. She held Luke responsible for her lack of trust in men and her generally bitter disposition.

Katie felt sorry for Shelly and was completely guilt-ridden about finding momentary pleasure in Luke's arms last night. He was the poison apple and she'd taken the forbidden bite.

Katie set out her utensils and staples: bowls, measuring cups, flour, sugar and eggs. She had begun measuring out her ingredients when the sound of boot heels clicking on the stairs reached her ears. Her nerves rattled a bit. It was Luke. Thank God, he was leaving.

"Coffee smells real good. Mind if I have a cup?" he asked.

She kept her head down, pouring sugar into the industrial-size bowl. "It's not ready yet."

"That's okay. I'll wait."

She glanced at the wall clock.

"Don't worry, I'll be out of your hair in a few minutes. I just want a little coffee before I head out. Lori will never know I was here."

"But I will," she muttered.

Luke chuckled.

"Don't laugh. None of this is funny."

He came up behind her, his nearness making her jittery. "Katie, I'm not laughing at the situation. I know this isn't easy on you. I'm laughing, because…well."

"What?" She turned to face him. He'd cleaned up nicely, his dark blond hair groomed and overnight beard extremely swoon-worthy.

He curled his hands around her waist and drew her in with those sky blue eyes. "You're cute when you're angry. Sexy, too."

"Hardly, Luke." She rolled her eyes.

"You doubt it, after last night?"

"Look, I know you think you're my husband and all, but from now on, I'd appreciate it if you didn't tell me I was amazing or sexy or cute. I'm none of those things...to you."

"Sounds like the coffee's ready." He ignored her comment and walked into the bakery.

She sighed. Maybe it was better not to argue with him. He would leave soon and she could go on with her baking.

"You want leaded?" he asked from the other room.

"God, yes," she called to him.

While he was pouring coffee, she combined all the ingredients for her base cupcake recipe and turned on the mixer. Then she started cutting up fruit for her fresh fillings; it was peaches and apples today.

Luke walked in with two steaming cups of coffee. "You take anything in it?"

"No, just black is fine," she said. She sampled too many of her sweets during the day to add any more sugar to her diet. She'd learned the hard way to always taste test her pastries before putting them on the shelves.

"I like watching you work," he said, handing her a cup.

She didn't know what to do with that comment. She clutched the cup to warm up her hands and wished he'd just leave.

"Do you get up at four every morning?"

She nodded. "If I want to open the bakery at seven, I do."

"It's a lot of work."

"It is, but Lori's a big help. Most mornings we're right on schedule."

He smiled, then sipped his coffee. He made her uncomfortable, eyeballing her the way that he was. She put her coffee down and got back to work.

"Okay," he said, taking a huge gulp. "It's time for me to get going, too."

"So soon?" she asked with a rise in her voice and once again, he chuckled.

"You know, I can stick around if it'd make you feel better."

"Out," she said, turning her back on him.

Luke didn't seem to take offense. Instead he roped his arms around her and she turned to frown at him. "What are you doing?"

"Giving you a goodbye kiss."

And then his mouth was on hers, and the melding of their lips felt like heaven on earth.

When the kiss ended, she backed away from him and pointed to the door. "Go."

He went.

She drew a deep breath and then let out a flustered sigh. Whenever the man kissed her, she felt helpless and needy.

It was all so terribly wrong.

Three days later, Drea entered the bakery just before lunch, a big smile on her face. Her bestie was smiling a lot lately and most of that had to do with Mason. Katie wasn't jealous of their happiness; she was thrilled for the two of them. It was just, at times, she thought she'd never meet the right guy, never know that kind of love.

She didn't get any encouragement from her sister and mom. They both thought a woman was better off without a man, but Katie didn't see it that way. She wasn't bitter or jaded, not yet anyway. But being around that sort of pessimism made it hard to keep a positive attitude.

Drea walked up to the counter and Katie greeted her. "Hi there. What brings you by so early this morning?"

"I have an invitation for you."

"Lunch? I'd love to." She wouldn't mind catching up with her friend.

"No, silly. Not lunch. Mason and I want to thank you for helping us plan the wedding and for being the best bachelorette party planner around. We want to take you to dinner tonight. Don't say no. We really, really want to do this."

Katie smiled. "Of course. I'd love to. Thanks."

"Can you be ready by six?"

"I can." She gave Drea a nod. Well, it wasn't lunch with her friend, but Mason was a pretty nice guy and Katie could use the distraction. "Where should I meet you?"

"Oh, no need for that. Luke will pick you up."

"Luke? Uh, why on earth?"

Drea shook her head. "Listen, I know he's not your favorite person, but you two seemed to get along just fine in Las Vegas."

The mention of Vegas brought up visions of their hasty drunken marriage and Katie's stomach squeezed tight.

"It's a thank-you dinner for him, too. We thought you wouldn't mind…much. I mean, you two have been working together at Red Barrel, right? And you seem cordial enough lately."

Oh gosh. Little did Drea know, Luke made her uncomfortable in too many ways to name. Being cordial to him in public was an act.

Yet Katie didn't want to come off as a scrooge. She didn't want to hurt Mason's feelings either, by refusing to break bread with his brother. What could she say? She was trapped, by no conscious doing by her friend. "No, that's fine. But maybe I should drive myself. You know, in case it's a late night. I wouldn't want to hold you guys up. You know I turn into a pumpkin by ten o'clock."

Drea laughed. "I promise Luke will have you home by ten."

"Can't we all go together?"

"We could, only Mason and I will be leaving earlier in the day for a final meeting with our wedding caterer and we didn't think you'd want to be dragged to that."

It was an impossible set of circumstances. Having maid of honor duties alongside Luke as best man, they were bound to be thrown together, but Katie hadn't seen this one coming. Not by a longshot. "Fine, have Luke pick me up. What should I wear?"

"Something dazzling. We're going to The Majestic."

It was a swanky non-Boone restaurant known for its classically romantic atmosphere on the outskirts of Boone County. "Nice," Katie said, feigning enthusiasm.

"Okay, great. We'll see you tonight." Drea clapped her hands. "I'm so excited. I've never been there before."

"Neither have I."

"It'll be a first for both of us then."

At noon, Katie and Lori were in the midst of their second rush hour, the first always coming around eight in the morning. This noon rush wasn't anything they couldn't handle, so when Shelly walked in with a man by her side, Katie greeted them both.

"Hi, Shel. Good to see you. What's up?" She darted a glance at the good-looking blond man standing beside Shelly.

"Katie, this is Dr. Moore. He's new in town and I told him about the best cupcakes in all of Boone County. Dr. Moore, this is my talented sis, Katie."

They exchanged greetings.

"Let me warn you, I have a sweet tooth," Dr. Moore said. "So you might be seeing me in here a great deal."

"Then you are my kind of person. Welcome. Do you have a favorite flavor?"

"I told him you make the best lemon raspberry cupcake

in the world." Shelly smiled and there was a light in her eyes that Katie hadn't seen in a long time.

"Sounds good to me. Love the shop, by the way," he said, admiring the pastel decor and dining area. He glanced at the bakery case. "And it looks like I'll be back to try everything you have in here."

"Good thing his brother is a dentist," Shelly said, teasing.

Katie chuckled. Her sister *never* teased, at least not recently, and it brought a lightness to Katie's heart. "I'd say so. So, will you two be eating here? We also have coffee, hot chocolate and chai."

"Another time. I'm afraid I have to get back to the hospital ASAP."

"Me, too," Shelly said.

"Okay then, let me box these up for you. And I'll throw in a few of my carrot zucchini specials and my newest creation, vanilla infused with peaches."

"That's very nice of you. Can't wait to try them later." His cell phone rang and he glanced at the screen. "Excuse me. I'm sorry, but I have to get this," he said, walking toward the front door. "Shelly, can you meet me outside?"

"Of course."

"Thanks again, Katie."

"Sure thing."

The second the doctor walked out, Katie couldn't hold her tongue. "He's really cute."

"I suppose."

"You mean to say you haven't noticed?"

Shelly caught her drift and rolled her eyes. "Oh, for heaven's sake. I was just being neighborly. Dr. Moore doesn't know too many people in town. I thought he'd like the shop and I wanted to introduce him to you."

"So, you're not interested in him? Because he seems

nice and you've never brought a guy into my shop before this."

"No, I'm not interested in him. Luke ruined me for all
men, I'm afraid. So don't even think it."

"Shel, really. It's been years and it's time you moved
on. Can't I think it a *little bit*?"

"Not even a smidge."

Katie sighed. She only wanted her sister to be happy.
But it looked like Shelly was fighting it tooth and nail.

Katie selected the cupcakes from the bakery case and
set them in the box, sealing it with two Katie's Kupcakes
stickers. "Okay then. Here you go," she said, handing the
box to Shelly.

"Thanks for the treats, sis."

"Shel?"

"What?"

"I like it when you come by to see me. You should do
it more often."

Shelly's expression softened and there was beauty in her
eyes and her smile just then. "I will. I promise."

Katie watched her sister leave and sighed. She had her
own problems to deal with.

Tonight, she had a "date" with the man who'd broken
her sister's heart.

Four

Luke scrutinized his reflection in the mirror after changing his shirt and tie several times trying to get the look just right. Normally, he didn't give two figs about looking sharp, but tonight he was going on a date with Katie. Well, not a date, but hell, the way his stomach was doing somersaults, it might as well be one. He hadn't seen her in three days. He'd kept himself busy, but no amount of work or play could keep him from thinking about her.

Once dressed, he headed to the parlor and found Aunt Lottie sitting on the sofa, all alone, sipping from a tumbler of bourbon. As soon as she noticed him, she gave him a wolf whistle and he chuckled. He never knew what she would do or say. She was genuine and quite a surprise and that's why all of his family loved her. But the desolate look he'd caught on her face moments before he entered the room tugged at his heart.

"You look handsome, Luke. Got a hot date?"

"Thanks. And you know I'm going to dinner with Mason and Drea tonight."

"And Katie, too? Is that why you've spruced up?"

"Never mind me. What's wrong, Aunt Lottie? And don't put me off. You've been unusually quiet lately. Is it Drew?"

She pursed her lips, but then finally nodded. "That man's got me all mixed up."

Drew MacDonald lived on the property now. He'd once been a land baron, with a ranch adjacent to Rising Springs, but he'd fallen on hard times when his wife Maria passed away. Lottie and Maria had been dear friends, and now years later, Drew and Luke's aunt were testing the waters of a relationship that unfortunately seemed to be drying up.

"It's clear you two care for each other."

"I suppose," she said. "But he's forever badgering me about this and that."

"That's nothing new. Even when Maria was alive, you two didn't much see eye to eye."

"Isn't that important though? Seems to me, a man and woman should have the same disposition."

"Boring."

"What?" she asked.

"Aunt Lottie, I know you. We all do. You have an adventurous nature. If you two got along like steak and potatoes, there wouldn't be any sparks. He's spirited, and you certainly are. Makes for a pretty lively union, if you ask me."

"I don't know. I always feel like I'm too much for him. Like he wants me to change."

"Does he tell you that?"

"No. But it's quite apparent to me."

Luke shook his head. "I don't know about that. I think he cares an awful lot for you. And you have deep feelings for him, too."

His aunt blinked. "The last time we were together was at the Founder's Day gala. We fought and he walked out."

Luke knew about the argument. Drew had been upset at Lottie for putting her life in danger, running into the street trying to save a wayward dog. And April, Risk's fiancée, had pushed her out of the way before a car almost hit her. It had all been caught on video and had made the news.

"That was a couple of months back."

"I know. Now, whenever we see each other on the ranch, it's awkward and we barely speak."

Luke took his aunt's hand. "You're a wonderful woman and I'll always have your back, but I can see Drew's point of view, too. He doesn't want you taking unnecessary risks."

"I made it all these sixty-two years."

"But he lost a wife. He's probably very sensitive about this stuff."

Lottie nodded. "How'd you get so smart about these things?"

"I wouldn't say I'm smart. I have issues." The biggest one being he'd married a woman who wanted out, as quickly as possible. And he was dragging his feet. "But I had a lot of time to think when I was in the service. Four years' worth. I guess you could say I see the big picture now and something's telling me that you two should go for it."

"You really think so?"

He nodded. "Yes, I think so. You're both being stubborn."

"I'll keep that in mind. Thanks," she said, giving him a kiss on the cheek. "Now, go. Have a great time with your Katie."

His aunt gave him a coy look. Sometimes he wondered if she had uncanny powers of perception.

"I'm going. I'm going."

From the minute Katie stepped into The Majestic, she felt transported into another era. The black-and-white-checkered floors, the elaborate table dressings with fine bone china and tiered, flickering candles gave way to sophistication and romance from a time long ago.

"You fit in this place, Katie," Luke said. "Especially tonight. I like your hair up like that."

She didn't want to hear his compliments. When he'd picked her up at her bakery apartment, he'd given her compliment after compliment, making her head swim, giving her ego a boost. True, she'd gone all out, putting her hair up in a messy bun, dressing in a long sleek black gown with a slit up the side and a thin rope of delicate rhinestones stitched into a sloping neckline. She'd bought the dress at an estate sale in Dallas. It was a gown she'd had to have, yet she'd never believed she'd have a place to wear it. Until tonight.

"This place is beautiful," she said, in awe of her surroundings.

Boone County appealed to many, but this place was one of a kind and definitely catered to the rich and fabulously famous.

"Like I said, you fit in perfectly."

She took his arm and stared into his deep blue eyes. Wearing a slate gray suit, his dark blond hair smoothed back showing off his strong jawline, he wasn't exactly hard on the eye. But that was shallow of her. He was much more than that. Mostly, he was off-limits. "Thank you. But please don't say nice things like that. This situation is hard enough."

She hoped her plea would set him straight. After hearing Shelly's bitter comment today about Luke ruining her for all men, Katie had to keep a firm resolve. There was too much at stake and she had to admit that Luke's compliments were charming her. Making her want things she had no right wanting.

"I'm only speaking the truth," he said in his defense.

"You see, that's what I mean." She squeezed her eyes closed for a moment. "Just don't. Please, Luke."

His eyes shuttered yet he didn't answer her.

The maître d' greeted them. "Mr. Boone, so good to see you again. Please, follow me. I believe your brother and his fiancée are waiting for you."

Luke pressed a hand to her back and guided her farther into the restaurant. It was only a moment before she spotted Drea and Mason sitting at a corner table overlooking the patio gardens. Thank goodness. She needed reinforcements tonight. Drea would make the perfect buffer.

The maître d' showed them to the table and pulled out a chair for her. She took her seat and Luke sat down next to her, his scent, his presence looming. She'd been intimate with him and was beginning to learn his mannerisms, like how his eyes turned a darker shade of blue when he was turned on, and how his mouth twitched when he tried to hide a smile, and how when he was exasperated, he'd run a hand along his jawline. She'd seen that one a lot since Las Vegas.

"Hi, you two." Drea smiled at them.

Mason reached over to shake Luke's hand. "Glad you both could make it."

"Thanks for the invite," Luke said.

"Yes…thank you," Katie added, though she'd rather muck a barn stall than spend any more time with Luke.

"Isn't this place spectacular?" Drea asked. "I feel like I'm in a 1940s movie or something."

"I feel the same way," Katie said.

"The food here is top-notch," Mason said. "The owner, Billy Meadows, was a friend of our father's. I think Henry Boone would've loved to top this place in grandeur, but Dad wasn't the greedy type. He saw his competition as a good thing."

"It's good for the town, too," Katie said. "Having choices, that is."

The Boone brothers gave each other a quick glance. Katie wondered what that was all about, but quickly Luke changed the subject. "So, your wedding is in less than a month. Hard to believe. If there's anything I can do for you guys, let me know."

"Same here," Katie interjected.

"Don't you worry, Katie my friend," Drea said. "I have a list of things I need help with. My final gown fitting is coming up and the bridesmaids' dresses are in."

"Exciting. Sign me up," Katie said.

"Aren't you helping Aunt Lottie with the bridal shower?" Luke asked her.

"Yes. And I'm looking forward to that. It's next weekend." Drea wanted a couples shower, and that meant more contact with Luke, but oh well, there was nothing Katie could do about it. Once the wedding was over, and Katie and Luke were properly divorced, she wouldn't have to spend any time with him.

"I feel bad taking you away from Red Barrel," Drea said. "I know you like to spend your free time there and it seems like I'll be usurping all of it."

"I…don't mind." The reminder of the rescue disheartened Katie. She hadn't been back since Snow died. "It's part of my MOH duties."

"That's maid of honor, in case you two didn't catch on," Drea added.

Mason smiled at her. "We're not that slow. I knew what it meant."

"Good thing you did. Because I had no idea," Luke said.

"You're not up on wedding speak, bro." Then Mason turned to Katie. "You looked sad when Drea mentioned the rescue. So sorry. Luke told me you lost a precious mare not too long ago."

"Yes. It was hard. She was a special one."

Drea's voice softened. "I've already told you how sorry I am that you lost Snow."

Luke touched her hand and she gazed into his eyes, seeing the compassion there. "She's at peace now."

Katie nodded, then pasted on a big smile. She wasn't here to bring everyone down. Yet the reminder of losing Snow, combined with her sister's bitterness today, gave her a stomachache. "I'm fine, really. Drea, I've been your friend since third grade and I'm looking forward to every minute of helping you with your wedding plans, so don't you worry about putting me out. We've fantasized about this day for as long as I can remember."

Drea blew her an air-kiss. "I know we have. And your day will come, too, and when it does, I'll be right there for you."

Katie's cheeks heated and she felt like such a fraud, sitting here next to her best friend and lying through her teeth. She couldn't even spare Luke a glance for fear of giving herself away.

Luckily, the waiter approached with menus and took their drink orders.

"Nothing for me please. Just water." She couldn't take a drink, not with her stomach in turmoil. And she'd sort of sworn off alcohol ever since Las Vegas.

Once the drinks were served, Mason asked everyone to raise their glasses. "Thank you both for coming. We wanted to show our appreciation for giving us a wonderful party in Las Vegas. Everyone had a good time, thanks to you both. Drea and I really appreciate your love and support. So, here's to a loving family and lasting friendships."

Everyone clinked their glasses and sipped. Then Drea gave Luke a kiss on the cheek and turned to give Katie a big hug and kiss, too.

"It was my pleasure," Katie said.

"Yeah," Luke said. "My pleasure, too. It was a great time for everyone."

Katie didn't have the heart to agree with him. It would be the biggest lie of all.

Musicians set up beyond the dance floor and began playing tunes her grandparents had probably loved. It was lively, big band stuff that seemed to bring out the best in people. After the waiter came by to take their orders, Mason grabbed Drea's hand and pulled her onto the dance floor. Drea turned to give Katie a helpless look as if to say sorry for leaving her alone with Luke.

"Would you like to dance?" Luke asked, after a minute of silence.

She shook her head. "No, thanks." She didn't want Luke holding her, touching her. They'd done too much of that already. Her stomach still churned and the only thing that would make it better was to be free of Lucas Boone. When she was sure Mason and Drea were well beyond hearing distance, she whispered, "I need an update on...on our divorce."

"What?" Luke leaned closer to her and she repeated what she'd said into his ear. His pure male scent filled her nostrils, and her mind flashed to the night they'd shared together. She wished those memories would fade, but every time she was close to him, they became sharper.

"I don't have an update. My attorney is still out of the country."

"Shh." Why was he using his regular speaking voice? "Surely there's something we can do," she said quietly.

Luke took her hand. "Sorry, Katie."

She didn't want his apologies, she wanted action. She could try to find an attorney herself, but unless she ventured to Willow County or some other town, she feared news would get out. It was the curse of living in a small town: the gossip hotline was long. Luke had promised her his attorney would use great discretion and she believed that, because nobody wanted to cross a Boone.

She pulled out of his grasp, but not before Drea and Mason returned to the table and eyed their linked hands. *Oh boy.*

Mason's brows rose, but dear Drea pretended not to notice.

After dinner was served, the conversation around the table was pleasant and engaging. Mostly they talked about wedding plans and the building of Mason and Drea's new home on Rising Springs Ranch property.

"Katie's going to help me design our kitchen," Drea said. "She's the expert in that area."

Katie had felt Luke's eyes on her most of the night and the look of admiration on his face right now made her uneasy. "I'm hardly an expert."

"You know more than a thing or two about kitchens, Katie. Admit it."

Mason spoke up. "She's right, Katie."

"Just take the compliment," Drea said, grinning.

Katie nodded, giving in. "O…kay, if you insist."

Luke laughed and she eyed him carefully. "What's so funny?"

His lips went tight and he shook his head. "Nothin'."

She was afraid he would say she was cute or something equally as revealing, so she dropped it. But she knew his laugh now and when it was aimed at her.

Dessert and coffee were served. The pastries, pies and cakes were beautiful, but Katie had barely eaten her dinner so the thought of dessert didn't sit well. Beef Wellington had sounded good on the menu, but as soon as the dish arrived, Katie had lost her appetite. She'd been feeling queasy lately, and for good reason. She'd married the enemy and the nightmare was continuing. She felt out of control, restless and confused about her feelings for Luke.

"I'll sit this one out," she said politely.

"Too much cupcake sampling at the bakery?" Drea asked.

"Uh, yeah. I'm really full," she said, and Drea gave her a look. She was astute enough not to ask her what was wrong, but she had no doubt her friend would be questioning her about it later on. "But you go on. Enjoy. Everything looks delicious."

After dessert, Mason and Drea took to the dance floor again. Her friend knew enough not to try to coax her out there with Luke. Thank goodness.

She glanced at her watch and noted the time. "Luke, it's after nine."

"Yeah," he said. "I know. You've been checking your watch every five minutes since we got here."

"I have not."

"You have." He ran his hand down his face in his classic frustrated move and it irritated her no end.

"Lucas Boone, exactly what is it you want from me?"

That stumped him for a second. He blinked his eyes and then stared at her. "You would be surprised."

Her heart started racing. "Would I?"

"I have absolutely no doubt you would, so let's drop it." He rose. "Grab your purse. I'll take you home now."

They waited until the dance ended to say goodbye to Drea and Mason. "Thank you for this evening, it was wonderful," Katie said.

"I'm glad you enjoyed it," Mason answered.

She hugged Drea goodbye, too, and then she and Luke were off.

The drive home was quiet, uncharacteristically so. Luke didn't spare her a word or a glance and she felt the tension down to her toes. "Are you mad at me?" she asked.

He inhaled a breath and shook his head. "No."

"Is that all you're going to say?"

"Yep. That's all." He kept his gaze trained on the road.

She folded her arms around her middle, and her stomach knotted up. She'd almost forgotten how unsettled it felt. It was all this stress, and she was put off that Luke, regardless of his denial, was angry with her. If anyone had a right to be angry, it was her. "Well, maybe I'm mad at you."

"What?" This time he did take his eyes off the road. He had an incredulous look on his face. "I'm not the one who spoiled the evening for Mason and Drea. They were trying to do a nice thing. And you refused to participate."

"I didn't refuse to participate. I just didn't want to… be with you. And for some reason, you don't seem to understand that."

"Oh, I get it all right. But couldn't you have shown some appreciation to my brother and Drea? You wouldn't dance, wouldn't eat. Why was that, *wife*?"

He said that just to rub salt in her wound. "Don't be an ass, Luke. I could never be your wife. And you know darn well I didn't spoil anything."

Her belly clenched and her face pulled tight as she absorbed the pain. "Uh." She glanced out the window, hiding her discomfort, hoping Luke wouldn't catch on.

"What's wrong?"

"Nothing." She wouldn't look at him.

Luke steered the car onto the side of the road and parked along the highway.

"What are you doing?" she asked, breathless.

"What's wrong with you?"

"I told you, nothing is wrong with me." Once again, her stomach rolled and she bit her lip. She didn't want to get sick in front of him. They were in semidarkness, the moonlight casting them in shadows. "But I would appreciate it if you took me home."

"Can we just talk a minute?" he asked.

"I'm not feeling well, okay? It's all this stress. I'm worried sick about my mother and sister finding out about... about what happened. And being with you makes me go a little nutty."

"Katie," he said, his voice ultra-soft now. "I'm sorry you're not feeling well. Why didn't you say something before?"

"I didn't want to ruin the evening. But according to you, I'm guilty of that, too."

"Katie," he whispered. "I was just being—"

"A jerk?"

"Okay," he said, defeat in his voice. "I was a jerk. Of course you didn't spoil anything. So I make you nutty? Do you hate me that much?"

"Luke, I don't hate you. I never did. Maybe my problem is that... I like you. And it's impossible."

"You like me?" His voice rose, filled with hope.

"Luke, we've been... Well, you know. I keep asking myself why I let that happen. True, it was grief over Snow, but—"

"How much do you like me?"

He was crazy to think anything could ever come of the two of them, yet he was asking as if there was a chance. "Not enough to destroy my sister and hurt my mother." Her stomach cramped and she put her hand on it. "Oh."

"Katie?"

"Luke, please, take me home."

Concern entered his eyes. "Okay, just sit back and try to relax. I'll get you home quickly, sweetheart."

She wasn't his sweetheart. She wasn't his anything, and she hoped this little talk would convince him of that.

A short time later, he pulled up in front of the bakery. "Hold on a second," he said and got out of the car to open the door for her. He took her hand and helped her out.

"Thanks for the ride." She turned away from him, but he didn't release her hand.

"I'll make sure you get in safely."

The front door was ten feet away. "I'll be fine."

"I'll walk you," he said stubbornly and he walked beside her as she made her way to the front of the bakery.

She unlocked the door and took a step inside.

"Katie?"

"What?" She turned to him.

His eyes were soft on her, his expression etched in concern. "Are you feeling any better?"

"A little."

He tipped her chin up and planted a sweet tender kiss to her lips. It instantly warmed her insides, soothing her. "Get some rest. I'll check on you tomorrow."

Before she could say "Don't," he had turned away and hopped into his car. A dreamy feeling flowed through her body as if she was floating.

Until she realized that Luke had just kissed her on the public street.

And someone might have seen them.

She took a peek, noting the sidewalks were empty, and there were no cars in sight, yet her belly twisted up again. And all feelings of warmth quickly evaporated.

Early the next morning, Luke pulled up in front of the bakery, wondering if he was making a mistake by showing up here. He had Katie on the brain, and just remembering how she'd looked in that sexy gown last night, how delicious her lips tasted when he'd given her a goodbye kiss, gave him some hope that she wouldn't mind him checking in on her.

She'd admitted she liked him. He'd been floored hearing those words come out of her mouth. It was more than he'd expected, more than he'd thought possible. It was a start. Keeping away from her for the past five years had been hard on him, but Las Vegas had changed all that.

He got out of the car and entered the bakery, disappointed to see her assistant behind the counter helping customers. He was hit with a knot of apprehension. Was Katie still feeling poorly?

And just then she walked out of the kitchen and into the bakery. They made eye contact. There was a spark in her eyes, a light that she quickly extinguished. But he'd seen it and she couldn't deny that for that one second, she'd been happy to see him.

He took a seat in a café chair and waited, watching Katie and Lori efficiently handle the morning rush. Finally, once the crowded bakery thinned out, Katie walked over to him. "I hope you're here to give me news…about you know what," she whispered.

She was speaking about the divorce.

"No change on that, I'm afraid."

She pursed her lips. "Then why are you here?"

He shrugged. "For coffee."

She tapped her foot. "Can I get you anything else?"

"Just coffee for now."

She hesitated. "Don't you have a coffee cart at Boone Inc.?"

"We do, but as you can see, I'm not at Boone Inc. at the moment. I'm here."

She sighed. "I'll get it for you." She turned to leave.

"Katie," he said firmly.

She gave him a deadpan look.

"How are you feeling?"

"I'm fine. Now will you go?"

"Coffee, please."

She gave her head a shake and left only to return a moments later holding a steaming cup of coffee. "Here you go." She set the cup in front of him.

"Sit with me."

"I can't, I'm working."

"Just for a minute." He pointed around the shop. "The place has emptied out."

"Only if you promise to leave as soon as you're through."

"Fine."

She sat down facing him, and once up close, he noticed the fatigue on her face and how her eyes were rimmed with red. She'd been moving slowly around the bakery. "How are you feeling?"

"I feel…good."

She was lying. "Don't take this the wrong way, but you look sluggish this morning."

"What every girl wants to hear. Thank you for that."

He shook his head. The woman was constantly sparring with him. Today, it wasn't cute or funny. "How's your stomach?"

"Luke, you don't have to check up on me. I'm perfectly capable of taking care of myself. So please, have your coffee and leave."

"Is that any way to speak to a customer? One you actually like."

She sighed. "Luke, I'm beginning to regret telling you that."

"Just for the record. I like you, too. A lot."

"Shh." She glanced at the door.

What was she so afraid of? Was she expecting to see her sister or mother walk in this morning? Was that it? Diana and Shelly had to know he and Katie had wedding business to discuss. They were both helping Aunt Lottie put on the bridal shower for Drea and Mason. Luke and Katie had been thrown together lately and it shouldn't be a crime that the two of them spent some time together.

He sipped his coffee. "Mmm, perfect."

"I'll tell Lori you enjoyed it. She makes a mean cup."

"So, I'll see you at the bridal shower on Saturday. Are we all set for that?"

"I am. I'm making the cake and helping with some of the activities."

"I'm good on my end, too." He actually wasn't asked to do much, just help the day of the shower behind the scenes. "I can pick you up and bring you out to the ranch."

"That's silly. You live at the ranch. You don't need to come all the way out here to pick me up. I'll manage."

She was good at shooting him down.

"I am sorry, you know," he said. "I don't like being the source of your stress. But I can't do anything about that right now."

"I'll...try to remember that. So no more sudden visits to the shop?"

"I can't promise that. I might have a craving."

Katie gave him a hard stare.

"For a cupcake."

She nibbled on her lip, trying to keep from saying something. Whatever it was, he was sure he didn't want to hear it. He finished his drink, then rose and reached out to help her up, but she ignored his outstretched hand.

"Just try to rest. Feel better, Katie."

The genuine concern in his voice caused a momentary tug in her heart. The truth was, she hadn't had anyone care about her this way in a long time. And it felt sort of nice. This was what she'd longed for, what she'd revealed to Luke in Las Vegas. She wanted more out of life. She wanted a partner, someone to share things with. She'd neglected that part of her life to make the bakery a success. Now, she had a thriving business, but no one to share it with.

Perhaps she should start dating again.

And then she remembered…she couldn't date anyone. She was married to Lucas Boone.

Three days later, Lottie opened the front door of the ranch house at Rising Springs to face Drew MacDonald. He was the last person she was expecting this morning and her heart did a little flip seeing him looking so handsome with a salt-and-pepper beard, his graying, windswept hair and his workout clothes the same shade of jade green as his Irish eyes.

It had been awkward between them lately but she wanted to rectify that. They were all going to be family as soon as Mason and Drea, Drew's daughter, were married. And this weekend, Lottie was throwing the two love-birds a couples bridal shower.

"Hi, Drew. I didn't expect to see you this morning."

Suddenly, she remembered what she must look like. She was cooking up a storm, baking apple cobbler and cookies for her nephews. Not only were her clothes a mess, but she probably had flour on her face and in her hair.

"I didn't come to see you."

"Oh."

"I mean, I'm happy to see you and all, but Luke asked me to stop by some time this morning. He needs a bit of advice about a company I used to deal with. Anyway, I decided to stop by after my walk."

"I see. I'm glad you're still taking walks, Drew."

"I enjoy it. But I sure liked it better when I had a walking partner." He gave her a direct look.

Warmth rushed up her cheeks. The man could always make her blush. "You need that much motivation?"

"No, ma'am. Just liked the company." And before she could react, he took a deep breath. "Something smells awfully good in here."

"I'm baking, in case you can't tell." She gestured to her

smudged clothes. "Apple cobbler and lemon supreme cookies. I'll send some home for you and Drea."

"Thanks. I'd never refuse any of your baking, Lottie. Though I'd probably have to walk farther every day just to burn off the calories."

"I don't think apple cobbler would do you any harm. You're, uh, looking fit these days."

They stared at each other for a few beats of a minute. "Well, if Luke's home, maybe I could see him now?"

"Oh, right. Sure, he's in the office. You know where it is. Go on in."

"Thanks. Oh, and it was nice talking to you this morning."

"Same here, Drew."

After he turned and walked down the hallway, she smiled. It seemed they could have a civil conversation if they put their mind to it. She went back to baking and thinking about Drew, her heart lighter than it had been in a long while.

An hour later, she came downstairs after taking a quick shower and changing her clothes. She wore a soft pink bell sleeve blouse. It worked well with her rosy complexion, and silly her, she found herself dressing to impress. She gave a quick knock on the office door and then entered.

Luke was sitting in front of his laptop computer, Drew nowhere in sight. "Hi, Aunt Lottie. What's up?"

"Oh, I thought you were having a meeting with Drew?"

"I was. He left a little bit ago." Luke grinned. "Don't you look pretty today. I thought you were baking."

"I was and I'm finished now. I meant to send Drew home with some cobbler and cookies for Drea."

"Just for Drea?" he asked, his mouth twitching.

She chuckled. She'd been caught. "Well, for both of them."

"So, what's stopping you? Take it over to them. I'm sure they'd appreciate it."

"You think so?"

"I know so. Drew loves his sweets."

"That is true." She mulled it over for half a second. She hadn't gotten all dressed up for nothing. "Okay, I think I will."

Luke smiled the smile of a matchmaker. The only thing missing was him rubbing his hands together gleefully. "Good idea."

And a few minutes later Lottie was set with a canvas tote containing the lemon cookies and a covered dish of still warm cobbler. She took off on foot; the extra bit of exercise today would do her good. Her heart was aflutter, thinking about Drew and how much he was beginning to mean to her.

As she approached the MacDonald cottage, Drew opened his front door and out stepped a pretty, dark-haired woman she'd never seen before. The two embraced in a passionate hug that lasted far too long. And then the woman took his face in her hands and kissed him right smack on the mouth.

Shocked, Lottie froze for a moment, not believing what she was seeing. She stood on the road, bag in hand, ready to make nice with Drew, and now she was hit with raw pangs of jealousy. She couldn't watch any longer. She turned on her heels and made fast tracks away from the cottage before Drew could see her.

Goodness, what an idiot she was. Had she been naive to think that Drew didn't have other options when it came to women? He'd straightened himself out, was ruggedly hand-some and had a good heart, for the most part. She'd always thought of him as hers in an odd sort of way. Had he led her on all these years? Or had she been blind to his needs?

Either way, she was roaring mad at him and his sweet-talking ways.

As her anger raged, she picked up her pace, walking as fast as her legs would take her. Running from the hurt, from the loss, from the betrayal as tears trickled down her face.

Five

"I'm here, Mama," Katie called as she unlocked the door and entered her mother's house Thursday afternoon.

She didn't find her right away. But soon Shelly appeared, coming in through the sliding back door. "Mom's in the backyard, getting some fresh air."

"That's a good idea. It's a beautiful afternoon. How're you doing, sis? Staying for dinner?"

"No, sorry. I hope you're okay with making Mom dinner without me. I'm… I'm going to a seminar tonight. It includes dinner."

"That's no problem, but another seminar? You know what they say, too much work and not enough play…"

Shelly smiled. "If I'm dull, then I'm dull. I happen to love my work."

"I get it. I love my work, too." Then Katie grinned. "Is a certain Dr. Moore going to this event?"

"Take that grin off your face, brat. And actually Dr. Moore is giving the seminar, part two of his Cardiology in the Twenty-first Century lecture. So of course he's going to be there."

"Now the evening's sounding more interesting." Katie smiled again.

Her sister picked up a pillow and tossed it at her, just like when they were kids. Katie was too fast for her. "You missed me."

"Only because I wasn't really trying."

There was a breezy lightness to Shelly tonight that she hoped would continue.

"So, Katie, any chance we can go shopping with Mom on Saturday? I have the day off and I thought it'd be nice to get her out of the house. You know, have a girls' day."

"Oh, that's a great idea, but I can't do it Saturday. It's Drea and Mason's bridal shower."

Shelly's perpetual frown reappeared. So much for light and breezy. "Oh, right. That's if Mason decides to show up for it. Boones are notorious for disappointing their fiancées."

"Shel, give it a rest, okay? Drea's crazy about him."

"Yeah, well, I was crazy about Luke and look how that turned out. I mean, he was an amazing boyfriend and fiancée until he wasn't."

"I know it hurt you, but you can't change the past," Katie said, trying to get through to her sister. Trying to ease her own conscience, too.

"I know that. But I also know I can't suppress my emotions."

"But you're suppressing living your life."

Shelly gave her head a tilt. "You really think so?"

"I absolutely do. You have a lot to offer someone. You should be open to that."

"Well, it's not as if anyone's busting down the door to get to me."

"How about you taking a chance. Walk out the door and find what you're looking for."

"I'm…scared."

Katie winced. It was hard seeing her big sister admit that. She took Shelly's hands in hers and squeezed. "Shel, you're strong enough to deal with anything that comes your way. You're a fantastic person, a wonderful nurse. You make people feel better, you care. People look up to you, they value your judgment. Never doubt that. I think that you'll find what you're looking for if you give yourself a chance."

Shelly drew a breath. "Maybe." She nodded. "I'll try. And thanks, sis. You're the best."

The conversation made Katie ache inside for the pain her sister had gone through. Hearing her admit that she'd been crazy about Luke was like a dagger to her heart.

Because Katie was starting to have real feelings for Luke.

And they were getting stronger every day.

Saturday morning, Katie rose extra early to get a head start on baking so she'd have enough time to put the finishing touches on the bridal shower cake. Though cakes weren't her specialty, she knew enough about them to design a one-of-a-kind cake for Drea and Mason that resembled the home they were building on Rising Springs land. It took a great deal of thought, but the cake when finished would be spectacular.

Halfway through the decorating, fatigue set in, and she took a seat to rest. She'd been stressed out lately, and for good reason, but she'd never felt so tired before. Her mother told her she was taking on too much, that she needed extra help running the bakery, but Katie didn't think that was it.

"You look as green as this pistachio icing," Lori said,

picking up a freshly frosted tray of cupcakes. "Are you feeling poorly?"

"I think I'm just tired. I worked hard on the cake last night and didn't get much sleep. I probably should've closed the shop today, so I could concentrate on Drea's shower."

"Why don't you go up to your apartment and get some rest? I'll finish up with the cupcakes, so you can be fresh for the bridal shower."

Normally, Katie wouldn't think of it, but her tummy was aching, the same queasy feeling she'd been having for days now. "I'll go up for an hour if you don't mind."

"Go, I've got things covered here."

"I have no doubt. You could run this bakery with your eyes closed. I'll be back soon."

"Take your time," Lori said.

"Thanks." Katie climbed the stairs to her apartment and once inside, her stomach cramped tight and she couldn't fight the nausea. "Oh no." Her hand on her belly, she dashed to the bathroom and made it just in time. When she was through, she sat down on the tile floor next to the toilet until her tummy settled down.

Where had that come from? She thought back to what she'd eaten these past few days but nothing struck her as odd. Could it be stress and fatigue causing such a disruption to her health?

She rose and took a shower, then tucked herself into bed. She'd rest for just a few minutes and then get up to put the finishing touches on the cake.

The sound of birds tweeting broke into her sleep. Katie opened her eyes and listened again. Those weren't real birds, it was her cell phone chirping. She grabbed it off the nightstand. Her eyes widened when she saw the time and she jolted out of bed, panicked. It was nine o'clock!

She was supposed to be at the ranch in half an hour. The shower was starting at noon.

The text read, Drea's sending me to pick you up. Stay put.

It was from Luke.

Oh God. She was late. She took a few minutes to dress and comb her hair and then raced downstairs. "Lori, I'm so sorry," she called out. She didn't have time to deal with Luke coming to get her. Actually, with the way she was feeling, she really could use his help.

"Hey, no problem," Lori said, coming into the work area. "It's slow right now, but I was beginning to worry. Are you feeling better?"

Gosh, she didn't have time to feel bad. She had to finish the cake and get to Rising Springs. "Yes, I'm better. The rest did me a world of good but I've got to finish the cake. Should only take a few minutes."

Katie pulled the cake out of the fridge and spent the next twenty minutes piping the perimeter and adding the names. When all was said and done, the two-tiered cake looked like a picture of serenity and love.

"There," she said, with a heavy dose of pride and relief.

"It's beautiful." Luke had sneaked up beside her. She hadn't heard him enter but she appreciated the compliment. "Thanks."

"A lot of work?"

"Yes," she replied. "But worth the effort."

"Funny, that's how I feel about you."

Katie turned to find a twinkle in his eye. "Luke."

He grinned. "C'mon. Let's get our butts to the house before the shower starts without us."

"You really didn't have to come."

"Drea insisted, and who am I to argue with my future sister?"

"Riiiight."

She wouldn't tell him she was glad he'd come to the rescue, that she had been sluggish lately and she hoped once they settled their "marriage" problem, her tummy aches would disappear.

Luke had driven with extra caution while Katie sat in the back seat of his roomy SUV with the double-tiered cake beside her. And now, thanks to Luke carefully carrying it inside, the cake sat on the kitchen counter, ready to be revealed once the shower began.

As Katie put up snow-white paper wedding bells along the perimeter of the spacious patio overhang, Luke held the ladder for her, watching her carefully. "You sure you don't want me to do that?" he asked her, for the second time.

"Not at all. These have to be spaced just right and hung a certain way."

"And a mere man can't figure it out?"

She laughed. She was having fun decorating for her best friend's shower and she didn't want anyone to take the joy away. "I think not."

"That's okay, I'm enjoying the view from down here anyway."

Katie immediately grabbed at the back of her dress, making sure she was well covered. The dress was tight enough to cling to her legs. But she noticed it was fitting a little more snugly around her waist than she'd remembered. She had to stop eating her own cupcakes. "You can't see anything, Luke, so stop teasing."

"Everything I do see, I like."

She gave him a look. "Shh."

"I meant the decorations are looking real pretty. Everyone's doing a great job."

She shook her head at him. He was so full of it. But in a sweet way that made her...nutty.

From her vantage point on the ladder, everyone was

pitching in and doing a great job. Risk and April were arranging the table flowers. April was an expert at staging homes so her expertise was spot on. The next home she would permanently stage would be at Canyon Lake Lodge, the old manor that Risk had bought for them to live in once they renovated it. The two were going to run the lodge together.

Drea and Mason were locked in an embrace watching the lily pads they'd set afloat in the pool drift off. Their happiness was contagious. Katie could be happy for them, and for this day. It was a dream come true for Drea, who'd been through so much in the past.

"Okay," Katie said, draping the last of the wedding bells. "I think I'm done."

She lowered herself down from the ladder and was hit with a bout of dizziness. Her head swam for a moment and Luke was right there, taking her hands, staring into her eyes. "Katie?"

"Whoa," she said. "That was weird."

"What happened?"

"Nothing." She gave her head a gentle shake. "I think I came down the ladder too fast. Got a little light-headed. I'm fine now."

He stepped closer to her. "Are you sure?"

"Yes," she said automatically. She stepped back from him, breaking their connection. She didn't want him worrying over her. She didn't want to see concern on his face or hear it in his voice. It was all too confusing.

Lottie approached with a gracious smile. "Katie, the cake is amazing. I can't wait for the guests to see it. We'll bring it out soon to show off your beautiful work."

"Thanks, Lottie. I'm—"

"She worked hard on it, Aunt Lottie." There was possessive pride in Luke's voice that had Lottie darting inquisitive glances between them.

"I can see that."

"It was a labor of love," Katie said.

Lottie patted her hand. "I bet you have a lot of love to give, Katie."

"I'm sort of married, uh…" She hesitated when Luke's eyes went shockingly wide. "To my job. I mean, right now I'm concentrating on the bakery. I haven't had time for anything else," she said quietly.

"Well, when you find the right one, you'll know it. There's no rush."

Katie nodded. "I agree. No rush at all."

Drew walked up and smiled at everyone. "Katie, I just saw the cake. You've outdone yourself."

"Thank you."

"I bet it tastes as good as it looks."

"Hope so."

"Drew's got a sweet tooth," Luke said good-naturedly. "I bet you enjoyed Aunt Lottie's cobbler the other day, too. Did you leave any crumbs for Drea?"

Drew's brows furrowed. "Cobbler? If you mean the day I stopped by to see you, Luke, I left your place before getting a chance to dig in."

"But she brought you some that day, didn't you, Aunt Lottie?"

Luke's aunt bit her lip and shook her head. "No, I never made it over."

She didn't give Drew a glance, and her expression was tight. After that, Lottie excused herself to speak with the caterer and Drew walked off in the other direction. Katie thought for sure something was up between the two of them.

She looked at the string and tape and scissors she'd left lying around. "Okay, well, I'd better clean up my mess. The guests will be arriving soon."

"I'll help," Luke said.

Katie couldn't shake the guy. He turned up beside her at every turn. It made mush of her nerves because she was getting used to him being around. She scooped up her mess before Luke could grab anything. "I've got this," she said. "But Mason might need your help. You should check with him."

"In other words, you want me to get lost."

She smiled.

And Luke took the hint. "I'll see you later."

"Okay," she said brightly and once he walked off, Katie entered the house and took a seat in the kitchen. Her tummy was still a bit unsettled and her energy was sapped.

She couldn't wait for the shower to begin and end. All she could think about was getting back into bed and sleeping.

Katie squinted into the bright May sunshine as she stepped out into the Boones' beautifully groomed backyard that they'd spent hours decorating. Everything had turned out perfectly. Drea's dream of true love and marriage was coming true.

The guests filed in as music played over hidden speakers. She watched as groups mingled and enjoyed appetizers and drank wine. Some of the girls in attendance were her friends, too, many of them either married, engaged or escorted by a boyfriend. She sighed and put on a happy face to mingle as well and catch up on their news.

Once the luncheon was served, everyone took their seats. Katie sat at the Boone table. Everyone was paired off with their counterparts, leaving her sitting next to Luke. Funny how it always worked out that way.

He seemed perfectly content with the arrangements and all she could do was smile and have a good time, for Drea's sake. Most of the guests played a silly game of who knew the bride and groom the best, and Katie ended up winning the bride half of the game.

Drea and Mason opened their gifts, and then Katie was asked to cut their cake, but not before a dozen pictures were taken of it. Katie was showered with compliments, which gave her spirit a lift. She found herself smiling and laughing a lot throughout the day.

"I'm glad to see you so happy," Luke whispered in her ear as they sipped coffee.

"I'm happy for Drea."

"Me, too. For Mason. The guy's gaga over his fiancée."

"As well he should be. Drea is awesome."

"So are—"

She put a finger to his lips to quiet him, and then realized what she'd done and quickly removed it, but not before a few heads turned her way. Oh God, had they seen her trying to silence his compliment?

Luke didn't let it faze him. He bit into a forkful of cake. "This is delicious."

She shot him a warning look, but that never seemed to work with him. "Thanks."

As the shower was winding down, Katie decided to remove herself from his presence. "Excuse me. I'm needed in the kitchen, and no, I don't need any help."

She escaped him and entered the kitchen, offering to help, but Lottie shoed her away. "You've done enough. The staff will take care of cleanup. Honestly, I think that's the best marble cake I've ever eaten. It's beautiful on the inside and out. You're a genius."

Drew walked into the kitchen and added, "That you are, Katie girl. I had seconds and would go back for thirds if I was twenty years younger."

Lottie feigned a smile and turned her back on him.

"Thank you both," Katie said. "Lottie, if you really don't need my help, I'll go outside and talk to Drea."

"Good idea," Lottie said. "Go have fun. I'll be out in a second."

* * *

Lottie watched Katie leave and then turned to Drew. "Honestly, I don't need any help here. You should go back outside, too."

"Kicking me out?" His mouth quirked up.

Lottie sighed. "No, you can stay or you can go. Do whatever you want, Drew."

Drew frowned. "Lottie, what the hell is wrong with you? You haven't spoken to me all day. Did I do something wrong, again?"

He was annoyed at her? Did he think she was a fool? The image of Drew kissing that woman on his porch flashed in her mind and anger roiled in her stomach. It was time to confront him. There was no other way. "Not at all. I mean, kissing a woman behind my back isn't wrong. Not if you read from the book of Drew MacDonald."

"What are you talking about?"

"I saw you, Drew. The other day, I was bringing you a dish of cobbler and I… I saw a woman coming out of your house. You two were very cozy. I guess I've been mistaken about the two of us. There is no us."

Drew's green eyes sparked and she couldn't tell what he was thinking. "There is no us?" He took her hand and tugged her close. "Lady, you have no idea."

Then he cupped her face in his hands and laid a kiss on her lips. Her heart fluttered and her mind dizzied as delicious sensations sped through her system. She kissed him back, trying to keep pace with his passion, his ardor.

She couldn't seem to get enough of him, and he must've been feeling the same way. He pulled her into his arms and she went willingly. His kisses went deeper, longer and nothing, nothing she'd experienced in this world had ever felt better. "Drew," she murmured.

He kissed her again, the melding of their mouths seamless and perfect.

Then he broke away and her eyes popped open. She stared at him and he said with a rasp, "Now, tell me there is no us."

"But the woman?"

"I'm her AA sponsor and she needed a one-on-one talk. Whatever you saw was gratitude. *She* kissed me and I set her straight right after that. My goodness, Lottie, she's half my age."

"So, you're not—"

"After the way we just kissed, you have to ask?"

Then he turned his back on her and walked outside. She touched a finger to her mouth, his taste still tingling on her lips.

On the drive home after the shower, Luke kept glancing at Katie. She sat in the passenger seat of his car, struggling to keep her eyes open as she laid her head against the headrest. Snuggled into her jacket, she looked warm and cozy and so peaceful, her body sinking into the contours of the seat.

He tried not to utter a sound as he drove along the quiet road, and before too long, she fell asleep. Luke drove on, feeling the rightness of this moment in his bones. He and Katie. There was no other woman in the world for him and as each day passed, the feeling grew stronger and stronger.

While she was hoping for a quick divorce, he was stalling...perhaps wrongfully so, but all those years while he was in Afghanistan serving his country, he'd felt hollow and empty inside. It was the worst feeling in the world, that aloneness, that feeling that aside from his brothers, there was no one waiting for him back home. Now, he had what he'd always wanted. It would be hard giving it up.

He could tell she was bone tired by the way she was huddled between the seat and the window, her breaths as noisy as they were weary.

Katie was a force, a dynamo in a very understated way. She'd made Katie's Kupcakes a success. And all the while, she'd continued supporting Red Barrel, donating her time and energy to neglected and abandoned horses. She was a great friend, a wonderful daughter and an ultra-loyal sister.

Luke sighed. He wanted to reach out and hold her hand, but that might wake her. That might put her on alert and it was the last thing he wanted, to make her wary, to have her erect walls that would keep him out. No, he was content to have her near him, to watch her sleep. Too soon, he would have to part ways with her.

Once they reached her street, Luke steered his car to the back door of her shop and parked. She'd want him to use discretion so the people strolling along the sidewalk wouldn't see him trying to get a sleepy Katie out of his car.

He didn't give two figs about being seen with her, so this he did for her.

"Sweetheart," he said gently, taking her hand trying to rouse her.

She didn't wake readily, only curled deeper into the comfort of her jacket.

"Katie, honey, you're home. You need to wake up."

She mumbled something incoherently and continued to sleep.

"Okay," he said on a whisper. "Looks like you need Prince Charming, only I don't see him anywhere around here."

He smirked at his bad joke and then got out of the car. When he opened her passenger side door, he hoped the cooler air would jostle her awake. When that didn't happen, he scooped her up in his arms, taking her handbag along with him.

"Luke," she breathed out and the sound of her sultry voice nearly did him in. His wholesome Katie was a very sexy temptation.

"I've got you."

He managed to dig the keys out of her purse, and once inside the bakery, he climbed the stairs to her apartment. Sleep tousled and still drowsy, she was light in his arms and relaxed enough to lie against his chest as he opened her apartment door. He carried her inside and wanted so much to deposit her onto her bed and lie down next to her.

Once in her living room, he set her on her feet and held on as she gained her footing. "Katie?"

She opened her eyes and gazed up at him. "Sorry. I was just so tired. I don't know why… I've never been that tired before."

Touching her cheek, Luke brushed a honey blond strand of hair off her face. "It's not a problem," he said quietly. "You've had a lot on your plate, sweetheart."

"I guess that must be it." The apartment was cool and dark and Katie looked so tempting, so soft. "Did I sleep all the way home?"

"Not all the way."

She covered her face with her hands. "Oh gosh. I'm so embarrassed. You're always seeing me at my worst."

"That's an impossibility, Katie."

"Luke," she warned, but with a smile on her face.

Yeah, he knew the drill. She was constantly giving him warnings. Yet Katie didn't know how hard it was standing this close to her while she looked so damn tousled and sexy. She had no idea how hard it was for him to say goodnight when he was legally married to her. He summoned up his willpower. "I'd better get going. Let you get some rest."

Was that a twinge of disappointment in her eyes? "It's probably for the best."

"Yeah," he said, hating to go. He touched a finger to her cheek and then kissed her there, softly, tenderly. "Good night then." He turned away from her, leaving her looking a little bit lost in the middle of the room.

When he was halfway to the door, she called to him. "Luke?"

He spun on his heels and faced her.

She took a big swallow. "Don't go."

Oh God. He drew breath into his lungs and approached her. "Why?"

"I mean you can go if you want to, but I'm just saying I'm not as tired now and if you'd like to stay for coffee or a drink, that would be nice. But you don't have to, you can always—"

"I'll stay."

"You will?"

He nodded. She had no idea how much he'd wanted to hear those words.

"But if I do, I'd want—"

"I, uh, sort of know what you want, Luke." She squeezed her eyes closed briefly.

He scratched his head. She was just so adorable. "I was going to say I'd want a cupcake with that coffee. If it's not too much trouble."

A look of relief swept over her face. "No, not at all. I'm your go-to for all things cupcake."

His go-to for all things, period.

"Just kick me out when you want me to leave," he said. They'd lingered after the bridal shower, Katie going gaga over Drea's gifts and talk of the wedding, while he had beers with both of his brothers, but it was still early in the evening.

She chuckled. "Don't worry. I will."

He didn't want to dwell on how easy it was for her to reject him, time and again. "So, are you always this peppy after a long nap?"

"I don't know. I usually don't take naps," she said as she walked into the kitchen and flipped on the light. She arranged half a dozen mouthwatering cupcakes on a dish and put them on the table, then began making coffee. "Have a seat."

Luke opted not to sit at the table. He leaned against the kitchen counter, watching her work. It smelled good in her kitchen, like sugar and warmth. "I plan on going to the rescue tomorrow. Haven't been back since Snow passed."

"Neither have I," she admitted. She stopped pouring ground beans into the coffee maker and bit her lip. "It's gonna be hard going back."

"Yeah. But there are so many other horses who need attention. After the wedding, I'm going to look into raising funds for Red Barrel. I've already spoken to Wes about it. They could use more financial support."

"It's a good idea, but I know your family—you, mostly—have been donating on a regular basis."

"How do you know that?"

"I hear things and that's all I'm going to say."

"You like keeping secrets, is that it?"

Her eyes grew as round as the cupcakes on the platter. "I certainly do not. I'm a very honest person and I hate secrets. You're the one making anonymous donations to the rescue and secretly marrying the first girl too drunk to know better." She blinked several times.

"First of all, sweetheart, it's not a crime to make a private donation once in a while. And second of all, you're not the first girl."

"Oh."

"You're the only girl."

She met his eyes and whispered, "Don't, Luke."

"Why'd you really invite me in tonight? And I want the honest truth."

She put her chin up, as if refusing to answer, but he stared at her for a long time and then her eyes fluttered and finally she admitted, "I get lonely…sometimes."

His heart pulled tight and he touched a finger to her

cheek, the skin smooth and soft there. "You don't ever have to be, not when I'm around."

She took a hard swallow, her eyes filled with regret. He hated seeing her looking so torn and scared. He couldn't have her afraid of him. She had to know he was her safe space. Leaning against the counter, he took her hand and brought her into the cradle of his arms. Her body pressed against his and all his willpower dashed out the window. *Oh man.*

"You don't have to say those things," she said quietly. "You're not really my husband."

"We have a marriage license to prove it," he said, kissing her forehead.

"It's just paper. It's not real."

"It's not just paper, sweetheart. And that's why you're fighting it so much."

"We've had this argument before," she said softly.

"Let's not have it again." And then he brushed his lips over hers and made love to her mouth until the coffeepot sizzled and the cupcakes were long forgotten.

Katie didn't want to have this uncanny, impossible attraction to Lucas Boone. Her brain was telling her no, no, no, while all other parts of her body screamed out yes. She'd never been in this kind of dilemma before. Usually she'd follow reason, but Luke had turned her rational thinking upside down.

Now, after abandoning the coffee and cupcakes, both stood naked and aroused in her bedroom facing each other. It was a blur how quickly they'd shed their clothes and wound up in here. One earthquake of a kiss was all it had taken. They were cast mostly in shadow with only a glimmer of moonlight peeking in through the shutters.

"I want to know all of you," Luke said, taking her hand

and kissing the inside of her palm. "I want you to know all of me, too."

Katie drew breath into her lungs. It seemed the harder she pushed him away, the more she thought about him, the more she wanted him. And now she was giving in to her true feelings, too tired to fight them any longer.

She knew what he wanted and as she touched him, caressed him, she could only relish his groans of pleasure, his quick breaths. It was too good, too delicious, the sensations wrapping them both up causing heat to climb rapidly.

And when she was through pleasuring him, he kissed her long and hard and then moved her onto the bed and returned the favor.

She was out of her mind with one burning hot sensation after another. He was a master with his mouth, his hands. He knew not only where to touch her, but how to touch her, making her feel worshipped and treasured. His kisses made her pulse with lust and need. Then when his broad, powerful body covered hers, sheathed in protection and moving deep inside her thrust after thrust, she cried out his name and climaxed to the highest peak.

It was beautiful. It was perfectly amazing. And scary as hell.

Minutes later, Luke tucked her close, spooning her, his breath soft on her neck. He reached around to cup her breast with one hand and fondle her with his masterful fingers.

"You're beautiful this way," he said, kissing her shoulder.

"What way?" she asked, smiling. She was still blissfully coming down from her release.

"Naked."

She laughed.

He kissed her again. "But I also like it when you're relaxed like this."

"Hmm. We do well like this," Katie admitted.

"Excuse me, did I just hear you say you think we're good together?"

"I wouldn't go that…far. Oh." He strummed his thumb over her nipple, sending immediate heat down to her belly. He was relentless, toying with her body, his hand stroking over places that could make her weep in pleasure.

"You wouldn't?" He brought his mouth to her shoulder and kissed her again and again. She squeezed her eyes tight. "Tell the truth."

"We can't be…together, Luke."

"Seems like we are together, sweetheart. And it's no use trying to deny it."

She turned to face him. She had to keep her resolve firm or they'd all live to regret it. "Luke, let's not argue about this. Not tonight. Can we change the subject?"

He paused, masking his feelings with a blank stare, which was fine with her. She didn't want to delve too deeply into his emotions. Or hers, for that matter. "What would you like to talk about?"

She turned onto her back and focused on the delicate patterns created by moonlight on the ceiling. "How about your father?"

"My father?" She'd surprised him, but she'd always been curious about Henry Boone. He'd been legendary, but she was curious about something that was said about him.

"Yes," she said. "He had a reputation for being sort of a… Well, there's no other way to say this. It was rumored he was quite ruthless in business."

"That's what happens when you're wealthy. People start thinking the worst of you."

"Really?"

"Happened a lot in my family. Before Drea learned the truth, she believed my father swindled Drew out of his ranch, Thundering Hills. Yet, all my father was trying to do was protect her from the truth. Drew had gone through quite a rough patch after his wife died and he'd made a secret deal with my dad to buy his ranch and put the money away for Drea's education. Drea wasn't told the truth until she fell in love with Mason."

"It was hard on Drea when her mom died. So, when you were talking with Mason the other night at dinner about how your father welcomed competition, you were speaking the truth?"

"Yes, my father was a fair man...to an extent. He always protected the town and made sure that the townsfolk came before dollar signs. It's how Boone Springs has thrived."

"And you and your brothers follow in his footsteps?"

"We try."

"I've always felt blessed that my shop has done so well. I thought for sure another bakery would've opened up by now. We're a growing community and—"

"You don't have to worry about that, Katie."

"What?" There was something in his tone, a finality in his voice, that worried her. She nibbled on her lip.

"You're the best baker in Texas."

"I'm sure I'm not. But just then, you seemed so confident. What are you not telling me?"

"Nothing, sweetheart. Just drop it."

"Luke, there's five bakeries in Willow County and I always wondered why I'm lucky enough to have a monopoly on the bakery business in Boone Springs."

"The grocery stores sell baked goods."

"Not the same thing. I've been in business almost seven years and in all that time, no one has tried to open a bakery that I know of. I think I'll ask April why that is." April, soon to be Risk's wife, was a Realtor. She knew both Willow and Boone counties very well. "She should know."

"Maybe, or maybe you should just count your lucky stars."

"What does that mean?"

"Nothing, sweetheart. Just don't involve April in this."

"In what?" Luke was being obtuse, deliberately trying to hide something. He kept his lips buttoned up tight.

When he reached for her, she pulled away. "Tell me."

He sighed and scrubbed his jaw. "You know the Boones own more than half of the properties in town."

"Yes, common knowledge. So?"

"So, we have a plan for the town, and each one of us has input."

"Okay?"

"That's it, Katie."

Baffled, she shook her head. "What's it?" Then a thought flashed in her mind and she couldn't let it go. She had to find out the truth no matter how the notion sickened her. "Are you saying the Boones have made sure I've had no competition?"

"Not the Boones. Just me," he said on an uncharacteristic squeak.

"Just you?" She didn't understand. Luke was confusing the hell out of her. "Why on earth would you do that?"

"It's not a bad thing, Katie. We've only had two inquiries and, well, they found better deals elsewhere."

"Because you made sure of it." Katie's emotions ran rampant. Anger, disappointment, betrayal. All of it made her heart ache. She rose from bed and threw on her clothes quickly.

"Katie."

"Get dressed, Luke. Right now."

As she watched him put on his clothes, she shook uncontrollably. Now that he was dressed and she didn't have to look at his striking body, she tried to make sense of this. She stood across the bed from him. "When did you do this? And I want the absolute truth?"

"Five years ago."

"Five," she whispered. *Five.* Frustrated, tears welled in her eyes. "Why, Luke? I don't understand."

"Don't you, Katie? Don't you know?"

She shook her head. She had no clue. Five years ago, he was dating her sister. Five years ago, he'd abandoned her sister. Five years ago, he'd joined the Marines.

Luke walked around the bed and came to face her. He placed his hands on her shoulders and she was forced to look into his melt-your-heart blue eyes. "Katie, I'm in love with you."

"No!"

"I am. And I've been in love with you for a very long time."

Oh God. She was afraid to ask. "H-how long?"

"More than five years now. When I realized I loved you, I had to back out of the wedding. I had to. I knew it was crazy and impossible. And so… I left town."

"That's why you joined the service?" She trembled from head to foot.

"Yes," he said on a long breath as if he was finally relieved to confess it. He stroked her arms up and down.

And then it all dawned on her and she flipped his arms off her and backed away. She was the reason Shelly's heart had been broken. "Oh no. Oh no. Oh no." She couldn't believe this. She couldn't comprehend what he was saying. But she knew deep down in her heart it was true. It all made sense now. "I never encouraged you."

"You didn't have to, Katie. You were just you."

"God, Luke. This is making me sick. Really sick. You have no idea how hurt Shelly was, how hard those first few years were for her. And now I find out it's all because of me! I'm to blame for all her pain." Tears streamed from her eyes now, big salty drops spilling down her cheeks.

"Nobody's to blame, Katie. You can't help who you fall in love with."

"Obviously you couldn't. And I'm not forgetting your duplicity about the bakery either. My goodness…you are certainly not like your father. You don't play fair."

Luke's eyes grew hot and he clenched his teeth. "All I wanted was for you to have a good life, Katie. I wanted you to be happy, to be successful."

"And you didn't think enough of me to let me go after that success on my own."

"My God, woman. You are being irrational."

"I'm being real, Luke. And honest. I don't want you to love me. I want a divorce as quickly as possible. And I want you to leave."

Luke looked her square in the eyes. "Fine."

"Well, good. Now go."

"I'm gone," he said.

After he slammed the door behind him, Katie's stomach gripped tight and she raced to the bathroom, throwing up into the toilet until there was nothing left.

Six

Katie stared at the stick in her hand, looking at it hard and praying the results would miraculously change, but that was too much to hope for. The stick wasn't changing, nor had it changed the last two times she'd taken the pregnancy test this week. The nausea, her late period and three pregnancy tests weren't wrong. She was going to have Luke's baby.

Luke, the guy who'd proclaimed his love for her last week. Luke, the guy who'd made sure her bakery wouldn't fail, regardless of her talent. Luke, the guy who'd caused her family undue heartache.

She fought the guilt that was eating away at her. What would Shelly think? What would she say?

Katie searched her mind, struggling with her memory, trying to recall her interactions with Luke back when he and Shelly were dating. Had Katie somehow given him the wrong idea? Had she done anything to encourage him? She wasn't a flirt. She'd never been good in that department.

No incidents came to mind, except her times working with him at the Red Barrel and sharing their love of horses.

It was hard to believe any of this, but now reality was staring her in the face on that stick.

Trembling, she touched a hand to her belly. Where could she turn? Who could she confide in? Drea was going to be married into the Boone family in a few weeks. Katie couldn't tell her best friend, could she? She certainly couldn't tell her sister or her mother, that was for sure. The news could very well send her mama back into the hospital.

"Oh, Katie, what are you going to do now? You're pregnant." Saying those words out loud, no matter how quietly, had impact. It made it real and there was no going back, no way to fix this.

She stared at herself in the bathroom mirror. How much longer could she hide her fatigue and nausea? And soon, she'd have a baby bump to hide as well. She had always wanted children, she wanted this one. It wasn't the baby's fault she'd gotten into this complicated mess. The child would be loved. Always loved.

A knock on her door made her jump. She tossed the box into the trash and straightened up her appearance.

"It's me, Drea," her friend called out.

Katie squeezed her eyes closed. Was it that time already? She was supposed to be dressed and ready to go with Drea for the final fitting on her wedding gown, but she was moving slowly this afternoon. "Coming," she said.

She opened the door and Drea took in her appearance. Oversize sweats weren't what she usually wore to go out. And well, Katie's face probably blended in with the shabby chic color on her walls. Only the paint was in style, and Katie was anything but.

Drea's big smile faded. "Katie, are you okay? You look a little...under the weather."

Of course her friend would think that. Perky Katie was

always ready for anything. She worked ten hours a day and ran around town like a spark was lit under her butt. She could juggle her career and her volunteer work and still have energy to spare.

"Nope, I'm fine," she said. "Come in."

"Okay, but we don't have to rush. We don't need to be at Clara's Bridal for an hour."

That sounded good to her. She still needed to get dressed and rushing around wasn't in the plan. "I've made a pot of jasmine tea. Would you like some?"

"Yes, sounds wonderful."

"Want anything to go with it?"

"No cupcakes for me. Remember, I have to get into my wedding gown today." Drea made herself comfortable at the kitchen table and Katie brought over her rose-patterned teapot. She sat down, too and poured the tea. "You have such a sweet expression on your face right now. I think love has gone to your head."

"I have to keep pinching myself that I'm getting such a great guy. Say, when we're through at Clara's, would you like to have dinner at the ranch with all of us?"

It was the last thing she wanted to do. She hadn't seen Luke in a week, and she'd rather it stay that way. After their last encounter, she'd contacted an attorney about the divorce, but that was just in the early stages. At least she was doing something about it. "Uh, I don't think so, but thanks anyway."

Drea pierced her with a curious look. "You look about as glum as Luke does. What's with the sour puss, my friend? Is something going on between the two of you? Because if it is, I'm here to listen."

Luke was in a bad mood lately? Why? Because she'd tossed him out of her apartment when he'd shocked her with his declaration of love? How on earth did he expect her to absorb that news? And now her best friend was asking probing questions.

"Oh, would you look at the time? I'd better change my clothes and get ready. Don't want to be late. I'll just be a few minutes."

Katie escaped Drea's questioning stare and walked into her bedroom. Her shoulders slumped and all the energy seemed to drain from her body. What in the world was she going to do?

"One thing at a time," she whispered. And right now, she had to put on a happy face and be the best maid of honor she could possibly be.

She took some time to gather her thoughts and then put on a floral sundress. She tossed her arms through a cropped sunny yellow sweater and slipped into a pair of pumps. Next, she rimmed her lips with rosy gloss and colored her lids with eye shadow, hoping to hide her pale complexion. Then she scooped her hair up in a twisty bun and was good to go.

On a deep sigh, she walked out of the bedroom. "I'm ready," she called out and found Drea just coming out of the bathroom.

"Apparently that's not all you are," she said, sympathy touching her eyes. She lifted the empty pregnancy test box. "I wasn't snooping, honest. But I saw this in your trash can, honey. Are you?"

Katie squeezed her eyes closed. She hadn't wanted to tell anyone, not yet. But now she was trapped and maybe that wasn't such a bad thing. She needed a friend, someone to confide in. "I am. I mean, I think so. Three pregnancy tests wouldn't lie, would they?"

"Do you have other symptoms?"

Katie nodded.

Drea walked over to her and gave her a big hug. "Oh,

Katie." The embrace lasted a long time and then Drea broke away. "Can you tell me about it?"

"We have to go to your fitting. It's important."

"You're more important. I'll change the appointment for tomorrow, not to worry." She pulled out her phone and called the bridal shop. They seemed to be accommodating her, and Katie felt terrible letting her friend down this way.

After she ended the call, Drea took her by the hand. "Now, come sit down on the sofa and talk to me." They sat facing each other. "I have a feeling Luke is the father. Am I right?"

"Yes, you're right," Katie said. "It's a long story."

"I'm here to listen. You can trust me."

"Luke doesn't know. And he can't know. Not until I can divorce him."

Drea blinked several times, shock stealing over her face. "Divorce him? Katie, you married Luke?"

She nodded, her emotions a wreck. Tears built up behind her eyes. "It's not what you think. It's worse. And I have to swear you to secrecy, Drea. Nobody else can know right now."

"Not even Mason?"

Several tears spilled down her cheeks. "You see, that's why I couldn't tell you. I don't want to put you in a compromising position. You shouldn't have to keep secrets from your fiancé."

"I, uh, I promise I won't say anything...until you tell me I can. Right now, you need my help and I need to be here for you." Drea took her hands and gave a gentle squeeze. "I want to help."

Katie nodded. "T-thank you. I know this isn't e-easy for you."

"I'm going to be fine, it's you I'm worried about. Now start from the beginning and tell me everything."

Katie started talking, the words spilling out of her mouth

easily now that she was finally able to unburden herself and share her innermost secrets with her best friend.

Luke sat as his desk at Boone Inc. staring at the computer screen, too absorbed in what he was about to do to concentrate on work. He glanced at his watch. It was almost time for him to end his marriage to Katie. However short-lived, he'd loved thinking of her as his wife. But that would be over soon. His attorney was due any second now.

Luke rose from his desk and walked over to the stocked bar in the corner of his office. He picked out the finest bourbon on the shelf and poured himself a drink. He needed fortification today to go through with this. It was what Katie wanted and the last thing she'd said to him as he'd walked out her door. She didn't want his love. She wanted a divorce.

And now he was about to grant her wish.

He took a large gulp. The alcohol burned this throat going down, but it also helped soothe his wrecked heart. He couldn't hold on to Katie if she didn't want him. Didn't love him.

Only, he believed she did. She was just too frightened to admit it.

Katie wasn't easy. She wouldn't have made love to him if she wasn't emotionally involved. He knew by the way she sizzled from his touch, the way she'd kissed him back so passionately she'd nearly bowled him over. The way she'd granted him her body so generously when he'd worshipped her. It wasn't just sex between them but if she refused to admit her feelings, what else could he do?

Every bone in his body rebelled at what was about to happen, but he cared about her enough to let her go. To free her from their secret marriage so she wouldn't lose the love of her sister, her mother.

The knock on the door came too quickly. He swallowed

another swig of his drink. "Come in," he said, setting the tumbler down on his desk. He stared at the door as if it'd bite him and was relieved to find his brother Risk walking in instead of Carmine Valencia, his attorney.

"Hey," Risk said.

"Hey back at ya. What's up?"

"Nothing much. April's out with the rest of the brides-maids, going for fittings or something. Want to have lunch at the Farmhouse Grill? My treat. I have a few hours to kill and I'm craving their pulled pork sliders."

Luke shook his head. He'd deliberately set his appointment with Carmine in the Boone Inc. offices rather than at Rising Springs. It wouldn't do to parade his lawyer in front of his relatives. "Sorry, no can do. I have an appointment in a little while."

"Someone more important than your brother?" Risk chuckled and then glanced at the near empty bourbon tumbler on his desk. "You're drinking this early? Whenever I used to drink before four, it had something to do with a woman."

"Those days are over for you. Lucky you."

Risk moved farther into the room and pinned him with a sober look. "Hey, why the bitterness? What's going on?"

Luke sighed. "Nothin'."

"Something. Who is she?"

"Mind your beeswax, Risker."

"Using my childhood name that always got on my nerves? Okay, now I know there's something wrong."

"Listen, Carmine will be here any second. So, I can't have lunch with you. Sorry, bro."

"Carmine, as in your personal attorney?"

"Yep."

"Are you okay? You've been quiet and, well, grumpy this past week or so."

Luke put on a smile. "I'm fine. Just let it be, Risk. Will you?"

His brother eyed him, concern in his expression. It was hard to fool his brothers. "Yeah, but…"

"I know. If I need your help, I'll ask. But trust me, this isn't anything you can fix."

Nobody could.

Luke's mood was about to go from gray to black. As soon as Valencia walked into the office and started the divorce proceedings.

Two days later, Luke drove to Red Barrel Rescue. In many ways the rescue had rescued him, giving him an outlet for his loneliness. Giving him a chance to think without anyone asking questions or judging him. Helping heal the neglected and sickly horses put life in perspective. It gave him balance and helped him recover from the hard times he'd had in Afghanistan, the soldiers who'd been left behind. While he was in the Marines, he'd longed for home, for Katie, and the hardest part of it all was not being able to tell another soul what he was going through. He'd kept his secret love for her locked away.

And now after making arrangements with his attorney, the divorce was in motion.

Even though Katie didn't want anything from him, he'd made a few stipulations that he believed to be fair. He wasn't going to leave Katie in the lurch. If she wanted a divorce, she'd have to agree to his terms.

Luke parked his truck and waved at Wes, who was in one of the corrals trying to calm a horse. The horse snorted and paced back and forth, a frightened look in her eyes. Wes wasn't making too much progress with her.

Luke walked over to the fence and Wes approached. "Hello, Luke."

He gave Wes a nod. "Looks like you've got a new guest."

"We do. She's a feisty one. Mustang. Probably lost her

way coming down from the hills. Either that or someone figured she was too wild to deal with and left her stranded. She was brought in two days ago."

"Does she have a name?"

He laughed. "Katie stopped by yesterday for a bit. She named her Cinnamon."

Luke smiled as he watched the mare huff and stomp around the far side of the corral. "That sounds about right."

"Katie tried to work with her a bit, but it was no use. The mare wouldn't let her get close. I don't know which of the two females was more stubborn. Anyway, Katie didn't look so good, so I sent her home."

Luke swiveled his head toward Wes. "How so?"

"She looked worn out, sort of drained. Never seen her look that way before. That girl does too much."

"She loves coming here." Luke always liked watching her work with the animals, whether it was to exercise them around the corrals, or bathe and groom them, or give them the loving caresses they needed. He enjoyed working beside her, seeing her energy and compassion. But it worried him a bit that she was fatigued. He wondered if she'd feel better once she received his divorce papers. It hurt to think it, but being rid of him might just be good for her health.

"We love having her here. Hell, she once told me this place was like her second home."

"I believe that." He sighed. He hadn't laid eyes on Katie in nine days and he missed her like crazy. "Well, I'm here and have a few hours. Put me to work."

Wes gave it some thought. "Pepper's up next. She could stand to take a dozen turns around the corral with the lead rope. After that, all the horses are due for their feed."

"You got it. No mucking for me today?"

"You feel like mucking?"

"Nobody feels like mucking." Except he wouldn't mind

yielding a hoe and working up a sweat in the stables. Anything to take his mind off Katie.

After several hours of hard work at Red Barrel, Luke arrived home after eight and headed straight for the shower. He'd mucked after all, needing the hard work, needing to blow off steam, and now his whole body ached. He walked into the shower and lingered, the hot spray raining down his shoulders and chest.

But every time he closed his eyes, he saw Katie. He wanted her here, with him now, giving both their bodies a good washing and afterward…

Luke shook his head, trying to clear his mind of her. He had to get a grip.

The shower door latched behind him as he got out and dried off. He put on his jeans and a T-shirt and wandered downstairs. The house was unusually quiet for this time of night. No lights were on anywhere, which was how he liked it. Quiet and dark, like his mood. His stomach growled. He hadn't eaten lunch or dinner today and he needed sustenance.

As he headed toward the kitchen, he heard Drea conversing with someone and stopped just short of the doorway, not wanting to interrupt.

"I'm sneaking a bite of lemon chiffon pie," he heard her say quietly.

He realized Drea was speaking on the phone. He turned around to leave, and then Drea said, "Whoops. Sorry, Katie. I shouldn't mention food when you're nauseous. I heard the nausea and fatigue will pass after your first trimester. It's still so hard for me to wrap my head around. You're going to have a baby."

Luke's eyes opened wide. He slumped silently against the wall, shocked at what he was hearing.

"No, I promised you, I won't tell a soul," Drea whispered so quietly he could barely hear. "Not until you're ready."

Luke backed away from the kitchen doorway, his mind racing. Katie was pregnant? She was going to have his baby. Climbing the stairs, he tried not to make a sound. Once he reached his bedroom, he lowered himself down on the bed. After the shock wore off, pure joy filled him up.

It was what he'd dreamed about for so many nights. To have a family with Katie. To *be* a family. Luke closed his eyes, absorbing the news.

But his joy only lasted an instant. Why hadn't she told him? How long had she known? She'd pressed for a divorce over and over again. Did she hate him that much to deny him their baby? Or was it fear that kept her from revealing the truth to him?

No wonder Katie had been tired lately. No wonder she'd been emotional. He'd seen a subtle change in her lately, but he'd always thought it was their secret marriage causing her stress. Well, stress or no stress, Luke wasn't giving her a divorce. Not now. Not when there was a baby to consider.

His baby. His child. A Boone.

Thoughts ran rampant in his head. Should he confront her? Make her fess up? Prod her into a confession?

He was no bully. He wanted Katie to tell him on her own. He wanted to be a part of the pregnancy, a part of the birth of his child. Did he have it in him to wait it out? Hell, he didn't know. He needed advice and he needed it quick. There was only one person who would know what to do.

Aunt Lottie.

The next morning, Luke put on his walking shoes and caught Aunt Lottie just as she was about to take her morning walk. "Mind if I join you today?"

His aunt tried to hide her surprise. "Sure, I'd love that." She eyed him curiously but with a smile on her face.

"Thanks."

"I remember a time when you three young boys would hike way up to the ridge with me. I loved taking you for walks."

"And you'd turn your head and pretend not to see us all roll down the grassy hill and crash into each other." The image made him smile. "It's a good memory."

"It is."

He opened the door for her and they made their way down the road. His aunt was always stylish no matter what she was doing. Today, she wore a dark raspberry jogging suit, her blond hair pulled back in a perky ponytail, her shoes sparkling clean as if she'd never worn them a day in her life, while he knew better.

"It's hard to believe Mason is getting married in a week," she said. "I know your folks will be dancing at their wedding."

"They will, if Mom has anything to say about it."

Aunt Lottie looked off in the distance. "I miss them."

"Me, too."

They were quiet for a while, and then when they were far away from the house, and out of earshot of the crew, Aunt Lottie spoke up. "As much as I love having your company on this walk, I know something's troubling you, Luke. Care to share it with me?"

"Aunt Lottie, you're sure perceptive."

"I just know you boys. And unless I miss my guess, this has something to do with that adorable girl, Katie."

Luke drew breath in his lungs. "It does. I married her."

"You married her?" His aunt stopped walking and tried her best poker face, but the shock in her voice gave her away.

"When we were in Vegas. It's the cliché drunken-vows-at-the-Midnight-Chapel sort of deal. Nobody knows. Well, one other person knows, but I'm in terrible need of advice."

Aunt Lottie nodded her head. "Why do I think you're not too sorry about this marriage?"

"Because I'm not. I'm in love with Katie."

"Oh dear," she said. "I see the problem. Katie's family won't abide that."

"They have no love for me, as you know. But actually, that's not the problem. The real problem is that I just found out by total accident, that…that Katie is pregnant."

"Pregnant? Oh my." Aunt Lottie smiled. "It's a blessing, Luke. Babies are little miracles. But does that mean she hasn't told you?"

"Right, she hasn't told me. I just found out last night by overhearing a conversation. And well, Katie's been pressing me for a divorce. She's worried about her family's reaction and what the news of our secret marriage would do to her mother's health.

"Honestly, Aunt Lottie, I think Katie is running scared. I know there are strong feelings there. She's just afraid to admit it. Now I don't know what to do. I've spoken to my attorney about filing for a divorce, putting the wheels in motion because Katie wanted to have this whole thing behind her. Unfortunately, my attorney is too efficient, and the papers have already been sent. But I won't sign them. I won't divorce her now that she's carrying my child. But do I confront her about the baby?"

"Oh dear. Luke, I understand your impatience. But Katie is in a tough spot right now. She's probably as confused as you are. Don't put more pressure on her. Give her time to sort it out in her head. She'll do the right thing."

He ran a hand through his hair and sighed. "That's easier said than done."

"I know." She turned to him, wrapping her arms around his shoulders, lending support and love. "Be patient with her. In the end, she'll be grateful for it. And one more thing."

"What is it?"

"Don't you dare divorce that girl."

He laughed, feeling a lightheartedness he hadn't felt in a long while. "I don't plan to."

Katie fumed, staring at the divorce papers she'd received by special messenger today. She couldn't believe the terms Luke expected her to agree to. What was with that man, anyway? Their marriage wasn't real. It had been a big fat mistake. She'd told him she wanted nothing from him, not one thing. But did Luke listen? No. He'd had his attorney draw up papers that went totally against her wishes.

She wouldn't agree to his crazy terms. She picked up her phone and tapped out a text to him.

I need to see you, right away.

Her text was answered five minutes later. I can be there in half an hour.

She didn't want Luke coming up to her apartment. She'd been getting curious looks from Lori lately, but her friend and employee was too discreet to question her. Aside from that, Katie didn't want reminders of the last time they'd been together in her apartment.

She didn't love the idea of meeting him in a restaurant either. There were too many people who might overhear their conversation. She couldn't believe she'd had to resort to so much secrecy lately.

Not here, she texted. Meet me at Red Barrel in an hour.

Luke's text came in fast. I'll be there.

A short time later, Katie's anger still simmered just under the surface as she drove up to the rescue. She parked her car next to Luke's steel gray truck in the back of the parking lot. Apparently, he'd gotten here early and as she scanned the area, she found him leaning against the barn wall, the sight of him making her heart beat harder. Angry or not, whenever she spotted him, her initial reaction was breathless attraction, one she couldn't quite seem to shake. It ticked her off that her body betrayed her mind.

She hadn't seen him in over a week, but now his eyes held hers from across the yard, watching her every move. She grabbed her skinny briefcase out of the car, one that made her look professional. Luke pulled away from the wall, his tan hat low on his forehead, his swagger making her swallow down hard. Dressed in jeans, a tan chambray shirt and snakeskin boots, he epitomized Texas, the image of a man who knew strength and power.

He approached her, his intense sky blue eyes trained on her. She held firm, trying not to let her heart overrule her mission here.

"Katie, it's good to see you."

She swallowed. "Hello, Luke."

"You want to talk?"

"Yes, I do."

"There's no one in the barn right now."

Privacy was of the utmost importance to her and the barn would provide that. It was a slow time for the rescue. Most of the volunteers had already gone home. And Wes was usually in the office by now, finishing up on business.

"Let's go," she said.

"How are you feeling?" Luke asked as they headed for the barn.

"Me? I'm fine."

"It's just that you've been feeling tired lately."

"No more than usual," she fibbed.

Luke nodded and was quiet until they entered the barn. Once inside she stopped, shaking her head at his gesture for them to sit on a bale of hay.

He frowned and faced her.

She pulled out the divorce papers and held them tight in her hands. "This is not what we agreed on."

"What's wrong?"

"What's wrong is that you are proposing to give me half a million dollars and then pay monthly alimony of three thousand dollars! I can't take that. I told you I wanted nothing and I meant it. I do fine on my own. At least I thought the bakery was doing well until I found out why."

"You'd be successful regardless. Can't you forget about that?"

"No, I can't. I feel terribly betrayed. I feel like a fraud, like my hard work didn't mean anything, I was pretty much ensured a monopoly in Boone Springs. The idea keeps me up at night."

"Katie, dammit. You need to rest."

Her jaw dropped. Was he kidding? He was responsible for many of her sleepless nights. "Then stop making me crazy. I don't need your help or your money."

His mouth grew tight for a few seconds, his face tensing up. And then all of a sudden, his eyes softened, the dark blue hue turning lighter, brighter. A big smile graced his face. "You know something, you're totally right, sweetheart." He took the divorce papers out of her hand. "This is all wrong."

He tore the paper down the center, then neatly placed the two pieces together and tore them again. "Here you go," he said, giving the squares back to her.

She stared at the ripped papers in her hand. "What are you doing?"

"I'm trying to give you what you want."

"No... I don't think that's it. You gave in too easily. What are you up to?"

"Nothing at all. You didn't want what I was offering. We have no deal now."

"For heaven's sake, Luke. It's not a deal, it's a divorce."

"One in the same."

A grotesque shrieking sound coming from outside interrupted them. It was so loud and ungodly, she had to find out what it was. She ran to the barn door and looked outside to the corral.

A giant hawk was swooping down on Cinnamon, winging over the horse inches from her head. The mare backed up and huffed, whinnying in panic as the bird continued to terrorize her. The hawk didn't back down. It kept on swooping and screeching at the horse.

Katie raced to the fence and screamed at the hawk. "Go! Get out of here!" She called to Luke, "He's relentless!"

Luke ran past her and the next thing she knew, he was behind the butt end of a rifle, taking aim.

"You're not going to shoot him, are you?"

He took his shot, the sharp snap of gunfire exploding in her ears. The hawk flew away, leaving the mare in peace finally.

"You didn't miss, did you?"

"Nope, wasn't trying to kill it. Just scare the damn thing away."

"I've never seen anything like that. Have you?"

"It's nothing more than a mama protecting her young, I'd imagine. There must be a nest around here. Or maybe one of her young'uns fell from the nest and Mama took it out on the closest one around."

"Cinnamon?"

"Just speculating."

She pointed at the rifle Luke held in one hand. "Where did you get that?"

"From my truck. I didn't see Wes's car and figured he was gone. It was up to me to take care of it."

"Well, that you did." She swallowed. "Could you please put it away?"

Surprise registered on his face. "Sure thing. I'll be a minute."

He turned and walked off, and Katie took a good look at the mare. She was still, motionless as if the hawk had put her in a state of shock. Maybe it was the loud ring of the rifle as well.

Katie opened the corral fence, looking into the mare's eyes. She didn't flinch, didn't seem to mind her approach. "Easy, girl, I'm coming," she said. She took several more steps toward Cinnamon. "That's it. Good girl."

She was making progress, speaking to the mare as she inched closer and closer.

"Katie, get out of there. Now." Luke's voice came from behind.

"Be quiet. She's letting me approach."

"You don't need to approach her. She's a wild one," he said through gritted teeth. Katie didn't dare turn to look at him. He was following her around the corral fencing.

"Not now, she's not. Stay put, Luke."

"Like hell I will."

"She'll spook if you try to come in and you know it."

"Are you *trying* to give me a damn heart attack?"

She smiled. He was being melodramatic. Katie knew horses just as well as anyone in Boone Springs, and she knew this one was ready to make friends.

"There, there, girl," she said softly. She put out her hand. "We're gonna be friends, you and me."

The horse snorted.

Katie waited and finally Cinnamon took a step toward her and then another step. The horse kept her eyes trained on her. Katie did the same. They were forming a bond, trusting each other, although tentatively.

Finally, the horse halted, going as far as she trusted, and Katie took the final step toward her. Inching closer, she touched her palm to the mare's nose. The mare held still as Katie stroked her up and down. "You're a good girl, aren't you?"

"Katie, you proved your point. Now get out of there." Luke's voice was low and strained.

"I know what I'm doing," she murmured.

Just then a blue jay flitted over Cinnamon's head. After what she'd just been through with the hawk, the horse spooked and kicked up her front legs. She came down hard and slammed into Katie's side. The jolt tossed her onto the packed ground. "Ow!"

"Dammit." Luke catapulted over the fence and scooped her up. "You are insane," he said, as he carried her out of the corral. He latched the gate, gave one deadly look over his shoulder at Cinnamon and headed to the barn.

The sun was setting now, casting long shadows on the land. Whatever sunshine was left didn't follow them into the barn. Katie could only make out the lines of fury around Luke's mouth, the dangerous slant of his eyes.

"You can put me down now," she said quietly.

"Can I?" His voice was harsh, impatient. "Maybe you'll decide to do another fool thing, like chase after a mountain lion or wrestle a bear."

"Luke."

"Hell. Are you hurt?" He kept her close and let her down slowly, her body brushing against his. Once her boots hit the ground, he probed her shoulders, her arms, gently applying pressure to her rib area. "Any pain here?" he asked.

"No."

Reaching behind her, he checked her spine and lower back, then laid his hands on her buttocks. "Here?"

She cleared her throat. "Nothing hurts."

Yet his touch was familiar, comforting and welcome. She couldn't lie to herself anymore. Her body came alive under his touch.

"Thank God for that. You could've been crushed."

"But I wasn't."

"Pure luck." His anger mingled with a look of genuine relief. "Don't worry me like that again."

Katie absorbed his words. She should be spitting mad at him for making demands he had no right making, yet she wasn't mad at all. His concern touched her deeply. She couldn't remember feeling this way about anyone before or having someone care so much for her. She approached him and laid her head on his chest, enjoying the sweet sensations rushing through her. She'd never admit it to him, but when the mare bucked up and then came down, Katie froze, knowing she was going to get shoved. And she'd sent up prayers that the jolt wouldn't harm the baby she carried.

She'd been lucky her prayers were answered.

Luke stroked her back, letting his hands glide up and down, easing the rough knock she'd taken. It felt right all of a sudden, more right than it should, and she gave in to the comfort.

He tipped her chin up and claimed her mouth in an inspiring kiss. He tasted delicious and her yearnings heightened, her breaths came faster. Luke broke off the kiss and grabbed her hand. "Come with me," he said.

He tugged her to the back of the barn and grabbed a quilted horse blanket. Throwing it down over a bed of straw, he straightened it out a bit, then lay down, bringing her with him.

She turned to him. "What about Wes?"

"He's gone. I told him earlier I'd lock up for him if he had to leave. We're alone here."

They weren't entirely alone. An image flashed in her mind of the three of them becoming a family, her, Luke and their baby. Tears burned behind her eyes. She wanted to tell him so badly about his child, about him becoming a father. But she held back. Call her a coward, but she wasn't ready for the backlash. She wasn't ready to own up to the truth. He'd expect something from her, something she couldn't really give.

She was silent for a few seconds and then Luke asked, "Sweetheart, you sure you're not hurt?"

She took his face in her hands and pressed a kiss to his lips. "No, I'm not hurt, Luke."

Then she unfastened his shirt, one snap at a time, eager to touch his skin, kiss his powerful chest. And fall deep into oblivion until the stars faded in the night sky.

Luke shed his clothes quickly, with Katie not far behind. Then he covered his body over hers, warming her up, kissing her senseless. He loved this woman and had wanted to die a thousand deaths when he saw that wild mare nearly stomp the life out of her. Katie had been lucky and he hoped to heaven she'd take better precautions next time. If not for her, for their baby.

Surely, she wouldn't do anything to endanger their child, but for a moment there, back in the corral, Luke hadn't been sure. He'd nearly blurted out that he knew about the baby, and only stark fear from seeing that mare knock Katie to the ground had shut him up.

He wanted her to come to him with the truth on her own. He didn't want to bully it out of her. Aunt Lottie had told him to be patient, and he was trying. Really trying.

Her little moans brought him back to the moment and he kissed her again, weaving his hands in her long silky blond hair. She was sweet and gentle and beautiful everywhere. He treasured every morsel of her body, caressing her breasts, their undeniable softness arousing the hell out of him. Next, he lay his palm on her belly and sweeping joy entered his heart, thinking of the child they'd both created. But he didn't linger there. He moved his hand past her navel to stroke her inner folds. She was soft there, too, and her heat caused his breath to speed up and his body to grow painfully hard.

"Katie," he murmured, finding her sweet spot. He caressed her there, over and over, her body moving wildly until she whimpered and cried out his name. There was no better sound. Then he sheathed himself and rose over her, joining their bodies.

"Ah, Katie. You feel so good."

Minutes later, he found his release, and the joy and peace that went along with it.

Katie had to be his.

There was no other way.

Seven

Katie woke with a blissful humming in her heart. The first image that came to mind was being with Luke last night. Having him inside her, and how he'd thrilled her with his masterful thrusts until they both came apart.

She sighed deeply. Then her alarm chimed, giving her notice it was time to rise and shine. Well, she didn't know about the shine part, but she rose from her bed. Luke had warned her last night she'd be sore today from the fall she took and he'd been right. Her shoulders and arms ached, but nothing hurt more than her rear end.

She readied a bath, throwing in a bath bomb scented with lavender. When she'd undressed and was just about to put her toes in to check the water, her phone pinged.

It was a text from Luke.

How are you feeling this morning? Are you sore?

Yes, a little bit. I'll live. Why are you up at this hour?

It was just after four. Luckily, so far she wasn't nauseous, but the day was young.

Thinking of you. I can come by and rub the soreness away.

Katie smiled. Wouldn't you just love that.

So much.

Sorry, have to go. Just getting in the tub.

Want company?

No thanks. Go back to sleep.

I'll dream of you. In the tub.

Katie signed off and set the phone down, the sweet humming in her heart speeding up. Last night, Luke had charmed her and she wasn't sure it was deliberate on his part, but rather an organic charm, like the way his blue eyes often set on her, as if he treasured her. She also felt it in the way he protected and cared for her.

Yet, he'd gone against her wishes for a simple divorce. She'd said she wanted nothing from him. And she didn't. She'd have to fight him on that. She wouldn't take a dime of Boone money. When they divorced, it should be as if they'd never married. A clean slate. She'd never be his wife in the real sense.

Yet, he was relentless in his pursuit, making her forget all the valid reasons she had to push him away. Her sister, her mother's health, the bakery deception.

After last night, they hadn't spoken of divorce again. Luke had simply walked her back to her car and given her a quick kiss on the lips, making her promise to get to sleep as soon as possible. He'd followed her home, just to make sure she'd arrived safely.

Of all the men in the world, why did it have to be Luke?

She stepped into the tub and slid down, luxuriating in the sweetly scented water, letting the heat soak away her soreness.

She thought about the baby she carried, just a tiny speck of life that would change her whole world. And she also thought about her carelessness in the corral. She couldn't afford another mistake like that and she was grateful Luke had been there. Grateful nothing worse had happened. She'd never take a chance like that again.

Hours later, Katie stood behind the bakery case and greeted one of her first customers of the day. "Hello again," she said.

"Hi, Katie. Remember me? Davis Moore."

Katie sure did remember him. He'd come into the bakery with Shelly one day. "I do, Dr. Moore."

"Call me Davis."

"All right. What can I do for you today?"

"I'm here for a dozen of your best cupcakes. Give me a variety of them, please."

"Okay, sure. That's easy enough."

"And throw in a few of Shelly's favorites. I think she said lemon raspberry."

"Yes, that's right. She loves them."

"Well, good."

She studied the good doctor. He was tall and nice looking and seemed pleasant enough. "So how is Boone Springs treating you so far?" she asked.

"I like it just fine. The people are friendly. And the work is satisfying."

"I'm glad to hear that."

She packed up the box and he paid for the cupcakes. And then he stood there, hesitating.

"Is there anything else I can get you?" she asked.

"Uh, well." He glanced around the shop. Other than a few customers sitting at the café tables, it was just the two of them. "Shelly's been so kind to me, making me feel welcome and all, I want to do something nice for her. Do you know her favorite flowers?"

"Not roses," she blurted. Shelly had had a fascination with roses and they'd ordered hundreds of snowy white roses for her wedding to Luke. Ever since then, she abhorred every kind of rose. "But I know she likes lilies."

"Lilies. Okay. Thanks for the tip. I might've blundered with the roses otherwise."

"I'm sure she'll appreciate the thought."

"Thanks."

"Hey, Davis?" She stopped him as he was scooping up the box, about to leave. "I just want to tell you Shelly really admires you. The flowers will make her happy."

A big smile graced his face, and his eyes were twinkling. "Good to know."

Well, wasn't that interesting? Katie didn't mind nudging the good doctor in Shelly's direction. She hadn't told Davis Moore anything that wasn't true and if only her stubborn sister would open herself up to let someone in, Shelly might find some happiness one day.

Three days later, Katie sat in her mother's kitchen trying to disguise her queasiness. "Mama, you didn't have to cook for us." Her stomach turned just at the smell of the spaghetti and meatballs. She wasn't eating heavy meals lately, but she couldn't talk her mother out of it. It was Katie's favorite dish and her mom worked so hard at preparing it.

"I want to cook for my daughters for a change. You girls

are always cooking for me. You're on your feet all day long. And goodness, Katie, you've been looking tired lately."

"I've noticed it, too," Shelly said, putting out pasta bowls. "You're looking pale. Not getting enough sleep? Or are you doing too much for Drea's wedding? There's always something happening. Can't miss it in the headlines. Whenever a Boone sneezes, the local papers feel the need to report it. They're holding the rehearsal dinner at The Baron."

"Yes, that's on Friday night."

"Soon it will be all over," Shelly said, "and you won't have any reason to deal with Luke. It must be so awkward for you."

"It…is. But we've—"

"You've what?" her mother asked, sitting up straighter in her chair. Her mother appeared healthier today, which also meant she was more engaged in the conversation.

"We've, uh, found a way to deal with each other. He's… not a bad person, Mama."

"Says who? Any man who breaks my daughter's heart isn't getting nominated for sainthood, I can assure you. We all embraced him and he turned his back on us."

"Mama, he didn't turn his back on you," Shelly said. "He turned away from me. He didn't love me enough."

Katie's chest tightened. She felt guiltier than ever, because she'd been actually entertaining thoughts of a life with Luke. But once again, her family brought her back to reality. If they ever found out the true reason Luke left Shelly—because he was in love with her—and that she was now carrying his child, all hell would break loose.

Funny, when she was around all this negativity, her situation looked grim, but when she was with Luke, she could envision a happy life together.

It was all so very confusing.

"That man doesn't know what he's lost," her mother said.

"I don't think he cares," Shelly said.

"He cares," Katie blurted.

Both heads turned to her. "What?" her sister asked.

"I mean, Luke isn't a horrible person. He knows he hurt you, hurt us all, and he's sorry about it."

"And you know this how?"

"I've spent time with him, remember? At the rescue and in preparing for Drea's wedding. But he didn't want to… Oh, never mind."

Katie could tell by their narrow-eyed expressions they weren't buying any of this. And they were looking at her like she was being a traitor to the Hate Lucas Boone Club.

"You're right. There's no need to spend another second speaking of him," her mother said.

Katie wanted to skulk in the corner but she wouldn't because she was too darn curious about Davis Moore. She took a pasta plate to the stove and dished up a generous amount for her mother. "Here you go, Mama. The least I can do is serve you."

"Thank you, sweetie." Her mom smiled and it brightened her face. Katie remembered a time when her mom smiled a lot. That was a long time ago.

Once they were all sitting and Katie was pushing her pasta around the plate, she casually mentioned Shelly's new friend. "Davis Moore came into the shop the other day, Shel. Seems he does have quite a sweet tooth."

Shelly stopped eating, the fork halfway to her mouth. "I suppose he does."

"Did you get the lemon raspberry cupcakes he bought specifically for you?"

"Yes, I did."

"He seems like a nice guy. He's settling into Boone Springs well, or so he says. I guess you've been showing him around town?"

"Yes, some. He's quite remarkable, actually. Has a long list of accomplishments in—"

"He's handsome," Katie said.

"Katie, are you interested in him?" her mother asked.

Shelly squared her a look and Katie tortured her for a few seconds. "Me? No, Mama. I think you're asking the wrong daughter."

"Shelly?"

"Mama, it's nothing. I mean, I like him and he did send me a beautiful bouquet of lilies the other day as a thank-you. But we're just friends."

"I think he wants to be more than friends, Shel."

"Why, what did he say?"

"All good things," Katie answered.

Shelly blushed and her mother gave her an approving look.

It was progress, albeit very little.

But both of them still had no use for Lucas Boone and nothing Katie could say would change that.

Luke knew the exact moment Katie entered the rehearsal dinner at The Baron Hotel's Steak House because the entire dining room seemed to light up. Or maybe it was just him. Everything seemed brighter when Katie was around. She stole his breath wearing a one-shoulder black dress and tall heels, her blond hair up in a messy bun with wisps of hair framing her face.

He sighed. She still hadn't told him about the baby and his patience was coming to an end. He couldn't see any physical evidence of her pregnancy yet, but he knew their child was growing in her belly.

Didn't she know how much he'd want to be a part of it? How much he would cherish their time together until the baby came? He thought for sure they'd gotten closer after the night in the barn, but after that one text, she'd never returned any of his other calls or texts.

She was avoiding him.

Risk stood beside him as the bridesmaids entered the restaurant. They were all giggles and laughter, and right in the middle of it all was the happy bride-to-be, Drea. Soft music played in the background as the rest of the wedding party filed in.

"Guess everyone's here," Risk said. "What happens now?"

"Now we have drinks and food and Drew makes a speech."

"Isn't he doing one tomorrow?"

"Nope, that's my job," Luke said.

"I suppose Katie's giving one, too?"

"I suppose."

"Don't tell me you don't know every little thing about her, bro. She's on your radar twenty-four-seven."

"I'm in love with her, Risk. So yeah, she's on my radar. And that's just between you and me."

"Okay. Wow. Want to talk about it?"

"There's nothing to say. You know the situation with her family."

"Yeah… I do. Man, oh man. Does she feel the same way about you?"

Luke shrugged. "She's trying her best not to but yeah, I think she does."

Risk gave him a sharp slap on the back. "Hang in there, and try not to look like you're going to your own execution. For Mason and Drea."

Luke nodded. "I'll do my best."

He wandered over to Aunt Lottie. She looked brilliant tonight in a sleek sapphire pantsuit. She always wore the most exotic jewelry from her many adventures around the globe. Today her necklace made of gold and Asian sculpted jade caught his eye. "Aunt Lottie, you're looking mighty pretty tonight."

"Thank you, Luke. That's nice to hear."

"Would you like a drink?" he asked.

"I would love one."

He guided her over to the bar. "What would you like?"

"Wine sounds wonderful. A hearty pinot," she told the bartender.

"I'll have your best rye," Luke said.

"Yes, sir."

Once the drinks were in their hands, Luke walked with Aunt Lottie over to a corner of the room. "How's your... situation, Luke?" she asked quietly, sipping her wine.

"She still hasn't told me. I have to admit, it angers me. She's denying me my rights."

"But you don't blame her, do you?"

"I'm trying not to. She's the *one*, Aunt Lottie. I can't stand just waiting around for her to come to her senses." Luke took a swig of his drink, the whiskey going down smoothly.

"Being patient isn't easy, especially when you know the truth. I'm excited for you as well. I almost can't wait myself. You'll be the first one in the family to become... Well, you know."

He nodded, searching the room and finding Katie in conversation with both of his brothers. She would talk to them but not him. A surge of jealousy had him gulping down his drink.

"She's a pretty one, isn't she?" Aunt Lottie remarked.

"Beautiful."

His aunt touched his arm. "Be patient. It hasn't been that long. And I'm sure Katie is mixed up right now, trying to work things out in her head."

"I hear you," he said. "I just wish she would trust what she feels. Trust me."

Drew walked up then, and Aunt Lottie gave him a warm smile. "Hello, Drew. Are you ready for the big day tomorrow?"

"I am. How about you?"

"Yes, of course. You know how I feel about Drea. She's like the daughter I never had. I'll be very happy seeing Mason and Drea say their vows."

"It'll be a good day. Well, I'll talk to you later. Didn't want to interrupt your conversation."

"It's okay, Drew." Luke kissed his aunt's cheek. "You stay and talk to Aunt Lottie. I'm about ready for another drink. Excuse me."

Lottie watched Luke walk off, wondering if she'd given him the right advice. She'd certainly botched her own love life, so who was she to give him guidance on his?

She turned to Drew. "You look nice this evening."

In his dark suit and string tie held with a sterling silver and turquoise clasp, Drew had never looked more appealing to her. His snowy hair and slight beard were groomed perfectly, giving him an air of sophistication.

"Thank you. Same goes for you," he said. "I like that color blue on you."

She smiled. "Thank you. Are you nervous about your speech?"

"I'm not much for public speaking."

"I think you'll do fine. After all, you'll be talking about Drea."

"And what a lousy father I've been."

"That's past history. Drea adores you."

"She didn't always."

"She does now and that's what you have to focus on."

"I guess so. I appreciate the pep talk. Well, just wanted to say hello. I'll be getting to my seat. Looks like dinner's about to be served."

"Sure, okay," she said, deflated. Why didn't she tell him she adored him, too? Why didn't she apologize for believing he'd been interested in another woman? The man had been nothing but true blue and honest with her, and yet she'd managed to alienate him. After the way he'd kissed her the other day, she had no doubt about his feelings for her or her feelings for him.

She just wished she had the nerve to tell him.

Before it was too late.

Katie sat next to Luke at the rehearsal dinner. There was no escaping it. Mason was paired up with Drea, Risk with April, and she didn't want to make a big deal of changing seats.

The truth was, she was falling for Luke, and the more time she spent with him the harder it would be to say goodbye. They couldn't be a couple. They couldn't stay married.

But when the baby came, she wouldn't deny Luke his rights. Her child needed both a father and mother. She'd been deprived of that in her own childhood, and sure, she'd faired okay, but it was hardly ideal. Her child deserved better than having come from a broken home, even before he or she was born.

Unfortunately, right now it was the only way forward. After the wedding, she'd have no reason to see Luke. She'd tell him in her own way and in her own time and…she'd have to confess to her family, too. She wasn't looking forward to that. She kept praying a solution would miraculously present itself.

The impossibility of it all hit her and tears moistened her eyes.

"What's wrong, sweetheart?" Luke whispered ever so closely in her ear.

She shook her head, summoning strength. "Nothing,"

she whispered, making sure no one was observing their exchange. She faked a smile. "I'm fine."

And then Luke's hand found hers under the table. The comfort he lent felt good even if he was the last person who should make her feel anything. But his encouragement, his compassion, seeped into her and soothed her raw nerves. She had to think about the baby and what was best. When she was with Luke, she had trouble thinking of anything else but being with him…as a family.

And yet her worry about her mom and sister always seemed to ruin that fantasy.

Mason stood up then and thanked everyone for being a part of the wedding. He'd put gifts on the table and encouraged the groomsmen to open their small blue boxes. Luke was forced to let go of her hand to open his gift. She was hit with a wave of relief and sadness at the same time as he broke their connection.

"Gold cuff links," he said, glancing at her.

She smiled. "Those will look good on you," she said. "They're very nice." And they probably cost a fortune.

At times, she forgot about the Boone wealth and what it meant. But Luke wasn't defined by his wealth. He was down to earth and kind and generous. He ran Rising Springs Ranch, shared the corporation with his brothers and owned half the town.

He was a man's man, a guy any girl would love to have by her side.

Tears touched her eyes again. She was being hormonal, her elevator emotions going up and down.

"Hey, if you don't stop looking so sad, I might have to kiss you into a better mood," Luke said softly.

She gasped and eyed him, giving him a don't-you-dare look.

"Smile, Katie."

"For Drea and Mason?" She glanced over to where they

sat at the table. They were busy eating their salads and chatting with each other, happiness on both of their faces.

He shook his head. "For me."

Goodness, what was with his ego? "I have no smiles for you," she said through tight lips.

Luke grinned. "Katie, you're forgetting about the work we did at the rescue," he said loud enough for others to hear, if they were so inclined. "You were very diligent."

Her nerves rattled. Of course, no one would know what they were talking about, but she knew, and it was a visual she couldn't get out of her head. Being naked in the barn with Luke and having him make love to her had been exciting. He'd always managed to draw her out of her wholesome shell and make her do wild and sexy things. "I... know. Sometimes I get carried away."

Luke stared into her eyes. "But it's very much appreciated."

Heat rushed to her face. "Is it?"

"Yes, you have a knack, with stallions especially, that's really inspiring."

She rolled her eyes, hiding a smile. There were no stallions at the rescue right now. "You give me too much credit."

"Doubtful."

Just then, Drea rose from her seat. "I, too, want to thank all of you for being a part of our special day. I can't wait until Mason and I become man and wife with all of you very special people in attendance. And I have gifts for my wonderful bridesmaids, too."

She walked around the room, giving the girls beautiful embossed gift bags made of soft lavender linen, the same color as their gowns. When she got to Katie, she kissed her cheek. "Thank you for everything, my bestie. This one is special, just for you. Because you're my maid of honor."

"Thank you," Katie said, giving Drea a smile straight from the heart.

"Please open your gifts," she said to everyone.

Katie opened hers by pulling a drawstring and then reached inside. She pulled out a black velvet box and opened the lid. "Ah! This is beautiful." She lifted out a gold-and-diamond drop necklace. She was touched and truly surprised. She'd never owned anything this exquisite before. "I don't know what to say."

"Say you'll wear it tomorrow."

"Try to stop me." She hugged the necklace to her chest. Drea grinned. "I had help picking it out."

"Mason?"

She shook her head. "Luke. Actually, he has pretty good taste."

"You picked this out?" she asked him.

He nodded. "It looked like you. Bright and sparkly."

She blinked and didn't know what to say. He was constantly surprising her.

"I will treasure it," she told Drea.

An hour later, Katie walked out of the restaurant and heard footsteps hitting the ground behind her. "Katie, wait up."

She sighed, stopped and turned around to Luke. "What is it?"

"Let me walk you to your car."

"That's not necessary."

"No, but I'd like to." His jaw set tight and it was no use arguing.

"Suit yourself," she said lightly and as she began walking again he fell in step beside her. He was quiet, pensive, and she didn't know what to make of his mood.

Once she reached her Toyota in the parking lot, she spun around to face him. "Well, here I am."

"I can see that."

"Thank you for walking me. Now it's time for me to get going."

"Where to?"

"Home to pick up my things and then I'm spending the night at Drea's cottage. We're getting our hair and makeup done there in the morning. Drew's getting the place ready for us right now."

He nodded.

"I really should get going."

A tick worked in his jaw. "Katie, where do we go from here?"

There was an urgency about him that she didn't quite understand. Why was he being so persistent? "Luke." She glanced around. There were a few people getting into their cars near her. "This is hardly the time or place."

"Then you tell me a good time and place and I'll be there."

She sighed. "I don't know. We have issues. And I can't think about them at the moment. Why are you bringing this up now?"

"Because you've been avoiding me. You haven't been answering my calls or texts. I didn't want to say anything tonight, but at some point you're gonna have to face reality."

"And what reality is that?"

Luke's eyes narrowed. He opened his mouth to say something, then closed it again.

"Look, I just needed a...break," she said.

"From what?"

"From...you."

His lips went tight and the look in his eyes darkened. "From me?"

"Yes, if you must know. I can't think when you're around."

"That's right, I make you crazy."

"Yes, yes, you do and it's horrible."

His brows rose in surprise and a hurt look crossed his features. "Fine. I'll give you all the space you need," he said, his tone sullen.

"You don't have to get mad."

"I'm not mad," he said, his voice a harsh rasp. He opened her car door and gestured for her to get in. She slid into the driver's seat, giving him a last look.

Then he slammed the car door.

And refused her another glance.

Eight

Katie cried on the way to the MacDonald cottage. She wanted to shed all her tears before she spent the night with Drea. This was to be their special before-the-wedding slumber party. Just the two of them, like they'd planned since they were kids. She wouldn't spoil the fun by being a miserable companion.

But she'd hurt Luke, made him angry. And she didn't feel good about any of it: the divorce, her deception about the baby. She wasn't lying when she told Luke he made her crazy. He did, because he was the right man for her, under the wrong circumstances.

Why did it have to be him? Recently, she'd asked that of herself every single day. She couldn't take it any longer. She didn't want to hurt the people she cared about. It was time to own up to the truth. She would reveal her secrets and finally deal with the consequences.

After the wedding.

With that thought in mind, her tears stopped flowing. At

least she had a plan now and it made her feel one thousand percent better. As she entered the gates of Rising Springs Ranch, she stopped the car and tidied herself up, wiping her tears and putting on a fresh coat of lip gloss. Tonight, she would be the best, best friend to Drea she could be and they would have a fun time.

Katie started her car up again and slowly drove down the road past the main house heading to the cottage. With her maid of honor dress and shoes in the back seat as well as her toiletries, she was totally prepared.

What she wasn't prepared for was seeing the flames up ahead, blazing bright and licking the night sky.

Her throat tight, she drove farther down the road and immediately stopped when she spotted Lottie and Drea with looks of horror on their faces. She parked the car on the side of the road and ran to them, the acrid smell of soot and ash filling her lungs.

"Oh no!" Half of the cottage was on fire. "What happened?"

Drea was shaking uncontrollably. "Oh, Katie. My d-dad's in there. I don't know how it h-happened. But he left the dinner early to come home and fix up the house for us."

"Luke's gone in after him," Lottie cried out.

"Luke? Oh my God. How long has he been in there?"

"He ran in as soon as he spotted the flames. Firefighters are on the way, but Luke refused to wait."

Katie's heart raced. This couldn't be happening. Not to Drew and Luke. Her Luke. She'd never forgive herself if something happened to him. She should've told him…she loved him. She did. She loved him, but was too frightened to confess. And now she was scared to death she'd never get the chance to tell him.

He needed to know she was carrying his baby. She needed him to know he was going to be a father. Maybe he wouldn't have taken such a chance with his own life.

But Luke was tough, a Marine, and of course he'd head straight into a burning house to save a friend.

She closed her eyes and prayed for both of them.

She couldn't lose Luke now, not when she was finally able to admit her true feelings for him.

The wind shifted and they were blasted with heat, forcing them to step back several yards. To think, Luke was in there, trying to save Drew. Smoke billowed up and they waited impatiently, holding hands, tears spilling down their cheeks.

From a distance, sirens could be heard. The fire engines were on the property now, but Katie kept her eyes trained on the front of the house. "Luke, please, please be okay," she whispered.

And then from out of the smoke and flames, Luke staggered down the steps, his face a mass of black soot, as he half walked, half dragged Drew with him.

"Thank God!" Lottie exclaimed, running over to the fence and opening it.

Both men looked worse for wear, but they were alive and breathing on their own.

"Daddy, are you okay?" Drea ran over to help.

"He will be," Luke said. "I found him knocked out on the floor by the back door. He's got a big knot on his forehead."

Drew looked up and gave his daughter half a smile. "One of the candles I set out for you gals got too close to your curtains and caught fire. I went running through the house to get the hose and tripped over a box of your softball trophies," he told her.

Drea's face paled. "Oh, Daddy. I'm so sorry."

"I wanted to surprise you and Katie with the trophies. I've been cleaning them up and damn fool that I am, I didn't quite…" He began coughing hard, his face turning red from the exertion.

"It's okay, Dad. No more talking right now."

Katie glanced at Luke. He looked exhausted, too, and coughed every now and then. She wanted to run over to him and hug him tight, but the firefighters had just pulled up and were shouting orders. Paramedics took Drew and Luke to their van for observation, while the firefighters set their hoses up to battle the flames.

Katie stood by the van, watching them tend to Luke. Every so often, he would glance her way and she'd smile and wave, wiping tears from her eyes. She'd been given a second chance with him and she wasn't going to blow it.

Lottie and Drea stood by Drew's side as he was being examined. "You really should go to the hospital for a complete checkup," the paramedic was saying.

"You said I'm fine. I don't need any more checking up."

"I said there's no sign of smoke inhalation. But that needs to be confirmed."

"My daughter is getting married tomorrow, and I need to be there."

"Dad, it won't take too long," Drea said.

"I'm just fine, Drea."

Lottie touched the paramedic's arm. "Let me speak to him, please."

"Okay, ma'am. I'll be back in a few minutes after I call this in."

Lottie smiled at Drew. "You had me in tears." She walked over to him, arms extended, and gave him a big hug. "I've never been so frightened in my life. To think you might've died in that house. And I can't have that. I can't lose you. I can't stand the thought of us not being together a moment longer. Drew Joseph MacDonald, I love you very much. And if you'll have me, I want to marry you."

Drew blinked and rubbed his sore head. "Did I hear you right? You want us to get married. Maybe I did hit my head too hard."

"Yes, yes and no. Yes, you heard me right. Yes, I want to marry you. And no, you didn't hit your head too hard. At least I hope not. You'd better say yes, because I'm not going to let you alone until you do."

"Promise?"

"I promise."

Drew smiled. It was a whopper, and Lottie smiled right back at him.

Katie and Drea exchanged glances. Drea had prayed for her father to find happiness. Now her prayers were being answered.

"I love you, Lottie. And I'm honored to marry you," he said. "Don't know if I'll have a house for us to live in though."

"We'll figure it out. It'll be our little adventure."

"Now you've got me looking forward to having an adventure with you."

"Oh, and one more thing, Drew," Lottie said. "You need to be checked out tonight at the hospital."

"No, I don't—"

"You do. And so does Luke. But don't worry, I'll go with you and make sure you get to the wedding on time."

"Bossy woman."

"You love it."

He grinned and pulled her close. "Guess I do."

And then he kissed her.

Once the paramedics were through checking over Luke, Katie walked over to him, put her arms around his neck and kissed him solid on the mouth. She didn't care who witnessed it, or what they thought. She just wanted Luke, period.

He snuggled her close, his eyes gleaming. "Are you going to propose to me?" he asked.

She brought her mouth to his and kissed him again. "Silly man. I'm already your wife."

"But you don't want to be."

"I'm rethinking that, Luke." She smiled at him and he blinked.

"You are?"

She nodded.

Luke's expression changed and his mouth spread into a grin.

Katie put her hands on his soot-stained face, looked into his blue eyes. "You saved Drew's life. It was a brave thing to do, but it scared me half to death."

"I just reacted. I couldn't let him die inside the house. I had to go after him."

"You risked your life."

"It was worth it. And there's an added plus."

"Oh yeah? What would that be?"

"You're here with me. And your eyes have a certain gleam. Sort of like the way you'd look at Snow, or one of your delicious cupcake concoctions."

"You do realize you just compared yourself to a horse and a cupcake," she said softly, admiring his handsome face and thinking of what might have happened to him.

He chuckled. "Katie, you're too much." He bent his head and kissed her, and it was better than anything in the world. But he needed more medical attention and she needed to wrap her head around loving him. She backed away, imploring him, "Be patient with me. For just a little while longer."

Before he could respond, Drea walked up with Drew and Lottie, all three holding hands. Drea stepped up. "I'll never forget what you did tonight, Luke." She was obviously rattled, the prospect of losing her dad keeping tears in her eyes. "You're a good man."

They embraced, Drea hugging him tight.

"Does that mean I'll be your favorite brother-in-law from now on?"

Drea smiled. "Risk would have to do something pretty great to top this. Saving my dad, that's a pretty high bar."

Drew walked over to him. "Let me shake your hand, Luke." Then he swiped the air and put his hand down. "Forget that." He wound his arms around Luke and gave him a big manly hug. "Thank you, son. I wouldn't be here if it weren't for you."

"You're welcome, Drew."

"I don't know what else to say. You risked your life to save mine. I'll be grateful to you for the rest of my life."

"No need for that," Luke said humbly. "Just make Aunt Lottie happy."

"I plan to." Drew gazed at Lottie with love in his eyes. It was beautiful to witness.

Lottie gave Luke a big hug, too. "Don't know what I would've done if I lost you both. You're like a son to me and I love you very much."

"Love you, too, Aunt Lottie."

"So then you'll get checked out at the hospital?"

"I'll make sure of it," Katie intervened.

Luke grabbed her hand. "You'll go with me?"

"Yes."

And if Shelly got wind of it, she'd have to tell her the truth. But luckily, she happened to know Shelly wasn't working tonight. She was taking her mother over to her friend's house for a nice long visit. It bought Katie a little time to reveal the truth.

When Mason and Risk showed up, everyone turned to them and filled them in on what had happened. They'd stayed behind to have drinks at The Baron before coming home.

As the fire was quelled, leaving only half of the three-bedroom cottage standing, everyone right then and there decided the wedding would go on as planned. It was set and ready to go.

They had something else to celebrate, too.

Drew and Lottie's engagement.

"I'm sorry for the way things turned out tonight, Drea." Katie handed her friend a glass of white wine. She happened to know this brand of pinot grigio was her favorite. The Boones had offered them the entire east wing of the second floor of their ranch house for tonight. They sat facing each other on the twin-size beds in one of the guest rooms. "Your dad's home is nearly destroyed."

"He'll rebuild, Katie. It'll give him and Lottie a chance to build something to their liking. Besides, I think my dad's happier than he's ever been. He and Lottie have been tiptoeing around each other for years. Now they'll finally settle down together. And he got a clean bill of health, thanks to Luke. If he hadn't rushed in to save Dad, the smoke would've gotten him before the fire did."

"Yeah, Luke's amazing. I'm happy he checked out just fine at the hospital, too. In that respect we were very lucky."

Drea smiled. "I saw you two kissing."

"I finally realized I love him. He's my guy."

"So, are you going to tell him everything?"

"I plan to. Very soon. I couldn't stand the thought of something happening to him before I had a chance to tell him he was going to be a father. It really put things in perspective for me. Our child deserves a loving home."

"I'm excited for you."

"Thanks." She bit her lip. "It's strange how things turn out sometimes, isn't it?"

"What do you mean?"

"Well, you hated Mason for what you thought he'd done

to your father. And I wasn't too keen on Luke, for what he did to Shelly. Now we're both in love with a Boone."

"You married one."

"And you're about to." Katie sipped her sparkling cider. "Let's not forget how much April disliked Risk when he first came back into her life, too. Their fake engagement led to the real thing."

Drea took a sip of wine. "Well, there's just something about those Boone brothers."

"I'll drink to that." She finished off her cider. "Oh my gosh, I just realized you probably lost a lot of your things at the cottage, too."

"I did, but I have what I need. I've been staying with Mason at the house, so half my stuff is here now."

"You're not panicked so I take it your wedding dress is safe and sound."

"Lottie picked it up for me from the bridal salon. It's here, at the house. She was going to bring it by the cottage in the morning."

"Thank goodness. Tomorrow is going to be a special day."

"You know, I wouldn't mind if you decided to wander over to the west end of the floor tonight, hon. Risk is at April's tonight and Mason decided to spend the night at The Baron."

"Because the bride and groom shouldn't see each other before the wedding?"

"Right...and we like the tradition. But tradition doesn't dictate anything about the best man and the maid of honor not seeing each other."

"Really...hmm. I wouldn't want to desert you."

"I'm starting to get super tired." Drea put her arms up and yawned. "And I need my beauty sleep."

"You're such a bad liar. But I would love to check in on him. Make sure he's okay."

Drea pointed toward the door. "Go."

"Gosh, now I'm getting thrown out of your room."

"Only because you've got something much better waiting for you across the hall."

Katie stood. "How do I look?" She fussed with her hair and straightened her dress.

"You could be wearing rags and Luke would think you were beautiful. You look great." Drea shooed her away. "It's down the hall and the last door on your right."

Katie blew her a kiss and made her way down the long hallway on bare feet, eager to see Luke again.

She knocked on his bedroom door three times. No answer. He was probably sleeping. Her desire to check in on him was stronger than her worry about waking him up, so she put her hand on the doorknob and opened the door.

As she stepped inside, she told herself she had a perfect right to check on her husband. He could've been injured or killed tonight running into those flames. But as she looked around, she found his bed was still made. Had he gone somewhere at this hour of night? She turned to leave, her hand reaching for the doorknob.

"Katie, where do you think you're going?"

She froze for a second and spun around. Luke was just stepping out of the bathroom, a towel draped below his waist. Moonlight glistened on his wet hair. Drops of water cascaded down his shoulders, falling onto his granite-hard chest. She itched to touch him there, to devour him and show him how much she loved him even though she had yet to tell him. "Luke, I didn't think you were here."

"I'm here." He smiled wide.

"Y-yes, you are."

He sauntered over to her. "Some nights I like to shower in the dark, with just the moonlight streaming in. It's quiet and peaceful that way."

"Oh… I didn't know."

"There's lots of things you don't know about me, sweetheart. I can't wait for you to learn all of them." He moved closer, the scent of his lime soap wafting to her nose.

"I came to check on you."

He opened his arms wide. "I'm healthy, Katie."

Her gaze flew below his waist and the bulge hidden under the towel. "That might be an understatement, Luke."

He laughed, a mischievous sound that got her juices flowing.

"You sure you're not tired, because I don't have to stay—"

"You're joking, right?"

She smiled at him. "Y-yes, I think I am. I don't want to leave."

Luke opened his arms and she stepped into them. Someone up above was granting her wishes, because as his arms wrapped around her and snuggled her close, her every dream was coming true. There was only one tiny flaw in her plans to be with him tonight, but she shoved thoughts of her family aside. She wanted to be fully in the moment. And as Luke's lips touched hers, his hard body pressing against her and his desire under the thin towel barrier reminding her of the thrills to come, she washed away everything and everybody but what was happening between them tonight.

"Katie." His voice held awe and wonder. "This is where you're meant to be."

She overflowed with emotion. It was almost too much for her, this roller coaster of a night. She shook, unable to control herself. "Luke, just kiss me and keep on kissing me."

He gripped her head in his hands and crushed his lips over hers, his expert mouth making every bone in her body melt. She could faint from the delicious sensations he aroused. And soon her dress was off and they were on the bed, under the covers, Luke worshipping her body.

His heat was contagious. She was nearing combustion, but she held on, wanting to enjoy every minute of this night with him. A night filled only with desire. No problems, no issues, just two people expressing their love in the most potent way.

Katie's body erupted first, her orgasm reaching new heights. "Luke," she cried out.

And he was there with her, rising above, his hard body tightening up, his powerful thrusts and groans of pleasure beautiful to behold. He held her tight as his release came and she kissed him until his breaths steadied and they both fell back onto the bed.

"Wow," he said, as he ran his hand up and down her arm. "Just checking that you're real."

"I'm real. Realer than real, after that."

He laughed and kissed her shoulder. "Stay with me tonight. Be my wife in all ways."

"I will," she answered, wanting that so badly, too.

Luke looked at the empty place beside him on the bed and smiled at the note Katie had left for him this morning on her pillow.

Dear Husband,
Sorry, had to leave early. Today is all about Drea and Mason. See you soon.
Your Wife

Luke rose from the bed, breathing in Katie's pleasing scent. In his humble opinion, she always smelled delicious and today was no exception. He couldn't believe she was finally his, after all his years of trying to do right by her, of trying to deny his feelings.

She hadn't said the words he wanted to hear. She hadn't confessed her love or told him about their baby yet, but they had made great progress. Finally, Katie thought of him as her husband. She'd come to him last night, and all it had taken was him racing into a house on fire for her to realize she cared about him.

He stepped into the shower, letting the water rain down his body, wishing Katie was here. It'd been a fantasy of his, to have her all soapy and wet with him, but they had time for that. Today, his brother was getting married, and Luke had the honor of being his best man.

He dressed in jeans and a T-shirt, and glanced out the window to the yard below. A team of event workers were constructing an open-air tent to house two hundred and fifty guests. A dance floor was going up as well as tables and chairs. Mason and Drea had opted to speak their vows on the steps of the gazebo Mason had built in the backyard.

Rising Springs Ranch had hosted many events, but this was the first wedding, and the Boones were doing it big.

Luke walked down the hallway and across the bridge that led to the east wing of the house. He heard the girls giggling, Drea and Katie giddy with excitement over the wedding. Warmth spread through his heart as he made his way downstairs.

In the kitchen, Aunt Lottie was drinking coffee with Drew. Early risers. "Mornin'," he said to them. Lottie and Drew had eyes only for each other.

Then Drew sat up straighter. "Luke, boy, how are you feeling this morning?"

"I'm feeling fit. How about you?"

"I'm…doing fine. Lottie's making sure of it. She won't hear of me worrying about losing my place, not today. Much of what I lost can be replaced but today is Drea's special day. And as long as she's happy, I'm happy."

Luke gazed at the loving look on Aunt Lottie's face

and knew instantly these two people were right for each other. "Congratulations again. Seems we've got another wedding coming up."

"Yep, but we're happy to focus on this one today. Drew's giving away his daughter."

"Now, Lottie, I'm not keen on that phrase. I'm not giving Drea to anyone."

Lottie laughed. "What would you call it then?"

"I'm allowing Mason the privilege of marrying my daughter."

"And Mason knows it, too," Luke added. "When's he getting here?"

"Not until just before the ceremony."

Luke poured himself a cup of coffee and looked under the covered dishes to see the brunch Jessica had made for the bridesmaids. "Wow, that's a lot of food for the girls."

"I agree, so help yourself, and then vamoose for a few hours. The girls need to get all dazzled up. Myself included."

"And men tend to ruin their party? Is that what you're saying, Aunt?"

"Something like that."

Luke got the hint. "I'll eat fast and then be on my way."

He had something he needed to do at Red Barrel Rescue anyway.

Something that would make Katie happy.

Katie stared at Drea in the oval mirror in her room, noting the gleam in her eyes, the joy on her face. All the bridesmaids had already gone downstairs, giving her and Drea some alone time.

"Drea, you are beautiful. I can't even describe how amazing you look. Now I know what they mean when they say blushing bride. That's you, and guess what? It's time to go downstairs."

"It is," she said dreamily. "I'm…a little nervous."

"No need to be. I've got your back."

"Thanks, hon." Drea gave her a peck on the cheek, making sure she didn't smudge her pale pink lipstick. "And you look amazing, too. I love your hair like that." Katie's hair was pulled up in a very loose updo, with blond curls framing her face. "The band of flowers in your hair makes you look like a princess."

"It's a miracle what a hair and makeup artist can do with a hot mess like me."

"Shush, none of that. You're not a hot mess as far as I'm concerned. You're a beautiful mommy-to-be."

Katie turned sideways and glanced at her reflection in the mirror. "Do you see a baby bump?"

Drea grinned. "Not yet, but it'll be here soon enough."

Katie sighed. She still had trouble believing she was having a baby, and then her crazy symptoms would appear to remind her. Today, she'd been lucky: no nausea. Only bliss this morning, waking up next to Luke. She had him on the brain, but she had to remember that this day was all about Drea and Mason. "I hear the violinist playing. It's time to go."

"Okay," Drea said. "You first. I'll be right behind you."

As Katie walked out the back door and down the path leading to the gazebo, she found Mason waiting for his bride, an eager look in his eyes. Katie didn't linger on Mason but rather on the guy standing next to him, his best man, the man she'd married weeks ago. And didn't Luke look smoking hot in his tuxedo?

Katie couldn't seem to look away until the music stopped for a beat, and then the familiar wedding march began to play. Drea stood beside her father, their arms entwined. She was holding a bouquet of white gardenias and roses. Everyone stood and then Drea made the walk down the aisle.

Katie teared up, her emotions running high. This was a monumental day. Her bestie was marrying a great guy. And before she knew it, they spoke sweet, funny, loving vows to each other and were then pronounced husband and wife. It was a glorious ceremony and Katie's tears flowed freely, from happiness for a change.

Mason and Drea were met with great applause and they waved to their friends and family as they made their first walk as a married couple down the aisle. Next it was Katie and Luke's turn to leave, and she met him in front of the flower-strewn gazebo. He took her hand possessively as they made their way up the aisle and away from the seated guests. Once they reached the reception tent, he stopped and quickly kissed her, his eyes beautifully blue and twinkling. "You look gorgeous."

"So do you, Lucas Boone."

His grin made her dizzy. "I expect to dance with you all night long."

"Don't I get one dance with the groom?"

His mouth twisted adorably. "One, since it's my brother."

Photographers were snapping photos and a videographer was recording the entire event. Katie had a mind to release Luke's hand and hoped the kiss wasn't captured on film. These photos were bound to make the newspapers in Boone County. But as she pulled her hand away slightly, Luke tightened his hold, making it clear he wasn't going to play that game anymore.

It meant she'd have to speak with her mother and sister soon. Like tonight after the wedding, or tomorrow, at the latest.

Chandeliers hung from the high beams and the drapes were parted in strategic places to give the tent an airy feel in the late afternoon. Hors d'oeuvres and champagne were passed around by white-jacketed waiters and Mason and

Drea took their places at the head table beside Risk and April. Mason waited until his guests were all inside the reception area before he picked up a microphone.

"May I have your attention please? First of all, I want to thank you all for coming and sharing our special day with us," he said. The crowd settled and all looked his way. "I have an announcement to make. Actually, it's really a wedding present for my bride."

Surprised, Drea gave him a curious look, though her eyes were still glowing.

"Tonight, our musical entertainment will be provided by The Band Blue."

Sean Manfred walked into the tented area, along with the rest on his band.

Drea looked from Sean to Mason, and then tears flowed down her cheeks. "Mason, how did you manage this?"

"He didn't have to twist my arm very hard, Drea," Sean said. "Congratulations to both of you."

Drea gave Sean the biggest hug and turned to Mason. For him, she had a major kiss. It was all so touching and sweet. The Band Blue had played a part in getting Mason and Drea together when they'd all worked on a fund-raiser for the Boone County Memorial Hospital. And now here they were after winning their first Grammy, playing at Drea and Mason's wedding.

"Pretty cool," Luke said to Katie.

"It's a wonderful surprise. Did you know?"

He nodded. "I knew. I helped Mason arrange it. It's what best men do, right?"

"Yes, but it's quite a secret to keep."

"No bigger than our secret."

"Yeah, about that, we should talk. After the wedding?"

He played with a strand of her hair, distracting her with the loving way he was looking at her. "I'm all in."

Nine

The Band Blue captured the guests' attention, their country pop music less drawl and more beat. Most of the wedding guests got up and danced like it was the best party they'd ever attended and some stood by in awe just watching the band do their thing. It was almost as if they were attending a concert.

Luke hadn't been joking when he said he'd dance with Katie all night long. She'd never had so much fun, but she wasn't at all sorry when The Band Blue began singing a slow, sexy ballad.

"Twinkle toes, let's dance to this slow one," Luke said.

"Thought you'd never ask," she teased.

She walked into his arms and rested her head on his shoulder. Two hundred and fifty guests had seen them stick together like glue this evening. They'd seen the way Luke looked at her when she was giving her funny little toast and they'd seen the way she hung on his every word when he'd given his toast to the happy couple.

She was sure it would get back to her sister, but there was nothing she could do about it. She couldn't hide her feelings for him anymore and slow dancing with him had lots of pluses. Like breathing in his swoon-worthy masculine scent, being held in his strong, powerful arms and enjoying his occasional and surprising kisses.

The crud would hit the fan later, but right now she wasn't going to think about that. She wanted to celebrate her best friend's wedding without fear or trepidation.

She lifted up on her toes and gave Luke a sweet kiss on the mouth.

He brought her tighter into his embrace. "What was that for?"

She gazed into his eyes. "Just because."

"That's a good enough reason for me."

He always made her smile. Well, not always, but recently she found herself breaking free of the binds of obligation to Shelly and her mom.

"This is probably the best wedding I've ever attended," she said dreamily.

"You mean, ours wasn't this good?"

"Ours? It's not even a blip on my radar."

"I know." He kissed the top of her head. "I'll make that up to you one day."

She gazed at him, finally finding the courage she needed. "Luke, will you come with me?"

"Sure, where are we going?"

"To the gazebo. It should be quiet there. And well, the reception's almost over. We'll be back in time for the last dance."

Luke took her hand and led her down the pathway leading to the gazebo. The sun was just descending, the sky to the west ablaze with hues of pinks and oranges. Once they reached the gazebo, she walked up the steps and took a seat. Luke sat directly beside her.

She got right down to business. "I don't know where to start, but yesterday when I found out you were inside Drew's house with fire all around you, I couldn't deny my feelings for you any longer. I love you, Luke. I don't know when it happened or why. Lord knows, I have half a dozen reasons not to care for you but I do. Very much."

His eyes closed, as if he were treasuring her words, as if he was trying to lock this memory away. He'd been patient with her. And obstinate and persistent. But she loved him, all of him, and she was glad to finally tell him.

"Katie, I've waited five long years for this. I love you. I've already told you but it wasn't the way I wanted to tell you. Not in the heat of an argument like that."

"I kicked you out of my house when you told me."

"I know. And I'll admit now, I overstepped my bounds by denying you competition at the bakery. It's just the way I love. I protect the people I care about."

"But you won't do anything like that again, will you?"

"I promise you, I won't."

She smiled and Luke ran his hands up and down her arms, soothingly, sweetly, and then he kissed her and kept on kissing her until she could barely breathe. She put a hand on his chest. "There's more."

"Tell me more." His eyes glistened as he gave her his full attention.

"I'm, uh… I'm…pregnant. You're going to be a father."

There, she'd said it. Telling him only made it seem more real.

"Ah, Katie." Tears misted in his eyes. "This is the best news," he said, relieving her qualms. She'd had no idea if he even wanted children. It had never been a topic of conversation. Why would it be, when all she'd been focusing on lately was divorcing him?

"So then, you're okay with it?"

"I'm...blown away. Did you worry I wouldn't be happy about this?"

"I didn't know how you felt about children in general. I've never seen you around them, but I see how compassionate you are around horses and all animals really, so I was hoping this wouldn't rattle you."

"I'm on top of the world right now. You and I created a baby, sweetheart, and I'll love that child as much as I love you. I don't care when or how it happened, it's a blessing."

"I think so, too," she said softly. "But I've always used protection. I'm fuzzy about our wedding night in Vegas."

"Me, too. I, um, I would never put you at risk, Katie. Not consciously. I hope you know that."

"I do. I guess we both blurred out."

"Yeah"

"It's just...well, I'm going to have to face my sister and mom very soon."

"The sooner the better, Katie. And I'll be with you every step of the way."

"T-thanks. But this is something I have to do on my own. Tomorrow. I'm gonna tell them tomorrow. Right now, I think we should get back to the wedding."

"I could sit here all night with you, but you're right." He cupped her face, laid a solid, delicious kiss on her lips and then stared into her eyes. "We should get back."

Hand in hand, they made their way down the gazebo steps approaching the twinkling lights of the tent, just as April came out to greet them holding a cell phone. "Katie, I think this might be important. Your phone's been ringing on the table almost nonstop."

"Oh, okay. Thanks, April." She glanced at her recent calls. "It's from Shelly. I'll be just a minute. Please excuse me." Alarmed, Katie hid her concern from Luke and April. Shelly knew where she was tonight and she wouldn't call unless it was super important.

"Want me to stay?" Luke asked.

"No, you go on. I'm sure it's nothing."

April hooked Luke's arm. "Come on, Luke. You owe me a dance."

Reluctantly Luke was led away and Katie paced back and forth until her sister picked up.

"Shelly? It's me. What's wrong?"

The news was not good. Katie's mom was in the hospital. This time it wasn't her heart, but a case of pneumonia and it was bad enough for Shelly to take her to the emergency room.

Katie took a minute to absorb it all, her heart beating fast, and then she went back to the reception to seek out Luke. She found him just finishing a dance with April. Grabbing his arm, she took him off to the side. "I have to leave. My mom's very ill. She's in the hospital. Will you please tell Drea and Mason I'm sorry, but I have to go?"

"I'll go with you," he said immediately.

"No."

"No? Katie, I'll drive you."

"Goodness, Luke. Don't you get it? I can't show up at the hospital with you."

"Are we back to that?"

"I'm sorry. But I'm going. By myself."

Luke's mouth hardened to a thin line and that stubborn tick twitched in his jaw.

She couldn't deal with him right now. She had to get to the hospital.

Katie sat by her mother's hospital bed, watching her sleep. Her breathing seemed labored right now and she hated seeing her hooked up to all that equipment. Outside in the hallway, she heard Shelly's voice and turned just in time to see her sister speaking to Davis Moore. When they were through talking, Dr. Moore took hold of Shelly's hand and promised to check in with her later.

Shelly gave the good doctor a hero-worship smile, one only a sister would recognize, and kept her eyes trained on him as he walked away.

If her mother wasn't so ill, Katie might find that amusing.

Shelly walked into the room and laid a hand on Katie's shoulder. "You must've come straight from the wedding."

"Your call scared me so I didn't bother to go home to change."

"I'm glad you're here."

She put her hand over the one Shelly had placed on her shoulder. "Of course I'd come."

"You look pretty," Shelly said. "That color suits you."

What? No snide remark about the Boones or the wedding?

"Thank you." Katie rose from her chair to face Shelly. "How's Mom doing?"

"Things have calmed down now. She had a fever when I brought her in and her coughing was bad."

"Thank goodness you were with her tonight."

"I, uh, wasn't. I was out, but I called to check on her and heard her hacking away. I knew it wasn't good. Davis thought that I should take her straight to the emergency room."

Davis? Shelly must've been out with him tonight. And hopefully not at a seminar. "I didn't realize Mom was ill."

"It came on suddenly. She was having trouble breathing and with her fever spiking, I didn't want to take any chances. She's where she needs to be at the moment."

Katie nodded, tears welling in her eyes. Her mother looked pale and so still. Fear stuck in her throat. She couldn't lose her mother. She was too young. She was going to be a grandmother.

Katie's stomach churned, her emotions roiling. Though her eyes burned, she wouldn't cry. She needed to be strong. "Do…do you think she's going to be okay?"

"Pneumonia is never good in an older person, but Mom should be able to recover from this now that she's being monitored," Shelly said in her nurse voice. "I do want to warn you, Mom's health isn't the best in general, so it may take a long time for her to get better."

Katie sighed, pain reaching deep into her heart. "Just as long as she does."

"It's important that she stay calm. She'll be medicated throughout the night. You don't have to stay, Katie. I'll call you if anything changes."

"No, I'm not going home. When Mom wakes up, I want to be here."

"Okay, sis. But at least go home and change your clothes. It gets chilly at night on the hospital floors. You'll freeze in that dress."

Katie hesitated a moment. "I don't want to leave Mom."

"I'll stay until you get back. Mom won't be alone."

"Okay, if you promise."

"Go, little sis. And of course I promise. You can always count on me."

Katie took those words to heart. Her older sister had always been her friend, had always had her back. She'd been someone she could rely on for all their years.

Katie's heart sank even further with guilt. She was torn up inside, worried sick over her mother and worried about Shelly's reaction to her news. All her life, she'd never wanted to let anyone down. And now, it seemed, she was letting down everyone she cared about. "I'll be back in fifteen minutes, at the latest."

She gave her mother an air-kiss and then walked out of the hospital room feeling a sense of desperation and sadness. She hated seeing her mother looking frail and weak.

As she walked toward the elevator, she pulled out her cell phone, ready to let Drea and Luke know what was going on. The screen went black. "Shoot." She was out of charge. Of course. She'd used her phone all day long during the wedding, taking pictures and texting Lori about bakery issues, never realizing she'd need it tonight.

Making her way through the lobby, she found her car easily in the parking lot and drove to her apartment. The drive only took five minutes. As she pulled into her parking space at the back end of the bakery, a car followed her and parked directly next to her. It was Luke.

She got out of her car, and so did he. She met him in front of her back door.

"Katie, I texted and called you and then I started to worry," he said. "What's going on?"

"Luke, I'm in a hurry right now."

"And you couldn't call me?"

"My cell has no charge. It died just as I was texting you and Drea. My mother's really ill right now. I only came home to change my clothes so I can sit with her during the night."

"I'm sorry to hear that. What's wrong with her?"

"Pneumonia. I'm so worried. They've got her hooked up to all these machines. It's scary to look at."

"Ah, that's too bad. Let me help. What can I do?"

He reached for her, and she scooted away. "Nothing. There's really nothing you can do. My mom's recovery could take weeks. Maybe longer. Shelly is waiting for me at the hospital right now."

He ran a hand through his hair. "Katie, why do I get the feeling you're pushing me away again?"

"I'm…not. I just can't focus on more than one problem at a time."

"I'm your problem?"

"You know what I mean. I'm really sorry, but I have to get upstairs."

"Okay, go. But you know how to reach me if you ever need anything."

"I do. Thanks."

She sidestepped him and went to the back door.

"Charge your phone, Katie," he said as he climbed back into his car.

"I will. I'll text you tomorrow."

Luke didn't look happy. He was right—she'd pushed him away. She couldn't afford having him around. How would she explain it? It was the same old same old, except now her mother was in even worse shape than before.

She raced up her stairs and shed her pretty maid of honor gown, throwing on a pair of comfy black leggings and a big cozy gray sweatshirt. She wrapped her feet up in a pair of warm socks and put on tennis shoes.

She had always thought falling in love would be easy and fun and thrilling. Well, loving Luke had caused her nothing but indecision and pain. It wasn't supposed to be this way. She did love him. The thought of not having him in her life destroyed her.

And she feared if she pushed Luke too far, he'd never come back.

When Luke returned to the ranch, he found his family sitting at a table under the tent, drinking a final toast to Mason and Drea. All the guests were gone. The caterers and waiters were just leaving and the tent was due to be taken down tomorrow.

The lights still twinkled, clashing with his dark mood.

He brought over a bottle of Jack Daniels from the bar and sat next to Risk.

All eyes were on him, including his Aunt Lottie's and Drew's.

"How is Katie's mother?" Drea asked.

"She's in the hospital with pneumonia."

"Oh no. Poor Diana. First a heart attack and now this. Is she bad?"

"According to Katie, she is. She's worried sick." Luke slouched in the chair and sipped from the bottle, raising a few eyebrows. He didn't care. He needed his family to know the truth. It was time. "My wife doesn't want me there."

His brothers exchanged glances and then Mason asked, "I'm sorry, did you say wife?"

"Yep. I married Katie in Las Vegas." He sipped from the bottle again.

"What," Mason asked, "are you talking about?"

"I'm married to Katie. It's true."

"I'm in shock," Risk said, glancing at April.

"No more than she was when she woke up next to me in Vegas."

"Wow, bro. You got married during my bachelor party?" Mason said.

"Yeah, I did."

"Okay. Well, Katie is a great person." Mason put out his hand and they shook on it. "Congratulations."

"Same here," Risk said, slapping him on the back. "Congrats."

Luke frowned. "Don't get carried away. It's not a marriage made in heaven. It was one of those too-drunk-to-know-any-better moments. Immediately, Katie demanded a divorce." He gulped down another swig of whiskey, finally feeling the effects of the alcohol.

"Well, I think you and Katie are meant for each other. You two make a great couple," April said sweetly.

It only made him feel worse. "She thinks her mother and Shelly would never accept it. She swore me to secrecy. She didn't want the word to get out. The truth is, I love her

nd she loves me. But it's taken a lot of persuasion on my
art to get her to admit it." He gave everyone at the table
n equal glance. "I'm sorry I haven't told you before this."

"So why now?" Aunt Lottie asked.

"Why now?" He gave them all another look. "Because
Katie is pregnant. We're having a baby."

"Wow! This is amazing. The best wedding present you
could have given us," Mason said, pulling Luke up and
hugging him. "And I didn't think anything could top you
getting The Band Blue here."

Drea stood, too, and they embraced. "I'm so happy for
you and Katie."

"I can't believe it. This is wonderful news," April said.

Risk pulled him in for a hug. "Wow, you sure know
how to liven up a party. Congrats." He slapped him on the
back. "Hey, I'm gonna be an uncle."

Tears swam in Drea's and April's eyes. "We're gonna
be aunts," they said at the same time as if just realizing it,
nd then everyone laughed.

When the laughter died down, Luke shook his head,
grateful for their encouragement. "And now for the hard
art. I'm gonna have to swear you all to secrecy. Just until
Katie feels like she can share the news with Diana and
Shelly. Right now, she won't hear of it. And she's doing
her best to push me away, too."

"Why?" April asked. "If she loves you?"

"It's what women do sometimes," Lottie said sagely,
glancing at Drew.

April nodded. "Yeah, I guess I did that with Risk, too."

"And I did that to Mason," Drea said. "But we all had
good reasons, at the time. Just don't give up on her. She
does love you."

"How can you be so sure of that?" Mason asked his
new wife.

Drea kissed his cheek and said softly, "Best friends

know these things." Then she turned to Luke. "I'm sure of it."

"Thanks, and don't worry. I've been very patient with Katie. She was ready to tell her family the truth until Diana got sick. I won't let her push me too far away. I have a plan."

"A Boone with a plan? Just make sure it doesn't backfire," Aunt Lottie said.

He'd had the same thought. But he had to try something.

His patience was at an end.

Katie was on a roll this morning. She'd finished baking cupcakes and frosted one hundred of them in less than an hour in her work kitchen. They were now ready to go in the dessert case.

"Lori, cupcakes are up."

"Coming," Lori called from the bakery. "I'll be right there."

Katie washed the bowls and utensils, and when Lori walked in she grabbed one of the large cupcake tins. "Wow. Working fast."

"I have to. I'm going to stop by the hospital to check on my mom after the morning rush. Thank you for holding down the fort for me this week."

"Of course. How's Mama doing today?"

"Getting better every day. Her doctor says she's out of danger."

"All good news."

"I know. Thank goodness. Her fever is gone and if it stays normal for one more day, they'll release her."

Katie had closed the bakery for the first three days while her mother was fighting pneumonia and had taken turns with Shelly to sit with her at the hospital. She reopened her shop once her mom's recovery took a good turn.

"That's great, Katie. It's been a hard week for you."

"As long as my mom gets to come home, it's all worth it."

"I'll keep good thoughts for her."

"Thanks."

Once Lori walked out, Katie checked her cell phone. No texts yet from Luke. He usually texted her first thing in the morning and then at night before bed. He always asked about her mother's health, and made sure she was feeling okay, too. She hadn't seen him since the wedding and it was killing her. She really missed him, but not enough to ask him to come over.

She couldn't take the pressure right now and she understood that this wasn't the way Luke wanted it. He wanted to be let into her heart and her life. She wasn't sure if Luke was trying to abide by her wishes by staying away, or if he was really angry with her. Maybe a little bit of both.

"Oh God," she murmured. She didn't want to push him away like this, but what choice did she have?

The morning rush was intense, Katie and Lori working their butts off, trying to accommodate all the customers' orders. Davis Moore walked in and Katie waved to him.

He gave her a quick smile. "Hi, Katie."

"Hi, Davis. Are you here for your usual?"

He'd become a regular customer and she had gotten to know him a bit. "Actually, I'm surprising the entire floor with your cupcakes this morning. Can you pack up two dozen for me to take back to the staff?"

"Sure." She turned to Lori. "We can do that, right?"

Lori nodded, getting two big boxes ready.

"Be sure to include Shelly's favorite, lemon raspberry," he told her. "Put in two of those. Your sister got me hooked on them, too."

"Shelly's good for business."

He grinned. "She's good all the way around."

Katie paused momentarily, holding back a wide smile. "I agree."

"Your mom's making progress on her recovery. I checked in on her this morning."

"Thank you. It makes me feel good knowing she's getting expert care. Actually, I'll be leaving here in just a few minutes to visit her."

"I wouldn't rush. She's got a visitor right now."

"Oh yeah? Do you know who it is?" Katie asked, making conversation as she totaled up the bill at the cash register.

"Well, someone told me it was Shelly's ex. He walked in with a big bouquet of tulips for your mom."

Katie nearly swallowed her tongue. Luke had gone to see her mother with a bouquet of her favorite flowers? "Davis, you know what? These cupcakes are on the house. As a thank-you to you and the rest of the staff."

"Well, that's nice of you—"

"Lori will finish up your order." Katie removed her apron and grabbed her purse. "I actually can't wait to see Mama another minute. I'll be back later," she told Lori. "Bye, Davis."

Then she dashed out the door, her stomach gripping tight. It wasn't morning sickness making her ill. It was a heavy dose of dread.

What in hell was Luke up to?

Ten

Luke hoped he wasn't making a big mistake. He stood outside Diana Rodgers's hospital room and took a breath. Holding a bouquet of Diana's favorite flowers in one hand, he gave her door a little tap with the other.

After a brief pause, she said, "Come in."

Her voice sounded strong. According to Katie, Diana was doing well. She'd make a full recovery and might even go home tomorrow. *Here goes*, he thought. He'd gotten the okay from Diana's nurse to pay her a visit.

He walked through the slightly open door and found her sitting up in bed. She glanced at him and the softness in her eyes disappeared. "Luke, what are you doing here?"

"May I come in?"

"You already have."

He nodded and set the tulips down on the bedside table. "For you."

Grudgingly, she glanced at the flowers. "They're lovely."

"I remembered your favorite."

She half smiled. "If only you'd remembered to marry my daughter."

Luke stared at her, understanding her wrath. "I came to speak with you, Diana. If you would hear me out."

"Haven't we said all there is to say years ago?"

"No, I don't think so."

Diana looked better than he expected. Her face hinted at a rosy sheen, her hazel eyes were bright and she seemed to have attitude, which he remembered about her. She was never a pushover.

"If you want me to leave, I will. But first, I want to say I'm glad to see you're making a full recovery. You look good."

"Thank you for that." She folded her arms over her chest.

"I'm here to speak to you about Katie."

"Katie? What about Katie?" Diana's eyes shifted warily.

"Well... Katie and I have been friends now a long time."

"I know. She always defends you."

"She does?" That made him smile. "I suppose I'm not your favorite person. But I'm here to explain about what happened. You see, I did love Shelly. I thought she was right for me and I was right for her. I suppose I'll always hold a special place in my heart for her."

"She was sick for months after you broke off the engagement. She crawled into a shell and didn't come out for a long time."

Luke pulled up a chair and took a bedside seat. "I'm sorry about that. But you might say I did the same by joining the Marines. I was hiding out, too, in my own way."

"And what were you hiding from?"

"My feelings. You see, I didn't mean it to happen and I certainly didn't want it to happen, but I fell deeply in love—"

"With another woman?" she asked quietly.

"Yes. I fell hard. I couldn't help it. This girl was everything I was looking for. She was bright and independent and funny. We shared the same interests and—"

"My Katie?"

"Yesssss." Luke closed his eyes briefly, then opened them to look straight at Diana. "I'm in love with Katie. It's the real reason I left town. I didn't want to come between Katie and her sister. I left my family, my work, all the things I loved, to keep peace in your family. She never knew. She never encouraged me."

Diana bit her lip and then sighed. "Now that explains it. We couldn't figure out why you broke up with Shelly days before the wedding. And you didn't stick around long enough to work things out with her. You left her high and dry."

"I know. I've apologized to her and to you. Many times. And well, I did a good job of staying away from Katie when I returned home to Boone Springs, except for the time we'd spend at Red Barrel together. Katie was the perfect protective sister. She never gave an inch and I accepted that. But then we were thrown together for Mason's wedding."

"And?"

"And I fell in love with him, Mama."

Katie entered the room and set a hand on Luke's shoulder. She gave him a look that said she'd take it from here *and don't you dare argue*. He wouldn't dream of it.

"You love Luke?"

"I do, Mama. He's a good man."

Her mother continued to nibble on her lip. "What about Shelly?"

"I'll speak with her tonight."

"Brave."

"I'm not, Mama. I should've told you the whole truth

myself. You see, Luke and I got married in Las Vegas during the bachelorette party weekend. A little too much tequila at night makes a girl do silly things. I was beside myself and panicked when I woke up seeing that marriage license. I was worried sick about how you and Shelly would take it."

"She tried to divorce me," he said. "But I stalled her."

"You stalled her until she fell in love with you?" Diana asked.

"Yes." He kissed the top of Katie's hand and looked into her beautiful eyes. She'd finally come around and nothing made him happier. "I couldn't let her go a second time. I love her too much."

"Mama, I finally realized my love for Luke when he ran into that burning house and saved Drew's life. He could've been killed in that fire and all of a sudden, everything became clear to me."

"I see. I read about your heroics in the newspaper, Luke. It was courageous of you. And what you sacrificed to spare Shelly's feelings is commendable. You stayed away from home for four years. You did an honorable thing. It makes me feel a little bit ashamed about how I've treated you."

"Don't be. I understand."

"You can't help who you fall in love with, Mama."

"I guess not."

"There's more," Katie said.

Luke stood up, grateful that Katie was finally revealing the entire truth. He wrapped his arm around her shoulder and brought her in close, showing solidarity.

"We're going to have a baby, Mama," she said. "You're going to be a grandmother."

Diana's eyes went wide for a few seconds, as if sorting out the words in her head, and once the shock wore off, a big smile graced her face. "You're pregnant?"

"Yes, Mama. And you're going to be the best Grammy ever."

"That's wonderful news, sweetheart. I can hardly believe my little girl is going to be a mother. And I'm going to be a grandmother." Diana put out her arms, and Katie ran into them. "All I've ever wanted is for my girls to be happy."

"I am, Mama. I'm very happy."

"Then so am I."

When Katie backed away, Diana stretched out her arms again. "Luke?"

He walked over to her and she hugged him tight. He'd always liked Diana, and she'd treated him like part of the family when he was with Shelly. Was it possible to regain that bond again? "I guess...you're my son-in-law now."

"Guess so."

"Well then, welcome to the family, Lucas Boone," Diana said. "In a million years, I never thought I'd say those words to you."

Luke felt a thousand times better than when he'd first walked in here. "Neither did I."

Katie knocked on Shelly's apartment door. She'd had this place ever since college; it was in a nice neighborhood surrounded by parks and gardens. Shelly had done well for herself. She'd become a highly respected nurse and was on her way to bigger things professionally. While Katie nurtured horses and all animals, Shelly loved patient care. She had a nurturing spirit, too, and it had taken her a long time after her breakup to get back to a good place in her life again.

Katie's nerves rattled as she waited for Shelly to answer the door. She prayed that her news wouldn't set her sister back. That had been her greatest fear of all—that her sister would be crushed all over again.

When Shelly opened the door, she seemed surprised. "Katie? I was just going to the hospital to give you a break. What is it? Is something wrong with Mom?"

"No, nothing's wrong with Mom. She's actually feeling much better."

"Oh good. For a second there, I got worried."

"Can I come in?"

Shelly's brows furrowed and she stepped aside to let Katie in. "That expression on your face has me puzzled. You look...scared. Are you shaking?"

"I, uh. Shelly, we need to talk."

"Okay," she said. "What's up?"

Katie's legs went weak and she took a seat on the living room sofa. She'd rehearsed what she would say to Shelly many times, but as hard as this confession was in her head, it was ten times harder in person. "I have something to tell you, Shel. But first I want you to know I love you very much and I'd never intentionally hurt you."

"Of course, I know that. Same here. Please tell me what's on your mind, because I'm starting to get a weird vibe here."

"Weird? No, that's not the word I'd use."

"Katie, you're being cryptic."

"Okay, okay. It's just hard to begin. It's about... Luke."

Shelly blinked a few times. "What about Luke?"

"I, uh, he's my... Remember, I love you."

She nodded.

"Well, when Luke came back home from overseas last year, we started bumping into each other at the rescue. It wasn't a friendship really, but we shared a mutual love for horses and we worked together there at times. But it never went beyond that. I swear to you. Then in Vegas, during the party for Mason and Drea, Luke and I both got blistering drunk. Luke offered to walk me back to the hotel.

Only we didn't quite make it back. Instead…we went to the Midnight Chapel and…got…married."

Shelly's eyes nearly bulged out of her head. "You got married? Am I hearing correctly? You and Luke are married?"

Bile rose in her throat. The last thing she wanted was to cause her sister grief. She took a breath and went on, "I t-tried to get a divorce, but Luke kept stalling me, saying his attorney wasn't available. And I didn't know what to do. Shel, I was panicked. We hid it from everyone. I just wanted the ordeal to be over. Luke and I were thrown together a lot because of Drea's wedding. And when Snow died, we bonded over that. And well, Luke shared with me the real reason he couldn't marry you. It killed me to hear it. But you have to know the whole truth. Luke had fallen in love…with me," she whispered.

Shelly seemed unusually calm, but Katie didn't take that as a good sign. "Luke fell in love with you?"

"Again, Shel, I never encouraged him back then. We were friends. He was going to be my brother-in-law. And well, that's when he decided to break up with you and join the Marines. He didn't want to hurt you anymore than he had. He left his home and family so that he wouldn't come between us. He kept away for four years and when he returned home… Well, you know the rest. I'm so sorry, Shelly. I didn't want this to come between us. Ever."

"Well, what did you think would happen? That I'd be jumping for joy?"

"No, just the opposite. That's why this is so hard."

"I was a mess after he dumped me. And you're telling me you knew nothing about this?"

"I truly didn't. I swear. I was just as shocked when he told me the truth as you are now. And I didn't want any part of it. I fought my feelings for him."

Shelly ground her teeth, trying for restraint but Katie

knew that look. Her sister wanted to scream to high heaven at the injustice of it all. How could she blame her? She'd held on to her bitterness for all these years. *"Your feelings for him?"*

Katie sighed deeply. "Yes, I have feelings for Luke. I love him. I mean, I didn't know that I'd fallen in love with him, until he ran into a burning building to save Drew MacDonald's life. After that, I realized how much he meant to me. How much I cared for him. How much it would hurt if I lost him."

"And so, you threw your sister under the bus for a guy."

Her words cut deep, but Shelly's anger seemed to lessen, and was there actually space between her tight lips now? Was she making a joke?

Katie reached for her sister's hands and hung on tight.

"Your hands are freezing," Shelly said. "You're really tortured about this, aren't you?"

"Of course I am." Katie held back a sob.

"I hate seeing you in such pain."

"And I hate knowing I've caused you pain. I know you have no use for Luke."

"You shouldn't have to choose between us."

"But you only have horrible things to say about him, Shel. And I know this is awkward as hell, but… I don't know what to do."

Shelly sat quietly for a while, holding her ice cold hands, thinking. Seconds seemed like hours, but then her sister released a big breath.

"You *know* what to do," Shelly said firmly. "You love him and he loves you. There's nothing to do except make a life with him. Look, I know I've been bitter, and I've been difficult. I was hurt, but I finally realized that I didn't want a man who didn't love me like crazy. What kind of marriage would that make? Luke wasn't right for me. Not the way…"

"Davis is?" Katie asked, hopefully.

Shelly sighed. "We're getting closer every day. He's amazing."

"The feeling is mutual, on his part. Whenever he comes into the bakery, he finds a way to tell me just that."

Shelly had a dreamy look on her face. "He does?"

"Yep. Every single time."

"We have the same interests and, well, we're taking it slow, but I've never felt this way about anyone before. Davis always makes me feel special."

"That's wonderful, Shelly. I'm really happy for you." Katie nibbled on her lips, hesitating. "But I have another bit of news. I'm afraid there's more."

Shelly tilted her head. "Can I handle more news?"

"Gosh, I hope so. This is important." She laid a hand on her abdomen, a protective gesture that any woman would pick up on, especially a nurse.

The words wouldn't come. This news could crush her sister and ruin their relationship for good.

But it seemed she didn't have to speak the words. Shelly's eyes riveted to her stomach and *she knew.* "You're pregnant."

Goodness, this was difficult. "H-how do you feel about becoming an aunt?"

"An aunt. Katie?"

"Yes, I'm, uh, we're going to have a baby, Shel. I hope this isn't too much for you, because I'm really gonna need you. I need my big sis."

"My gosh, Katie. This is a lot to take in."

"I know," she squeaked, and gave Shelly her best little sister pout. It used to work when they were kids. "But I hope you can, 'cause I'm gonna really need you."

Shelly's shoulders relaxed and her expression changed. "You know what? I'm through being miserable. It's like meeting Davis has shined a bright light inside me. So, yes, of course I'll be there for you. You're my baby sister."

Tears dripped freely down Katie's face as she gave her sister a gigantic heartfelt squeeze. "Oh Shel, this means everything to me. Thank you."

"Have you told Mom?"

"Yes, just before I spoke with you," Katie said. "She's gonna be a grandma, and that makes her happy. I think she's accepted Luke, too. She said she just wants her girls to be happy."

Shelly smiled for the first time since Katie walked into the apartment. "Then, I think she's gotten her wish."

When Katie arrived home, she slumped on her bed, drained of energy. It had been an emotional day and all she could think about was getting into bed and falling asleep. It didn't matter it was only six in the evening, she was bone weary.

Her cell phone buzzed and buzzed and she dug into her purse. It was Luke. Immediately, she smiled. Her husband was calling.

She chuckled and then answered the phone. "Hi," she said.

"Hi."

Just hearing his voice brought her peace.

"How did it go with your sister?"

"It was difficult, but Shelly will come around. She's in love with someone and I think it's going to be okay."

Luke released a big sigh. "Glad to hear it, sweetheart. That makes this day perfect. Well, almost perfect. If you look outside now, you'll see there's a car waiting for you out front."

"A car? Luke, what are you up to?"

"You'll see. The driver knows where to take you. Trust me, Katie."

She took a deep breath. "Can I have twenty minutes? I need to shower and change."

"Okay, but remember I'll be waiting."

After she hung up the phone, she took a quick shower and put on her favorite floral sundress, one that wouldn't be fitting her too much longer. She tossed a short denim jacket over the dress and then slipped her feet into a pair of tan leather boots. Then she brushed her hair to one side and let it flow down her shoulders. She stared into the mirror for a second, wondering how on earth she'd gotten to this point in her life. This time, her thoughts weren't filled with dread and fear but with hope and promise.

The "car" Luke had sent was a limousine. Of course. At times she forgot how incredibly wealthy he was. The driver opened the door for her and she climbed in the back seat and stretched out.

"Miss, there's food and snacks and apple cider in case you get hungry," the driver said.

"Why, where am I going? Is it far?"

"Not too far. Mr. Boone wanted to make sure you were comfortable."

"I am, thank you. So, you can't tell me where you're taking me?"

"And ruin the surprise?" he asked with a grin before closing her door.

Surprise? Goodness, she didn't know how much more her heart could take today, but she leaned back, closed her eyes and relaxed. Luke had asked her to trust him. And she did.

A short time later, the limo turned down the path toward Red Barrel Horse Rescue. Katie sat up straighter in the seat and peered out the window. Her curiosity aroused, she scanned the area. There was no sign of Luke. The driver parked in front of the office and then got out to open the door for her. "Miss, Mr. Boone is waiting for you in the barn."

She glanced over to the big red barn and saw Luke approaching, wearing his black Stetson and a stunning dark suit, a string tie at his neck. Her heart raced. He was handsome and wonderful and all hers. She picked up the pace and soon she was in his arms, his mouth devouring hers, laying claim, making every bone in her body melt.

"Luke," she murmured between kisses. "What's this all about?"

Luke kissed her one last time. "Come with me."

He placed his hand on her back and led her into the barn. She gasped when she saw what he'd done. A dozen arrangements of flowers and tiny white lights surrounded a round linen-clad table set for two. Sparkling cider sat in a bucket of ice. The whole place appeared magical. "This is beautiful."

"I hoped you'd like it."

"But what are we—"

Luke dropped to one knee and took her hands in his. "Katie, I want to do this right. I want you to have all the things a bride should have, including a proper proposal."

"Oh, Luke." Tears swam in her eyes.

"I brought you here because this is where I fell in love with you. We have good memories here, you and me. It's fitting that this is the place I bare my soul to you. Katie Rodgers Boone, I'm crazy in love with you and have been for a long time. You're the only girl for me and I'm asking if you'll have me for your husband. To live and love with me for the rest of our lives. Will you, Katie?"

He reached into his pocket and presented her with a ring. Not just any diamond ring—this one was designed with emerald and marquise cuts of diamonds in the shape of a barrel. Red rubies surrounded the whole ring. "Do you see it?" he asked.

Tears streamed down her face now. Her every dream was coming true. "I see it. It's very special. And I see you for the good and honorable man that you are. I love the ring and yes, yes, yes. I'll have you for my husband, if you'll have me as your wife."

A smile spread across his face and he rose up. "Are you joking?" he teased as he placed the ring on her finger. Then he kissed her, a good, long, joyful kiss that warmed her heart. "You're all I've ever wanted. You, me and our baby, Katie, we'll be a family. I can't wait. But for now, I'm grateful our families know about us. We can stop pretending."

"Yes, I'm glad about that, too. I love you very much and now I get to show it."

"There's more."

"There always seems to be with you."

He chuckled and took her hand again. As they walked out of the barn, the sky was a shock of tangerine and pink hues, as if Mother Nature had summoned up such wonder for this moment.

"Katie, I said I didn't want you to miss out on being a bride. So today I'm giving you your wedding present."

"It's not necessary. You've already given me too much."

"Not even close, sweetheart. And I think you're going to like this gift." He led her to Cinnamon's corral. The horse looked her way, those big brown eyes capturing her attention. "I made arrangements to adopt her. She'll be yours."

"Really?" She'd never dared to dream of having a horse of her own. She loved every horse at the rescue, even the feisty ones, but she had a feeling Cinnamon was extra special. "She'll be mine..."

"Yes. And when she's ready, we'll take her to Rising Springs. I've already contacted a trainer to work with her."

"Luke, I don't know what to say but thank you." She buried her face in his shoulder and hugged him tight. "This is all so very much."

He put his hand over her belly. Any day now, the evidence of their love would be pushing the limits of her body and bumping out. "I love this little one already," he said.

She placed her hand over his. "Me, too."

He spoke softly, his arm snugly around her. "We should go in and have our dinner. Gotta keep the baby nourished."

"We do," she said. "And afterward?"

He kissed her, leading her inside. "Afterward, we'll have a proper start to our honeymoon, making hay inside the barn."

Katie laughed as Luke closed the big barn doors.

She was one lucky girl. Waking up wed to the Texan sure had its perks.

Epilogue

Three months later

Drew and Lottie stood before the minister in front of the backyard gazebo on Rising Springs Ranch, saying heartfelt vows of love and devotion. Luke looked on with Katie beside him. Her peach chiffon bridesmaid dress rounded over her growing belly, and her expression was light, bright and happy. The sight of her carrying their child always put a smile on his face and reminded him of his great fortune having married her.

Drea stood as Lottie's maid of honor and Mason as Drew's best man. Risk and April were also in the wedding party, along with a few of Drew and Lottie's good friends.

"I do," said Lottie, staring blissfully into Drew Mac-Donald's eyes. Drew was eager to repeat those same vows to her. The wedding was a family affair with fewer than thirty people in attendance. It was how Drew and Lottie wanted it. Only the most special people in their lives had received an invitation.

Theirs was the final piece of the puzzle that was the Boone family.

Drew's cottage was under repair, with the addition of new rooms and a modern kitchen for Lottie. The renovations gave the whole place a face-lift and soon, their Tuesday night poker games would resume there.

Mason and Drea had just moved into their newly built home on the property. Word had it that Drea was eager to start a family and Mason was more than willing to oblige.

Risk and April were just finishing the work at Canyon Lake Lodge, hoping to open their new venture this June. The Boones would receive the first invitation to test out the lodge, before paying customers made reservations.

Luke and Katie were living at the ranch, his wife delegating duties between Lori and a new hire at her shop. She didn't want to give up Katie's Kupcakes entirely, and on her workdays they stayed at Katie's apartment. Things would get a little more complicated when their baby came, but they'd work it out. He had no doubt.

"You may kiss the bride," Minister Gavin declared.

Drew landed a passionate kiss on Lottie's lips, one that made the minister turn a shade of bright red. He pronounced them husband and wife and the couple turned to their guests.

"Ladies and gentlemen, I give you Mr. and Mrs. Mac-Donald."

Luke took Katie's hand and squeezed it tight as applause broke out for the newly married couple. Katie gazed at him, her pretty green eyes clear and full of love.

As the wedding party and guests dispersed, heading toward the reception area, Luke tugged Katie away to a private corner of the yard. "What is it?" she asked.

"Just wanted a kiss, the good kind."

She laughed and then obliged him, her mouth sweet on his. The touch of her lips never failed to make him fall even harder in love with her. "I love you," he said from deep in his heart.

"I love you right back, Luke," she said sweetly. "And you still make me nutty."

"I still do?"

"Yes, you still do, and I wouldn't have it any other way."

* * * * *

COMING SOON!

We really hope you enjoyed reading this book. If you're looking for more romance, be sure to head to the shops when new books are available on

Thursday 9th January

JOIN US ON SOCIAL MEDIA!

Stay up to date with our latest releases, author
news and gossip, special offers and discounts, and
all the behind-the-scenes action
from Mills & Boon...

 millsandboon

 millsandboonuk

 millsandboon

night just be true love...

MILLS & BOON
MEDICAL
Pulse-Racing Passion

Set your pulse racing with dedicated, delectable doctors in the high-pressure world of medicine, where emotions run high and passion, comfort and love are the best medicine.

MILLS & BOON
True Love
Romance from the Heart

Celebrate true love with tender stories of heartfelt romance, from the rush of falling in love to the joy a new baby can bring, and a focus on the emotional heart of a relationship.

LET'S TALK
Romance

For exclusive extracts, competitions
and special offers, find us online:

- facebook.com/millsandboon
- @MillsandBoon
- @MillsandBoonUK

Get in touch on 01413 063232

For all the latest titles coming soon, visit
millsandboon.co.uk/nextmonth